# SNOW
# GOING
# BACK

# BOOKS BY EMMA TALLON

# EMMA TALLON

# SNOW GOING BACK

bookouture

Published by Bookouture in 2024

An imprint of Storyfire Ltd.
Carmelite House
50 Victoria Embankment
London EC4Y 0DZ

www.bookouture.com

Storyfire Ltd's authorised representative in the EEA is Hachette Ireland
8 Castlecourt Centre
Castleknock Road
Castleknock
Dublin 15, D15 YF6A
Ireland

ISBN: 978-1-83525-054-9
eBook ISBN: 978-1-83525-053-2

*For the reasons I breathe, Christian and Charlotte.*
*And for my dad, from whom I got my sense of humour – and who*
*I shall shortly emancipate myself from, if he doesn't actually read*
*this one.*

# ONE

There was a very specific smell that belonged to old church porches, Kate deduced as she stared at the centuries-old yellow stone walls either side of her. It was a mixture of the incense they burned inside, old wood and something else, something... damp. Yes, it was definitely damp. Though that wasn't surprising. The outer archway had no door, and the narrow windows on either side were glassless, leaving little protection against the wet British weather.

She barely registered the low excited chatter behind her, shivering as the cold October air bit at her bare arms. Folding them tightly, she wished – not for the first time – that they'd chosen a date in the summer. Or spring. Or early autumn. Any time of the year that was warmer than this.

The first bars of Johann Pachelbel's Canon in D wafted out from the organ inside. That was her cue. Taking a deep breath, she lifted her chin and pulled her shoulders back, trying to ignore the nerves that jittered around her stomach.

'Ready?'

She turned to see Amy, her best friend in the world, smiling at her.

Kate nodded, touching her dark hair one more time to check it was still in place as the heavy wooden door opened. Light and warmth spilled out, and she stepped forward into its inviting embrace.

Her bluey-green eyes softened as she walked to the top of the aisle and looked around. The light from the tall wrought-iron candelabras dotting each side of the room turned the yellow stone walls to a shimmering gold and warmed the dark wood of the pews. Clusters of white roses wrapped with trailing ivy hung on the end of each pew, matching the bouquet in her hands and the sprays on each side of the altar. She'd seen it all before, of course – she'd finished off the last little touches just hours before – but the effect was truly magical, now it had all come together.

A sea of smiling faces stared back at her as she forced herself onward, one step at a time, to the music. The planning had been the fun bit. *This* was the part she hadn't been looking forward to. Her long walk down the plank, with everyone watching. *Aisle*, she corrected. As naturally confident as Kate was, being at the centre of such pointed attention made her feel like a zoo attraction.

People craned their necks to see around wide-brimmed hats and feathery fascinators, and the clicks and flashes of the cameras began. Ignoring it all, she focused instead on just one familiar face ahead of her. The face of the man standing beside the vicar. A face that instantly warmed her heart and widened her smile. The face that belonged to Lance.

He smiled back at her, the action lighting up his handsome face. Lance looked incredible in the tailored dark grey morning suit, silver waistcoat and white cravat. Then again, with his athletic figure and preppy-yet-devilish good looks, Lance looked good in pretty much anything. Despite the fact it was October, he still retained a summery sun-kissed glow, which was complimented by his wavy flop of sandy hair and warm hazel eyes.

Eyes which twinkled at her from behind round tortoiseshell glasses as she finally reached him.

'And here you are,' he said quietly. He looked down to her dress and back up. 'You look sensational.'

'As do you,' Kate replied warmly. 'Both of you,' she added, to include the man beside him.

'Thanks,' Rick said, hooking his fingers under his shirt collar. 'Is yours tight?' He glanced at Lance. 'Mine feels tight. *Too* tight. I can't breathe.'

'You need to relax, old boy,' Lance replied. He placed a reassuring hand on Rick's back and leaned in towards his ear as Kate moved to the other side of the vicar. 'This is your wedding, not a colonic.'

Kate decided she'd probably prefer the colonic, given that choice, but luckily for Amy, Rick was not of the same opinion. She hid a grin and then looked back down the aisle with anticipation as the other bridesmaids filed in beside her. As maid of honour and lifelong best friend, it had been Kate's job to make sure today was everything Amy had ever wanted, and she was pretty confident that she'd pulled it off. The church was perfect. The reception venue was ready, down to the very last detail. Everyone was where they were supposed to be – the guests, the suppliers – and if some disaster did occur, she was confident that she was prepared for absolutely anything.

# TWO

The melodic sounds of the string quartet filled the grand ballroom, where everyone was thoroughly enjoying the wedding reception, and Kate leaned back against the bar, sipping the ice-cold champagne she'd just been handed by one of the waiters.

'It really is a fabulous wedding,' Lance said, joining her.

'It is,' Kate agreed. Across the room, Rick leaned in to kiss Amy's cheek for the hundredth time since they'd left the church, and Kate smiled fondly. 'It's everything she's ever wanted. She's always had *very* specific ideas.'

'Well, of course. Doesn't every woman have their wedding planned out in their head?' Lance asked, tipping his head back to finish the last of his champagne.

'Not *every* woman,' Kate replied.

Lance's eyebrows rose, and the corner of his mouth tugged upwards, but as he opened it to reply, a high-pitched indignant voice suddenly cut through the air.

'*There* you are!'

Kate turned with a resigned smile. 'Hello, Mother.'

'Where have you *been*, Katherine?' Her mother's expression was as indignant as her tone. 'I've been looking all *over* for you.'

'Right here,' Kate replied brightly.

'Can I get you a drink, Eleanor?' Lance asked.

'Oh, go on then,' she said, immediately more cheerful. 'I'll have a gin and tonic, thank you, Lance.'

'A double gin and tonic and a Laphroaig on the rocks,' Lance said to the barman. 'Have I mentioned how lovely you look today, Eleanor?'

Eleanor preened and patted her salt-and-pepper pinned-up curls. 'Well, thank you, Lance. You are a good boy. And you're looking dashing as always, of course. Grey suits you, dear.' She eyed Kate's dress, her smile morphing into a look of disapproval. 'Though it's not a colour that suits *everyone*. I really don't know why Amy put you girls in grey, too.'

'It's silver,' Kate replied, ignoring the insult. She was too used to her mother's critical and unfiltered opinions on her general appearance for it to be a surprise. 'Where's Dad, anyway? You haven't left him alone, have you?' She looked around hopefully.

'He's fine, and it's *grey*,' Eleanor replied. 'You can dress it up all you want, but silver is simply grey with a shimmer, darling.' She tutted. 'I don't understand why she didn't pick a nice bright colour. She *knows* you're too pale to wear grey.'

'It's silver,' Kate repeated flatly. 'And that's the colour theme, as you know.'

Kate eyed her glass, wishing she'd gone for something stronger than champagne. Her mother was a dish best paired with something like whisky or vodka.

'Well, I think she looks fantastic,' Lance stated, handing Eleanor her gin.

'Oh, don't get me *wrong*, Lance. She *can* look fantastic, of course, in so many colours. In fact, almost *any* other colour. Just not grey.' Eleanor shook her head again, looking at Kate with sympathy. 'It's like she *wanted* you to look washed out.'

'Thank you,' Kate replied wryly.

'Well...' Eleanor gave her a conspiratorial look. 'Perhaps that was *exactly* what she was thinking. You *have* always been prettier than her.'

'Mum!' Kate exclaimed. 'Would you *keep your voice down*. What a thing to say – and at her wedding!' She double-checked no one else had heard and exhaled a long, stressed breath.

'*What*? You are.' Eleanor shrugged. 'And no one wants to be outshined by a bridesmaid.' She caught Kate's look of disapproval. 'Oh, don't give me that look, you'll be *just* the same when it comes to *your* wedding. You wait.' A devilish smile spread across her face. 'You should have seen what I did to your aunt Helen and Jenny.'

Kate frowned warily. 'What *did* you do to them?' The only picture she'd seen from her parents' wedding was of the two of them.

Eleanor's eyes twinkled. 'I had their dresses made up from your grandmother's old curtains. Brown and orange swirls. They looked *awful*. Big flowers along the neckline and full puffed sleeves.' She giggled naughtily, and Kate couldn't help but grin.

'You're terrible,' she accused wryly. 'Aunt Helen would have been so happy for you, too.'

'Oh, she was fine.' Eleanor waved her hand dismissively. 'As was Jenny. They both made me wear *hideous* creations at theirs. As Amy has done to you...' She gestured towards the elegant silver slip dress that, until ten minutes ago, Kate had rather liked. 'It's a time-honoured tradition.'

Kate sipped her champagne, bored of the subject, and looked across the ballroom, wondering once more where her father had gone. He was probably quietly enjoying the peaceful respite from her mother somewhere, she supposed.

'When *will* we be cooking up plans for bridesmaids dresses, anyway, Katherine?' Eleanor asked, arching an eyebrow with a sideways look at Lance. 'I'm not a young woman, you know, Lance. I can't wait forever to become a grandmother.'

Kate's eyes widened in mortified shock. '*Mother!*'

Lance choked on his whisky and coughed, thumping his chest as he put his drink back down on the bar.

'I'm only speaking the truth. Nearly all of my friends have grandchildren now, and some of them are a lot younger than me. And *you're* not exactly a spring chicken either anymore, you know, Katherine,' Eleanor continued, ignoring her daughter's horrified expression. 'She's thirty-five, Lance. Nearing the winter of her childbearing years. And you'll want to be married awhile before starting a family—'

'OK, that's *enough*,' Kate snapped, feeling angry and embarrassed. 'Firstly, I'm not in the *winter* of *anything*, thank you very much. Secondly, and more importantly, we're here to celebrate Amy and Rick, so I suggest we all get back to *that*.' She glared at Eleanor warningly.

Eleanor, however, was not backing down. 'I'm not saying it's a *bad* thing, Katherine. You've been busy with your career, and I'm very proud of how much you've achieved. I'm just pointing out that—'

'Eleanor.' Lance stepped between them as Kate opened her mouth, cutting them both off. 'I'm *sure* I just saw Hilary Lane follow Henry outside.'

'*What? Where?*' Eleanor's eyes flew wide and she swivelled around.

'Yes, I think – I *think* it was her. I might be wrong,' Lance continued.

Eleanor grasped his arm. 'Come, you must show me where they went. I *knew* that hussy had eyes on my Henry...'

Lance squeezed Kate's hand and led Eleanor off on a well-timed wild goose chase, defusing the situation with expert precision. Hilary Lane was a friend of Amy's mother who'd been widowed a few years before, and who Eleanor had firmly, and completely unfairly, decided was now trying to steal all their husbands. She was also currently on holiday, in Aruba.

Kate silently seethed as she watched them leave. Eleanor had *always* bulldozed her way into Kate's private affairs with all the grace of a rhino and intentionally blind to any normal boundaries, but to bring up something like that in front of Lance was way over the line. She and Lance weren't anywhere *near* the point of discussing weddings or children. They were still just dating – they didn't even *live* together! They'd met just over a year ago at one of Rick's parties that she'd attended with Amy. She'd been drawn in by his charismatic charm and interesting conversation, and they'd ended up talking all night until the weak rays of early morning light had rudely interrupted. Upon realising the time, Lance had invited her out for breakfast, and they'd been dating ever since.

It had been a refreshingly easy relationship to slip into. Although they worked in different fields, both she and Lance were lawyers, which meant they understood how hectic life could get. They spent weekends together and grabbed the odd date night in the week, and totally understood each other's need for space when a case became all-consuming. Their setup worked perfectly for them both.

Amy sidled up with a knowing look. 'The last time I saw you throw daggers at your mother's back like that was the time she made us miss the school disco to help out at that charity festival.'

Kate laughed at the memory. 'I'd forgotten all about that.'

'*I hadn't*,' Amy replied. 'I'd planned to declare my undying love to Kevin Barker that night and he ended up copping off with Cheryl McCall instead. I was heartbroken.'

'It was probably for the best. I bet he's really ugly or in prison now,' Kate joked.

'Actually, he's drop-dead gorgeous, owns a string of hotels and lives in Tuscany,' Amy replied, sipping her champagne.

'*Really?*' Kate asked, surprised.

'Yes. But he's also married to a six-foot Italian called Antonio, so you're right, it probably was for the best,' Amy told her. 'Anyway, what's Eleanor done this time?'

Kate sighed irritably. 'She basically outright asked Lance when he's going to marry me and get me pregnant, like I'm about to hit my expiration date and fall to the shelf of barren old maids!' She shook her head. 'It was so inappropriate.'

Amy's jaw dropped. 'Wow. And you didn't strangle her to death with the strap of your handbag right there and then?' She blew out a long breath. 'Well, I applaud you.' She patted her on the back. 'Seriously, well done.'

Kate laughed and linked her arm through Amy's, pulling her away from the bar. 'Come on – let's dance. We're here to celebrate your wedding, not plot the early demise of my excruciatingly embarrassing mother.'

'Who says we can't do both?' Amy replied.

Kate laughed again, but there was an edge to her tone, and she threw a dark look towards the door Lance and Eleanor had disappeared through. 'Don't tempt me...'

# THREE

The fortnight following the wedding passed in a blur. At least it did for those who *hadn't* been relaxing on a beach in the Bahamas sending photos of delicious-looking cocktails and perfect sunsets to everyone back home in a cold, grey and drizzly London.

Kate yawned as she leaned back against the passenger-seat headrest of Lance's car, feeling drained after a whole week of working all day and night into the early hours. She'd barely caught four hours of sleep the night before – *two* the one before that. All she wanted to do now that she'd made it to the weekend was turn off her phone, draw all the curtains, lock the door and fall into a deep uninterruptable sleep. But that wasn't an option today. Instead, they were now en route to her parents' house in the country for the afternoon. These visits were a monthly arrangement. They gave Kate the chance to catch up with her parents properly, and for the most part, to Kate's relief, it had stopped Eleanor turning up unannounced at her flat in London whenever she felt like it.

As the sharp, greyscale lines of the city made way for the countryside's frost-kissed hedges and hills, Kate closed her eyes

– just for a moment. But when she reopened them what felt like a second later, Lance was suddenly turning into the quaint Cotswold village she'd grown up in.

'Oh, I'm so sorry!' she exclaimed, realising she must have slept for the entire journey. She felt a flood of guilt at being such terrible company on the long drive.

'Don't be,' Lance replied. 'You looked like you needed it. I didn't want to wake you.'

'Thanks,' Kate replied.

'What time did you leave the office last night?' he asked.

Kate blew a long breath out through her cheeks. 'I think it was about three,' she said. 'I don't know.'

Lance frowned. 'What's complicated things?'

'OK, so, the client wanted to sell off what is, effectively, a failing arm of their company,' Kate explained. 'They split it up into smaller pieces to sell off separately, to make it look more appealing.'

'*Is* it?' Lance queried.

Kate shrugged. 'I guess. Less of a loss showing in the financials of each smaller piece, but it's still exactly the same. Nothing was hidden though, so that was fine. It meant more complex contracts, and many more of them, of course, but again, this was still all fine.'

'So what *wasn't* fine?' Lance asked.

'The amendments they made to my contracts and all the unstoppable wheels they set in motion too early, in the hope they could push some dirty details through each one without me noticing,' she replied with clear annoyance. 'It's been pure crisis management all week with an almost impossible deadline.' She rubbed her forehead, feeling stressed.

'*Seriously?*' Lance replied in surprise. 'How on *earth* did they come to the conclusion that they could hide details in a legal contract from their own contract lawyer?'

She shrugged and pursed her lips, glaring out of the window

as the reminder of what they'd tried to do made something inside her bubble irritatedly once more.

Kate was a senior associate at her law firm, her speciality international contract law. Unlike Lance – who was used to sudden case dramatics, being a criminal defence lawyer at a firm across the city – she very rarely needed to enter this level of crisis mode. And had this crisis been a genuine one, due to a mistake or unforeseen circumstance, she wouldn't have minded so much. But she bitterly resented this particular case and the clients responsible now because they'd caused this mess knowingly, and in an attempt to screw other people over for money they'd neither earned nor deserved.

And it wasn't just the clients they would have screwed over for it, either. They'd also been about to screw *her*. They'd tampered with her documents, which, if she hadn't caught it, could have landed her in real trouble. If it wasn't for the impact it could have on herself, she'd have dropped them immediately and left them to figure out their own mess. But as it stood, she had no choice but to pull them all through it, then she could drop them afterwards. *Ideally off the edge of a really high cliff*, she thought bitterly. It was clients like those that made her hate her job some days.

With a sigh, Kate checked herself over in the mirror and tried to rub some life back into her pale skin, then pulled her loose wavy hair forward to better frame her face and trail down the front of her cream cable-knit jumper.

'Don't worry – you look fine. Eleanor will never know you've indulged in a nap.' He shot her a grin, a teasing twinkle in his eye.

'You underestimate my mother,' Kate replied with a wry smile.

She looked out of the window at the familiar sight of the yellow stone cottages and the higgledy-piggledy stone walls edging their front gardens, her mind still worriedly circling everything that was still waiting for her to pick back up on Monday. Maybe she'd try and get a few hours in tomorrow, after she'd caught up on some sleep.

As Lance rounded the corner that led to her childhood home, Kate pulled on her cream beret and gathered her things.

'It really is beautiful all year round here, isn't it?' Lance remarked. 'It must have been a great place to grow up.'

'Mm,' Kate replied noncommittally. She hadn't been the biggest fan of the place as a child.

'I could definitely live here,' he continued, swinging onto the wide gravel drive at the front of the house.

Kate blinked in surprise. 'Really?'

'Swap the view of city skyscrapers for cultured countryside? Absolutely,' he replied. He parked between her parents' cars and cut the engine. 'I mean this is exactly the sort of place you aim to settle down in, isn't it?'

The front door opened and Eleanor leaned out, waving excitedly. Lance waved back and got out of the car, and after a moment, Kate followed suit, pursing her lips and choosing not to answer that question. She personally couldn't think of anything *worse* than living back here. A childhood full of mundane community tea parties, neighbourly one-upmanship and intense focus on lawn and plant care had put her firmly off that particular idea.

'*Darling.*' Eleanor held out her arms and pulled Kate in for a hug.

'Hi, Mum,' Kate replied.

Eleanor stepped back and held her at arm's length. 'Let's take a look at you.'

Kate waited, resignedly, to discover what her mother disapproved of today, but after a short silence Eleanor simply smiled.

'As *beautiful* as ever,' she chirped. 'Have you done something new with your hair? I love it!'

Without waiting for an answer, Eleanor grabbed Lance's arm and ushered him inside.

Kate frowned and followed them, feeling unnerved. The last time Eleanor complimented her so unconditionally, she'd gone on to tell her the family dog had died. But there were no more pets in the house.

Suddenly her eyes flew wide and she sped up. '*Dad?*'

Ten minutes later, Kate sipped on her lukewarm tea and watched her parents warily over the rim of the delicate bone-china cup that her mother usually guarded against the use of with her life. The tea set was Eleanor's pride and joy, kept only for important visitors, such as the vicar, or the Queen.

'Another Chocolate Oliver, Lance?' Eleanor asked, holding out the plate of dark-chocolate-coated biscuits.

'Oh, er, no, thank you.' Lance smiled tightly.

'Oh. Don't you like them?' Eleanor looked disappointed.

Kate and Henry exchanged a private look, and Kate had to bite her inner cheek to hold back a grin. No one in their house actually *liked* them – her mother included, not that she'd admit it – but after reading an article in *Hello!* magazine that it was the Queen's favourite biscuit, she'd insisted on serving it to anyone who visited.

'They're lovely,' Lance lied, 'I just need to watch the old waistline.'

'Of course,' Eleanor replied, placing the plate back on the table. 'Your dedication to keeping yourself fit is admirable, Lance. If only *everyone* possessed such discipline.' She turned and swept her gaze pointedly over her husband.

Henry, who'd been carefully guiding a sugar lump between the bowl and his cup with the tongs, glanced at his wife with a slight pause, then dropped it in and began to stir with a defiant smile. Kate had to turn away this time as Eleanor's face twitched with irritation.

'How's work going, Kate?' Henry asked. 'Much going on?'

'Oh, let's not talk shop today, Henry. It's Saturday,' Eleanor said quickly.

Kate looked at her, surprised. Eleanor usually *loved* to talk about her work. The fact her only daughter was a successful lawyer was her favourite bragging right. She also usually enjoyed offering her detailed opinion on what Kate *should* have done on a case, as though she were a retired law oracle and not a suburban housewife whose only flirtation with work had been a stint selling Avon to the neighbours.

Eleanor stared at Henry, holding his gaze a fraction of a second too long.

'Yes, I guess you're right,' he said. 'There's more to life than work.'

Kate frowned. Something was definitely off here today. But *what*?

'You OK, Dad?' she asked.

Henry shot her a quick smile. ''Course. Did I tell you I finally finished the rockery down by your cherry trees?'

'No, you didn't. That's great,' she replied, frowning suspiciously.

Lance stood up and stretched. 'I think I need some fresh air after that drive, you know,' he said. 'I might wander down and take a look at it, Henry.'

'Sure.' Henry shrugged and picked up his tea.

'Oh, you should. The centrepiece is *quite spectacular*,' Eleanor enthused.

'I'll join you,' Kate said, standing up. 'I'll grab our coats.'

'No, no! You sit there, darling. I'll grab them,' Eleanor insisted. She jumped up and swept past them, out into the hallway.

'What is *with* her today?' Kate whispered, directing the question at her father as soon as Eleanor was out of earshot.

'What do you mean?' he asked.

'What do you mean *what do I mean?*' she replied, glancing at the door. 'The tea set, offering to get my coat – she even told me my *hair looked nice.*' Her voice dropped to an urgent hiss. 'The last time she complimented my hair, someone *died.*'

'Someone *died?*' Lance's eyes widened.

'No one died,' Henry said in a flat tone.

'*Pippi* died,' Kate countered stubbornly.

'Who's Pippi?' Lance asked.

'Pippi was the dog. She's being dramatic, Lance,' Henry replied.

'Dad, you're *sure* there's nothing you need to tell me? You're not *dying* are you?' Kate checked.

Henry sighed. 'Kate, other than the unavoidable oxidisation process we call aging, and the chronic neck pain also known as Eleanor, I assure you I'm as healthy as a horse.' He topped up his tea and dropped in another lump of sugar. 'And your mother is still complaining daily about every ache and pain under the sun, so she's absolutely fine, too. It's when she goes quiet that we'll need to worry.'

He glanced at Kate with a mischievous twinkle in his eye, and she couldn't help but grin.

Eleanor breezed back in with an armful of coats.

'Here we are,' she said in a singsong voice. She handed everything out and sat back down. 'Just go out here. No need to go all the way round.' She gestured to the French doors.

Kate pulled on her long grey coat and her scarf and hat, still eying her father, but his attention was firmly on the tea. She moved her gaze over to her mother, but Eleanor turned away and walked to the window. Kate's frown deepened. She was *sure* her mother was avoiding eye contact.

'Shall we?' Lance put a hand on her back, gently moving her towards the door.

Kate bit her lip, resigning herself to a pause, and her stomach turned uneasily as she stepped outside into the late autumn chill. There was definitely something strange going on.

*But what was it? And why were they so intent on hiding it from her?*

# FOUR

Kate's breath crystallised in the air and drifted off in white hazy curls as they made their way down the long frosty lawn, and the sight of it made her smile. Eleanor had once told her, when she'd been very small, that when the air was so cold it froze breath, it was actually the yearly reminder from Jack Frost to start preparing the Christmas cake. Kate had been so young she'd taken it literally, and for years had spent the fading days of autumn running outside to check whether he'd been by to tell them it was time.

Their family home was over a hundred years old, built in an era when it was the norm for back gardens to stretch on for an eternity, well before people worked out that small patches of land were more practical. The garden sloped gently away for just over two hundred metres, a small grove of apple trees and a low fence separating it from the rolling fields beyond.

'I'd go for a garden like this, too,' Lance said.

It took Kate a minute to realise he was continuing from his earlier comment in the car. She looked out at the view, and her forehead puckered in a small frown. 'It's lovely, but it's a lot of maintenance. You hate helping your mother weed her tiny front garden. Why would you want something *this* size?'

'Because that view screams *success*, Kate. It says, *This person made it.* I'd like that reminder with my morning coffee each day. We don't work as hard as we do in the cutthroat world of law for nothing, do we?' He glanced at her. 'We do it because we're competitive creatures. People like us, we crave the best. *Being* the best, *having* the best.'

They slowed as they neared the two cherry trees stood to one side of the garden, and Kate pushed the loose tendrils of hair being tousled by the wind back off her face. She didn't fully agree with Lance's statement. Although she was as competitive as any other lawyer, she didn't care about status symbols the way Lance did.

As they reached the rockery Henry had installed between the cherry trees, her eyes instinctively moved up to the branches.

'Did I ever tell you how these got here?' Kate asked.

'Er, don't think so,' Lance replied distractedly.

'I was about seven. We'd learned how to grow trees from pips at school, and that weekend I decided to give it a go,' Kate told him with a grin. 'I saved a handful of cherry pips and gave it a shot. These were the only ones that grew.' Kate looked up at the two twisted trees. 'You should have seen my mother's face. She'd planned to deck this area. These were just shoots at the time and she very nearly dug them up. But my dad found me crying, and when he found out why, he told her not to touch them under *any* circumstances. Really put his foot down. She was *furious*.'

Lance laughed. 'Oh, wow. I don't think I've ever seen Henry stand up to Eleanor over anything.'

'Oh, he does. When it really matters he can be quite unmovable. And for some reason, these mattered.' She stared at the knotted branches fondly.

'And now he's completed the area,' Lance added, gesturing to the raised circle of rocks dotted with succulents between the trees. 'One could say this area has come full circle.'

'Mm,' Kate mumbled absently, her mind still in the past as an icy gust of wind crept under her scarf and made her shiver.

She yawned and stared tiredly up at the racing clouds as she fought the achy weight of her eyelids. She wasn't sure she could make it through the entire day without falling asleep. Maybe they could slip away a bit early.

'Aren't you going to look at what he's done?' Lance asked.

'Oh, it's OK. I saw it a couple of weeks ago,' Kate replied dismissively. 'I can never tell the difference between all Dad's little green plants anyway.'

Lance wandered over to the rocks, and Kate's thoughts moved back to her parents. The way they were acting was unnerving her. If it had just been her mother, the odd behaviour wouldn't have been quite so alarming. Eleanor was routinely unpredictable. You never knew *what* she would do next. But for her father, this was completely out of character. Nothing ruffled him usually. And he'd always been straight with her. He didn't hide things.

'Some of these rocks are *magnificent*, Kate,' Lance said, squatting down to take a closer look.

'Yes,' she agreed politely, not really listening.

*What could possibly be so bad that her dad would actively keep it from her?* She racked her brain.

'In fact, this one in the middle is *really* unique,' Lance continued. 'Not something you find every day. Come take a look.'

The wind picked up and whipped some of her hair into her face, and she pulled it away. Almost instantly it whipped back again, and she turned into the wind to force it back with a frown of annoyance.

'Kate?' Lance pressed. 'Come on – turn around and give me your legal verdict on this rock.'

'What are the charges?' she joked back, hiding her annoyance. She didn't care about plants and rocks. She just wanted to be told what was going on. But she turned anyway, ready to feign interest. She immediately got another mouthful of hair and quickly tried to spit it out. 'Oh, for God's sake,' she muttered, failing miserably to tuck it neatly behind her ears where she wanted it. Realising the wind was going to win this fight, she gave up and grabbed all her hair into one hand, twisting it up under her hat instead.

'*Kate?*' Lance prompted her again, and she felt her irritation spike sharply. *Surely he could see what she was struggling with?*

She swivelled around, forcing a bright smile to soften the snappiness she couldn't quite bite back out of her response.

'*Yes!*'

She held his gaze pointedly to show him he had her full attention. *Slow breaths*, she reminded herself. *You're annoyed with your hair, not Lance.* She opened her mouth again to ask which rock it was that had so deeply taken his interest, but as she did, Lance's smile lit up so brilliantly that she hesitated, confused.

It took a fraction of a second from this point for her eyes to clock the small blue box in his hand. It took another fraction for her brain to register that the rock he'd been referring to was the giant pear-shaped diamond gleaming back at her and *not* one from her father's rockery. In the following fraction she tried to suck in a deep breath, but then it stuck in her throat and she froze as the realisation dawned that Lance was *proposing* to her. Proposing *marriage*! And then finally, another full second later, shock zapped through her like a bolt of lightning as she realised that he'd taken her *yes* as an answer to his proposal rather than as a simple answer to her name, as intended.

As Lance leaped to his feet with an elated punch to the air, Kate searched for the words to protest, to explain he'd made a mistake. But before she could, he declared it to the skies in an elated bellowing cry.

'*She said yes!*'

'Oh,' she breathed. 'No, Lance—' She reached out towards him, but in that moment a roaring chorus of cheers erupted from somewhere behind her.

Kate's heart lurched sharply as she turned towards the noise, then sank to the pit of her stomach like a cold hard stone as she saw the crowd of their closest family and friends gathered by the house. As she realised they'd all been *watching*. That this had all been planned, and that they'd *all* accepted her *yes*.

'Oh my God,' she uttered.

*How is this happening?* she cried internally. *And why? Am I being punked? Is Ashton Kutcher hiding somewhere?*

'I know, you're stunned,' Lance said with a light happy laugh. He took her hand and slipped the ring onto her finger.

Kate stared down at it, frozen. Reeling. Unsure how to proceed. *This has to be a nightmare*, she reasoned. *That's it. I'm dreaming. This isn't real.* But when Lance pulled her to him and lifted her chin it certainly *felt* real. She swallowed, vaguely aware that the sound of the cheering crowd was growing nearer. She felt sick.

'You know, I had a whole speech prepared, about what a great team we make and about our future together.' Lance's warm amber eyes sparkled as he looked down at her with a wide smile. 'But you didn't even give me the chance.' He laughed and then stroked her face gently. 'Well, that's fine. Because all that really needs to be said is this. I love you, Kate Hunter. And I'm so glad you said yes to becoming my wife.'

Kate opened her mouth, desperate to say something – *anything* – to stop this gross misunderstanding from going any further. She wasn't ready for *marriage* – they didn't even *live* together! But as Lance turned her to face the crowd of people coming towards them, she realised, in horror, that it was already too late.

# FIVE

There was a loud pop as another bottle of champagne was opened and poured over the tower of glasses on the round central table. Kate watched in a stunned daze, still unable to get her head around the fact this was actually happening. But it *was* happening. Because Ashton Kutcher hadn't appeared to tell her she'd been punked, it was nowhere *near* April Fool's Day, and as far as she could tell, Lance wasn't blind drunk or doing this for a laugh. Which meant that this was all horrifyingly real. She really had accidentally accepted a marriage proposal – and she'd done it in front of *all* her family and friends.

There had been no time to work out how to rectify her mistake before she and Lance had been bombarded by the excited group of spectators. Eleanor had cried, hugging Kate tightly before telling Lance how proud she was of him and how overjoyed she was to be welcoming him into the family. Amy had squealed and jumped up and down, promising to be just as amazing a maid of honour to Kate as Kate had been to her, while Rick offered similar sentiments to Lance. One by one, everyone had stepped forward with their congratulations and hugs, and before she'd known it, they'd been ushered back up to the house and into the formal dining room, which was all set up with banners and balloons and the ridiculous champagne tower in the middle, to celebrate.

Eleanor, never one to miss a chance to play hostess and talk at a willing crowd, immediately took to a stool and gave an emotional speech about how worried she'd been, as the years had passed, that she'd never see this day. She declared Lance her hero and told Kate how proud she was of her for finding such a wonderful man. If Kate hadn't been in a state of complete shock, she might have felt wryly offended by her mother's focus, but she had bigger things to worry about now.

'Here.' Henry handed Kate a glass of champagne as she finally managed to slip away from the stream of well wishes and hugs.

'Thanks,' she replied, moving to the less crowded side of the room and standing back by the wall. She put a hand to her forehead, feeling hot despite the cold weather.

She'd done *nothing* to undo this colossal misunderstanding. *Nothing.* She'd just *stood there* with a forced smile, nodding her acceptance as each person spoke to her. As Lance proudly held her waist and accepted praise for choosing such a wonderful ring. She'd just stood in stunned, horrified, awkward silence, and every second that passed made it more and more impossible to go back. *What was she doing?* Realising her father was watching her with a small frown of concern, Kate forced another smile and raised her glass to meet his.

'Cheers,' he said quietly. He took a sip and looked over at Eleanor for a moment. 'Well, you've certainly made your mother very happy,' he commented.

'Yes,' Kate managed, following his gaze.

Her mother's excitement and joy set off a fresh wave of despair. There was no way out of this. She couldn't backtrack *now*. It was too late! Both Lance and her mother would be absolutely crushed and embarrassed after their various declarations and speeches in front of everybody. And on top of that, Eleanor would never forgive her. Lance was everything she'd ever wanted in a son-in-law.

Kate blew out a long silent breath as she tried to remain calm. It had surprised her, the strength of her natural reaction to the idea of marrying Lance. Why *was* she so horrified at the idea? They were great together. They were happy, they were in love, and everything about them as a couple made total sense. So what *was* it? She twisted the stem of the glass in her hand for a moment.

The idea of marriage had always just been somewhere far off in the mental distance for Kate. An idea she'd parked as something to get round to thinking about *someday*. But someday was another thing she'd always felt a distance from. How on earth had *someday* become today? And without any warning whatsoever? She took in a deep breath, forcing herself to expel it slowly.

It wasn't that she was *against* marriage. But while girls like Amy had dreamed of dresses and made wedding scrapbooks, Kate had dreamed of adventures and made bucket lists. To her, marriage was something that came *after* she'd conquered the dragon and sailed the seven seas and found an ancient cure for all the world's ills wearing Indiana Jones's hat. But she hadn't even bought the hat yet.

Kate looked over at Lance as he held court, his handsome face animated and full of life. Why hadn't he brought the idea of marriage up in conversation first? Why had he made it so public?

Amy walked over and wrapped her arm around Kate, squeezing her in a sideways hug with another small sound of excitement. 'So, when can I start organising everything?' she asked. 'This is perfect timing, by the way. I was getting *serious* post-wedding blues. All those years of planning and then it's over, just like *that*.' She snapped her fingers, then leaned forward and glanced around Kate to Henry. 'You ready for this, Mr H? I'm going to put you in a wedding suit so sharp you'll outshine all the other groomsmen on the day. Won't take much, of course. Handsome chap like you.' She winked at him, and he chuckled.

'Buttering me up for the budget already, Amy? She's only been engaged an hour.'

'Well, you know what they say. The early bird catches the worm,' she replied with a cheery shrug.

'Right. Well, on that note, I think I'll leave you early birds to it,' he said. 'Catch you in a bit.' He wandered off towards Eleanor.

'You and me, Mr H,' Amy called after him. 'Savile Row, suit shopping. Only the best for you!'

He nodded and raised his hand in acceptance.

Kate couldn't help but grin. 'You're shameless, Amy Ellis.'

Amy shrugged, unbothered. 'Shame is for bores.' She sipped her champagne then turned and took Kate's hand in hers to take a closer look at the ring. 'That really is an *insanely* big diamond.'

'Yes,' Kate replied, the grin fading as she stared at it.

Amy's brow dipped in brief concern, and she lowered her voice. 'Do you not like it?'

Kate let out a troubled sigh. 'It's a very beautiful ring—'

'But it's not *you*,' Amy said, cutting her off with a grim nod. 'I thought that when he showed me, but he'd already bought it. It's very *Lance* though.'

'It *is* very Lance,' Kate agreed. She'd didn't wear much jewellery, but what she did have was delicate and subtle. The complete opposite of this dazzling statement ring. She sighed. 'It's not that though, Amy. It's *everything*.'

'What do you mean?'

Just as Kate tried to answer, there was a loud cheer. More champagne was being poured over the tower of glasses. She closed her mouth and exhaled tiredly.

Amy squeezed her arm and pulled her to the door. 'Come on. Let's talk in the kitchen. And give me that. We both know you hate champagne.' She took Kate's glass as they slipped out of the room. 'I shoved some Prosecco in the fridge for you earlier.'

'Thanks,' Kate replied gratefully. That was *exactly* what she needed right now.

She made a beeline for the glass cupboard and pulled one out, while Amy grabbed the Prosecco and placed it on her mother's large kitchen island. Glad to be away from all the noise and the people, she sat down on one of the bar stools as Amy popped the cork and poured.

'Here.' She passed it to Kate and sat down, taking a sip from her own glass. 'So what's going on? Talk to me.'

Kate sighed and shook her head. She wanted to tell Amy everything, but as she sat there, she realised she couldn't. Not unless she was prepared to tell everyone. It wasn't fair to place that burden on her. She fiddled with one of her nails.

'This was all just really out of the blue,' she said finally. 'It just completely blindsided me.'

'Surely you'd considered the possibility of this happening at some point though?' Amy asked. 'You've been together about a year now, right?'

'No. I really didn't,' Kate answered honestly. 'And yes, just over, actually.' She rubbed her head and looked up with a troubled frown. 'It's just, we've never talked about it. I thought we were *good*, you know? As we are. I didn't think we were *here* yet. We don't even live together. And then this today, everything is just, I don't know...' She pushed her hand back through her hair and felt all the knots from the wind snag on her fingers. 'Why didn't you *warn* me he was planning this?'

'*Warn* you?' Amy repeated. 'Kate, it was a proposal, not the four horsemen riding into town! I didn't want to spoil the surprise.'

'But I *hate* surprises,' Kate reminded her. 'I always have. *You* know that.'

Amy's forehead creased, and her eyes clouded with guilt. 'I'm sorry, Kate. I thought this was one surprise you'd *want*. I didn't mean to let you down.'

'No. *No*, Amy you haven't done that,' Kate replied quickly. She was being unfair. 'You're an amazing friend. I'm sorry. It's *me* who's being weird.' She kneaded her forehead, stressed.

Amy rubbed her arm. 'Listen, it's been a lot today. You're just overwhelmed. That's all this is. And you really *are* terrible with surprises. You're right – I should have told you. You've never reacted well.' She pushed her long blonde curls back over her shoulder then propped her elbow on the breakfast bar and rested her head on her hand with a smile. 'Remember that time I tried to surprise you on your birthday by jumping out of a box on your doorstep dressed like a clown? We must have been twelve or thirteen. You cried for an hour and didn't talk to me all day.'

Kate stared at her accusingly. 'That was my *ninth* birthday and that was the scariest thing – to this *day* – that has ever happened to me. I *still* get nightmares about it now and then.'

'Oh, come on, it wasn't that bad,' Amy said with a dismissive wave. 'I was even holding your birthday present. It was cute.'

'It was a doctor's kit,' Kate said flatly. 'I could see the fake syringe and pill box through the front, which really *didn't* look cute in the hands of a clown, I assure you. Anyway...' She shook off the memory with a small shudder.

'*Anyway*,' Amy echoed, 'my point, though I could have perhaps used a better example, is that you're right – you *don't* take surprises well. That's all this is. You and Lance are one of the best couples I know. You're perfect together. And don't forget, despite being surprised, you said *yes*,' she said with a smile. 'You wouldn't have said yes to marrying the handsome, charming, successful boyfriend you love while in shock if you didn't really mean it. *Would* you?'

'No,' Kate replied, looking down at the bubbles rising in her glass. 'I guess not.'

'Well, there you go then,' Amy said. 'You just need another three glasses and a good sleep, and in the morning you'll feel much better, I promise. You always do in situations like these.' She took another sip of champagne. 'Except for that time with the clown. Admittedly that was an exception.'

Kate forced a smile and sipped her Prosecco. *But I didn't say yes, Amy*, she wanted to scream. *I didn't say yes. So what am I supposed to do now?*

# SIX

The sound of Eleanor's voice wafted into the kitchen from the hallway just as Kate and Amy finished off the bottle of Prosecco.

'It's a trick *every* woman should know and a good way of impressing a man,' she said briskly. 'I'll show you now, so you have it up your sleeve for when you find a good prospect. With the Christmas season coming up, there will be plentiful opportunities to find young men. Parties and gatherings.'

'Really, it's fine,' a voice replied. 'You've given me those instructions. I'll just give it a go at home later on.'

Kate and Amy exchanged a wide-eyed look, and Amy quickly shoved the bottle in the bin.

'What are you doing?' Kate whispered, amused. 'We're thirty-five.'

Amy clapped a hand over her mouth and let out a muffled giggle. 'Well, we'll probably still be in trouble for *something*.'

'Nonsense,' Eleanor continued firmly. 'There's a knack to it, Beth. You need to see the subtleties in the art of soufflé making first-hand or you'll never master it. And *no* man wants a woman with a flat soufflé, *let me tell you!*'

Kate had to bite both her lips together to stop herself laughing as her mother walked into the kitchen with Beth, another of Kate's close friends.

Eleanor stopped short and frowned. 'What are you doing in *here,* Katherine? You need to get back to your guests.'

'Lance has it handled,' Kate replied, covering the snort of amusement at Amy's *I told you so* expression with a cough.

Eleanor frowned. 'Katherine, are you *drunk*?'

'No!' she exclaimed. 'Of course not.' She glanced at the bin. 'I don't think.'

'Right, well you'll need to move over, girls. I'm showing Beth how to make a good chocolate soufflé.' Eleanor rolled up her sleeves and marched around to their side of the island. 'Come on now – spit-spot.'

Beth shot them both an accusatory glare as they stood up and moved aside, followed by a silent plea for help. Kate bit her lip with a silent look of apology, feeling bad. They should have brought her in here with them. Eleanor had probably pounced on her ages ago.

'Do you know how to make a soufflé, Amy?' Eleanor asked.

'Of course,' Amy lied. 'Kate taught me your wonderful method years ago.'

Kate closed her eyes and waited for the inevitable.

Eleanor's head popped up, and her sharp gaze honed in on Amy. 'If *Kate* taught you how to make soufflés, then you're in even more need of this lesson than Beth,' she told her bluntly. 'Despite a lifetime of my attempts to teach her, Kate could never quite grasp it. Her soufflés are terrible.'

'Thank you, Mother,' Kate said wryly.

'Sorry, darling, but they are. You know they are,' Eleanor said, her tone completely unapologetic. 'I'll need to *unteach* you whatever Kate showed you and reteach you the correct way. Beth, open that drawer and grab three pinnies out, please.'

Beth gave Amy a withering look of disappointment. None of them were getting out of it now it seemed.

'Now, it's *all* in the egg whites. I'll show you when we get there, but just mentally note that, girls, and keep repeating it in your head so you don't forget. It's *all in the egg whites*,' Eleanor instructed.

'Definitely, will do *just that*, Eleanor,' Amy said, nodding seriously. 'And I'm *really* excited to do this at some point, but we should really get back to the party, shouldn't we?'

'If you can be in here for this long *drinking*, Amy Ellis, you can spare a little longer to learn something *useful*,' Eleanor reprimanded, raising one eyebrow at her.

'Yes, Mrs H,' she replied with a resigned sigh.

She reached for a pinny, and Beth's arms flew up in the air as her gaze moved back and forth questioningly between the two. Amy shrugged back and mouthed, *What can I do?* Kate held her hands up to show them she had nothing, either, as they both turned to her.

Eleanor popped back up and pulled up her sleeves. 'Right, ladies. So—'

'Actually, Mrs H, I'm so sorry, but we really will have to do this another time.' Amy said with a sad grimace. 'It's just that, um, it's, er...' She looked around helplessly for a moment, then her gaze landed on Kate's hand and a lightbulb pinged up behind her big blue eyes. 'It's just that with Beth and I both being here at the same time, I thought Kate should take the opportunity to talk us through her wedding ideas.'

'*What?*' Kate asked, her eyebrows shooting up.

'Oh, of course!' Eleanor chimed at the same time. She clapped her hands together with a wide smile. 'You do have both your bridesmaids here together, Kate. That's an excellent idea, Amy. OK, the soufflé can wait.'

She began putting everything back again, and Kate shot

Amy an accusatory glare. *What the hell?* she mouthed. Until her mother had walked in, she'd been starting to calm down, but now all her panic and guilt and worry and confusion rushed back at full force. The *last* thing she wanted to do right now was talk about a wedding. Amy's reassurances had given her hope that she might wake up tomorrow and feel differently. But right now, this still felt like some strange, awkward nightmare.

She suddenly realised Beth was looking at her with a wobbly emotional smile, and she looked at her questioningly.

'I know we always used to say we'd be each other's bridesmaids when we were kids, but when it actually happens, when you hear one of your best friends wants you as their bridesmaid...' Her voice rose to a squeak, and she flapped her hands wildly at her face as tears filled her eyes. 'It means the world. Thank you, Kate.' She sniffed, and a couple of tears fell down over her smile.

'Aw, Beth!' Amy pulled her into a hug. 'It's so special, isn't it? You were both mine, now we're Kate's and one day we'll be yours, and we'll have gone full circle.'

Kate forced a smile as they looked at her, but she didn't trust herself to make it a group hug right now, in case she broke down. They'd always been her people, Amy and Beth. Her safe place when she felt vulnerable and needed to ugly-cry over things no one else would understand. But this was different. This was something she needed to get her own head around before she pulled in anyone else.

'Alright then, girls, let's go!' Eleanor said. Her eager gaze moved over to Kate. 'Where shall we start, Katherine? We're all ears.'

Eleanor stared at her expectantly, and Kate fought hard to keep her true feelings out of her expression as she was thrust unwillingly under the spotlight. 'Um...' She racked her brain, trying to come up with a suitable answer.

'Thinking about venues, there's Kirtlington Hall,' Eleanor suggested with a spark of excitement.

Kate's eyebrows shot up. 'Kirtlington Hall is *huge*,' she reminded her.

'And *very* grand,' Eleanor added, missing Kate's meaning entirely. 'It's ideal.'

'*Too* grand,' Kate said with a frown. 'Not ideal at *all*.'

Her pulse began to quicken at the thought. The fact they were talking about a wedding *at all* was enough to send her heartrate clanging through her chest like an old fire alarm, but the sort of royal circus it would be at *that* place was beyond comprehension.

Eleanor frowned. 'How can somewhere be *too* grand for your wedding?'

'If you'd prefer something more country-style, Caswell House is really nice,' Beth offered. 'It's a big stone barn, really pretty.'

Eleanor gasped and put a hand to her chest. 'My daughter is *not* getting married in a *barn*! Of *all* the suggestions! Honestly, Beth, she's not a *cow*.'

'No, it's not like a farmyard barn,' Beth replied. 'Seriously, it's really nice.'

'Wouldn't you rather a London wedding?' Amy jumped in. 'That's more you. City sleek. Contemporary sophistication.'

'Of *course* she wouldn't,' Eleanor argued, seemingly affronted. 'She'll have a *traditional* wedding, somewhere around here, where she's *from*.'

Kate watched them argue and suddenly wished that she could just tap her heels together three times and disappear, like Dorothy in *The Wizard of Oz*, back to her flat in London. Or to anywhere, really. Anywhere but here. But as the argument went round in circles and Eleanor began to bristle, Kate realised she was going to have to step up and take control of the conversation before it escalated any further. There was no escaping it. She took a deep breath.

'Listen, the thought of a big wedding really just doesn't appeal to me at all,' she said carefully. 'I think maybe something intimate would be better. Just something small, nothing too crazy. OK?'

Her mother drew back from her with a look of shock. 'What do you *mean*, Katherine?' she asked, flustered. 'Darling, I love you dearly, but if you're about to suggest some awful elopey-style registry-office dash, then you can think again. I mean *really*, Katherine, how could you even ask me to consider it?'

Kate blinked. 'I wasn't—'

'And I doubt Lance will be OK with that – he has such *vision*!' Eleanor cut her off. 'And this is his wedding, too, remember. It's not all about *you*, Katherine.' She gave Kate a disappointed stare. 'Really, you can be quite selfish sometimes, darling.'

Kate's mouth dropped open. 'But—'

'No.' Eleanor cut her off firmly. 'I'm sorry, but you can toss that idea right out of the window.'

'*Mum*,' Kate said, holding her hands out to halt her. 'No one said anything about a registry office. OK?' This wasn't going well at all.

'Well, what *are* you thinking then?' Eleanor asked.

'Um...' Kate looked out of the window, searching for inspiration, but all she found was a bird staring back from a nearby branch. It took off, flying away into the distance. *Lucky sod,* she thought.

'Well?' Eleanor prompted.

Kate exhaled heavily and admitted defeat. 'I don't know, Mum.' She spread her arms with a shrug. 'It's all happened so fast, I haven't had time to think.'

'Haven't had time to think about what?'

They all turned at the sound of Lance's voice. He walked

into the room and over to Kate, resting an arm across her shoulders.

'Hello, fiancée,' he said warmly.

Kate looked up and forced the threatening cringe into a smile, squeezing his hand. She couldn't answer him. Her stomach twisted uncomfortably at the sound of the word *fiancée*. As he turned his attention to the rest of the group, she rested her head against his taut torso and felt a wave of helplessness wash over her. There had to be a way to back out of this. But *how*, without hurting and embarrassing everyone she cared about?

'We were just discussing possible options for the wedding, Lance,' Eleanor told him. 'I suggested Kirtlington Hall,' Eleanor began.

'That's a great idea,' Lance said enthusiastically.

'Isn't it? And I was thinking—' Eleanor pushed on like a runaway steamroller, and Kate quickly sat upright, knowing she had to rein her mother in now before she got too carried away.

'Actually, I really don't want it there. I'm sorry, but a big wedding would be my worst nightmare,' she said honestly. 'I know it's probably not what you had in mind, but I'd just prefer something small. More intimate.'

'Gosh, OK.' Lance pushed his tortoiseshell glasses up his nose and let out a small laugh. 'Well, I can't say I'm not surprised, but if an intimate wedding is what you want, then that's what we'll have. Whatever makes you happy.'

Kate shot him a small smile. Despite the fact he'd caused this waking nightmare, she was grateful for this support. It would make containing her mother a lot more manageable.

'There are some great smaller venues in London we could look at,' Lance continued. 'We could maybe book one of the Michelin-star restaurants for the wedding breakfast. Galvin La Chapelle would be quite fitting.'

There was a chorus of agreement, and Eleanor jumped on

board immediately. Kate's relief swiftly faded, however, as Eleanor began listing which magazines might be interested in covering the event and Lance met these suggestions with great enthusiasm.

'So, when are we thinking?' Eleanor asked. 'A spring wedding? Autumn?'

'Actually, I've always rather liked the idea of getting married on New Year's Eve,' Lance said. 'Saying goodbye to the old year and celebrating the start of a *new* one as a married man. What do you think, Kate?'

Kate hesitated, feeling like she was being backed into a corner with this question. Did they really have to make that decision now? 'Um, New Year's Eve?' she repeated.

She thought it through for a moment. It was the end of October now, so that would make it over a year away. Perhaps agreeing to that wasn't the worst idea. It would put a decent amount of time and distance between her and the wedding. Her hopes lifted a little, and she slowly nodded.

'Yes,' she said, a little more enthusiasm in her tone now. 'I think that's a perfect idea.'

'Yeah?' Lance queried.

'Yes,' she said firmly. 'New Year's Eve is ideal.' *Fourteen months*, she told herself encouragingly.

'Perfect!' Eleanor clapped her hands together. 'Then that's settled. New Year's Eve it is! Oh, Katherine, what an exciting Christmas this is going to be! Not long to plan, but that's OK. What is it, nine weeks away?'

'*This* new year?' Kate's eyes widened in alarm as her strategic agreement completely backfired. This hadn't been the idea at all.

'It's impossible,' Amy said, horrified.

'No, it's not,' Eleanor replied. 'It's just been agreed that it will be a small wedding, hasn't it? No need to organise endless suppliers or hundreds of guests. We'll simply book the venues, then buy the dresses, the suits and a cake.'

Kate opened her mouth to argue, then realised there was no argument there to use. She'd well and truly screwed herself over.

'It could work,' Lance said thoughtfully.

'*Really,* Lance?' Amy exclaimed.

'I can't see why not,' he replied. 'Alright. Let's do it! What do you say, Kate?'

Kate felt the back of her neck grow hot, and she placed a cooling hand there as she tried to think of *any* valid argument she could throw in against the idea, but there wasn't one that didn't betray her true reluctance.

'I can't see why not, either,' she said eventually. *Literally,* she added mentally. *I literally cannot find a valid reason.*

'That's settled then!' Lance exclaimed. 'The date's set. We're getting married!'

There was a small eruption of cheers, and Lance lifted his glass. Kate lifted hers, too, automatically clinking it against everyone else's with a fixed smile as she internally screamed. As she imagined herself leaping up from the bar stool and throwing herself through the window to escape. Because this was all moving too fast, and in a direction she hadn't even *chosen.* This wasn't a miscommunication over which restaurant they were going to eat at tonight or what style she asked her hairdresser for. Those things were temporary. This was *forever.* Heat crept up her neck into her cheeks, and she pulled at the neck of her jumper.

Standing up abruptly, she flashed everyone a quick smile. 'I'll be back in a minute.'

Not pausing to explain, Kate made her way through the house to the furthest point away from the party and the kitchen. The furthest point away from *everyone.* As she slipped out the side door, she sucked in a deep breath of air and bent over, giving in to the panic attack that had been hovering over her since she'd first seen the ring.

Pulling in great deep noisy gulps of air one after the other, she finally let it all out. All the panic and the horror and the guilt and the helplessness. It all flooded out of her in a series of big ugly anxiety-filled sobs, each one tripping over the next as they rushed to escape, to the point she could barely breathe. Her sobs grew faster and faster until she felt like she couldn't get enough oxygen in her lungs. It was only when she started to feel faint that Kate forced her emotions back under control and sat down on the ground, exhausted. She leaned back against the wall, and slowed her breathing, staring bleakly out at the garden.

There was something wrong with her. She knew that. Anyone else would be thrilled to be in her position. But knowing that didn't make it any easier. She rested her head back and closed her eyes. She needed to clear her head, but it was impossible here. She needed to get away somewhere quiet, somewhere where she could get a grip on everything without everyone buzzing around her.

A quiet ping broke the silence, and after a few seconds Kate pulled her phone from her pocket to see who it was. It was from her boss, Simon. She opened it with a small frown of surprise. He never usually disturbed her on a weekend.

*Sorry to do this to you on a weekend, but you're needed in Boston urgently. If I can get you a flight tomorrow, could you make it work? I know tomorrow's Sunday. I wouldn't ask this of you if it wasn't absolutely necessary. Too complex to explain over text. Bob will fill you in when you land. Please let me know ASAP. –S*

Kate blinked and sat up, grasping the unexpected and perfectly timed lifeline with both hands.

*Yes, I can make it work. Book it. Whatever flights available. —K*

Pressing send, she glanced back towards the door, then typed out a second message.

*Actually, if you can get me on one tonight, even better. I can be at the airport in three hours. Let me know. —K*

# SEVEN

After breaking the news that she'd been urgently called away to everyone – and dealing with her mother's very vocal disapproval that she'd even *consider* leaving the country so soon after being proposed to – Kate had finally managed to slip away from the party and head back to London, with the excuse that she needed to pack. Faced with two hours alone with Lance in the confines of his car, she'd exaggerated her exhaustion and pretended to fall asleep a few minutes into the drive. She didn't actually sleep a wink on the long trip back, her head too busy spinning to rest, as she tried to process the events of the day. But she kept up the pretence until Lance had dropped her off at her flat, as she just couldn't face talking about it all any further.

Her flight the next morning passed in a wonderfully peaceful blur, and after landing in a grey, rainy Boston, Kate taxied to her hotel and took some time to freshen up. By the time she was ready to get to work, she *almost* felt normal again.

Grabbing her phone from the table by her window, Kate placed a call to Bob, one of the senior partners in their Boston office and the man she answered to whenever she worked on this side of the pond. She looked out across the skyline as the

US dialling tone hummed in her ear. The rain had finally stopped, and flight trails were now the only thing graffitiing the clear blue skies over the city.

Bob picked up on the second ring. 'Kate, hi. You here? Flight OK?' He sounded tense.

'Yes, all checked in. Where shall I meet you?' She glanced at her watch. 'Have you eaten? Want to catch me up over lunch?'

'I figured you'd be hungry, so I've ordered in,' he replied. 'Chinese food from that place you like. It just arrived, so head on over while it's still hot.'

Kate frowned suspiciously. Bob hated Chinese food.

'OK,' she replied. 'I'll be right over.' She put the phone down and picked up her jacket.

A year or so before, Sophie, her counterpart in the Boston office, had upped and left without notice, after dumping the contents of all her case files in one big defiant *screw you* pile on the floor of her office. It was her parting gift to Derek, a slick-talking junior partner she'd been dating, after finding out that not only had he cheated on her with one of the interns, but he was also married with two children. Kate had worked closely with Sophie, their international clients often needing services on both continents, which made her the only person who knew enough to piece all the files back together correctly. It was supposed to have been a temporary arrangement for Kate to fix the files and just keep things ticking over until they recruited Sophie's replacement, but as time went on, Kate had realised she really enjoyed the variety of working between the two offices. And as she was happy to continue that way, Bob had been in no hurry to change things.

The office was just two buildings down from the hotel, so a few minutes later Kate let herself in and made her way up to Bob's office on the sixth floor. She knocked and then walked in.

'Kate!' Bob held his arms outwards with a wide winning

smile. His unnaturally white teeth gleamed against tanned leathery skin, and his blue eyes twinkled with a sharpness that belied his years. 'You look well. How are you?' He beckoned her further in. 'Come. Sit, sit, sit. You must be tired.'

'I'm great, thanks,' Kate lied, allowing him to gently push her towards the lounge area of his office, comprising of four sofas facing inwards in a neat square.

The coffee table in the centre was covered in unopened boxes of food along with two tumblers filled with ice and a dark amber liquid she suspected was probably whisky. Raymond, one of the other partners, lay casually back on the sofa facing her, his arms draped across the back, one leg crossed over the other. The relaxed stance didn't fool her.

'How are things here?' she asked, looking at them both in turn.

'They're good – things are good,' Bob replied brightly, nodding as he sat down next to Raymond. 'But we'll get to all that. Come – take a load off. Let's have some food and catch up first. Can I get you a drink?'

He stood back up, but she halted him with her hand.

'With all due respect, Bob, and I really don't mean to be rude, but I'm not having a drink until you tell me what's going on.' She looked at them both in turn. 'All Simon told me was that I had to jump on an emergency last-minute flight, out of the blue, with absolutely no explanation attached, and I *did*. So now I'm here. On a Sunday.' She placed her hands on her hips. 'I think it's about time someone told me why. *Before* trying to soften me up with alcohol.'

Raymond let out a low chuckle. 'I told you she wouldn't let you beat around the bush.' He looked up at Bob with an amused smile.

Bob sighed and sat back down, scratching the almost bald – save a few white hairs that were still clinging on – top of his head. 'OK, we'll get right to it then.'

Kate nodded and sat down opposite them.

'How much do you know about when this company was started?' Bob asked.

Kate frowned. 'The basics, really. That it was started here in 1962 by Jacob Morris. Philip Schuster became a named partner in '75, and then he opened the London office in '81.'

'OK.' Bob nodded, then leaned forward onto his knees and laced his fingers together. Kate eyed the boxes of food on the table as her stomach grumbled at her. They smelled amazing.

'Please, eat,' Bob urged, following her gaze.

Raymond sat up and reached for one of the boxes. '*Yes*,' he agreed, with feeling. 'Please do. I've been daydreaming about the Kung Pao chicken since we ordered. I so rarely get to order it here, with Bob around, and my wife has me on a seemingly lifelong diet.' He shot her a pained look.

Kate laughed and reached for the nearest box. She tonged some noodles and waited for them to continue.

'Coreaux Roots was one of the accounts you took over when Sophie left,' Bob said, picking up his drink. 'They likely haven't called on you for much, but are you familiar with their business?'

'Yes,' Kate said, mentally sifting back through their brief encounters. 'Timber company. Up in Vermont?' Bob nodded. 'Medium-sized enterprise that turns over pretty decent profits, if I remember rightly. A lot of land assets.'

'That's right,' Bob said. 'What you may *not* know is that they were Morris's first-ever client.' He took a sip of his drink. 'Jacob Morris came from very humble roots. Family had nothing. He was smart though. And *driven*. Got himself a full scholarship to university, studied hard and graduated top of his class. He made a friend there, who stayed in touch after he returned to Boston.'

'Let me guess – the founder of Coreaux Roots?' Kate asked.

'One and the same,' Bob replied. 'When Jacob started this

firm a year or so after college, his old friend William was first in line. He signed up on a retainer for the firm to handle all legalities related to Coreaux Roots, *and*' – Bob paused – 'himself and his wife, too.'

Kate frowned. 'What do you mean?'

'From what I gather, William didn't trust lawyers. But he trusted Jacob. Asked him to take all of it on, not just the business,' Bob told her with a grim shrug. 'Jacob was just starting out. He needed clients... So while his firm officially only dealt with corporate law, he agreed to William's request, too, as a favour.'

Raymond cleared his throat. 'They worked out quite a specific contract which included us being legally responsible for their affairs after they passed.'

Kate's eyebrows briefly shot up. That was unexpected.

'William died a few years ago and it was pretty straightforward, as he left everything to Cora,' Bob continued. He shifted in his seat and fiddled with his glass. 'But last week, we got a call informing us Cora had passed.'

'I'm sorry,' Kate offered.

'Oh, we didn't know her. But, as I said, the contract was very specific,' Raymond replied. 'It states that in the event of the second of the two passing away, whoever officially holds their account here has to take up temporary residence in their home within one week and personally log all assets and possessions, then divide everything according to the terms of the will. In the absence of clear named parties, that person must make an informed decision about how everything is divided after spending no less than six weeks in their home and around the people who were in their lives.'

'*What?*' Kate exclaimed, looking back and forth between them. 'You can't be serious?'

'Very much so, I'm afraid,' Bob replied.

Kate shook her head. 'No,' she said firmly. 'Bob, I *can't*. I have cases coming out of my ears. I can't just drop everything to go and fanny about listing frilly curtains and fine china. With all due respect, that's something you can send a junior to do. They can be spared, and it all sounds straightforward, if a little odd...'

Bob held his hand up and cut her off. 'Kate, I already thought of that, and that *was* the initial plan.'

'*Was?*' Kate echoed warily.

Bob sighed heavily and pulled a newspaper out from under the food-laden table, passing it over. '*This* is why we can no longer switch you out.'

'Of course you can,' Kate countered, taking the paper from him. 'As long as we put the right people in place, it won't matter that it's not *me*. Who would even know?'

'*Oh*, quite a lot of people,' Raymond said heavily.

He pointed at the paper in her hands, and she looked down.

'Oh.' As she stared at the bold black headline and the pictures underneath, her hopes of getting out of this suddenly plummeted.

# EIGHT

Kate stared down at herself. They'd taken her headshot from the company website, a very stiff corporate picture that she hated.

'What *is* this?' she asked, scanning the lines of text.

Neither answered, giving her time to find out herself. She sat back and read the article properly. It was front-page news for some small-town paper. An interview of sorts with Cora's great-niece, Aubrey Rowlings. Kate skimmed over the ramblings about how much Cora and William had done for the town and for Aubrey – and cut to the part that involved her.

> 'In death, as in life, my great-aunt Cora made sure that things would be carried out with the best interests of the people who worked for Coreaux Roots in mind,' Aubrey Rowlings tells us with a look of pride shining through the veil of grief she currently wears. 'My great-uncle William, God rest his soul, had a contract written up many years ago with the founder of Boston law firm Morris & Schuster. It promised that Morris & Schuster would always have their best and finest lawyer handling their legalities, and that when they died, this lawyer

*would come here to our town in person, to carry out their wishes to the letter. My great-aunt Cora made sure I had a copy of this contract, so I knew who to call to help me bring us all through this difficult transition.'*

*Aubrey Rowlings confirmed that the top lawyer who looked after Coreaux Roots and the Moreauxs' personal legalities is British national Kate Hunter. Kate works across the company's Boston and London offices and will be here in Pineview Falls, according to this agreement, within a week.*

*In a final statement, Aubrey Rowlings addresses all the people whose livelihoods rely directly on Coreaux Roots: 'We are all grieving the loss of my cherished great-aunt Cora, and this change naturally has a lot of people worried about the stability of their future. Well, I can assure you that with the help of the highly esteemed Kate Hunter, I will continue to drive Coreaux Roots forward and make sure our thriving company remains the same pillar of the town it always has been.'*

Kate groaned, mentally picturing her next few weeks go up in flames, and Aubrey Rowlings holding the match. She pursed her lips, looking to the picture next to hers. Slightly large, neat white teeth beamed out of the page from the wide-eyed, plump-cheeked smile of a thirtysomething blonde, in smart cream tweed and a matching hairband. Kate threw the paper down on the table and rubbed her forehead.

'There's more, Kate,' Raymond said gently.

She looked up grimly. 'Go on.'

'Right now, you're probably thinking this could be solved by explaining your situation to Aubrey Rowlings and sending someone in your stead,' he guessed. 'But this girl isn't all she seems.'

'She *is*, as the article states, Cora's great-niece,' Bob confirmed. 'And she *does*, as her words make it appear, work within the company. But in a low-level role with nothing that indicates the company or any part was to be left to her. The will that stands, surprisingly, is the original, and the instructions are simple but clear. In the instance that they had no children – which they did not – what is left to whom must be decided by you after assessing all viable options. Reasonable proof also has to be shown that this decision is made in the best interests of all who work there, and, rather frustratingly,' Bob sighed, 'it clearly states that if anyone thinks our decision was rushed or is not in the best interest of the workers, they can take us to court.'

Kate pulled back. 'Why would William put *that* in the contract if he trusted Jacob so implicitly?'

Bob threw a hand up in the air as if to say, *Who knows?* 'Whatever game this Aubrey is playing, it could do us some real damage now that it's hit the press.'

'Of a small-town newspaper that no one probably even reads,' Kate argued. 'It's not like it's *The New York Times*, Bob. This article will be tomorrow's chip paper and soon everyone will have forgotten all about it.'

Both men looked confused. '*Chip* paper?' Raymond asked.

'Yes. *Chip paper*. Oh, never mind,' Kate said dismissively. 'It's a British thing. But look, my point is, no one that knows us is ever likely to see this.'

'No,' Bob agreed. 'But since Cora died, we've had three separate family members contact us with lengthy arguments as to why they're entitled to the company, the house and everything else, and an equally lengthy argument as to why the others shouldn't get a dime. And when the ball drops into whoever's hands it eventually does, the others aren't going to go away quietly. This contract and your position are now public knowledge.' Bob grimaced apologetically. 'Which means—'

'Which means you can't risk not following it to the letter, because whatever we do, they'll denounce us to appeal the decision, and a breach of contract like sending someone in my stead will be their first port of call,' Kate stated the point he was getting to flatly.

Bob nodded. 'And then it *will* hit the bigger papers. We'd lose all credibility. There's no way around it, Kate. You have to go. I'm sorry. And the reason we asked you to come today is because the seven days are officially up tomorrow. We've hired you a car. You'll need to head out to Pineview Falls first thing in the morning as it's about a five-hour drive away, up in northern Vermont.'

She closed her eyes and dropped her head into her hands. Six weeks would take her almost to Christmas – and that's if she was lucky and could tie it all up in that time.

'Your cases are all being taken care of while you're out there, so there's nothing else to worry about,' Raymond told her. 'Your assistant will start the handover in the morning.'

'And you'll have access to Erica for anything you need,' Bob added.

Kate raised her eyebrows underneath her hands. Bob *never* shared his assistant. Not with anyone. That he was doing so now spoke volumes on its own. Her ring stabbed into the side of her finger, and she jerked her head back up at the sudden reminder.

'Oh! I got engaged yesterday!' she exclaimed, fresh horror setting in as she realised the new predicament she was now in.

'Congratulations!' they both replied in cheerful unison.

'The wedding is New Year's Eve,' she whispered.

'Oh.' Raymond's eyes widened, and Bob blew a long breath out through his cheeks.

As an awkward silence fell across the room, Kate chewed the inside of her cheek. If she was being honest, part of her felt absolutely elated that she had a legitimate reason to run away from all her problems back home. But the bigger part of her knew that it would only delay and add to them in the long run. She'd also have to break it to Lance that she wouldn't be there to plan the wedding, that she'd have to do what she could from here. That wouldn't be a fun conversation at all. Nor would the following conversation be, with her mother. She exhaled heavily and dropped her head into her hands. Why did life have to be so complicated?

# NINE

Kate flicked down her indicator and pulled off the highway with a smile.

She'd been on the road for five and a half hours, stopping only once to briefly stretch her legs, not wanting to draw the journey out any longer than necessary. To her surprise, snow had been steadily falling for the last hour, and as it coated the ground in a thick, fluffy white blanket, the wet grey world she'd woken to that morning had morphed into a bright and cheery winter wonderland.

The satnav led Kate down a much quieter road, and the sounds of the highway soon melted away to nothing. As she wound through the dense evergreen forest, the sun briefly broke through the clouds and every fallen snowflake began to wildly glisten. Kate smiled, drinking in the incredible natural beauty of the place, and for a while she almost forgot all her problems even existed. After another few miles, she passed the welcome sign for Pineview Falls, and as she reached the main high street, she slowed to a crawl.

'What on *earth*...' she muttered, looking around.

Picturesque buildings lined each side of the street, some

brick, some colourful timber, all of them unique. Quaint shopfronts and restaurants advertised their wares in pretty window displays and on hand-painted signs, and the coffee shop in the centre, with its pitched roof and wooden window shutters, was so inviting she almost pulled over there and then. The whole high street was thoroughly enchanting, as though it had been plucked right out of the pages of a fairy tale. She'd never seen anywhere quite like it.

The red-framed glass door fronting one of the larger brick buildings swung open and two small boys ran out, scampering away clutching paper bags. A frantic-looking woman chased after them a moment later. Kate glanced up at the sign: *The Old Firehouse Sweets 'n' Treats*. Her gaze moved up to the old bell in the brick tower above it.

'Seriously, what *is* this place?' she breathed.

Driving on, Kate left the curious little town centre and made her way to the address Bob had given her the night before. She stopped on the side of the road and peered out of the window, as the satnav declared she'd reached her destination. A white picket fence separated a generous garden from the sidewalk, opening up at one side into a wide sweeping driveway. The brick walls of the large home were painted white, with grey shutters decorating the outer edges of each window. Steps led up a covered porch that ran half the length of the house and to a green front door with a big brass knocker.

After pulling on to the drive, Kate parked and rummaged in her bag for the keys. She found the one marked *Front Door*, then, hesitating only a moment to brace herself against the cold, she finally got out of the car.

'Jesus *Christ*,' she yelped as she grabbed her handbag and dashed across to the front of the house. Pulling out the key, she blew in and out in swift bursts, shivering violently. Her hands shook as she tried to insert the key into the lock, and she cursed under her breath. 'Come *on*,' she pleaded. 'Come on, come on, come on... *Yes!*'

The key slid in, and soon she was inside with the door closed firmly behind her. Her joy at being out of the cold was short lived, however, as she swiftly realised it wasn't much warmer inside.

Wrapping the practically useless tailored red coat she'd chosen for Boston's mild autumn temperatures around herself a little tighter, Kate tucked her hands under her armpits and looked around the wide entrance hall, wondering where to start. She flicked on the lights and began to explore, walking from room to room and admiring the polished hardwood floors and pale greens and greys in the tastefully decorated rooms. She found the hot water and heating controls and whacked them up high, then checked the kitchen cupboards and fridge. She'd forgotten to stop en route for supplies, which her stomach was now pointedly reminding her.

A carton of milk stood in the door of the fridge, and she eyed it dubiously before pulling it out to check the date. Remarkably it actually *was* in date, and as the only other things she could find were half a box of Cap'n Crunch and a jar of instant coffee, she settled for exactly that.

'*Ugh!*' She grimaced as she tasted the first mouthful of cereal. It was awful. She glanced disgustedly at the box. 'Well, Cora,' she muttered, 'you have great taste in furniture, but cereal, *not so much...*'


A couple of hours, another grudging bowl of Cap'n Crunch and a hot shower later, Kate changed into her pyjamas, thankful that she'd packed her thick winter ones. She'd only packed a couple of outfits, not realising she'd be over here for more than her usual couple of days, and neither were even remotely suitable for the freezing temperatures that had fallen over northern

Vermont. As she'd unpacked, the local news had informed her that the area was experiencing an unexpected cold snap, the usual mid-November weather having apparently decided to make its entrance a little early this year. She'd have to go out first thing and buy some more suitable clothes, she decided. And a coat that actually stood a chance of doing its job.

Her phone buzzed, and she looked down to see Lance's name flash up on the screen. She took a deep breath in to steel herself and then answered with a smile.

'Hey, how are you?' she asked.

Despite the stress of the situation, it still felt good to see his face. She'd worked so late the night before, going over everything with Raymond and Bob, that she hadn't had a chance to talk to him.

'I'm good,' he replied with a yawn. He lifted his glasses and rubbed his eyes, dropping them back into place and pushing back the stray hair that flopped forward. 'Just having a bit of a crazy night. Client went psycho in the courtroom and now there's months' worth of damage to try and undo.' He shook his head. 'How're things there? What was the big emergency?' There was a short pause as he squinted at the screen. 'Where *are* you?'

Kate sat down on the bed she'd commandeered as her own and looked around. 'Long story,' she said heavily.

'I've got time,' Lance replied.

'Have you?' Kate looked at her watch. 'It's gone *midnight* there. You must be exhausted.'

'It's fine.' Lance held a full glass of Scotch up to the screen. 'I need to decompress anyway. Call it a bedtime story.'

'I'm not sure it's one you'll like,' Kate warned.

'Try me,' Lance replied, a touch impatiently. 'Come on – what was this emergency they flew you over on a *Sunday* for?'

Kate shifted into a more comfortable position. He'd been less than impressed when she'd broken the news that she had to leave for Boston just hours after he'd proposed, so *this* news was going to go down like a lead balloon.

'Short version, there's an old contractual agreement that falls outside our usual remit and that I'm responsible for carrying out. The terms are explicit with no room for movement, and it requires me to be in Vermont for the next few weeks,' Kate told him frankly.

'*What?*' Lance looked horrified. 'Kate, we're getting *married* in a few weeks!' His expression darkened. 'No. This is too much.' He shook his head. 'You need to turn it down and get on a flight back home *tomorrow*. Tell Bob he can find someone else.'

'*Excuse* me?' Kate's eyebrows shot up in surprise.

She could understand his feelings, but that didn't mean he could tell her what to do and how to speak to her boss.

'Kate, this is *preposterous*,' Lance continued. 'I mean, what do they expect you to do? Put some case you shouldn't even be on in the first place before your own wedding and then fly back last minute and hope you make the ceremony?' His voice rose as the sarcastic side of his temper went off like a firework. 'Sorry, Vicar, she's somewhere over Birmingham – if she parachutes into the wind just right though, she still might make it...'

'Lance, come on,' Kate said gently. 'I'll come back and forth to sort whatever I need to for the wedding. Bob even put his PA at my disposal to make things as smooth as possible.'

'Why? Where's Pam?' he asked.

'Busy handing all my cases over to other people.' Kate paused, but Lance had fallen into a brooding silence. 'Look, I'll explain everything properly when I get back, but just know that I tried to get out of it. I really did, but there's no other way.'

Lance opened his mouth to speak but then clamped it back shut and just shook his head.

'It's not ideal, I know. But Amy and Mum are both absolutely itching to get involved. I'll speak to them tomorrow and let them loose.' She forced a smile, trying to break the tension. 'They can make sure things are going to schedule and cover anything I can't. It'll be fine. Really, the only thing that I can't delegate is finding my dress.'

Lance sighed sharply. 'It will have to do, I guess.' He ran his hand back through his sandy gold hair and sighed. 'I hope they appreciate what you're doing for them here.'

A frown flickered across Kate's brows. 'I'm just doing my job, Lance. You know how it is, the weekends, the late nights – you've just got in yourself. It's what we do.'

'For *now*, sure,' Lance responded. 'But we're getting married soon. I just hope they understand what that means.'

Kate blinked at the screen. 'What *does* that mean?'

'Well, you won't be at their beck and call to jet around the world putting out their fires forever, Kate. We'll be *married*. Your priorities will change.'

'To *what* exactly?' she asked slowly.

Lance tutted. 'To *us*, to our *future*. We'll be building a proper home somewhere soon. Finding the right place, turning it from house to home. That alone will be a huge project. And when our children come, that'll change things considerably. Raising them will be a full-time job. They won't be able to pull you away like this then. If you're even still working at that point.'

Kate's eyebrows flew sharply upwards. 'I'm sorry, *what*?' she asked. 'Why wouldn't I be working? Surely if we have kids, we'd juggle them and our careers between us.'

It was Lance's turn to look surprised. 'That wouldn't be a very stable environment, Kate, being tossed between two busy overloaded parents. Children need their mother to be a constant.'

Kate felt the prickly heat begin to rise from her chest up and around her throat again. She placed a hand on the back of her neck and rubbed it.

'There's nothing wrong with two working parents, Lance. And I haven't worked as hard as I have for my career to give it all up and become a stay-at-home mum,' she said in an apologetically stubborn tone.

'There's nothing wrong with being a stay-at-home mum, Kate. Raising children is the most noble job a woman can do,' Lance berated.

'I didn't say otherwise, but it just isn't what I've personally spent all these years working towards,' Kate responded, feeling the heat reach her face. 'And why are we debating all this? We've not even discussed kids yet – whether we even want them, and if so when, in the distant realm of *someday* that might happen. We've barely been engaged two days!'

'*Someday*?' Lance repeated. 'Kate, we're not starstruck kids with all the time in the world ahead. For two people of our age about to get married, I assumed it was a given that kids aren't in the too distant future at *all*. That *is* the point, after all, isn't it? A family? And with the utmost respect here, and though I truly *hate* to sound like your mother, you *do* only have so much time biologically.'

Kate stared at him in disbelief. 'I'm thirty-five, Lance, not sixty! Women have kids well into their forties all the time.'

'I know, but there's a lot to think about. What if we struggle to get pregnant? What if we want a gap between each child? What about the *health* risks that increase with age?' Lance let out a long breath. 'I'm just thinking about things practically. When you take everything into consideration and plan backwards from the outer edge of your physical ability, it lands us pretty much here.'

Kate opened her mouth to respond but just ended up shaking her head, for once lost for words.

'Look, we don't have to talk about this now,' Lance said finally. 'But you do need to think about it. I mean, come on, Kate. You're the biggest planner I know. You run your life with the precision of a military general, so why would this be any different?' He raised an eyebrow in question. 'Set all the variables out and work the plan back. You'll see what I'm saying. We can come back to this conversation then. Now, when will you be back?'

Kate paused and bit her lip, staring back at him through the screen. Her flight back was booked for Friday night, but after this conversation, she suddenly wanted to go home even less than she had before.

'I'm not sure yet,' she lied. She'd get Erica to cancel it for now, she decided. Then she could rebook when she was ready.

'You're not *sure*?' Lance repeated.

'I need to see what dates are best to come back, but it won't be too long,' she told him vaguely. 'This place is just a lot further than Boston, so I need to sit down and figure it all out properly.'

Lance let out a resigned sigh and rubbed his eyes once more. 'Right. OK,' he replied. 'Just let me know as soon as you can. I'll book a nice restaurant for when you get back, take you for dinner.' He smiled at her tiredly. 'We haven't actually celebrated our engagement just the two of us yet.'

Kate nodded. 'Life gets in the way of everything, right?' she joked.

Lance nodded wryly. 'I'll speak to you tomorrow. Sleep well.'

'You, too,' she replied.

The call ended, and Kate stared at the screen. Two days ago, she'd just been minding her own business and living her life, happily chugging along in her own lane with her easy-going boyfriend and her annoying but manageable clients, and now her whole life had been turned upside down. Two days ago, she'd thought she and Lance were on the same page, but suddenly he was ambushing her with proposals and arguing over her body clock. Planning out their future with a bunch of kids they'd never discussed but who he suddenly expected her to give up her career for to raise full-time. Kate didn't know what she expected the picture to look like when, or if, she had children one day, but she knew it wasn't that. She moved her gaze to the small iceberg sitting on her finger and sighed.

Why would Lance assume she'd be happy to throw away her career after all the years of hard work she'd put into building it? She'd always thought he respected her career. That he'd respected *her*. At the very least enough to ask for her opinions. She'd always thought they saw each other as equals. But suddenly she wasn't sure. In fact, after the last few days, Kate wasn't sure she knew Lance very well at all.

# TEN

Kate woke up bleary-eyed and momentarily confused. She squinted one eye open, noting the slow pound of a brewing headache, and looked around.

Rolling over, she picked up her phone from the bedside table and checked the time. It was already past nine.

'Crap,' she muttered, instantly following it with a sneeze. She reclosed her eyes. '*Double crap.*'

She really couldn't afford to get ill right now. Not if she was going to get this tied up and sorted before Christmas. And there was no way on earth that she was spending Christmas away from home.

She sat up and stretched, pausing to gaze through the window after opening the curtains with a tired smile. Snow was still falling steadily outside in thick fluffy clumps. It was beautiful. As the sight stirred up memories of building snowmen and snowball fights, Kate's thoughts naturally drifted to Christmas.

Eleanor always went all out at Christmas. From the first of December the house was taken over by Christmas in every way possible. Every room, door and hallway was decorated with perfect precision. Matching pyjamas would appear – a tradition her father always complained about, though they all knew he secretly loved it. There would be eggnog constantly warming and games by the fire every night, while the Nat King Cole and Michael Bublé Christmas albums took turns on endless repeat.

Kate would go with her dad to find the perfect tree for the living room. Then, as it was the only part of the decor Eleanor ever allowed them to touch, they'd dress it together, purposely overfilling the branches with every contrasting colour and shape known to man, just because they could. Eleanor would smile afterwards and tell them it looked wonderful, unaware of her complete inability to hide her true feelings from her expression. And Kate and Henry would pretend to believe her. Just like they'd pretend they never noticed that their tree decorations always looked a little tidier and their baubles more neatly spaced the next day. Eleanor would sing cheerily along to the music in the kitchen as she baked enough festive goods to feed a small army. And, as she actually had quite a good voice, and as Kate loved to hear her mother happy, sometimes she'd just sit quietly on the stairs for a while to listen. The warm spicy aroma of cinnamon and nutmeg would fill every corner of the house, and the three of them would tramp through the fields on long family walks with flasks of hot chocolate between stints of curling up on the sofa with a good book.

Christmas had always been her favourite time of year. And the one time of year she usually tried to spend as much time as possible at home. This December was going to look a little different though, it seemed.

She rubbed the sleep from her eyes and Christmas from her mind and got dressed, layering up and stuffing a decent supply of tissues up her sleeve in between increasingly snotty blows. She made a mental note to stock up on enough cold medicine to knock out a small elephant, then set out on her quest to find the nearest Walmart.

She carefully backed the hire car off the drive, slowing to a snail's pace after sliding on the frozen ground almost straight away, then navigated her way out to the main road, relieved to find this one was well gritted. Fifteen minutes later she was there, and after an hour inside the large superstore, Kate reappeared, laden with bags and wearing a coat that made her feel like the Michelin Man with its padded white rolls. It was a fashion sacrifice she was willing to make though, as it kept her toasty warm from head to mid-shin. After dumping the bags in the boot, Kate took a quick swig from a bottle of cold medicine, then set off back towards the house feeling much more prepared.

When she reached the suburban edge of the town, Kate slowed to a crawl, careful to stop at each intersection, as Bob had reminded her to do. The rule in America about coming to a complete stop even if there were no other cars around was something she'd never understood. But the law was the law, especially for a lawyer.

Coming to another stop, Kate glanced down the road to her left. A black pickup truck was headed towards the intersection, but as it was still a little way off, she pulled forward to cross. Partway across, she suddenly realised that the pickup wasn't slowing down the way it should have been. A zap of panic shot through her body and she instinctively slammed her foot on the brakes. To her horror, her car kept moving, sliding on through the snow as she lost traction.

'Shit! No! *No, no, no...*' She tried to get the car back under her control and just about managed it, but it was too late. She'd stopped right in the middle of the intersection. Kate felt a cold stab of terror as she watched the pickup hurtle towards her, and she braced for impact, realising she was out of time.

She cringed, waiting for the explosion of pain she knew was coming, but at the last second the driver finally seemed to wake up and the truck jerked sharply away, missing the front of her car by inches. It veered into a spin across the icy road, then crashed, nose first, into a tree.

'Oh my God!' Kate exclaimed.

Smoke began to rise in thin ribbons from the top edges of the truck's doors, and she quickly got out of the car, leaving her door open as she rushed across the road.

The driver's door swung open and a man stumbled out, coughing and waving the smoke that accompanied him out of his face as he walked a few paces and then turned back to look at his truck. He bent forward and rested his weight on his thighs for a moment.

Kate closed the distance quickly, searching for any obvious sign of injury as she stopped. 'Are you OK? Are you hurt?' she asked urgently.

He didn't answer her, instead just stared back at his truck with a pained expression.

'Excuse me?' Kate eyed the smoke still filling the cab. 'Er, you really need to move away from the vehicle. With smoke coming out like that it's not safe to—'

'*Smoke?*' he repeated in an incredulous tone, straightening up and turning towards her. He looked her up and down, his expression contemptuous. 'That ain't *smoke*. It's just the powder from the airbags. Any idiot above the age of *twelve* knows that, ugh...' He looked back at his truck.

Kate stopped short, her eyes flashing with annoyance. 'There's no need to be so *rude*. I was just trying to help.'

'*Help?*' He reached up and gripped two fistfuls of thick silver-streaked dark hair. 'Look what you've done to my *truck!*'

'What *I've* done?' Kate exclaimed indignantly, angry now. '*You* were the one who didn't stop at the intersection. *I* was already on it!'

'*Yes*, and if you'd just kept moving instead of losing control of your car like the amateur tourist you clearly are, you'd have been well away by the time I passed,' he yelled, raising his voice to match hers. 'I mean, *Christ*, who lead-foots the damn *brakes* on *ice!*'

'*You did!*' she reminded him, gesturing towards his truck.

'Because I *had* to!' he retorted accusingly. 'There's a damn *ditch* across that verge.' He pointed to where the truck would have naturally ended up had he not changed course. 'It was either roll it in the ditch, hit you, or hit the tree and pray it only damaged the bodywork.' He shook his head and dropped it to his chest. 'Either way, you've cost me *considerably* today.'

Kate stared at him with furious disbelief. She opened her mouth to give him a piece of her mind, but before she could, the short, sharp blast of a police siren screamed out from right behind her. She jumped nearly out of her skin at the unexpected sound and they both turned around.

The squad car was just a few feet away and an amused-looking police officer leaned out of the window, watching them from behind a pair of dark aviators. The rude truck driver groaned. Kate took a deep breath and regained composure. The officer stepped out of the car and walked towards them leisurely, readjusting his gun belt and hooking his leather-clad thumbs into the front belt loops.

'Well, well, well,' he said with an oddly wide grin. 'What have we here?'

Kate glanced at his badge. 'Officer Healy, hi. My name is Kate Hunter.'

'Hello, Kate,' he replied in a cheery tone.

She smiled but watched him warily. She didn't know much about American police officers, other than that they were stereotyped on the TV as donut-loving car-chase enthusiasts, and as the outsider here, she knew she held an immediate disadvantage. She needed to explain what happened before the other driver could twist things. 'Officer, I was crossing this intersection after the appropriate pause on the stop line, when this *lunatic*, who came from—'

'He *knows*,' the rude driver said, cutting her off.

Kate's head whipped round, and she glowered at him before turning back to the officer. 'He was way back there,' she continued, nodding down the road, 'when I...'

'*He knows*,' the driver repeated impatiently, interrupting her again.

Kate made a sound of frustration and glared at him once more, opening her mouth, determined to finish her sentence. 'I...'

'It's OK, ma'am.' Officer Healy halted her with his hand. 'I know. I saw it all.'

'Oh. Right.' She blinked and cleared her throat.

'Like I said,' the rude driver said flatly. 'Douche's been hiding in the bushes just waiting for a free meal ticket.'

Kate glanced at the officer, but he just shook his head unfazed.

'Oh, Langston, you really do make things *so easy*.' He unhooked a thumb and reached for his handcuffs. 'Walk to me and turn around.'

'*Bite me*, Healy,' he replied, complying anyway.

The driver met her gaze as the officer cuffed him, his piercing blue eyes shooting out hot daggers above the unkempt beard that covered the bottom half of his face. Kate shook her head and looked away. The guy could have killed them both. He was lucky all he'd damaged was the truck.

'Failing to come to a full stop at an intersection, dangerous driving, insulting a police officer,' Officer Healy reeled off with a low whistle. 'That's a lot you've given me this time, Langston.'

'You'd better get my truck over to Marl's garage ASAP, Healy,' the man she now knew as Langston growled.

'You're in no position to be making demands,' Officer Healy replied.

He'd been walking Langston towards the back of the squad

car, but Langston abruptly stopped. 'I *need it* for *tomorrow*,' he said in a low, angered tone.

Healy stared back, his smile dropping, and Kate wondered if he was about to snap. But after a tense pause, Healy just glanced downwards with a sniff.

'I'll have it to Marl by lunchtime, alright?' He pushed Langston towards the car and reached to open the back door. 'Now get in.'

He pushed Langston's head down and closed the door, walking back towards Kate with the wide grin back in place.

'I'm sorry you had to experience that, ma'am. As both you and your vehicle are unharmed, I'll just need to take your name and number for the record and you can be on your way,' he told her.

'Will you not need a statement?' she asked, pulling her wallet out of her pocket. She handed him one of her business cards, which he glanced at and pocketed with a nod.

'Shouldn't do – it's all pretty straightforward, and my dash cam caught it all,' he replied. He pushed his aviators up his nose and glanced back at the squad car. 'I'm just glad I was around when it happened. Langston's a mighty *unsavoury* fellow, I'm afraid.'

Langston narrowed his eyes at Healy through the window, clearly able to hear everything they were saying.

'Who knows *what* might have happened were I not here.'

'Well, I'm glad you *were*,' Kate replied, shooting one last look at the man now in the officer's custody. 'Thank you.'

'You're more than welcome,' Healy answered. 'You mind yourself now. I can tell you're no local, so enjoy your visit to our little town. It's a nice place for the most part. Just steer clear of trailer trash like Langston here, and you won't go far wrong.'

Kate nodded. She wanted to ask Healy what he meant, exactly, by *unsavoury fellow*. Was he violent? What *would* have happened if Healy had been around? But instead she just smiled. The man was in custody now. There was no need to know.

'Noted.' She walked back to her car. 'Thanks again, Officer.'

'Anytime,' he called back.

Kate watched him drive away and then turned to continue her journey back to the house with a loud sigh. She pulled a tissue out of her pocket and blew her swollen red nose. It had certainly been an eventful day already, and it wasn't even lunchtime! She *had* planned to venture out to the main street later, but she wasn't sure she could take anything else going wrong today.

*No*, she decided firmly, discarding the idea. She was going to wrap up warm and sit inside with a ridiculously over-mallowed hot chocolate, then make a start on everything she needed to do. She wasn't venturing outside of the house again today.

Not for *anything*.

# ELEVEN

Kate's run of bad luck had unfortunately not quite been over. She hadn't noticed the gentle slope of the road leading up to the house the day before, when the snow had still been settling, and on her way out she'd felt too fuzzy to give it much thought. But she'd realised the moment she'd seen it on her return that she wouldn't get the car back up. She tried anyway, but no matter what she did, it just slipped casually from side to side as soon as it hit the slope. After fifteen minutes of attempts, Kate had given up and parked on the side of the road, then walked the rest of the way, regretting some of the heavier items in her shopping bags.

After a well-earned hot chocolate topped with a gravity-defying mountain of mini-marshmallows, Kate had succumbed to her cold-induced lethargy and simply curled up with a blanket in a cosy chair beside a window overlooking the garden. She'd watched the snow fall slowly to the ground, each flake carrying another whisper of that special magic that only snow can bring to the world. And in the peaceful silence Kate felt herself finally relax into an unfamiliar state of complete calm.

She must have fallen asleep, because the next thing she

knew, the snow had stopped and the sky had turned a deep inky blue, devoid of sun or snow cloud. Somehow, she'd slept away the entire afternoon, and although she knew she could easily continue through the whole night, too, she did feel considerably more energised than she had. There were several missed calls and messages from her mother, the messages filled with links to different wedding articles and services. Kate debated sending a quick reply to say she'd call tomorrow, but knowing Eleanor would ignore that and take the fact Kate was beside her phone as an invitation to call straight back, she decided against it.

Sitting cross-legged on the floor of the bedroom, Kate laid out three sheets of paper in front of her. There wasn't an awful lot of information to take in just yet, but they were a starting point. She picked up the first one and studied it thoughtfully. Erica had managed to pull a fair amount of information from Aubrey Rowlings's social media profiles. Aubrey was thirty-two, a college dropout who'd gone through a string of jobs, never lasting more than a year, other than at Coreaux Roots. Aubrey had been *there* for just over three years.

Though the rest of Erica's findings were of no use legally, they still gave Kate some insight into who she was dealing with. Aubrey's online persona showed her living the sort of lifestyle Kate imagined might befit a mediocre motel heiress. Not quite the private jets and yacht summers the Hiltons could afford, but the champagne flowed freely and the Chanel was pointedly placed in every regally posed selfie.

It was clear though, when Kate read further, that this was all a facade. Aubrey rented a one-bedroom apartment in a very average part of town and earned only a modest wage. All in all, she appeared to be more interested in faking appearances than actually working for anything.

According to Aubrey, Cora had been grooming her to take over and become the sole leader of Coreaux Roots. But unless there was a lot she was missing from this picture, Kate couldn't see why Cora and William would want to hand their beloved company to Aubrey.

Placing the profile back down, Kate picked up the one beside it. Evelyn McEwan was Aubrey's grandmother, Cora's sister and a failed actress who had, when the sporadic small-time roles she occasionally won dwindled to nothing, written and self-published an equally unsuccessful book titled *Me, Myself & the Flickering Spotlight of Hollywood*.

Evelyn hadn't properly worked a day in her life from what Kate could tell. But she'd still been busy. She'd had one daughter with her husband, Fred, who'd died ten years before. Since then, Cora had been paying Evelyn's rent and living costs through a monthly stipend.

Evelyn claimed to have a letter from Cora expressing that *she* should be given the house, along with a fifty per cent share of the company – but that she didn't need to actually *run* the company. That she was to become a silent partner and live out the rest of her days in comfort from the income. This seemed as suspicious to Kate as Aubrey's claims, from what she knew about William and Cora so far.

Moving on to the last of the three, Kate read the few sparse lines of information that had been available on Edward, William's brother. There was no photo, as he had no online presence for Erica to search through. All they knew was that he was twelve years William's junior and ran a small news press a few towns over. Public records showed that he had a son living in Australia, but that was it.

Edward had sent one short correspondence to the office, expressing that he wished to lay claim to the company and other assets in full. He claimed it was his duty to ensure Coreaux Roots survived, as the only blood relative who understood what it took to run a company and to protect it from those who would run it into the ground. That he owed this to his brother's memory.

Kate let the paper drop to the floor. All three had requested a meeting with her, but she'd asked Erica to field them for now until she could get a better overview on things. Ideally, she wanted to figure out how close William and Cora had been to each of them first. And where better to do that than right here?

Photos, lovingly saved birthday cards, frequent plans in old diaries. Those would be pretty good indicators. She just had to figure out where to find them.

Kate twisted round and grabbed the second steaming cup of cocoa she'd made herself today, from the bedside table. She blew on it gently, breathing in the sweet, comforting smell as she looked around the room. This room wasn't quite as modern as the other rooms in the house. The salmon-pink walls, frilly cream curtains and bedspread, and the lace doilies on the bedside tables all told tales of a very different time. But something about the room had drawn her in. Perhaps it was because it was the one room she could actually get a sense of Cora in. The desk in the corner had an old sewing machine out on top, the case open and a tub of cotton reels left beside it. The scissors were out, too, slightly open, as though Cora had been midway through using them and had meant to come back.

Kate had thought about tidying the desk to work at, but she couldn't bring herself to move any of it. It seemed wrong some-how, like she'd be removing the last living traces of Cora. She stared at it now, imagining the old lady she'd seen in many photos around the house, sitting there, threading the needle.

Her phone rang, and the sudden interruption made her jump, hot cocoa splashing over the rim of her mug and down her front.

'Ouch! *Ugh*, great...' Kate stared down at the brown stain on the front of her green button-up pyjamas with a look of tired annoyance, before reaching for the phone. She closed her eyes and debated ignoring it again but then reluctantly answered, knowing she would only be delaying the inevitable. 'Hi, Mum.' She leaned back against the bed and pulled up her knees.

'*Finally!*' Eleanor exclaimed accusingly. 'So your phone *is* working and you *are* alive then, Katherine?'

'Yep,' she replied. 'It would seem so. How are you?'

'*Don't* you how-are-you *me*, young *lady!*' Eleanor replied indignantly. 'I've been worried *sick!*'

Kate instantly felt guilty. 'Sorry, Mum. I'm fine though, honestly.'

Eleanor tutted impatiently. 'I know *you're* fine, Katherine. I'm not worried about *you*. I'm worried about this *absurd* idea of you working from another *continent* when you need to be at *home* planning your *wedding!*'

Kate pressed her lips together in a long thin line and shook her head.

'Katherine? Did you *hear* me?' Eleanor demanded.

'I did,' Kate replied wryly. 'You've spoken to Lance then?'

'Of course I have,' Eleanor replied. 'I wanted to make sure he was OK, poor boy. He put so much into that amazing proposal and then you *swan off* halfway across the world the very next day! Honestly, Katherine, what is the *matter* with you?'

The six-inch tall doppelganger devil who Kate liked to imagine lived on her shoulder from time to time poofed to life. It nudged her neck and whispered a wickedly tempting response into her ear, but her angel counterpart appeared on the other shoulder just in time and leaped across with a well-aimed rugby tackle. As her two fantastical mini-mes fell away, Kate simply sighed.

'I have to say, I'm amazed the man still wants to marry you at *all*, the way you've been acting,' Eleanor continued.

Kate's eyebrows shot up. 'What's *that* supposed to mean?'

'I *mean*, Katherine, the way you've been acting since the moment he popped the question hasn't been very nice,' Eleanor replied, her tone still huffy. 'You think you hide it well, but you *don't*. At least not from *me*. I know you better than you think I do, you know.' There was a pause as she sighed. 'I know you aren't a fan of surprises. You never have been, but you spent *all day* looking like you'd rather have been anywhere else. And you covered it well enough. Luckily, men don't tend to notice anything that's not spelled out for them in black and white, in my experience. But Lance *will* notice that his future wife is so uninterested in her wedding that she's run halfway across the world.'

Kate rubbed her eyes. 'I'm not running away from anything, Mum. I'm *legally obliged* to be here, and it's bound into a very specific contract that it has to be me.' It wasn't a total lie. 'If I could have avoided this, I would have. I've looked for any possible way out, but there just isn't one.'

'Hmm,' Eleanor mused. 'Send the contract over to me. I'll give it a look over, see if I can find anything.'

Kate had to pull the phone away as the little devil began to scramble back up.

*You are not a lawyer!* she silently mouthed at the screen. Then, taking a deep calming breath, she put the phone back up to her ear.

'... because there could be something in that, Katherine – that's the sort of thing people often overlook.'

'Mm,' she mumbled noncommittally. 'Anyway, look, I'll be back as much as I can between now and the wedding. I'm just so glad I have you and Amy back there to hold the fort.' She dangled the bait and waited.

Eleanor sniffed. 'Well, yes. You *do* have us.' Her tone brightened. 'And I've had some utterly brilliant ideas, even if I do say so myself. I think I have a bit of a knack for this, actually. Small or not, I can promise you now, with all I have planned, your wedding is going to be absolutely spectacular. It really is. You should *see* the design boards I've had made up. They should be coming back from the printer first thing in the morning, just in time for the first meeting tomorrow. I called the girls to arms the *moment* I heard about all this, so *don't* worry. Mother has it *all* under control.'

Eleanor's words sent a little ripple of dread through Kate's middle. The devil cringed and the angel twisted her clasped hands with a worried grimace.

'Right,' she managed, her tone sounding much calmer than she felt. 'Well, um, I actually need to go now, Mum.' She put Eleanor on loudspeaker and sent a frantic SOS text to Amy. 'And you probably need to go, too, I imagine. It's past three in the morning there.'

Anyone else calling at this time would have surprised her, but this was Eleanor. A woman more stubborn than a hundred mules could ever hope to be collectively. After Kate had ignored her calls, she'd probably set an alarm to try again now.

'Yes, I probably should sleep. There's a lot to do tomorrow.'

There was a short pause.

'You know, you're a beautiful girl when you show it, Katherine. You know, when you don't have your hair up in that horrible bun or wash yourself out with one of those awful grey suits. You work hard, you're interesting and you're *clever*. *Really* clever. All in all, you have a lot to offer the world. To offer a partner.'

Kate squeezed her gaze with a suspicious frown. 'Thanks, Mum,' she said cautiously.

'You truly *dazzle*, Katherine,' Eleanor said simply.

Kate glanced at the screen to double-check it was actually *her* mother on the end of the line. Apparently it was.

'But there's one advantage you don't have and never will,' Eleanor continued.

*Ah, here it comes*, Kate thought with resigned amusement.

'You're not a *man*. Men have the luxury of *time*. When they hit forty, their looks just get better. Fifty? They call them silver foxes. Do you know what they call us?'

'Silver cats?' Kate quipped.

'No, darling, and your sense of humour won't help you then, either,' Eleanor replied. 'What I'm getting at is that while men look better with age, we do *not*. You're at your peak, Katherine. Forty is around the corner, and I can assure you, if you found yourself back on the single line again then, you wouldn't land another Lance.'

Kate let out a burst of laughter. 'Wow, OK. Thanks, Mum!'

'You'll still look good for your age, but you'll be tired around the edges,' Eleanor continued, ignoring her. 'You'll be labelled – wrong as it will feel – as being the woman who chose a career over having a family. Past her sell-by date for any man shopping for one.'

'Emmeline Pankhurst is turning in her grave right now,' Kate said flatly.

'*Emmeline Pankhurst* was married to her husband at twenty-one,' Eleanor shot back, unfazed. 'Don't try to out-feminist *me*, Katherine. You'll lose.'

Kate shook her head with a wry smile. She and her mother had two very different ideas about what feminism was today, but now wasn't the time.

'I'm not saying it's fair, but it *is* the way of the world,' Eleanor continued. 'Lance is a gentleman. He's intelligent, successful, *ridiculously* handsome, a good man and he *loves* you.'

'Mum, I *know* all this,' Kate said, stifling a sigh. Clearly her mother noticed more than she gave her credit for. She pinched the bridge of her nose. 'Look, I don't know what's brought this on, but there's really no need to convince me. OK? Especially at three in the morning. Seriously, you should get some sleep.'

'Alright, well...' Eleanor paused reluctantly. 'Goodnight, darling.'

'Night, Mum.' Kate ended the call and ran her hands over her face. Glancing back down at the screen, she realised her battery was nearly completely dead. '*Damnit.*'

She'd accidentally left her adaptor in Boston and had forgotten to buy a new one. Luckily there was one socket in the kitchen that had a USB port, so she'd been using that sporadically. Standing up, she padded out into the hallway and down the stairs to the kitchen.

She connected her phone to the charger and then stopped to get a glass of water. Leaning back against the kitchen counter as she sipped it, she thought back to Eleanor's words about how spectacular she planned to make this wedding. Those words had filled her with dread, and that dread now lurked in the pit of her stomach. Once Eleanor had set her course, there was very little anyone could do to stop her. She was too powerful a force. Unstoppable. A battleship stuck on full speed, parting every wave it crossed without pause.

Kate closed her eyes as a wave of helplessness washed over. She had no control over anything from here. Then again, it didn't feel like she'd had much control back home, either. It was all moving too fast, and she felt like life was simply dragging her along in its wake. Would it ever calm down enough for her to dust herself off and get her head around everything? Or was she stuck in this nightmarish state of overwhelm for good?

# TWELVE

After trudging back upstairs, Kate decided to call it a night. She blew her nose and sat down on the bed, reaching for the cold medicine and taking another swig of the potent syrup straight from the bottle. Something Eleanor would have been mortified to see her doing.

As she placed it back on the bedside table, Kate accidentally knocked her pen off the edge, and it rolled under the bed. With a tut, she kneeled down and lifted the frilly valance, peering into the darkness underneath. She squinted as her eyes adjusted, then her expression suddenly brightened. 'Now *that* is *exactly* what I need.'

Kate picked up the pen, then pulled out the big box behind it. A box that was helpfully marked *Cora's Diaries*. She crossed her legs and placed it in front of her, her tiredness forgotten, then she pulled off the lid and cast her eye over the contents. Inside were a number of diaries in varying shapes and sizes. Some were hardback, some leather. There were patterned ones and plain, old and new. An old worn diary right at the bottom caught her eye, and she picked it up, running her hand gently over the intricate pattern embossed on the soft leather. She paused as her thumb reached the initials in the corner: *CD*. If this was Cora's, it had to have been from before she was married.

She opened the cover and saw that she was right. Just inside, in neat, old-fashioned cursive was the name Cora Dawson, alongside the year 1955.

Kate glanced back at the other diaries in the box. She needed a more recent one, to glean any information about Cora's relationship with the three vultures now circling. But eying the diary in her hand, she hesitated, feeling strangely curious. After a few seconds of deliberation, she decided to indulge her curiosity and stood up, taking the diary with her into bed.

She shuffled down under the covers, propped herself half up with pillows and turned to the first page. The first few lines immediately caught her interest, and by the end of the first paragraph, Kate was fully engrossed.

*1 January 1955*

*It is with a deeply troubled, painfully conflicted and yet thoroughly alive heart that I walk into this new year. I cannot bring myself to complain about my predicament, because that would mean I wish not to be in it. And that is something I could never wish. For to be without these troubles would also mean to be without the feeling that has awakened my soul from the dreamless sleepwalk it existed in before. The feeling that lights every dark corner of my being like a hundred flares all fired at once. The feeling we all think we know, until the moment we really do. The feeling of love.*

*I have never had reason to write with caution before, and I withhold nothing for myself now, for I am not ashamed of my feelings or opinions. But for the sake of another, whom I hope to protect should this fall into the wrong hands and be read by an unsympathetic party, I shall, from here on, refer to all outside of my household by one initial only.*

Kate's eyes sparkled with intrigue, and she turned the page.

*We attended the party at the manor last night to see in the new year, and, as usual, W's father spared no expense. It was a grand affair, with music and dancing and champagne. Mother disapproves of alcohol, so she did not partake in the drinking of the champagne, nor would she approve of me doing so. But after a particularly energetic dance with W, we retired to the library to cool down, and he brought along two glasses. I should perhaps have declined, but I decided that, as I only have one life, and as W is a good friend whom I trust to keep a secret, I would go ahead and try it. It turns out that it is rather delicious. I wouldn't mind drinking it again, should the opportunity arise. I said as much to W, who said he would make sure that it did.*

W must be William, Kate realised. She grinned at young Cora's idea of rebellion. A glass of champagne among family friends was a far cry from the cheap beer on park benches that *her* generation had cut their teeth on as teenagers.

There was a sudden noise downstairs, a dull clang, that cut through her thoughts. Having grown up in an old house, Kate initially ignored it. Old houses made all sorts of noises.

The second sound made her pause. This time it was a bang, like something hard knocking onto something else. She turned to the door with a small frown. The third noise was a scrape, and this time Kate sat bolt upright, her face draining of colour. These weren't just the sounds of old floorboards and pipes.

*Someone was in the house.*

# THIRTEEN

Ice flooded Kate's veins, and her heart began to thump against the wall of her chest. She instinctively reached for her phone and then remembered with horror that it was downstairs. She put her hands to her mouth, the grisly details of all the true crime shows she'd ever watched flickering through her mind in startling detail. They all mashed together into the image of her mother's face boxed into a TV screen with a text ribbon running across her chest, reading *Eleanor Hunter, Kate's mother*.

'*It was a week before they found her,*' TV Eleanor said tearfully. '*Parts of her, anyway. They never did find her arms.*'

Kate jumped sharply out of bed, pushing the image of her body being hacked into small pieces firmly out of her mind. Someone being in the house was bad enough without her imagination making it worse. She looked around, searching for something she could use as a weapon. Whoever was down there most likely thought the house was empty, so if she was smart – and armed to at least *some* degree – there was a chance she could get out of this safely. She just needed to keep a cool head.

She suddenly remembered seeing a baseball bat in the bedroom next door. Creeping to the door, she peered through the crack into the hallway, then, seeing it was clear, she hurried over and grabbed the hollow metal bat. She tested it out in her hands and tried a couple of practice swings, then with deep reluctance she forced herself out of the room and down the stairs.

She moved slowly, her heart pounding in her chest, pausing halfway down where the stairwell opened up to peer over the banister towards the kitchen. Light spilled out, and she could tell by the ongoing sounds that this was where the intruder was, though she couldn't see much from where she stood.

She had to stifle a gasp as a shadow suddenly crossed the floor. He – or she – hovered just around the corner for a moment and then retreated towards the other end of the kitchen again. Realising that this was probably the best opportunity she was going to get, and not giving herself time to talk herself out of it, Kate mustered all the courage she had and rounded the bottom of the stairs.

She ran into the kitchen with the bat held high and let out a fierce warrior cry. 'Arghhhh!'

Skidding to an aggressive stop, she glared down the long room towards the intruder, but as she registered his face, her mouth dropped open and she gasped.

'*You!*' she accused, horrified. It was the driver who'd nearly rammed her with his truck. The man the police officer had carted off and warned her to steer clear of. *Unsavoury*, he'd called him. As the scene replayed in her mind, she suddenly remembered his more chilling words. *Who knows what might have happened were I not here.*

Her eyes flickered between his face and the kitchen knife in his hand. 'Oh my God,' she breathed, her insides turning to ice. *He was here to kill her.*

'*You,*' he growled back.

His voice cut through her fear, reigniting her survival instincts, and she lifted the bat higher. *Langston,* she suddenly recalled the officer calling him. Kate's throat constricted, but she batted back the panic, focusing on him instead. She stared at his wild beard, shaggy unkempt hair and rumpled clothes, and wondered how he'd tracked her down.

He let out a dark growl and took a step towards her. 'What the *hell* do you—'

'*Don't* you move a *damn* muscle, you *psychopath*!' Kate roared, cutting him off and jolting the bat back with a threatening half step towards him, as though about to attack.

Kate knew she had to make herself look threatening, even though she wasn't. It was simple psychology but the key to survival throughout the animal kingdom. Something she'd learned from the many hours of David Attenborough documentaries she'd watched over the years.

Adrenaline coursed through her body, and blood rushed through her ears as she edged towards her phone. Langston had paused, confusion colouring his angry glare. Was he buying it?

'That's right, *back off*,' she continued aggressively. 'You try *anything* and it's this bat versus your skull! And not that steel needs much help against bone, but I've got good aim and I'm stronger than I look, *buddy*.' She reached out and grabbed her phone.

Langston glanced at it. 'Yeah?' His hard gaze glinted in challenge. 'You really like your chances?'

He took a pointed step towards her, and a frisson of ice-cold alarm ran up Kate's spine. It wasn't working! She swung the bat in a swift arc, cutting through the air between them viciously.

'*Don't test me*,' she hollered, puffing out her chest with fake confidence. 'I will *end you*. I'm no damsel you can distress, *mate*. I'm from *London*. And in *London* we eat bully boys like you for *breakfast*.' Kate jutted out her chin, putting on her very best ghetto-girl impression.

Langston's eyebrows shot up, and she internally winced, wondering whether the breakfast comment had been a touch over the top. She'd clicked the wake button on the side of her phone five times down by her side and then, risking a quick glance at the screen, quickly swiped her finger across the emergency call option. She pointed the bat towards him with a dark glare, aware she needed to keep him distracted.

'You think you're bad, but you have *no* idea what dangerous is,' she bluffed. 'You picked the *wrong* victim today.' She swiped the air with the bat again.

'You think you're a *victim*?' He shot back. '*You* didn't end up with your car wrapped around a tree. *You* didn't end up being hauled to the police station and held there for hours by an ass on a power trip. And now you stand there threatening *me*, holding *that*.'

'Yes, I *damn well do*,' Kate shouted, cutting him off. 'Because I sure as hell am *not* going to be murdered here tonight! Here, standing by the back door of the *damn kitchen* at the back of this *lovely house*, barely a *week* after *Cora Moreaux* died here!' She prayed she was giving the police enough information to find her. She'd heard the quiet sound of the call connecting.

Langston's face darkened, and anger flashed anew in his eyes. 'Cora didn't *die* here,' he growled.

'Oh yeah?' Kate blustered. 'And you know that *how* exactly? Murder her with that big knife in your hands, *too*, did you?'

Langston blinked and pulled back as though repelled by her words. He glanced down at the knife and then back up to her, suddenly clocking the live call on the phone in her hand. He shook his head.

'No. *No*. That's not... Here.' He placed the knife down on the kitchen counter and stepped away with a sound of frustration. 'You've got it all wrong. Just put the phone down, OK? And the bat. This is all a complete misunderstanding.'

He was spooked. He now knew the police had heard it all and were likely already on their way. There were only two ways out of this kitchen, and he'd have to get past her to reach either of them, while it was all being recorded by the police. He was trapped.

'*How* is this a misunderstanding, exactly?' she asked. 'Clear it up for me.'

'I...' He faltered and placed his hands on his hips with a sharp, irritated sigh. 'I can't,' he admitted. 'But you need to just *stop*,' he demanded. 'Put the damn bat down, and we—'

'I didn't think so,' Kate snapped, cutting him off sharply. 'But that's fine – you can save your story for the police. And as for putting down the bat, not on your *damn life*.' She raised the phone to her ear. 'Hello? *Yes*, I'm here. The address is one-oh-one... Yes. Yes, that's it. Two minutes out? *Thank you.* Thank you so much.'

Relief rushed through her. She eyed Langston, wary that he might still try to barge past her as the walls closed in on him. 'The man whose voice you've just heard was arrested after nearly running me off the road this morning and being aggressive to the officer who attended the scene.' Kate ignored his derisive snort. 'The officer warned me to steer clear, and now that same man has broken into the house with a knife and pretty clear intentions. I have a bat raised, ready to defend myself if he makes another move. Please warn your officers.'

She felt her heart jump as Langston lifted his arm, but he simply threw it in the air and dropped it again. She tried to focus on what other information the police would need. 'H-He's a white male, around six foot, broad, muscular. Er, dark messy hair and beard, red checked flannel shirt and jeans.'

Langston glared at her, and Kate tightened her grip on the bat. It was getting harder to keep it in the air, and her arms were starting to ache.

'How far out are they now?' she asked, terrified Langston would soon see how weak she really was.

The responder assured her they were pulling into the street just as Kate heard the sirens.

Sighing loudly, Langston shook his head. 'You're going to regret this.'

'You just made that threat on a recorded police call,' she replied coolly, hearing the car doors slam. They were here. It was going to be OK. 'Thank you. That will help in court.'

'In court?' he repeated.

'When they decide the length of your sentence. And trust me' – she reached over and unlocked the back door as the dull thud of approaching boots grew louder – 'you'll have many years to look back and regret what an epic, *epic* mistake you made tonight.'

Two officers burst in, guns pointed forward. One of them hooked his free arm around Kate and manoeuvred her quickly behind him, shielding her with his body. She dropped the bat with a clatter and sagged with relief.

'*Nobody move!*' the second officer boomed. He darted forward, turning in swift jerky movements as he checked the room. '*Where is he, Sam?*'

Kate looked expectantly at the officer shielding her, but it was Langston who answered.

'You're looking at him.'

'*Yes*,' she said strongly. '*That's him!*'

'Where?' the officer asked, repeating the jerky swing of the gun around the room.

Kate's brows knitted together, and she frowned with frustrated disbelief. Was this guy serious?

The officer shielding her moved away from her towards the hallway. Exposed again, Kate glanced nervously at Langston and found him staring back at her oddly.

'*Sam*,' the officer barked. 'Come *on* – where'd he go?'

'Put your gun down, Mike,' Langston said. 'You too, Jerry. There's no one here but us.'

'*What*?' the officer asked.

'Yes, *what*?' Kate echoed, watching them lower their weapons. 'What are you *doing*?' she demanded in a panicked tone. 'Don't put them away. *Christ*! He's – he – you...'

Kate fell silent, putting one hand on her hip and the other to her forehead, rubbing it agitatedly as she tried to make sense of what was happening. Both officers were now eying her suspiciously. They moved to stand near Langston, and there was a short silence. Kate watched the three men with a deep frown, and the uncomfortable feeling that something was very wrong here settled in the pit of her stomach. Something she couldn't see yet. Something that she had the distinct impression was about to get a whole lot worse.

# FOURTEEN

The officer Langston had called Mike narrowed his gaze. 'We got told there was an intruder, some violent guy with a knife trying to kill people.'

'That would be me.' Langston opened his arms outwards, and both officers' expressions widened in surprise.

'What the *hell*?' the one he'd called Jerry exclaimed. 'Sam, what's going on?'

'Sam, this was put out as a highest-level emergency,' Mike said, sounding angry now. 'I had a shoplifter I had to turn *loose* because of the priority level of *this call*. And you're telling me it was, what, a – a...' He threw both hands up, flummoxed. 'Well, what *is it*? Because I *know* you'd never be stupid enough to pull a damn prank call!'

'Well...' Jerry tilted his head to one side, giving them a meaningful look. 'There was that *one* time.'

'Oh, *come on!*' Langston exclaimed.

'Jesus, we were *fifteen*, Jerry!' Mike said, joining him. 'Are *you* the same idiot you were at fifteen? Actually, don't answer that.' He shot Jerry a filthy look.

'I'll remember that, Jerry,' Langston said accusingly. 'Next time I'm talking to your wife. You wait.'

Jerry opened his arms wide, a slightly panicked smile on his face. 'Aw, come on, guys, I wasn't *serious*...'

'*Shut up*, Jerry,' Mike ordered, annoyance still sharpening his tone.

'Yeah, let Mike think, *Jerry*,' Langston said, a trace of amusement in his voice now as he stepped back and folded his arms over his chest. He turned his gaze to meet Kate. 'He's still tryin'a figure out what's going on here.'

'Which *is*?' Mike asked him exasperatedly.

'Beats me,' Langston answered. His casual shrug and easy half smile were at odds with his intense glare. 'I got back into town this morning and ended up crashing my truck, when some crazy tourist decided to stop in the middle of an *intersection*,' he began.

Kate let out an affronted gasp at the unfair spin he'd put on the event and glared back, but kept quiet, still not exactly sure what was happening here.

'You stop?' Mike asked, cocking an eyebrow.

Langston – or Sam, as it appeared was his first name – gave a scornful look that clearly said, *Come on, who cares about stop signs?* Mike shrugged back as if to say, *Well that's your own fault then, buddy.*

'Well, that wasn't the end of my karmic kick up the ass for it,' Sam continued verbally. 'Squad car rolled out from behind the bushes and there was my old friend *Healy*.'

'*Damn*,' Jerry said with a low whistle.

'I wasn't in the best mood,' Sam admitted. 'So he managed to book me.'

'Ahh, he'll dine out on that for *months*,' Mike said with disgust.

'Yep.' Sam took a deep breath in and released it slowly, his deep blue eyes still boring into Kate's.

The jittery panic in her chest heightened, and she looked away, wondering why she suddenly felt like *she* was the person in the wrong. She definitely *wasn't*, she reminded herself. *She* was the victim here.

'I got out about an hour ago,' Langston continued. 'So I *finally* came home, took off my jacket, walked in here to—'

'This *isn't* your home!' Kate blurted out, jumping on the lie like a lifeline. '*You don't live here.*'

'*What?*' he asked, seemingly shocked.

'Lady, *he lives here*,' Mike replied, looking at her like she was insane.

'No, he doesn't! This house is – *was* – Cora and William Moreaux's house. I have no idea where *you* live, but it's not – it's – it's...'

She trailed off as her brain suddenly connected the fact that these cops had known him since adolescence, to the probability of them knowing where he lived. She bit her lip grimly and eyed him warily.

'You live *here*?' she asked slowly.

He nodded.

'Who *are* you?' she asked with a frown. 'Who were you to—'

'Who *is he*?' Mike almost yelled in disbelief. 'Lady, who in *the hell* are *you*? You come in here and stir up all sorts of crazy and then ask *him* who *he* is?'

There was a crackling noise, and a voice on the end of the police radio asked the officers to report in. Jerry walked out of the room to reply.

'I-I'm the lawyer,' Kate stuttered, feeling like a complete fool. 'I didn't know you existed,' she said to Sam, hearing how lame that sounded as the words came out. 'No one told me...'

'Ahh, of *course*.' Realisation dawned on Mike's face. 'I completely forgot.' He turned to Sam. 'You've been away. You won't have seen the paper.'

'The *paper*?' Sam asked blankly.

'Yeah, I, um…' He rubbed his stubble awkwardly. 'You know what, it doesn't matter. She's legit. Cora left instructions for her lawyer to stay here while sorting everything. The rest ain't important,' he replied quietly.

Sam studied her with an uncertain frown. Kate cleared her throat and straightened up, trying to appear in control – which was no easy task, standing as she was in cocoa-stained pyjamas with bare feet and a bright red nose.

'Look, I think we started out on the wrong foot,' she said resentfully. 'Not that you can blame me for jumping to conclusions. I was simply following the road laws, *like I should*, and then after nearly killing us both, you were *very* aggressive and rude.'

'*Aggressive*? Lady, rude, you can have, but the rest couldn't even be classed as full-blown irritation,' Sam retorted.

'Well, it is where I come from,' Kate replied.

'Well, *you* ain't in Kansas anymore, Dorothy,' he exclaimed. 'And I have to say, I find it hard to believe my annoyance at wrapping my truck around a tree offended the delicate sensibilities of a woman who, not ten minutes ago, threatened to wrap a bat around my head.'

Kate felt the heat rush to her cheeks.

Jerry walked back in quietly.

'Yes, well, *obviously* I had to try *something*,' she argued. 'Like I'd stand a chance if you *had* decided to go for me. I mean, look at the *size* of you.' She gestured to his broad muscular physique. 'Imagine being five-foot-three in a town you don't know, and then after the encounter *we* shared this morning, finding that guy *downstairs*, late at night, holding a knife.' She gave him an accusatory stare. 'And as if that wasn't already reason enough to assume you had bad intentions, you're hardly putting out choirboy vibes, either.'

'What does that mean?' he asked.

'Oh, *come on*. The crazy hair and beard and…' She stopped

abruptly mid-flow, not wanting to be rude herself, but she didn't quite stop her gaze quickly enough, and he caught her glance at his dirty rumpled clothes.

'Wow.' He nodded and leaned back on the counter. 'OK.'

She tried to cover. 'I just mean, your shirt, it's buttoned wrong. And – and – alright *fine*,' she sighed. 'You look pretty dishevelled. You can't exactly blame me for noticing that, considering everything else.' She shrugged unapologetically.

Sam just watched her silently.

Mike looked Sam up and down. 'You *do* look like crap right now,' he agreed apologetically. 'And you could do with a bath.' He leaned in and lowered his voice. 'With all due respect, my friend, *you stink.*'

'I'm aware,' Sam replied. 'And that *had* been the plan. You know I wouldn't usually be around other people while I'm in need of a shower and clean clothes, but then I lost my truck' – he took a couple of steps towards Kate – 'and an entire *day* to a jail cell. And then I get home, and I'm jumped in my kitchen by a complete stranger.' His glare simmered. 'A stranger who's moved into my house without my knowledge *or permission*, and who not only tried to have me arrested for the *second* time today, but who had the *audacity* to threaten me with my own baseball bat – which, by the way, *lawyer girl*, is *not* steel, it's *aluminum*,' he told her witheringly. 'And *now*, Mike, as we enter the last hour of this forest fire of a day, this *British bee sting to the ass* insults my appearance, too.' Finishing his angry list of grievances, Sam eyed Kate with a hard stare.

Mike nodded and patted Sam's shoulder.

'Well...' Kate exhaled heavily through her nose. *British bee sting to the ass, indeed.*

She knew, reasonably, that the best thing to do right now was just concede and apologise for the sake of peace. But after all she'd been through today, Sam's attitude had burrowed right underneath her skin, and she ignored the pleading angel tugging on her shoulder.

'*No*, you know what, I sympathise with your shitty day. I *do*. But I'm *not* sorry,' she told him. 'I'm not apologising for a damn thing. You brought this morning on yourself. And maybe if you hadn't been such a *jerk*, I wouldn't have assumed you were here to kill me tonight.'

The devil on her other shoulder jumped with glee as the angel sat down and gave up. Kate held Sam's gaze stubbornly, and the room fell into silence until Jerry broke it with a casually loaded question.

'She's a *complete* stranger, you said, Sam?' One side of his mouth hitched in a hint of a smile.

A slow grin spread across Sam's face. 'I did indeed. You always were good with details, Jerry.'

Mike chuckled. 'The *best*,' he agreed.

Kate's eyes darted warily around the group as she realised where they were going with this. 'I'm a *lawyer*,' she reminded them strongly. '*Cora's* lawyer. I'm supposed to be here, and you *know* it.'

Mike pulled out his cuffs. 'Do *you* know that, Sam?'

'No, I do not,' he replied, watching the proceedings with open amusement now.

'*Yes, you do*,' Kate argued. 'For God's sake, this is *ridiculous*. I'm in my pyjamas for crying out loud.'

'Not the best choice of outfit for a break-in, huh?' Sam quipped, clearly enjoying himself.

'Turn around please, ma'am,' Mike said.

'I'm not turning around,' she said irritably. 'And I haven't broken into *anything*. I'm allowed to be here, and I have proof.'

'What proof?' Mike asked.

'The contract,' she replied, getting her confidence back as *his* visibly lessened. 'It states *very* clearly that Cora wanted me here whilst sorting the details of her estate.'

Mike scratched his head and looked back at Sam.

'Does it name you personally?' Jerry piped up.

Kate narrowed her eyes. Jerry was becoming a real pain in the ass.

'It instructs the lawyer in charge of their account, which is *me*,' she replied icily.

He smiled. 'And who can officially *confirm* that's you, Kate?'

'I can show you emails—'

'Emails can be faked,' Jerry said. 'No, we're going to need a senior representative of the firm to *confirm* you are who you say you are before we can accept your story. None of us have ever seen you before. For all *we* know, you could be one of those con artists we hear stories about from that big city of yours.' Jerry exaggeratedly changed his accent. 'This is a small town, ma'am, and we're simple folk. We gotta be careful of strangers now, so you'll need to come with us until this is all cleared up. But don't you worry – someone will look into this just after nine tomorrow. Contact your boss for you. Now, will you be needing a *lawyer* while you're staying with us?' he asked, not quite hiding his grin.

'*Nice*,' Kate said sarcastically. 'Good one, Jerry. OK, you guys have had your fun and made your point. Let's just move on now and start over.'

'Oh, I don't think so, lawyer girl,' Sam replied with a low chuckle. 'Take this intruder away, boys. But be careful now. I think she may be crazy. What with breaking into my house in her nightwear and with her hair all wild like that.' He grinned, taking great pleasure in turning the tables on her.

Kate narrowed her eyes at him and shook her head.

Sam gave her an exaggerated shrug. 'Sorry. But between that and the threats with the bat, you can see how I've reached this assumption, I'm sure.'

'Turn around,' Mike ordered.

'Seriously?' Kate exclaimed, raising her knotted brows in disbelief. 'Mike, come on. You're a police officer. Surely you take your job more seriously than this?'

'Oh, I do take it seriously. And *you* cost me a perfectly good shoplifter. Now turn around,' he ordered, his tone brooking no nonsense.

Kate's mouth dropped open, but she complied, knowing she couldn't afford to be cited for resisting arrest. 'This is *ridiculous*,' she repeated furiously as Mike cuffed her.

'*Hey*, you're lucky I haven't booked you for wasting police time,' he snapped. 'I'm only *not* because I believe you really did think Sammy here was coming for you, and I know you can't afford that on your record, but don't *push* me or I will.'

'You're wasting your *own* time if you actually go through with this,' she responded. 'And you'll waste more of it still after I report this baseless arrest tomorrow, I *assure you*.'

'Try it if you like; you won't get far,' Mike told her. 'Jerry's the detail king. He'll have all the Ts crossed and Is dotted on the paperwork by morning. Go get her coat and shoes, Sam.'

Kate twisted to look back over her shoulder and saw him walk out of the room. They were really going to *do* this, she realised. They were actually going to make her spend the night in jail!

Sam arrived back and draped her coat over her shoulders, before dropping her new snow boots to the floor. The smile on his face pushed Kate over the edge.

'You're going to regret this,' she seethed, the lid popping off her anger as it boiled over. 'I am *not* kidding, Sam. This is *so* far beyond the line it's a bloody *dot in the distance!*'

Mike propelled her forward with a tut. 'Come on – let's go.'

'Don't worry, Kate,' Sam called after them, echoing her earlier words as she was led away to the squad car. 'You'll have *many hours* to look back and regret what an epic, *epic* mistake you made tonight.'

# FIFTEEN

Kate glared over the counter at the young policewoman bent over the desk taking an age to sign her very few personal belongings back to her. She'd lost all patience in the seventeen hours she'd been left in here. Aside from the fact she'd spent not just the night in jail but an entire *day*, too, the awful thin plastic-covered mattress and the drunken ballads coming from the cell next door had meant she'd not slept a wink, either. She'd waited all morning to be collected for release. As morning had turned to afternoon, she'd been crawling the walls, furious that this ridiculous situation had gone so far. Finally, just before seven in the evening, the young girl in front of her had finally collected her for processing out.

Catching her glowering reflection in the glass separating them, Kate calmed her expression and rubbed her temples tiredly. It wasn't *this* officer's fault that she was here.

'Here you are, Ms Hunter,' the young woman said chirpily, finally looking up. 'Everything accounted for.'

'Thanks,' Kate replied, slipping her coat on and checking her phone.

Dozens of notifications glared back at her, mostly from her

mother and Bob. She shoved it in her pocket, wishing she could ignore them all until after she'd had a hot shower and eight solid hours of sleep. But she couldn't.

Zipping up her coat, Kate walked outside into the snowy evening. She stopped and held her phone up in the air, trying to get a signal so she could summon an Uber, but it seemed to be a dead zone. She cursed under her breath and looked around the small car park. A man stepping out of his vehicle briefly drew her gaze, but she immediately moved on, searching for some sort of public transport option. The police station was in an annoyingly remote area, with nothing but forest surrounding it and the one empty road.

'You gonna stand there all night, or shall we try to *avoid* losing limbs to frostbite?'

Kate turned towards the voice with a frown, realising that the man who'd stepped out of his car was Sam. She stared at him silently for a moment, surprised at how different he looked today. She could actually see his face now that he'd brushed his hair and trimmed the wild beard back to a more flattering short stubble. His blue eyes stood out more, strikingly bright between two layers of thick, dark lashes. He had a strong jaw and deeply etched dimples either side of his mouth, and a prominent classically sculpted nose that lent him a proud air.

Irritation suddenly ran through her as she realised that the arrogant douche who'd nearly killed her and made her spend a night in *jail* had the *audacity* to be good-looking – and not just slightly good-looking, *incredibly* good-looking. It seemed cosmically unjust. She knew as it registered that this was a completely irrational thought, but that made no difference to her feelings whatsoever.

Sam pushed his hands down further into the trouser pockets of the smart suit he wore today and hunched his shoulders, shifting from one shiny black shoe to another in an attempt to keep warm. 'Well?' he prompted.

Kate stared at him icily and then turned away without a word, lifting her phone back up and praying for signal. She heard him sigh.

'Kate, would you please just get in the car? I'm not kidding about the frostbite.'

She turned back with a furious glare. 'Not a chance! I'll make my own way back, thank you very much!'

'Yeah?' Sam challenged, glancing down the dark empty road to where it disappeared into the forest. 'How? You made some friends in the short time you've been in there? Joined a prison gang maybe? You got an old cellmate coming to pick you up?'

Kate's hatred for the man increased. '*Hilarious*. I'll get an Uber,' she replied coldly.

A ghost of a smile flitted across Sam's face. 'We don't have Uber here, lawyer girl. This ain't Boston. There is a cab company in town, but they're closed today.'

Kate cursed and put her phone away. '*Fine*. Then I'll walk.'

'You'll walk?' Sam repeated flatly.

'*Yes*,' she replied stubbornly.

'All seven miles?' He raised an eyebrow and waited.

Kate pressed her lips together hard to stop herself from exploding in a fit of frustration and looked back at the road, desperately willing a bus stop to appear. It didn't. She stood there for a few more moments, trying to think of another option.

Sam followed her gaze. 'Look, you can stay out here and freeze to death, or you can get in the truck and let me drive you back. But either way, *I'm* getting in the car.'

He paused as Kate warred with the two options, not sure which one she hated less.

'It's got heated seats...' he added temptingly.

Kate held out for another few stubborn seconds, then turned and stalked past him to the passenger side. '*Fine*,' she snapped as he opened the door for her. 'But don't expect any gratitude. You're the reason I'm stuck here in the first place.

And don't think picking me up makes up for what you did, either. Far, *far* from it.'

Sam let out a short laugh of surprise and shook his head as she stepped up into the plush black pickup. 'Whatever, lawyer girl.'

'And *don't* talk to me,' Kate snapped, his casual tone like kindling to her fury. 'I might need the ride, but I sure as *hell* don't need to speak to you.'

He flashed her a swift sarcastic smile. 'S*uits me,*' he replied before slamming the passenger door shut.

# SIXTEEN

After a tense and thankfully silent drive, Kate jogged straight upstairs and treated herself to a long hot shower. When she stepped back out, she felt ten times better, the jailhouse grime washed off and her cold eased by the steam. She rifled through her bag of new clothes and threw on a pair of soft beige lounge pants and matching top, before blasting her hair with the dryer and fanning the long dark waves around her shoulders to let them finish drying naturally. Feeling ready to tackle the many waiting messages, she unlocked her phone and began wading through them while she creamed her skin.

Although there were a lot from Eleanor, they were mainly talking *at* her, so she hadn't actually noticed Kate's prolonged absence. Lance had, in his usual way, just assumed she was busy and told her to call when she had time. After flicking through the rest, she placed a call to Bob.

He answered almost instantly. '*Kate.* Are you alright? What the hell happened?'

'I'm fine,' Kate replied. 'I'm out now. *Finally.*' She leaned back against the chair and ran her fingers through the damp ends of her hair.

'I'm so sorry,' Bob said crossly. 'They assured me when they called that they were releasing you straight away. That was around eleven.'

'They didn't call you until *eleven*?' Kate asked in disbelief.

'When I hadn't heard from you by one, I called back and kept calling all afternoon, making myself as big a pain in their asses as I could. By then it was too late in the day to send anyone.'

'Don't worry. There was nothing you could do. Even if I wasn't five hours away, who could do something I can't?'

'True. What *happened*? The story they gave me made no sense at all.'

'That's because it was nonsense,' Kate told him, the reminder reawakening her annoyance. 'But don't worry about it. It's sorted, the charges are dropped and I'm fine. Honestly. By the way, did you know Cora had a great-nephew called Sam Langston?'

'Name doesn't ring a bell,' he replied.

'Well, apparently he lives here. In Cora's house,' she told him.

'Oh. That complicates things,' Bob mused. 'Or possibly not. It's certainly a stronger claim for the house.'

'Mm,' she agreed. 'Maybe.'

Kate watched the snowflakes falling outside her window and felt a spear of homesickness. It was the first of November, which meant Eleanor would be baking the big family Christmas cake, ready to spike with honey whisky liqueur – her secret twist on the more traditional brandy – every few days between now and Christmas Day.

'There anything else you need?' Bob asked. 'Anything I can do?'

Kate focused back on the call with a sigh. 'No, I'm fine. Really. I just want to get on and wrap this up as soon as possible.'

'Alright, well...' Bob lingered.

'Honestly, I'm *fine*.'

'Alright. I'll leave you to it then. Keep me updated.'

'I will. Night.' Kate ended the call and chewed the inside of her lip, staring down at the blank screen. If they'd called Bob at eleven, why had she been kept in that cell for another eight hours?

Kate stood up and made her way downstairs and into the front room, where she could hear Sam pottering around. As she walked in, he pretended to jump and put a hand to his chest, letting out an exaggerated whoosh of air.

'Oh, it's just *you*. *Thank God.* For a moment, I thought there was some crazy British psycho in my house who wanted to kill me with a baseball bat.'

Kate gave him a withering look. 'It's still tempting. Why was I not released this morning?' she demanded. 'My boss was called at eleven, but I wasn't released until nearly seven. I want to know why. Your moron friends understand that I'm a *lawyer*, right? I could easily end both their careers if I decided to pursue this, and yet they wanted to push their luck by another *eight hours*? Really?'

'Hey, Mike's no moron,' Sam replied, dusting off his hands as he turned away from whatever he'd been doing by the fireplace. 'He's actually a very clever guy. And as for when you were released, that was the time I asked them to let you out at.'

He walked past her, through to the kitchen, and Kate's jaw dropped. She stood there, momentarily too stunned to move, then hurried after him.

'I'm sorry, *what* did you just say?' She caught up and stepped in front of him with a deep frown.

'I said that's the time I asked them to keep you to, so you didn't get in my way,' he repeated with a shrug, opening one of the cupboards.

'How *dare* you?' she demanded, a fresh wave of anger

rushing through her. 'As if last night wasn't bad enough, you told them to put me through that hell for a whole *day, too*? A *workday* for me, by the way.'

'Yeah, a whole day in there is fun, huh?' he replied, shooting her a pointed look before returning to his search of the cupboards. 'You started this, remember? I was simply returning the favour.'

'*What*?' she exclaimed. 'You got *yourself* arrested!'

'It could be argued that you did, too, *lawyer girl*. You cost Mike a good arrest by wasting police time.' He tutted as he reached the last cupboard. 'Hey, did you eat all my Cap'n Crunch?' he asked with an accusing frown.

Kate stared back at him in disbelief. '*Yes*,' she shouted, losing her temper. '*I did*! And it tasted like *crap*! In fact, *Crap'n* Crunch would be a better description of that sugar-coated cardboard.'

Sam pulled back with a gasp, looking genuinely shocked and insulted, and Kate shook her head, unable to comprehend how a human being existed who thought nothing of sending someone to jail for fun but was offended by her opinion on his choice of breakfast.

'I— You know what...' She threw her hands in the air and walked away from him. It was clearly pointless trying to have a conversation with him. 'I'm done. No, actually' – she turned and marched back – 'I'm *not* done. I have one more thing to say.'

'*Oh good*,' Sam replied dryly.

'I'm here to do a job, and I don't appreciate my time being wasted,' she told him hotly. 'So *do not* get in my way again. Because next time I won't be so lenient. And whether you like it or not, I will be here for the next few weeks until I can settle Cora's estate. Got it?'

'There's a perfectly good hotel down the road, you know,' Sam said. 'Where the people might actually *want* you around. Or want your money, at least.'

'I don't care who wants me around. The contract specified I have to stay here, so I'm *staying*,' she responded.

Sam rolled his eyes with a tut of annoyance. '*Fine*,' he snapped. 'But if you're staying here, let's get a few things straight – the room at the top of the stairs is mine. Go through whatever else you want, but that room is off limits.'

'Fine by me,' she replied, making to turn away.

'I'm not done.' Sam walked towards her, stopping just close enough that it felt slightly uncomfortable. Kate's breath caught in her throat as he stared down at her sternly. 'Keep your stuff out of the living room. The TV area is mine. I sometimes have friends over to watch big games. I don't want the room to be turned into your damn office.'

Kate rolled her eyes and stepped back. 'I had *one notepad* in there – it was hardly a hostile takeover. And I haven't even *seen* a TV,' she said, confused. The living room was beautiful but oddly devoid of any technology.

'You wouldn't have. I built it into the wall behind the mirror. The glass clears to show the screen when it's switched on. Which reminds me, *do not*, under any circumstances, move the remote from the coffee table,' he stressed. 'The TV is sunk into the wall and hooked up to the electricity through the drywall to hide the cables, which makes the manual switches unreachable. So, I'm serious, *do not* move that remote.'

'I heard you the first time,' she replied tersely.

'Good – don't forget it,' he retorted.

Kate raised her eyebrows. 'OK, *my turn*,' she said, placing her hands on her hips. 'While we have to be under the same roof, you can show me the courtesy of *basic manners*. There's no need to be so rude all the time.'

Sam shook his head. 'No, you don't get a turn, lawyer girl. This house may not be mine in legal terms, but it's still my *home* for now. And in *my home*, I will do as I damn well please.

Which, after recent events, does *not* include making *your* life easy.'

A strange ripple of pain flashed across his face for a moment, then he abruptly turned and walked over to the fridge, opening the door to look inside.

'*Nice*,' Kate said, nodding to herself. 'Well, that's fine, Sam. At least we both know where we stand.'

'Oh,' he said, glancing back at her. 'One last thing. Don't touch my cereal.'

'Whatever,' she muttered.

She got herself a glass from the cupboard and walked over to the sink. As water gushed out, her gaze wandered to the two used wine glasses to the side and she absently noted the hum of the dishwasher going round underneath. Her glass full, Kate turned off the tap and almost walked away before stopping abruptly with a frown. She looked back at the wine glasses. A bright red ring of lipstick clung to the top of one of them. As she stared, Sam's earlier flippant admission played back in her mind.

*That's the time I asked them to keep you to, so you didn't get in my way.*

She swung around, hot bubbles of anger starting to form as she thought it through. She had to be wrong, surely. Even *he* couldn't be that awful.

'Sam, what are those?' she asked, pointing to the glasses.

He pulled out the orange juice and closed the fridge, glancing over. 'Those are *glasses,* Kate. We Americans drink outta them. Hadn't realised the Brits were that behind.'

'*Right*.' She ignored the insult. 'Wine glasses,' she clarified. 'One's yours, obviously, and the other used by a woman, unless one of your male friends has a thing for lipstick.'

'Amazing,' Sam replied, sounding bored. 'You should have been a PI.'

'So you had a woman over here today to share a bottle of wine?'

Sam's gaze tightened, and Kate waited for another dry, disparaging comment, but after a few moments, he simply answered, 'Yes. I did.'

Her eyes slipped down to his smart suit and shoes, and she had to work to contain her steadily rising anger.

'Sam...' She pressed her palms together and briefly touched her fingers to her mouth. 'Please tell me you didn't ask them to keep me locked up in a jail cell for an entire day, just to keep me out of the house so you could have a woman over.' He met her gaze unwaveringly, and that anger began to boil over. 'Please tell me I did not get put through a day of *hell* for *that*. For you to pop some *cheap* bottle of Chardonnay on an uninterrupted date.'

There was a short pause. 'Actually, it was Sauvignon Blanc. And a pretty decent one, too.'

Kate's jaw dropped, and she just stared at him, for once too angry even for words.

'From what little experience I have of you, *lawyer girl*, I've learned you're very unpredictable.' His words were calm now and devoid of the quick-witted arrogance Kate had begun to expect. He pulled a glass out of the cupboard and placed it on the side. 'And *destructive*, too. You're like a little hurricane that's rolled in here upturning everything you touch.' He poured the juice into the glass. 'Truth is, I didn't want to risk you coming here this afternoon and ruining things. Making it all about you, acting like you own the place and destroying the peace. I didn't need today torn up by another storm.' He put the carton back in the fridge and then turned to look at her again, taking a long sip of his juice. 'So yeah.' He wiped his top lip. 'I told them to keep you locked up until my company had gone home.'

Kate bit her lip and took a second to contain her raging fury before she spoke.

'You know nothing about me. You've *experienced* nothing of me. If you had, a hurricane is the *last* word you'd have just used. My whole life orbits around order and logic and reason. But right now, after hearing that...'

She felt all the anger and disbelief and hatred she felt towards the man swell up inside and break through her last thread of sanity. Sam had gone too far now. *Way* too far. The devil on her shoulder booted the sleeping angel off the edge of the other, and then both she and Kate pulled themselves up to full height.

'I'm done playing nice. You're going to regret today. Because karma's a bitch, Sam,' Kate said determinedly. 'And she's coming for you. *That's* a promise.' Turning away from him, she walked determinedly out of the room.

'Game on, *lawyer girl*,' he called after her. 'Game on.'

# SEVENTEEN

Kate threw herself into her work the next day, sorting the house into categories and delving deeper into Cora's and William's lives. There was so much more to sort out than she'd initially anticipated. The attic ran the length of the house and was full of boxes and furniture and old filing cabinets. The basement, which she'd only glanced at briefly when she'd first arrived, turned out to be almost as big and almost as full. She wandered through and looked around bleakly, wondering how she was supposed to get through all of it in just a few weeks.

Reaching one end, she stopped and read the labels on some of the boxes. The top box on one stack read: *Photo Albums '90s–'00s*. The lid was half open, and she peeped inside before reaching for one. She flipped through a few of the cardboard pages with photos stuck under the film and smiled, the sight bringing back memories of putting together albums like this with her nanna. The same swirly writing from Cora's diary noted dates and places, and she scanned a few of them.

*William, Cora, Grant and Alma, Rocky Peak Café,*
*Aug '96*

*William and Matthew Opening the Coreaux Roots Workers Café, Oct '96*

*First Christmas with Sam, Dec '96*

Kate paused, a small crease forming between her brows. The Sam in this picture was around ten or eleven she guessed from his size. He'd been particularly skinny back then, and there was a deep vulnerability in his expression and in the way he stood between William and Cora, who had her arm wrapped comfortingly around his shoulders.

Kate read the notation again. *First Christmas with Sam.* She flicked onto the next page, and then the next. There were several *firsts* with Sam. First day of school, first baseball match, first birthday party. Kate put the album down and glanced across to the stairs that led up to the house. Sam didn't just live here *now*; he'd been *raised* by them. She had no idea how or why that had come about, but his connection with Cora clearly went far deeper than she'd thought.

Kate walked upstairs and made a beeline for the garage, where she'd last seen Sam headed. He stood at a tool bench fiddling with something, small screws littered all around him. He glanced over as she entered, then ignored her.

'Why didn't you tell me you were raised here by your aunt and uncle?' she asked bluntly.

'Because it ain't your business,' he replied. 'Do *you* go round telling strangers your life story?'

Kate rolled her eyes. 'It literally *is* my business right now. My *entire purpose* here is to work out who meant what to them, so I can make sure everything is left to the right people. And you didn't think to tell me that you're basically their *son*?'

Sam began picking up the screws and dropped them in a small box. 'I'm their *nephew*,' he stated firmly. 'I lived here, yeah. But that doesn't change facts.' He dropped in the last screw and picked up the box, sliding it into a gap on the shelf above. Turning around, he dusted off his hands. 'I'm not staking any claim to my aunt and uncle's business. So it really doesn't matter either way. Just make sure you give it to someone who'll look after it the way they did,' he told her, the words sounding like a subtle warning.

He walked past her and paused by the doorway into the house. 'Who's in the running, anyway?' he asked.

Kate studied him thoughtfully. Nothing about Sam made sense. He'd shown himself to be self-serving and thoughtless for the most part. Yet he wasn't interested in being handed a thriving business and the keys to the home he grew up in, which was worth around a million dollars in today's market. That didn't add up at all.

'Well?' he prompted. 'Who's laid a claim?'

'I can't legally share that information with you,' Kate replied.

One corner of his mouth hitched up wryly. 'You should go down to the offices,' he suggested, turning into the house. 'See what it's all about.'

'I plan to,' she replied.

'Good. Try not to wreck anything big while you're there,' he added. 'And maybe thaw out that personality of yours a bit before you go. The whole cold, mean British thing won't get you very far with the nice folk over there.'

'Oh, you don't need to worry about that. I bring out the ice just for you,' Kate responded smoothly, deciding to meet his sarcasm with a dose of her own. 'And *you* try not to crash into any more trees while I'm gone. Maybe book some driving lessons.' She put on a wide fake smile. 'I found a great book for you, actually. It's called *Basic Road Rules for Idiots*.' He let out a small laugh and her eyes twinkled back with sarcastic sweetness. 'It's a picture book, so it's one even *you* should be able to get on with. I got you one for Christmas.'

'I'm touched,' Sam said, placing his hand on his heart. 'I haven't got you anything.'

'Oh, your glittering personality rolling pointlessly around the house while the rest of civilisation actually work is already *more* than enough,' Kate replied.

Sam laughed and shook his head. 'Ahh, lawyer girl...'

He met her gaze, and she thought he was going to continue, but then he suddenly closed the door instead. A second later, he switched the light off, leaving her standing there in total darkness.

She nodded slowly, pressing her lips together in a wry line. 'Yep. Should have seen that coming.'

# EIGHTEEN

Kate smiled at the picture Lance had sent through of the two of them dancing and laughing at a party last New Year's Eve. Amy had taken it, she recalled. It had been a brilliant night. But as she remembered how good it had been, her smile began to fade. Things had been fun then. They'd only been dating a couple of months and had still been enjoying the rose-tinted honeymoon period that new couples go through. She typed out a quick response to Lance.

> *Great pic. Hope you're OK. It doesn't look like I'll get home this weekend, after all. Will see if I can make it work for next week and let you know. –K x*

Her phone vibrated with his response just a few seconds later.

> *OK. Talk later. –L x*

Kate slipped the phone back into her coat pocket, then got out of the car and trudged through the snow to the main double doors of the Coreaux Roots offices. As they closed behind her, she stamped her feet on the welcome mat and looked around. The reception area was small and simply decorated. A few sturdy practical chairs lined one wall facing a small, and currently vacant, reception desk. Kate leaned over to look down the hallway that led off behind, then peeped through the small window in the only other door in the room. She couldn't see a soul.

Resigning herself to a wait, she pushed her hands down into the pockets of her big white coat and wandered over to the framed pictures hung beside the door. The first one was very old, a handful of people standing together in front of some trees. She recognised the young smiling faces of William and Cora. The second picture was a few years later, a larger group beside a cleared section of forest, William and Cora front and centre once more. The company snapshots continued every few years, right up to the most recent, where one space was noticeably empty beside Cora. Kate looked at her sadly, noticing she still smiled, but without the excitement and hope that had been there before. Kate tried to imagine how it would feel to lose someone you'd spent a lifetime with.

'They're all taken in the same spot,' a voice said behind her.

Kate turned to see a woman who she guessed to be in her late twenties watching her from behind the desk. She was dressed in a vertically half-black, half-blue knee-length dress, her shiny dark hair loose around her shoulders.

'The pictures,' she clarified, pointing to the photos Kate had been looking at. 'All taken in the same place, from the first to the last.'

'Really?' Kate looked back across them. The background evolved from trees to cleared ground to a wooden cabin that grew and was eventually replaced with the building she now stood in. She smiled. 'I like that. That's almost as interesting to watch as the change in the people.'

'They're one and the same, this place and its people,' the woman replied. 'That's what Cora used to say. The body and soul, both equally as important.'

Kate nodded. 'Wise words.'

'She was a wise woman.'

Kate walked to the desk and held out her hand. 'I'm Kate. I'm—'

'I know who you are,' the woman said, cutting her off. 'Sam called to tell us you were coming.'

'Ah.' Kate let her hand drop. 'I see.'

The woman grinned. 'Don't worry,' she said. 'We make up our own minds about people around here.'

'Oh.' Kate felt her hope lift, and she smiled back. 'Good.'

'I'm Jenna,' the woman said. 'I manage the office. Make sure the contracts are all in order and operations are running smoothly. Field incoming requests.'

This jogged something in Kate's memory. 'We've exchanged emails before, haven't we?'

'We have,' Jenna confirmed.

Kate nodded. Things were run so smoothly here that her involvement had always been minimal, and this was the person responsible for such easy dealings. She noted Jenna down as the person to come to when she needed to delve deeper, which she inevitably would.

'I was hoping to look around, get a general idea of how things work here,' Kate said.

Jenna nodded. 'I thought you would, so I arranged for one of the senior site managers to take you on a tour and answer any questions you have.'

'Oh. Thank you,' Kate said, impressed. 'That's actually perfect.'

'I think you'll enjoy it. This is a really special place.' Jenna grinned again, her brown eyes twinkling with the quiet confidence of someone about to share something they clearly loved.

'Take a seat – he won't be long. I have to get back, but if you need anything else, don't hesitate to call.'

'Great, thanks. It was nice to meet you,' Kate replied.

'You, too!'

Jenna disappeared down the hall behind the desk, and Kate stared thoughtfully after her.

The door beside her swung open a second later, and she turned to see an older man in faded blue overalls poke his head in with an expectant expression on his weathered face.

'You Kate?' he asked.

'That's me,' she replied, following him through to the building beyond.

The various clunks and whirrs of heavy machinery grew louder as they walked through the production area, and the man raised his voice to be heard above it.

'I'm Matthew,' he shouted. 'I'm one of the senior site managers. Ain't nothing I don't know about this place, so feel free to ask away. I joined back when it was still pretty small. I'll have been here fifty years next month.'

'*Wow*!' Kate exclaimed.

'Came here right outta school. Started at the bottom and worked alongside Will and Cora and the others to grow this place to what it is today.' He looked around, and Kate could see the pride in his eyes. 'It's been a real journey.'

'That's amazing,' Kate said. They reached one of the machines, and she squinted at it. 'What does this do?'

'OK, so we make three different products here, all of them from wood.' Matthew led her to a bench along the back wall. 'Come sit. My legs ain't what they used to be.' He eased himself down, and Kate sat beside him. 'That's better. Will and Cora came here when this town was nothing. And I mean *nothing*. There was probably a hundred people or so, a church, few houses and one general store. And that store was nothing like the ones you see today, let me tell you.'

'Did you grow up here?' Kate asked.

'I did,' he confirmed. 'This place had nothing going for it at all, but Will saw things differently. He saw the forest as wood that could be turned into something useful. And they were practically giving land away back then, so Will saved up and bought a whole lot of it. Moved over here with his new wife, knocked up a little cabin to live in and got to work.'

'A cabin?' Kate asked. 'So they didn't build the big house straight away?'

'No, that came a few years later. They didn't have much at all when they started out. Built up everything they had with their bare hands.'

Kate frowned. In Cora's diary, she'd made it clear William had come from money. His family must have lost that money or cut him off. She resolved to continue reading and find out.

'Will started out making furniture. Decent stuff. Sturdy. Back then plastic was all the rage, but Will stuck to wood, saying that eventually quality would win out over flimsy fashion. And of course he was right. It was a slow start, but that's what got them on the map.' Matthew scratched his head. 'It was Cora's idea to branch out into making wood charcoal with the cutoffs, few years on.'

'I was wondering about that. Surely with so much wood around here people just burn that?'

'Some do,' he told her. 'But charcoal made from untreated wood burns hotter and for longer. It's a flameless burn, too, so no smoke.'

'Huh.' Kate raised her eyebrows. 'I never knew that.'

'Third product is cellulose film. Fake plastic. Started production a couple of years back. It's still small, but it's catching on now, and we're getting some bigger orders in.'

'And that's made from wood, too?' Kate asked, intrigued.

'Yep. We break down the wood fibres with a chemical compound and then put it through a process that turns it into a

clear single-use film. It can be made into bags, food wrap.'
Matthew grinned. 'Anything plastic can do, it can do better.
And after it's done with, it can be thrown on the compost heap,
and it'll break down in just three weeks.'

'That's incredible,' Kate said, impressed. 'That's the kind of
product that will change the world.'

'That's the plan,' he told her. 'That's kinda been at the soul
of this place from the start. Everything Will and Cora ever did
helped others in some way. They created jobs, opportunities for
people like me, who didn't have any. They plugged money into
the town. They actually *built* more than half of it, renting out
the shops cheap to people who were just getting started, then
selling them the premises when they were doing well enough to
buy them.'

'Seriously?' Kate's eyebrows shot up.

'Yep. They were the best people I've ever known.' He
looked away sadly. 'The world is a better place for them being
in it.'

He fell silent, and Kate gave him some space to ride out his
thoughts. The more she learned about this place, the more she
could understand why its people loved it so much. What they
did here *mattered*. And the sense of community was deep and
strong. She could see now why the contract had so clearly specified that she had to spend time here. This place wasn't something that could be described. It had to be seen to be
understood. It had to be felt.

'Come on.' Matthew stood up. 'I'll show you how it's all
done.'

She followed him down the side of the room and glanced up
at the windows of the offices above. 'Is Aubrey Rowlings here
today?'

She didn't really want to meet her yet, but after all the
messages the woman had left, she knew it would be rude to
leave without at least introducing herself.

Matthew's expression fell into a grim frown. 'I doubt it. After Cora got ill and couldn't check in on her anymore, she's been here less and less. It's been a whole lot more peaceful.' He glanced at her. 'I probably shouldn't say that to you, with her about to take over, but...' He squinted into the distance and scratched the back of his neck. 'When you get to my age, you get a bit tired of toeing the line with people like that. When she takes charge, I'll probably just retire. Would make the wife happy, I guess.' He sighed. 'Company won't last much longer, anyway, in her hands.'

Kate pursed her lips as he confirmed her suspicions about Aubrey. 'Actually, it's not been decided who'll inherit yet. That's the *real* reason I'm here, to work all that out.'

Matthew looked surprised.

'I know. She made it sound more like it was pre-decided in that article.'

'She's been outright telling people that, too,' Matthew told her. He tutted. 'Will and Cora must be turning in their graves watching that girl right now.'

'Is she really that bad?' Kate asked.

Matthew sighed. 'When she first came here, she worked for Jenna as an assistant. Though *worked* is really too strong a word. She'd swan in late, leave early, do nothing but make personal calls between complaints that she was *born for better things*.' He rolled his eyes. 'Jenna put up with it for as long as she could, not wanting to upset Cora. She was very close to Cora. Most of us were. But one day she caught her red-handed dipping into the office safe. We always have a few hundred dollars or so in there for cash flow. Jenna saw her slip some cash into her pocket and called her on it. Aubrey kicked up a stink and left, and when Jenna checked, the books balanced fine. But when she dug in further, she discovered a whole load of fake receipts – *good* ones. A lot of them, too.'

'You're *kidding*?' Kate asked, shocked. 'Didn't she tell Cora?'

'She did,' Matthew replied.

Kate frowned. 'Why didn't they fire her?'

'Oh, Aubrey turned on the tears, swore blind she knew nothing, hadn't taken nothing. Made up some tale for why she'd been in there. No one believed her, not even Cora, but no one could prove it, either. And even when it stung, Cora was a strong advocate for innocent until proven guilty, so...' He shrugged, his disapproval clear. 'Cora moved her over to marketing and tightened up the access to the safe. Aubrey still treats people like crap and walks around up there like she owns the place, and she does no more up there than she did down-stairs. Not that anyone expects her to at this point. Except *Cora. Cora* did.'

Kate felt troubled as they walked outside, feeling the weight of the responsibility she'd been handed grow heavier on her shoulders. She had to get this right. The last thing she wanted to do was hand over control of the company to someone who'd use that power to treat all the people Cora and William had cared about badly.

'Who would *you* have take over this place?' she asked.

'Well, *anyone* would be better than Aubrey, I reckon.' Matthew skewed his mouth to one side as he thought it over. 'You'd think there'd be a clear choice at this point, but there ain't. The only person who knows the business *well enough* is Sam. But he doesn't want that, from what I gather.'

'No.' Kate stopped and looked out at the blanket of snow-topped pine trees that covered the valley below. 'This is an incredible view.'

'Yeah.' Matthew moved to stand beside her with a fond smile as he looked out, too. 'See that big one on its own there?' He pointed to it and chuckled. 'Every year Cora heads down on the first of November with one of the forklifts and covers it in enough Christmas lights to blind a space station.' His smile faded. 'Or she *did*, anyway.'

'I'm so sorry for your loss,' Kate said gently. 'I'm learning a lot about Cora, and I'm sad I never got to meet her. She seems like someone I'd have really liked.'

Matthew turned and directly held her gaze for the first time with a warm smile. '*No*. You'd have *loved* her. And I think she'd have rather liked you.'

Kate looked out at the beautiful valley where William and Cora had created so much and enriched so many lives, and wondered once more how the boy they'd raised had turned out to be such an arrogant idiot.

# NINETEEN

Kate grimaced at her phone as it rang yet again and flicked it on to silent before slipping it into her back pocket. Her mother had called four times already today, not at *all* happy with the news that Kate wouldn't be coming home for the weekend as planned. She'd answered the first time, but knowing the other calls would just be more escalated variations of her mother's upset indignation, Kate was now pointedly ignoring them. She was the harbinger of bad news all round, it seemed. Lance hadn't exactly been happy with the change of plans, either. Though at least *he* had kept his annoyance to just one call.

Crossing her arms, she stared out at the garden through her bedroom window. The sky was clear today, a dazzling blue, and the deep snow that seemed to be in no hurry to disappear glistened and sparkled in the sun. Her pocket vibrated again, and she closed her eyes with a groan. Waiting for it to stop, she pulled the phone out and opened her messages. She typed out a quick text to her dad and read it over with a squint before deleting and rewriting it in a more jokey fashion.

*Dear Mr Hunter, could you kindly stop paying your phone bill or perhaps drop said phone in a lake, so that your wife can't keep trying to break the world record for number of times calling the same person in one day? Would be much appreciated. With love, your favourite child.*

Kate knew she needn't worry about his reaction to her ongoing absence. Where Eleanor was the storm, her father was always the calm. She pressed send and turned to grab a jumper.

The reply pinged back swiftly.

*Tony? Is that you?*

Kate grinned and took a moment to think up a fitting response.

*Don't tell me you have a secret second family \*now\*. You already had your shot at childhood trauma infliction. You don't get another go.*

She watched the three dots move on the screen and quickly pulled the jumper over her head.

*Oh, it's you, Kate! Never mind. I always thought if I had a favourite child, it would be a boy. And he'd be called Tony. You'll do though.*

Kate laughed and typed back.

*I totally get it. I always thought if I had a favourite dad, he'd be Sean Bean. I think Mum agrees with me on that one, too.*

She chuckled as she pressed send. Sean Bean was her mother's big celebrity crush. A laughing face instantly popped up, followed shortly by his reply.

*Touché! OK, you win. Don't worry about your mother. I'll take her out and distract her for a bit. She'll have calmed down in a few hours. You doing OK though? Give me a call sometime to catch up. No pressure, just whenever you're free. X*

Kate smiled sadly and felt a pang of homesickness. She felt thoroughly detached from everyone right now. This was partly her own fault. She'd been avoiding her mother and Lance – and even Amy at times – unable to face thinking about the ever-evolving wedding plans and the alarming focus Lance was suddenly putting on the future.

She typed one last reply, seeing that her dad was still online.

*I'm fine, just really under it here. I'll call in the next few days, I promise. Love you, Dad. Xx*

*Love you, too. Stay safe. Xx*

Kate closed her screen feeling a little hollow. She'd have loved to talk to him now, but that would mean dealing with her mother, and she couldn't deal with Eleanor's hysterics or the guilt she'd try to put on her for not being there to help plan the wedding.

She couldn't even blame her mother for feeling the way she did, either. Kate *should* be there. She should be the one planning and excitedly organising everything. That's what brides did. But then most brides hadn't accidentally accepted a proposal without being given a chance to even think about it, and then somehow landed themselves with a wedding just weeks away, before being called halfway around the world for a job! She sighed and decided to head down to the kitchen. A cup of tea was what she needed to sort her out and make her feel a little less glum.

Sam sat at the breakfast bar eating a bowl of his favourite fake sea captain and reading the newspaper. He looked up as she passed, and she pointedly ignored him, not in the mood for another interaction with him right now, though she saw him lean back and stretch, his white T-shirt pulling taut over the well-defined lines of his muscular frame. She subtly studied him out of the corner of her eye. He'd paired the seasonally unsuitable T-shirt with jeans, and between this simple tightly fitted outfit, his stylishly messy hair and strong stubbly jawline, he looked like he was trying out for some sort of vintage Levi's commercial. The devil on her shoulder gave an appreciative facial shrug and the angel appeared with an accusatory glare. Kate pursed her lips and turned to the cupboard to grab herself a mug with a sniff. Why was she even looking at him?

'What's up, lawyer girl?' he asked. 'You look annoyed. How have I offended your delicate sensibilities *today*? Did I leave the toilet seat up?'

She put the mug down and dropped in a teabag. 'Actually, *yes*,' she replied. 'You did. But I expected no less, so *no*, that hasn't upset me.' She had no intention of sharing her personal life with him so didn't bother to elaborate further.

She filled up the kettle and switched it on, Sam's words bringing back her visit to Coreaux Roots yesterday. She'd been left in awe of William and Cora after all she'd seen and learned. The place was so much more than just a business. It was a family. The beating heart of a town *they* had built. A whole community that wouldn't even be there had it not been for them. They'd changed and enriched so many people's lives. They'd given their lives to the people of this town. And Sam, the boy they'd raised as their own, couldn't care less about the legacy they left behind. It made no sense, and that selfishness made Kate hate him even more than she did already.

'Hmm.' Sam chewed his cereal. 'I'll have to try harder.' He poured another helping of cereal into the milk still in his bowl and watched her with an unreadable expression. 'By the way, I've got company round tonight, so if you could either stay upstairs or maybe go out for a ride on your broomstick, it would be appreciated,' he said. 'Whatever works best.'

'*Eugh*, you're detestable,' Kate replied with a tut, turning to pour the water into her tea. 'I don't know how you even get this *company* to come over in the first place. Your handsome face might draw them in, but surely the moment you open your mouth, these women drop away like flies?' she asked scathingly, her temper getting the better of her for a moment as the faces of all the wonderful people she'd met the day before flew through her mind.

These people depended on that place for their livelihoods. They needed a leader, someone to keep it safe, and hearing Matthew, one of the most experienced workers there, confide that *Sam* was the only person he felt could do that had filled her with deep concern.

Sam laughed. 'Oh, you find me handsome, do you, lawyer girl?' he asked, amused.

Kate realised her mistake and shot him a withering look. 'Not personally, no,' she lied, annoyed with herself. 'But I know your particular look appeals to some women.' It was a weak backtrack and she knew it, which just annoyed her even further.

He grinned, and she turned away crossly.

'You think I'm handsome,' he gloated. 'Is that what's bothering you, lawyer girl? That you're attracted to me?' His eyes twinkled with amusement.

'*No*,' she replied, slamming the cutlery drawer shut and walking over to the fridge. 'The only thing that's currently bothering me about *you* is how you could have been raised by two such incredible people and still end up as *awful* as you are.'

That seemed to hit home somewhat, Sam's grin faltering

and the amusement fading from his eyes. Kate turned away and searched the fridge for the milk.

'You've got everyone figured *right* out from up there on your high and mighty perch, haven't you, Kate?' Sam said quietly after a long pause.

'Not everyone,' she replied. 'But I've seen *more* than enough to have figured *you* out.'

Sam watched her as he ate his cereal, a much sharper edge to his gaze now. *Good*, she thought. *It should hit every nerve you've got*. She scanned the fridge again and frowned.

'You looking for this?' Sam asked.

Kate turned and realised the milk had been beside him on the island the whole time.

'Oh. Yes.' She closed the door and reached over towards it, but Sam scooped it up out of her reach.

Kate frowned. 'What are you *doing*?'

Sam shrugged. 'I'm picking up my milk.'

Kate's eyes tightened. '*I* bought that milk.'

'But it's in *my* fridge,' he countered.

Kate glared at him and sucked in a deep breath before replying in a perfectly level tone. 'Fine. Could you please pass me *your* milk?'

'This milk?' Sam asked, pointing at the carton with his free hand.

'Yes,' Kate replied, holding on to her patience with great difficulty.

'For your tea? Don't you like it black?' He stared at her expectantly.

Kate considered dropping it and walking away, but after the series of strained conversations she'd already suffered with Lance and her mother, she really did desperately just want to sit and enjoy a nice soothing cup of tea.

'*Yes*, I want it for my tea,' she said flatly. 'And *no*, I don't like it black.'

Sam shook the carton, bringing attention to the little it had left in the bottom, then looked down at his bowl. She followed his gaze. It was still half full of milk but now had just a couple of stray milk-sodden beige squares floating around the top.

'Nope,' he said finally with a tight smile. He opened the milk and tipped what was left into his bowl.

Kate's mouth dropped open, and she stared at him with pure hatred. That was the *final straw*. The man had clearly never been told how dangerous it was to get between an Englishwoman and her tea, but he was about to find out.

Sam picked up the bowl, put it to his lips and tipped it back, drinking the entire contents without stopping. Kate's eyes narrowed. She'd never been a vindictive person, but she was creative, so even if it took her all weekend, she'd figure out her revenge.

'*Ahhh...*' Sam put down the empty bowl with a loud sound of satisfaction and wiped the back of his hand across his mouth. 'I *love* a bowl of milk in the morning.' He laced his fingers together behind his head and leaned back on the stool. 'All that calcium. Important for building strong bones, my uncle used to say.' He grinned.

Kate stared back at him coldly. 'Well, it's certainly thickened your skull, so I guess he was right,' she replied.

Sam laughed. 'O-ho! Touché, lawyer girl.'

Kate stalked over to the sink and poured away her tea, wishing all kinds of hell on him. She took a deep breath and forced herself to think about the day ahead instead, then gritted her teeth, realising she needed to run something by him. 'I'm sorting stuff in the basement today. There's a box at the back—'

'Wait, hold that thought,' he said, cutting her off.

She turned to see him answering an incoming call.

'Hi, Cassie, how's things?' he asked in a bright genuine tone. '*Mhm. Mhm...*'

She watched him for a moment with a murderous glare as

his face creased into a smile. Without really meaning to, she flicked her gaze down to his bare muscular arms and over the sculpted lines of his chest and torso. As she did, Sam suddenly turned and looked straight at her. He hitched an eyebrow, and his grin widened as Kate's cheeks flushed red. She turned away, furious with herself. She hadn't been *looking* looking. Not like that. But with his level of arrogance, that would be exactly how he'd take it.

'Oh yeah?' she heard him say. 'And how's that new bed of yours doing?'

Kate rolled her eyes. Cassie must be the Wednesday wine girl.

The chair creaked as Sam stood up. 'Maybe I should come and just check it over, see if I can sort that out for you.'

'Dear *Lord*,' Kate mumbled with another eye roll.

'I'll see if I have one here and I'll be straight over.' Sam walked out and jogged up the stairs.

Kate turned back around as he left and noticed his coat hanging from the back of the stool, and his keys and wallet on the island. She bit the inside of her cheek and glanced into the hallway as the devil on her shoulder grinned and whispered an idea into her ear. Sam was in his room, the floorboards creaking above her as he walked around.

Wandering over to the island, she stopped beside his things and half turned away, drumming her fingers on the side as she pondered the opportunity to get a little petty revenge on the man, for all the horrendous things he'd put her through so far. It would be more than fair, really. But she *shouldn't*, she reasoned, as the angel popped up with some moralistic reminders. It would be wrong. *Really* wrong.

She sneaked a sideways peek at the wallet. No, she *couldn't*. The devil and angel squabbled, the disagreement swiftly escalating into a full-on fistfight. They rolled around her shoulders, and Kate took a couple of steps away, then turned to walk back.

The wallet *was* very close to the edge of the island. And the bin was butted right up against that end. It wouldn't take much... She tilted her head and arched an eyebrow. The devil pressed home her advantage, and the angel teetered on the edge.

Taking one step forward, Kate pressed her foot onto the bin peddle and eyed the bread ends and potato peels below. The creaking above her moved towards the hall, and before she could change her mind, she reached out her hand and swiped Sam's wallet into the bin. She felt an immediate thrill of both alarm and deliciously naughty revenge.

Sam jogged down the stairs, and she darted back to the sink, just as he walked back into view.

He shrugged on his jacket and picked up his keys, still on the phone. Glancing over at her, he gave her one more smile clearly designed to tease, but this time it didn't bother her.

'I'm headed to you now, so I'll stop at the store and pick one up on the way,' he said, walking out of the house and closing the door behind him.

'Good luck *paying* for that,' she said quietly with a smile. 'Because like I told you before – karma's a bitch, Sam Langston.'

# TWENTY

After a few hours spent sorting through another stack of basement boxes, Kate took a well-earned break and drove back out to Walmart to stock up on milk and a few other supplies. She rolled back up to the spot she'd claimed as her own on the road, just before the slope she couldn't conquer, and turned off the engine. More practically prepared this time, at least, she zipped up her warm winter coat, pulled down today's fuchsia-pink bobble hat then shrugged the backpack full of her purchases up over her shoulders.

Tramping up the slope through the snow, Kate breathed in the fresh air and looked around at the pretty street with a cheerful smile. A few of the houses had already begun to put up their Christmas lights, and those that hadn't still looked wonderfully festive next to them, with every pitched roof, cosy porch and picket fence already decorated with the fluffy white blanket and glistening crystals of Mother Nature. Surrounded by all of this, it really was impossible not to be filled with a warm cheery feeling of anticipation for Christmas.

She reached the house and paused outside for a moment to catch her breath.

Two people two doors down were busy covering their roof with Christmas lights, and as the woman holding the ladder saw Kate there, she let go of one side to wave hello. Kate waved back with a smile as she opened the front door, but this swiftly turned to an alarmed grimace as the ladder wobbled and the man at the top grabbed the gutter with a yelp. The woman quickly righted it as he called out in panic, and Kate ducked inside with a cringe.

After closing the door, she quickly turned to check on them through the side window. The man had luckily *not* fallen to his death due to her distracting his wife and had returned to decorating his roof.

She let out a sigh of relief. '*Phew.* I do not need *that* kind of guilt right now.'

'No?'

The sharp question caught Kate off guard, and she jumped as she turned around.

Sam stared at her with a hard, accusatory glare. 'Already got enough guilt weighing you down?'

Kate suddenly remembered Sam's wallet, and she shook her head slowly, twisting her lips to one side as if thinking it over.

'Mm, nope,' she said breezily. 'Can't really think of anything.'

Sam stood in the walkway through to the rest of the house, his feet planted squarely apart and arms crossed tightly over his chest as he continued to stare at her. Kate squirmed, feeling a mixture of deep guilt at being caught out and gleeful amusement that she'd finally got to him.

'Really?' he queried flatly, his disbelief obvious.

'Nope.' She held his gaze and smiled, raising her eyebrows smugly.

Sam nodded, narrowing his eyes. 'Nice. Well, you'll be pleased to know my plans tonight are now cancelled, because after driving nearly thirty miles out and realising I couldn't actually pay for the things I needed, and driving all the way back to discover my wallet's suddenly *missing*, I've had to waste time getting cash out of the bank so that I can start off all over again. *Four hours later*,' he told her with only barely contained anger.

'Oh *no!*' she replied, feigning surprise. 'How *terrible*. What happened?'

Sam gave her a withering look before grabbing his jacket off the hook and walking past her to the front door.

'You know, you really should be more mindful of things like your wallet, Sam,' she said with fake concern. 'I guess today really taught you that lesson, huh?'

Sam glared at her and opened his mouth as if to reply, then promptly shut it again with a small growl of frustration before walking out without a word.

Kate leaned over to peep through the window as the front door slammed shut, a wide satisfied smile on her face. 'You'll think twice before taking my milk again, *won't* you, Sam Langston?' she said quietly.

As he backed off the drive, she turned and walked through to the kitchen, then hopped onto the counter and reached up to the space above the cupboards, retrieving the wallet she'd gone back and stashed there earlier. She hadn't been able to leave it in the bin, with the risk it might actually be thrown out. She wanted revenge, but she wasn't *that* cruel.

Kate took the wallet upstairs and made a beeline for Sam's bedroom. She could just leave it in the kitchen, but he'd banned her from entering his room, so the extra dig of leaving it on his bed was just too tempting. Walking in, she looked around with fresh eyes.

It was the room next to hers, the one she'd taken the bat from. But she'd paid it little attention then, assuming it was just another spare room. Now though, she saw the small details that told the tale of its inhabitant. For the most part, Sam kept it pretty minimalist. The bedsheets and curtains were white and navy. A small wooden wardrobe and matching drawers lined one edge of the room, along with a small desk. This had nothing much on it, other than a small lamp and a toiletry bag. The only personal items on show were a flannel shirt hanging off the back of the chair and a bottle of aftershave on the bedside table.

Kate picked this up and took the lid off, raising it to her nose to breathe in the scent. It was musky and woody, with a hint of sweetness and a warmth running through it. Though she hated to admit it to herself, she'd found herself admiring the scent on Sam when he'd walked close by. It was impossible to ignore things like that, living, as they were, in such close quarters. Now though, up close, the smell was utterly intoxicating. She closed her eyes, feeling an inviting heady sense of it pulling her in. To what, exactly, she wasn't sure. Just *in*.

Opening her eyes again sharply, she quickly put it down and backed away, feeling unnerved. What on earth was she doing? That was the smell of *him*. Of *Sam*. What was *wrong* with her? Thoughts of Lance filled her mind, and a deep feeling of guilt swiftly followed.

No, she wasn't doing anything wrong, she quickly told herself. She was simply admiring an aftershave, that was all. There were lots of nice aftershaves. Though they were probably best tested in shops, she reasoned, rather than the bedrooms of men who *weren't* her fiancé. She wasn't even supposed to be in here.

She stared at the aftershave for a moment longer, then slowly turned and walked out of the room with a troubled frown. Maybe she would leave the wallet in the kitchen, after all.

# TWENTY-ONE

*3 January 1955*

*This morning was one of the most wonderful of my existence in this world so far. I am still ablaze with the most vivid energy, as though I am a battery that has been charged by way of lightning bolt.*

*It may seem as if I must be referring to some sensational event, and when I write the basic facts, it will be clear that it is not. Because it was simply a walk to the river and back. The same river I have walked to a thousand times. But today it was different. Today all the colors glowed brighter and the trees stood taller. The river glittered and the skies sang out my name. Because after all our lingering moments and snatched conversations, I finally enjoyed an hour-long, perfect walk with M.*

'M?' Kate sat up sharply in shock.

She'd decided, after shaking off her weird moment in Sam's room, to distract herself with a few entries of Cora's diaries. To revisit the beginnings of the wonderful love story she knew Cora and William's to be. Theirs was a story of the deepest love and of a deeply happy, fulfilling life together. All the pictures around the house and the endless albums full of their many adventures had shown her that much. So to suddenly see Cora writing about another man like this – even if it *was* before she married William – suddenly felt like a complete betrayal.

Kate pursed her lips and raised her eyebrows in disapproval, turning towards a framed photo of Cora on the wall.

'If you turn out to be a hussy, I'm going to be *very* disappointed,' she warned.

She shuffled back down under the covers and read on.

*It was everything I'd hoped it would be. We walked to the willow tree with the low branch and sat watching the sunrise over the water. We talked about philosophy and the universe. About places we wanted to see and what possibilities the future holds. The possibilities for the future of our world, and of great evolutionary change through science.*

*I've never known anyone whose depth and passion for the unordinary so perfectly match my own. It's like being with the other half of one whole. I wanted time to stop, so we could talk forever.*

*But inevitably it did not, and in what seemed like the blink of an eye, it was time to return. I couldn't risk my mother finding out, not when she is so set on pushing me into a serious courtship with W. If she were to find out about M, she would most certainly put an end to our meetings. And I really couldn't bear if that were to happen.*

*But our meeting ended on the most heavenly of notes. Because as I said goodbye, M pulled me close and kissed me. And it was wonderful. I felt sparks fly through my entire body, and his lips felt soft and warm and strong all at once. And I don't know if that's what every kiss feels like, but I felt as though I were floating in the air, tethered to the earth only by his hands around my waist.*

> *Monday mornings are our only time to meet, so for the next*
> *six days, I'll only see him briefly when he delivers the post. It*
> *feels a painfully long time. But so long as we get letters, I'll at*
> *least be able to steal a few moments at the gate.*

Kate shut the diary with an unimpressed clap and turned an accusatory stare towards Cora's picture. 'The *mailman?*' She shook her head. 'He was probably romancing a different girl in every postcode! Your mother's right not to approve. He lured you away in secret, charmed you with words then brazenly kissed you on the first date – which is ballsy *now*, let alone in 1955, *Cora Dawson.*' She shook her head again but this time at herself. 'And now I'm talking to a photograph, as if that's not a sign of being clinically insane. I need to go to sleep.'

Turning her back on Cora's picture, Kate put the diary down and turned off the light. But although she was tired, sleep evaded her. Cora's words floated around in her head, the girlish thrill behind them so clear she could almost feel them herself. It was ridiculous, she knew, to feel so bothered by silly words written nearly seventy years before, by a naïve young girl she'd never even met. But despite this, Kate still wanted to travel back in time and shake her. She still wanted to urge her to see William for the great man he clearly was, to tell her what an incredible future she'd have ahead of her, when she finally made the right choice. Just as Cora's mother was clearly doing, by the sound of the side note in the diary entry. But that was the wisdom of mothers, Kate supposed. The women who'd been there and done that and understood the no-return policy of the T-shirt they'd got along the way.

Kate turned over and kicked one leg out of the covers irritably as this line of thought brought her back to the conversation she'd had with her own mother about Lance. The not-so-subtle warning Eleanor had given her of the perils of not marrying him. But this wasn't the same, she decided, throwing herself onto her back and lying an arm over her head. She stared at the ceiling through the darkness. Or was it?

Kate wasn't a young unworldly girl like Cora, her head easily turned by a few pretty words. She *did* understand life and the pitfalls of reality. But wasn't she *also* pulling away from the prospect of a future with a man who was clearly an ideal match? Wasn't *her* mother trying to guide her towards the right choice with all the wisdom of *her* generation? There was no man in the shadows turning her head, but *something* was. The only difference between them, really, was that she didn't know what that something was.

This realisation was sobering, and Kate frowned through the darkness. Taking a mental step back, she looked at herself from a detached distance. As though hers were the diary she was reading. Analysing herself as an outsider looking in, just as she had Cora.

There she was. Kate Hunter. A thirty-five-year-old woman with a good career, good friends and family, and a boyfriend who wanted to marry her. A boyfriend who was handsome and successful, and whose career aligned with her own. A boyfriend who her friends and family loved. A boyfriend who ticked every box there could be on the list for perfect marriage material. He wanted everything with her. The whole shebang. A full, all-encompassing future.

She replayed her reaction to Lance's proposal. Even from this viewpoint, she still understood her initial reaction to the shock. Anyone who accidentally accepted a proposal before realising it's happening has the right to feel a bit horrified. But when she looked at her reactions from that point, her confidence faded.

She'd wanted to shake Cora for her foolish disregard of William, the man who was all of the same things Lance was today. Because the world spun on reason and logic. Not on flighty fancies and stolen kisses with the mailman. And the incredible happy life she'd eventually led with William, after coming to her senses, just went on to prove that.

Kate felt a troubled churn in her stomach as she realised there was no great difference in what Cora had been doing and what she was doing now. And she realised then that, whatever it took to do so, she needed to start focusing on what was best for her future and stop festering in the destructive, unwarranted panic that had been driving her every move since Lance proposed. It was time to focus on the big picture in life, rather than the – clearly malfunctioning – pixels of today.

But despite making the decision to do that with as much determination as she could gather, Kate still couldn't escape the hopeless sinking feeling of being trapped in a room with the walls closing in.

# TWENTY-TWO

The following few days passed in a blur of paperwork for Kate, broken up only by the various acts of war that were thrown back and forth between her and Sam.

The day after the wallet escapade, the water wouldn't turn on in either of the showers or the bath. At first Kate assumed it was a plumbing issue but quickly realised it was no unfortunate coincidence when Sam swaggered out of his room wearing nothing but a towel and a smug grin.

'Great day for a shower, don't you think?' he asked cheerily.

Kate's eyebrows had shot up in surprise, but she simply folded her arms and let him pass without a word. She listened at the door and heard the squeaking of metal on metal, which sounded suspiciously like the sound of a wrench reopening the pipes. A whoosh of running water followed right after, and her mouth dropped open in outrage.

Glaring at the door, Kate thought it over for a few moments, then lifted her chin and marched downstairs to fill up a bucket of water from the kitchen tap. If Sam wanted to play water games, then water games were what he'd get. Carefully walking the full bucket back up the stairs, she promptly emptied it over the contents of his clothes drawers, soaking every item of clothing he owned.

Not wanting to miss Sam's reaction, she settled in the hallway to wait, leaning against the banister with a smile of anticipation. He eventually walked out in a cloud of steam, the same towel wrapped around his waist and with water dripping from his dark hair. Seeing her there, he stretched out exaggeratedly with a sound of contentment.

'Ahh, there's just nothing better, is there?' he asked before continuing to his room, whistling loudly.

As the whistling abruptly stopped and was replaced by shouts of frustration, Kate's grin widened broadly.

'Nope,' she said, turning to her room with a satisfied chuckle. 'Nothing better.'

Sam's response to that had been to blast heavy metal through the house-wide sound system over the following few days every time she tried to take a call or had a Zoom meeting. He even did it during the night a few times, too, jerking her awake. After the second night of being woken this way, Kate began to debate whether prison might just be worth it if it meant she got to strangle the man with her bare hands, but then a better opportunity suddenly presented itself: Sam's game night.

Kate was curled up in the lounge checking off the assets she'd documented so far when Sam walked in and stopped beside her, hands on his hips.

'What?' she asked.

'You need to be elsewhere tonight,' he said. 'Same deal as before. Upstairs, on a rock leading sailors to their deaths, I don't care which. Just anywhere else but here.'

'Charming,' she said wryly. 'Why?'

'It's game night. And it's the biggest game of the season, so...' He tilted his head and upper body towards the door. 'Off you go.' He glanced out of the window with an anxious frown.

Kate folded her arms. 'Not until you ask me nicely.' She arched a challenging eyebrow.

Sam's face flashed with annoyance, then he forced a smile. '*Kate... please* would you kindly take your British backside out of this general area for the rest of the evening?' he asked.

'Not quite what I meant, but fine,' she replied flatly. 'I'll finish reading this, then I'll go.'

'Well, read fast,' he ordered rudely. 'I'm headed out to grab some drinks and I'll be back in ten minutes. I need you gone by then.'

Kate watched him leave, feeling the same irritating fizz of frustration his presence always incited. The man was just *infuriating*. Rude and obnoxious and infuriating.

She watched him leave through the window as she gathered her things. She knew she should just ignore him, but they were locked in this maddening game of petty revenge now, and she just couldn't seem to step away from it. Stopping in her tracks, she glanced over at the remote. The remote he'd told her never, under any circumstances, to move.

She picked it up, turned on the TV and flicked through the channels until she found a particularly dramatic Spanish soap opera. As two women began to argue passionately on screen, she grinned and turned the volume up. She glanced out at the drive to check Sam had definitely left, then jogged upstairs and let herself into his room. Pointedly ignoring the aftershave on his bedside table, she slipped the remote under Sam's pillow, then made her way next door to her own room with a low, mischievous giggle. That would be the very last place he'd look, even if he turned the house upside down trying to find it.

After changing into a pair of jeans and a thick woolly jumper, Kate filled her satchel with enough work to keep herself busy for a few hours. She slung this over her shoulder just as she heard Sam pull into the drive. Several other male voices joined his as he neared the door. It seemed his company had arrived to watch the game. Well, they were in for a bit of a surprise.

The voices grew louder as they moved inside, then there was a pause before they all began talking again in more serious tones. Kate listened to the pound of feet on the stairs and waited for the inevitable knock on the door.

'Kate?' Sam called tersely.

'Yes?' she answered, swirling her bronzing brush over her cheekbones in the mirror.

The door opened and he appeared, his face thunderous. 'Where is it?' he demanded.

'Where's what?' she replied. She applied a touch of lip gloss.

'Don't play with me,' he ordered. 'I'm serious. Where is it?'

Kate screwed the cap back on and rubbed her lips together, making him wait before she answered. 'If you're referring to the remote, I can assure you it's still in the house and it's perfectly safe,' she told him, turning to look at him. 'Or maybe it isn't. We *sirens* do love to destroy things, after all. Ships, men... The list does grow when we're feeling cranky after being woken up by loud music several times a night. So who knows?' She shrugged.

The muscles around Sam's jaw worked back and forth as he turned away and scratched the back of his neck.

'Kate, this isn't funny. I have a houseful of people down there ready to watch the game. Give it back,' he demanded.

'I have to disagree. I find that *incredibly* funny.' She stood up and picked up her satchel. 'It *is* in the house. I'll give you that clue, to get you started. Excuse me.' She waited until he moved back into the hall and then closed the door behind her. 'Oh, and I'll give you one more. *Well*, actually it's more of a warning. It's not in my room, and my room is off limits.' She held his gaze. 'And just to ensure you don't feel tempted to ignore that, I've set various booby traps around the place that are more than a little dangerous. So if you value all ten fingers, I'd keep out.'

Sam scoffed. 'You're bluffing.'

'Am I?' She raised an eyebrow, and as doubt flickered through his expression, she knew her words had hit the mark.

Leaving him there, she walked down the stairs and put on her boots, glancing into the lounge. A group of men stood together looking miserable, Mike included.

'Kate,' he said, catching sight of her. 'How you doing? You're looking good.' He walked over with an awkward smile. 'I, er...' He glanced back at the group. 'We were wondering if you could maybe find it in you to, er...'

'No,' she replied with a smile. 'I couldn't.'

Mike nodded, shifting his weight uneasily between his feet. 'It's just, er, this game, it's an *important* game...'

'Oh, am I ruining your night, Mike?' she asked, her words laced with sarcasm as she pointedly lifted an eyebrow. 'I *hate* it when people do that.'

Mike nodded, mashing his lips together, suitably shamed. '*Yep*. Yeah, that, er... OK, you have a good night!'

There was a chorus of groans from the group of men as he returned, unsuccessful. Kate suddenly realised Jerry was sat on the sofa stuffing popcorn into his mouth, transfixed by the Spanish drama unfolding on the TV.

'Jerry,' Mike prompted him. 'Hey. *Jerry*.'

'Mm? Oh, hey, Kate.' Turning briefly, he grinned. 'Sorry about the other night,' he added casually. 'Hope all's good with you.'

Kate stared back at him, amused. 'All's great, thanks, Jerry.'

'Good, good.' The dramatic music increased, and his hand paused mid-air as his eyes widened.

Sam walked past her to stand with his friends, looking furious. 'This really isn't cool, Kate. Look around – this isn't just my night you're ruining. It's *everyone's*.'

'That's not true,' she argued cheerfully. 'Look at Jerry. He's having a *wonderful* time!'

'I am,' he agreed with a nod. 'Why don't we just watch *this*? It's really good. Sarah and I watch it at home. This chick has a—'

'*Shut up*, Jerry,' Mike snapped, throwing a packet of pretzels at his head.

Sam stared at Kate determinedly. 'We are *watching* the game tonight. No matter what. Give me the damn remote, Kate. I *mean* it.'

'Oh, you *mean* it?' Kate asked, a slow smile curling up her face.

Mike leaned in towards Sam and spoke in a quiet, urgent tone. '*Listen*, you ain't married, so there are some things you have yet to learn, and one of them is that if a woman smiles like that—'

'I don't give a damn, Mike,' Sam exploded. 'This is *my* damn home, that is *my* damn TV, and if I want to watch it, I'm not letting some stuck-up tea-drinking pain in the ass *stop* me!'

Mike shook his head with a resigned expression, and Kate's smile broadened.

'Happy hunting, boys,' she said brightly before turning around and walking out.

She grabbed her coat off the hook and set off, Mike's voice drifting through as she shut the front door.

'*Now* what are we gonna do?'

'Oh, we're watching the game, Mike,' Sam replied determinedly. 'And if she thinks she's stopped that happening, then she's got another thing coming.'

## TWENTY-THREE

With a chuckle, Kate pulled on her hat and gloves then set off towards Main Street, deciding to work in the quaint-looking coffee shop she'd spotted on her way into town that first day. The sound of cheerful Christmas songs rang out as she passed the raised bandstand where a local choir practised. White twinkling lights wound around each wooden beam, bathing the singers in a warm ethereal glow. It somehow made everything look even more magical, and Kate smiled, feeling the festive warmth fill her heart.

Much as this place had been thrown at her, and much as she truly despised Sam, she realised she'd begun to fall deeply in love with Pineview Falls, with its pretty town centre, caring community and beautiful history. And suddenly she was glad that she'd been given the chance to experience this place in the run-up to Christmas. Even if it was causing all kinds of chaos back home. Pineview Falls was a rare hidden gem – and one she hoped stayed that way, for its own sake. Wonderful aesthetics aside, it was a town with a true beating heart. A town with a soul in a world where most places had sold theirs to the highest bidder long ago. It was simply and quietly beautiful. To be part of it for a little while, even as an outsider, was a gift she knew she was unlikely to experience again.

Reaching the coffee shop, she walked inside and ordered a peppermint hot chocolate before setting herself up to work in a cosy-looking corner. Soon absorbed in what she was doing, Kate zoned out, oblivious to the time and the world around her as both continued moving forward. When she was finally pulled from her focus, two hours had passed.

'Kate?' She looked up to see Jenna, the office manager from Coreaux Roots, smiling at her tentatively.

'Jenna, hi!' Kate smiled back, folding her file over to the side.

'Sorry, I didn't mean to disturb you. I just thought I'd say hi,' Jenna told her with an apologetic look.

'No, no, you haven't,' Kate replied. 'I'm done, anyway. How are you?'

'I'm OK, thanks,' Jenna replied. She held up a take-out cup. 'I have a rare weekend off from the kids so thought I'd go wild and wander down here for a hot chocolate.' She laughed, sounding slightly embarrassed.

'Ah.' Kate held up her empty cup. 'I've chosen the wild side, too.' She grinned. 'How old are your kids?'

'Five and nearly seven now.' Jenna's warm brown eyes lit up as she spoke. 'They're staying with their grandpa for a couple of days, and my husband works nights, so it's just me tonight.'

'Would you like to join me?' Kate offered, gesturing towards the empty chair opposite her. 'I'd welcome the company.'

'Sure, that would be nice.' Jenna smiled and sat down.

Kate ordered a fresh drink, along with two of the cookies she'd previously been eying. She offered one to Jenna.

'Oh, thanks!' Jenna smiled. 'These are *really* good.' She took a bite. 'So, what about you? Do you have a family back home? Kids?'

Kate shook her head. 'No, not yet. But I'm engaged,' she

added, trying to sound upbeat. 'Getting married on New Year's Eve, actually.'

'Congratulations!' Jenna said. 'Gosh, it must be so stressful being here with all that going on. Though you're probably all set by now, I imagine.'

Kate forced a bright smile. '*Few* things left to do, but, er, yes. Mostly.'

'How are you getting on at the house? You have everything you need?' Jenna asked.

'It's going OK,' Kate replied. 'There was a lot more to sort than I'd anticipated, but I'm making some headway. I'm learning so much about Cora and William, too. That's probably what's slowing me down the most, to be honest.' She laughed. 'The more I discover, the more I want to know. They seem like they were pretty amazing people.'

'They were,' Jenna said with a smaller smile this time. She took a sip of her drink.

Kate's mind wandered back to Cora's diary and the sweet-talking mailman. 'So, you and Cora were pretty close. Can I ask you a question about her? It's quite personal.'

'Sure, go ahead,' Jenna said, her eyes filling with curiosity.

'Did Cora ever mention another man? From her past, I mean. A first love, perhaps.' Kate sipped her hot chocolate.

Jenna's forehead puckered into a frown. '*No*,' she said, shaking her head. 'No. William was the only man Cora had ever loved. She'd say that a lot. Those two were the most perfect couple there ever was.' Jenna smiled fondly and looked away. 'I knew them both my whole life. I've never known a couple so deeply in love, so happy, no matter what was happening or how many years passed. They—' Jenna stopped abruptly as her bottom lip wobbled and tears filled her eyes.

'Oh, gosh, Jenna, I'm sorry,' Kate said, aghast. 'I didn't mean to upset you.'

'No, you didn't,' Jenna told her, wiping her eyes as the tears began to fall. 'Really you didn't. I just really miss her.' She gave Kate a sad smile as more tears followed, then reached into her pocket and pulled out a tissue. 'Cora was like a mom to me, you see. Mine died when I was just a baby, and when my dad couldn't figure out how he was going to work *and* take care of me, Cora was the one who made it possible. She had a corner of her office set up with baby equipment and arranged it so that when he worked, she'd look after me there. Wouldn't take no for an answer, my dad said. And would never accept a word of thanks, either. She was amazing. Threw me a birthday party *every* year. Took me shopping for my first bra, showed me how to style my hair, nursed me when I was sick.' She closed her eyes and bowed her head in pain.

'Jenna, I'm so sorry,' Kate said, feeling heartbroken for the woman.

Jenna sniffed and wiped her eyes. 'No, I'm sorry. You're here just tryin'a work and enjoy your night, and here I am bawling all over you.' She laughed, visibly forcing back the tide of grief. 'I'm fine. Really. It's fine. Death is part of life.' She shrugged, her eyes still glistening but the tears subsiding. 'That's what Cora told us when William died. As long as we remember the good times, people live on through us.'

Kate nodded and reached out to squeeze Jenna's arm. 'If there's anything of Cora's you'd like to keep, let me know, OK? I'll see it comes to you.'

If *anyone* was deserving of being left something by Cora, it was her. Kate found it strange, knowing as she now did how close the couple had been to people, that they'd never written an updated will. She frowned, and Jenna looked at her questioningly.

'What's wrong?' she asked.

'Nothing,' Kate said, waving the question away. 'It's...' She squeezed her gaze, suddenly realising that if anyone knew why, it would likely be Jenna. 'Actually, there's just something that strikes me as odd.' She looked down at the table, gently tapping her finger on the grainy wood as she picked her words carefully. 'The last will we have on record is from 1962. It doesn't specify any names, only gives instructions on how I'm to decide based on different possibilities. I'm just surprised they never wrote an updated one.'

Jenna met Kate's gaze with a frown. 'But they *did*,' she said with certainty. 'I remember. I was there when they had the witnesses round to sign.'

Kate sat upright, her eyes widening. 'Are you *sure*? *Absolutely* sure?'

'Yes,' Jenna replied. 'I was off school sick, so Cora had me laid up on the sofa in her office.'

'Was there a lawyer there?' Kate pressed.

'No.' Jenna shook her head. 'I remember, Cora wanted one there, but William told her that he'd already run it past their lawyer friend, who'd said that so long as they got witnesses to sign, it was legally tight.'

'Jacob,' Kate breathed.

'They had some friends of theirs in, got it signed, had some coffee and then they all left except Cora. I was curious, being a kid, so I asked, and Cora explained what a will was,' Jenna told her.

'Where did it go?' Kate asked urgently. This would change everything. Her mind whirled. 'Their lawyer friend, Jacob, he was my firm's founder, but we never got a copy of this. Do you know what it said or where it went? When did this happen?'

'Er...' Jenna's eyes darted from side to side as she tried to recall the details. 'I was about nine, I think. Yes, I was because it was around Sam's sixteenth birthday.'

If she was seven years younger than Sam, then Jenna was thirty-one, Kate noted, adjusting her mental profile of the woman. She looked much younger.

'Where it went, I couldn't tell you. It's not in the company safe or in Cora's office, and she's never told me. I just assumed Sam knew or that *you* had it.' Jenna grimaced. 'As for the contents, I have no idea. So, what does this mean now?'

Kate took a deep breath and blew it out through her cheeks, lying back against the chair. 'Well, unless we find it, it means *nothing*,' she told her. 'Legally we have to abide by the last known will on record. Without it physically in front of me, legally speaking, it doesn't exist. What about the witnesses? Do you remember who they were?'

'I do, but that won't help. They both died in a crash a few years back,' Jenna replied.

Kate grimaced.

'You should ask Sam,' Jenna advised. 'If anyone knows, it will be him. I'm surprised he hasn't brought it up already though.'

'Hmm,' Kate agreed, biting her lip. 'Why *hasn't* he?'


Kate finished up her text conversation with Lance and walked through the door, disappointed to hear the sounds of men watching sport coming from the lounge. Clearly her hiding spot wasn't as clever as she'd thought. She hung her coat and slipped off her boots, then walked towards the kitchen, but as she passed the archway to the lounge, she jerked to a halt and turned to stare in amazement.

Pieces of plaster and drywall littered the floor, and a jagged gaping hole that revealed the timber frame behind now surrounded the TV. A sledgehammer leaned on a piece of wall that was still intact below. Someone hit a ball, and a loud cheer erupted. Only Sam's head turned towards her, his glare piercing into her from across the room with a mixture of anger and defiance. Kate closed her mouth, suddenly aware it had dropped open, and then slowly turned to continue into the kitchen, completely lost for words.

She'd give him *one* thing – he was certainly determined.

After putting away the few grocery items she'd picked up on her way home, Kate grabbed a drink and headed up to bed.

She lay staring up at the ceiling for some time, thinking over her conversation with Jenna. Eventually she heard the men downstairs trickle away, and then Sam went up to bed. She bit her lip and listened closely, waiting for the moment he found the remote. She still couldn't believe he'd actually *destroyed a wall* to watch that game rather than miss it. Hearing him curse and march back out of his room, Kate quickly grabbed a book and pretended to be reading. Her door almost instantly flew open, and he appeared in the doorway.

'Didn't your mother teach you to knock?' she asked dryly, not looking up from the pages.

'*No,*' he answered shortly. He held up the remote in the air accusingly. '*Really?*' he asked. '*Seriously?*'

Kate just shrugged, keeping her eyes on the page and watching him in her peripheral vision. 'I told you it was in the house.'

Sam made a low growling sound in the back of his throat and wrung his hands in the air as if imagining her neck was between them.

'Shut the door on your way out,' Kate said sunnily, but as he turned, she remembered what she'd wanted to ask him. 'Oh, Sam?' She sat up, putting the book aside.

'*What?*' he seethed.

'The will I've been working from – it's an old one. *Very* old. Jenna told me they wrote a more recent one, about twenty-two years ago.' She watched as his frown lessened slightly and couldn't help but notice how much nicer he looked when he wasn't glaring at her or plotting something. Her gaze slipped from his face down to the curve of his collarbone and she pulled it away quickly, clearing her throat. Why did she keep doing that? 'Do you know where it is? Have you seen it?' She paused, but he didn't answer. 'It would really help speed things up.'

Sam looked away down the hallway, then shook his head. 'I haven't seen any will.'

'OK. Well, if you come across...' Kate trailed off as the door was swiftly shut again and Sam's angry stomps returned to his own room. His door slammed, and she turned to the picture of Cora on the wall. 'Where did you hide it, Cora? And why have you made it so hard to find?'

# TWENTY-FOUR

*9 January 1955*

*W took me to the movies last night, to see* White Christmas.
*Christmas was obviously over weeks ago now, but when I told
W I hadn't seen it, he insisted we go. And I'm glad he did. It
was a simply wonderful film. Vera-Ellen danced around the
screen with the most glorious skill. And in one scene with
Danny Kaye, it was as though she barely even touched the
ground.*

*W made me laugh by twirling me around on the pavement
outside. But he said the characters played by Bing Crosby and
Rosemary Clooney reminded him of us, which was the moment
I was pulled right back to earth, because I am far from the quiet
and cautious older sister. And that he thinks that made me
wonder if he knows me at all. Vera-Ellen's character was the
one who called to my soul. She had such spirit and bravery.*

*Upon returning home, I said as much to my mother, who
told me that the film was just fantasy and that true braveness is
much less obvious. She also said that adventures are created
wherever you decide to have them. She told me that some are*

quieter, that any movement forward in life is a new adventure. And I suppose she is right.

W has openly declared his love for me now. My parents couldn't be happier about it. I told my mother that I don't see W that way. That I love him as a friend. She tells me that this is the most important type of love one can have in a marriage, that after a while, romantic love fades, and if friendship is what's left, then life will be good.

Mother also told me that now I am a woman, I cannot think of my current happiness, I must think of my future happiness and what is necessary for a comfortable life. With W, I would have a very good life. I would never have to worry about the prospect of poverty or resentment after the shine of romance has faded.

I suppose I should heed her words. But the thought of entering a marriage with someone who lights no fire in my soul fills me with desolation. Not that W has proposed marriage yet, but I think he eventually will.

Sometimes, for just a second, a part of me wishes I had never met M. For then I'd never know what I was missing; no flame would have been set alight. But that thought flickers away quickly, because I know, even if that fire were to be put out by the cold rains of life's storms, I would never live to regret it. Because I'd know, even if I never found it again, that for one brief shining moment, my heart truly lived.

# TWENTY-FIVE

Kate looked up from the photo album she was poring over cross-legged on the basement floor and tilted her head to the side. Had that been the doorbell or was she imagining things? After a second, it sounded again, and she tutted, dragging herself up with reluctance. Sam wasn't in, so she'd have to answer it.

She checked her watch as she climbed the stairs, surprised to see it was almost five. She'd been wading through the basement boxes all day and had decided to stop and reward herself with a little break and a look through more of Cora and William's old photo albums. They'd been on so many adventures together. Safaris and sailing trips, with snaps from the tops of snowy mountains to the bowls of desert valleys. But the one thing Kate noticed in all of them was that, whether they were on an adventure, or simply sitting in the garden, the happiness and love shining from their faces never altered.

The doorbell chimed a third time as she reached the top of the stairs.

'Just a sec!' she called, quickly patting the basement dust off her trousers.

Kate opened the door with a polite smile, then froze as she came face to face with Aubrey Rowlings.

The gleaming smile, militantly straight blonde hair and eerily wide blue eyes hit Kate like a glitch in the Matrix, being such a perfect match to her posed photo. But unlike the photo, this Aubrey couldn't be ignored.

'Oh my *gosh*!' Aubrey gushed, ascending into a high muted scream and throwing her arms outwards. 'It is *so good* to *see you*! Come *here* – let's *hug*!' She grabbed Kate and squeezed her against her ample bosom.

'Oh, er, *oop*! OK...' Kate muttered awkwardly, feeling alarmed.

'Ah, Kate, how *are* you?' Aubrey released her and twisted her around in one swift move, linking her arm through Kate's and walking her forward into the house. 'How're you holding up? Are you *OK*? You doing *OK*?' She was nodding at Kate encouragingly now, her forehead puckered in concern as though worried about her.

Kate blinked, thoroughly confused. 'Er, yes, thank you. I'm – I'm fine.' She stared back at Aubrey, who was now nodding faster and making crooning sounds of sympathetic agreement. 'But it's *me* who should be asking *you* that,' she said slowly, trying very hard to keep the instant distrust she felt towards Aubrey out of her expression. 'You're the one who just lost your great-aunt.' She gently but firmly removed her arm from the other woman's grip, softening the move with a smile and a gesture to walk through to the kitchen. '*Tea*?'

'Oh my gosh, you're so *British*!' Aubrey exclaimed with a laugh of delight as she moved to walk ahead of Kate.

'Er, *yes*,' Kate responded awkwardly, shooting a wary frown at the back of the woman's perfectly styled head. 'So I've been told.'

'*Tea*,' Aubrey repeated, amused. 'I thought that was just a *joke*, that offering tea is the first thing you British people do.

Like something that went viral from a stand-up or something. I didn't realise it was *true*.'

She let out another sharp burst of laughter, and Kate's frown deepened, but she swiftly smiled as Aubrey reached the kitchen and turned around.

'Er, *yes*. I guess it *is* true,' she agreed. 'So...' She walked over to the kettle. 'Would you like one?'

Aubrey grinned and sat down on one of the bar stools, running her fingers through the ends of her perfectly straight hair. 'You are *adorable*, Kate, *honestly*.'

The little devil on her shoulder popped up with a look of question and an array of choices, and even the angel pointedly studied her nails between hopeful glances. But Kate simply took a deep breath and smiled, leaving them to share a disappointed look.

'Well, I'm having one,' she said firmly. 'Let me know what you decide.'

'I'll join you,' Aubrey replied. 'I can't pass up the opportunity to enjoy a cup made by a real *British person* now, can I?'

Having turned around, Kate was free to roll her eyes.

'How do you take it?' she asked.

'Oh, I'll have it however you take it, Kate,' Aubrey replied. 'You show me how it's done.'

'So, Aubrey, it's great to finally meet you,' Kate said as she readied the cups and boiled the kettle. She turned and leaned back against the side. 'Please accept my apologies for not reaching out before now. I've just been trying to get everything in order first before meeting any of you to discuss things further.'

Aubrey's smile twitched, and her head tilted a little to the side as she let out a tight tinkling laugh. '*Any* of us?' she asked. 'What do you mean?'

'Everyone who submitted a claim on the estate,' Kate

replied. 'There are a number of you, so I'll need to arrange some meetings to assess everything.'

'*Well!*' Aubrey's eyebrows rose upwards, and she pulled her chin backwards with another delicate laugh. 'I am personally *shocked* that anyone else has had the *audacity* to try and claim *our company,*' she declared.

'*Our?*' Kate queried, holding her gaze. 'I was under the impression that the company was owned solely by Cora. At least, that's who it's filed under.'

Aubrey's big blue eyes flashed with irritation, and something dark began to show through the cracks of her fixed smile.

*There you are*, Kate thought.

Aubrey was an anomaly in Kate's world. She possessed a personality type Kate hadn't crossed before, but what Kate *was* familiar with was the attempt to hide behind a mask. Everyone did it to some degree, but the people with the worst intentions always worked the hardest to disguise themselves.

'I'm sure you *also* know that I'm the *only* member of this family who actually cares enough about our company to work there then,' Aubrey replied.

Kate nodded, turning to pour the water as the kettle came to the boil. 'I do. You're a junior marketing exec, right?'

She stirred the tea, noting the pause.

'I *am* in marketing at the moment, yes,' Aubrey said, her tone more professional now as she tested the waters. 'My great-aunt wanted me to work across different areas of the company in the time before I took over,' she continued. 'So I started off in the general office, learning payroll, scheduling, contracts, all those sort of things. After I mastered that, I moved on to marketing. Because you *know* what they say, don't you?'

Aubrey shot Kate a winning smile as she walked over with the two teas.

'What do they say?' Kate asked.

'You can have the best product in the world and still fail if

you *don't understand how to market it.*' She gave Kate a look as
if to press home a lesson, then took a sip of her tea. 'Gosh, this
tea is divinity itself,' she gushed. 'How do you make it? You
*must* tell me so I can make this at home.'

'Teabag, water, milk, two sugars, stir,' Kate replied, adding a
smile to take the sharp edge off of her delivery.

She watched Aubrey nod along seriously as if taking notes
and resisted the urge to shake her head.

'Thank you,' Aubrey enthused. 'I shall remember that.' She
smiled. 'So, who else has put in a claim for *our company*, Kate?
This *is* something I take quite seriously, and as you are our
lawyer, I *would* like to discuss that with you further.'

Kate took a deep breath and exhaled, immediately seeing
the trap Aubrey was trying to lay. She sidestepped it with a
snap decision.

'Actually, until the ownership of the company is decided,
Jenna, the office manager, has been appointed as temporary
CEO. So I'll be discussing anything relating to the business
with her at this point in time, and you'll be made aware of any
decisions accordingly.'

As soon as she said it, Kate realised it made perfect sense.
When it came to management, Jenna had been, in all but title,
Cora's second in command. Who better to keep things running
smoothly? She decided to make it official first thing in the
morning.

'*Excuse* me?' Aubrey said, the friendly tone beginning to
wear thin. 'I'm sorry, but *what* did you just say?'

Kate held her gaze levelly. 'I said I've appointed Jenna to
stand as temporary CEO until matters are settled. She's best
placed to do so, and as an impartial party, she's also best placed
to help me decide on the best candidate to take over long-term.'

'Yes, that's what I thought I heard,' Aubrey snapped. '*You*
telling *me* that you've made a decision about my family's business without even asking my *permission*. How *dare* you?' she

demanded, her anger beginning to redden her cheeks. 'I'm *family*, I *work* there, I have *rights*.'

'Actually, you don't,' Kate replied, turning her head at the sound of the doorbell. She lifted a finger to stop Aubrey in her tracks as the woman opened her mouth to speak again. 'Hold that thought.'

She nipped out to the front door, thankful for whoever was on the other side of it for shattering the tense exchange. Her thankfulness was short-lived, however, when she opened the door and found Evelyn, Cora's sister, standing on the other side.

'Oh, for the *love of God*,' she muttered under her breath, wondering if it was National Harass a Kate Day and no one had bothered to tell her.

Wrapped in a vintage mink fur coat that had seen better days, Evelyn clutched her handbag to her chest with both hands. Her pale cheeks were dotted with a little too much blusher, and her red lipstick bled out through the fine lines around her lips, which she squeezed together as if sucking on a lemon.

'*Where is she?*' Evelyn demanded, sweeping past Kate with barely a glance. '*Where* is my granddaughter?'

'*Please,*' Kate muttered wryly, shutting the door. '*Do come in.*'

She followed Evelyn through to the kitchen.

'*I knew it,*' Evelyn declared in angry triumph.

Aubrey glared at her grandmother. 'I said I would sort this out, and I *will*,' she replied.

'*Oh really?*' Evelyn asked with obvious disbelief. 'Let's see, shall we?'

She swung round to face Kate, quickly shifting her expression to a calm sweet smile. The sour battle-axe who'd stormed in moments before was gone, replaced with a soft elderly woman who looked like she probably spent her days in a rocking chair crooning at babies and knitting them hats. Kate marvelled at the woman's ability to flip an instant personality change. Perhaps she hadn't been that bad an actress, after all.

'Kate, *hello*,' she said, her voice distinctly slower and weaker. Evelyn placed her handbag on the side and walked over with a new stiffness in her gait, reaching out to grip Kate's hand between both of hers. 'It's a pleasure to meet you, my dear. An absolute *pleasure*. I'm Evelyn, Cora's sister.' She cast her gaze down a little too perfectly, raising it again with a sad smile.

'It's nice to meet you, too,' Kate said, drawing her hand back.

'I've been trying to call you,' Evelyn said, screwing up her face to look a little confused. 'I've been terribly worried, you see. I have a letter from my sister that—'

'Oh, Gram, *stop*,' Aubrey ordered angrily. 'I said we'd cut a deal and I *meant* it, but right now we have a bigger problem. *Kate* here has decided to make some decisions of her *own* without consulting me, putting the control of the company in the hands of Cora's *office girl*.'

'*What*?' Evelyn demanded, the soft-knit grandmother disappearing instantly. 'What do you *mean*, Aubrey? She can't *do* that, can she?'

Kate sighed, looking between their angry faces as she tried to work out how best to proceed. '*Look*, let's all just calm down and have a civilised discussion.' She flicked the switch to reheat the kettle. 'Evelyn, would you like a cup of tea?'

'*No*! She does *not want* a cup of your *damned tea*,' Aubrey exploded.

'*Well*...' Evelyn tipped her head sideways as if she wanted to disagree, glancing at Aubrey's mug with interest.

'*No. No tea*. Tea does not fix this. *You* fix this.' Aubrey pointed at Kate.

Kate stared back at her coldly, having had enough of the woman's tantrum. 'I don't know who you think you're talking to, but I can *assure* you, you're not helping yourself at all right now.'

She recalled Bob's warning to tread carefully with Aubrey and stopped there. With Aubrey's love for attention and clear desire to be in the media, they didn't need her walking off with any ammunition. Still, that didn't mean she had to accept this kind of behaviour. So long as she remained calm and professional, she could still tell the other woman to take a hike.

Aubrey slipped off the stool and stalked towards Kate. Kate watched her warily and felt a ripple of unease as Aubrey's eyes turned glassy, a darkness flickering just behind. The woman no longer looked anything like the preppy cheerleader type from her picture. Now, with her vacant stare and obvious anger, she just seemed dangerous.

'*You* don't know who *I* think I am?' she asked in a low, shaky tone, taking another step towards Kate. '*I'm* the person you're going to hand the company to, Kate. Because it's what I'm *owed*. Because it's rightfully *mine*, by *blood*. You'll hand me this house, too, and everything else you've listed. And *I* will decide who gets what out of it. And you'll do that *now*.'

'*Damn* right,' Evelyn snapped waspishly.

Kate glanced at the older woman and at the sour look on her face, then turned back to Aubrey, taking a measured step backwards to the counter as the woman moved into her personal space.

'Aubrey, I think I should remind you that I'm a *lawyer*,' she said in a calm but firm tone, feeling anything but those things. 'Threatening me into putting my legal stamp on anything is a federal offence, which you could, and *would,* go to prison for, if I were to report you.'

A smile briefly played on Aubrey's lips. 'Oh, you won't be reporting *anything*, Kate,' she said with confidence. 'You'd turn yourself into a joke and never be taken seriously again.'

Kate frowned. 'I don't think you understand what I'm saying, Aubrey.'

'No, I don't think *you* understand what *I'm* saying,' Aubrey shot back.

'Why don't you explain it to her a little better,' Evelyn hissed menacingly.

The kettle came to the boil and clicked off, and Aubrey glanced towards it with a glint in her eye. Kate frowned as a warning prickle travelled up her neck, but she didn't catch Aubrey's dark train of thought until it was too late.

Snatching up the steaming kettle, Aubrey moved closer to Kate with a manic look. Kate darted backwards, startled, and held up her hands defensively.

'*Hey*! *Whoa,* what the *hell* are you doing?' she demanded.

Aubrey brandished the boiling-hot stainless-steel kettle like a weapon and backed Kate into the corner of the room. Her teeth clenched, and her lips curled back.

'I did not pander to that woman for *three whole years* to walk away now with nothing,' she growled.

'Aubrey, *stop* this. This is *crazy*,' Kate pleaded, genuinely afraid now. 'I've never said you'd walk away with nothing. All I said was that I'm in the process of working things out. Nothing has been decided.'

Aubrey let out a sharp laugh. 'Oh, but you *did*, Kate, when you told me you'd be taking advice from Cora's little *paper pusher*. That spiteful little thing *hates* me, just because I was actually *related* to Cora and *she* wasn't. She'll make sure to steer you *anywhere* but me, with all *sorts* of lies that are really just a cover for her *jealousy*. And I can't have that. I *need* this money and so does Gram. So *get to it*, or I will burn that pretty little face of yours so bad you'll never look the same again.'

Kate's eyes flew fearfully to the kettle as she took in the threat. Was Aubrey really that crazy? How had things flipped so drastically? Kate was right in the corner now, with no way out, as Aubrey loomed over her.

'*Well*?' Aubrey suddenly roared. 'What'll it be, Kate? You gonna make up the papers, or am I going to burn your face off?'

'She don't bluff, child,' Evelyn threw in with a nasty smile. 'So I'd choose wisely.'

'You're *crazy*,' Kate breathed.

'You're not the first to call me that,' Aubrey replied. 'And you'll doubtful be the last. Now, *make your damn choice!*' She leered in. 'Let's see if we can't persuade you, huh? Test it out on your arm first.'

'*No!* Aubrey, *stop* this!' Kate begged.

'*Gimme* your arm.' Aubrey lurched forward and grabbed her arm viciously. Kate yelped and tried to pull away, but there was nowhere left to go. 'Let's see this pale English skin of yours *burn*.'

Kate squeezed her eyes closed, her heart thudding hard and the internal roar of blind panic filling her head until it was all she could hear.

A deep voice suddenly boomed through the room. '*What the hell are you doing?*'

Aubrey's vicious grip suddenly ripped away from her arm, and she opened her eyes to see Sam flinging the woman across the room towards Evelyn with one hand as he cast the kettle across the floor with the other. Boiling water splashed out everywhere as Aubrey collided with her grandmother, and fear briefly flickered across her face. She quickly straightened, watching Sam warily as she smoothed her hair.

'Sam—' she began, but he cut her straight off.

'*Get out of my house!*' he bellowed. '*Now!*'

Evelyn backed away from Aubrey and was now feigning shock. 'Thank *goodness* you arrived, Sam,' she simpered. 'I was just—'

'*Both* of you,' he shouted at her. '*Get out* and don't you *ever* come back here. I find you threatening Kate like that again, *so help me God...*'

'*OK, OK!*' Evelyn raised her hands in surrender and turned to join Aubrey, who was now waiting for her in the hall, shooting evils at Sam.

'You don't know what she's *done*,' Aubrey hissed.

'I don't *need* to,' he shot back furiously. 'If it's pissed *you* off, that's enough to know she's on the right track. Now *get out* before I throw you out myself!'

Sam marched a few paces towards them, and they quickly scuttled out of the house, slamming the door behind them. Sam's torso sharply rose and fell a few times as he stared after them, then he stepped back and forced a couple of deep calming breaths before turning back towards Kate.

Kate stood frozen in the corner, her fists tight against her chest.

'Are you OK?' Sam asked, genuine worry in both his tone and eyes.

Kate wetted her lips and then tried to clear her throat. She nodded slightly, her gaze flickering past him to the hallway.

'Yes,' she said in not much more than a whisper. 'Yes, I'm OK.'

She moved forward off the wall and lowered her arms shakily as Sam moved towards her, looking her over.

'Here, let me see that.' His voice was surprisingly gentle now, and she instinctively wanted to comply, but she frowned, not understanding. 'Your arm,' he clarified.

She looked down at her arm and blinked in surprise at the three angry red gashes. 'I'm *bleeding*,' she said with a strangely detached voice. 'I can't even feel it.'

'That's the adrenaline,' Sam told her. 'But it'll wear off. Let me sort that out before it does. It'll be easier.'

Somewhere in the back of her mind, she knew she should decline. Sam was the enemy, not a friend. But in the face of

Aubrey's attack, something had changed in his voice. In his eyes. So instead, she simply nodded, holding her arm out with an inexplicable feeling of trust. As he went to touch it, she gasped and pointed to the angry red burn that ran up *his* arm.

'Yeah, *that* I can feel,' he told her with a small, grim smile.

And that was what tipped her over the edge. She wasn't sure if it was the burn or the shock wearing off, or a combination of everything that had happened, but as Kate opened her mouth to speak, she suddenly let out a loud sob. Tears filled her eyes, and she shook her head helplessly, trying to force them away, but they wouldn't go, and as the second sob followed, she covered her face with her hands.

'Hey, it's OK,' Sam told her gently. 'You're safe now. They're not coming back.' He hesitated for a moment and glanced over to the kettle on the floor, scratching his head. 'You know, er... I heard a cup of tea is the ultimate solve-all solution for you Brits, but how do things stand after one's been terrorised by the kettle?'

Kate laughed through her sobs at the perfectly timed joke and wiped the tears from her cheeks. Her grin softened to a thankful smile. 'You know, I don't think there's anything that can strip the therapeutic qualities of a good cup of tea for us Brits. Not even being terrorised by the kettle.'

# TWENTY-SIX

Sam walked over to the sofa Kate was sitting on with two steaming mugs and handed one over. The kettle had been unharmed, other than a small dent in the side, much to Kate's relief.

'Thanks,' Kate said, blowing on it before taking a sip. '*Oh.*' She pulled back. 'That's one *strong* tea.'

'I figured we could both use a touch of the Irish in there tonight,' Sam replied, sitting on the opposite end of the sofa and twisting to face her. 'Well, technically Scotch,' he added. 'Let's call it a Celtic tea.'

Kate smiled and pulled her feet up to give him more room. Cosied up in a warm blanket, she'd now regained full control of her emotions since Sam had joked her initial shock away. She was grateful to him for that. It had been exactly what she'd needed. She was grateful, too, for the gentle care he'd then given her patching up her arm. And for saving her from Aubrey's psychotic attack. Out of nowhere, Sam had gone from being the most maddening adversary she'd ever faced to being her all-round hero. Life really was funny sometimes. She glanced at him over the rim of her cup as she took another sip.

'Thank you,' she said quietly. 'You know. For earlier.'

Sam rested his arm across the back of the sofa and shook his head with a grim expression. 'I should have warned you about those two. I'm sorry.'

Kate frowned. 'It's not your fault.' She tipped her head to the side with a wry expression. 'Which actually makes a change compared to everything *else* that happens to me around here.'

He let out a short sound of amusement. 'True,' he admitted. '*That* was definitely not me though.'

'So sending someone to *prison's* acceptable, but you draw the line at permanent scarring?' Kate asked with a laugh.

Sam thought it over, then nodded. 'I'd say that about sums it up.'

'I'd better cancel that tattoo artist I had booked in for you then,' she joked.

Sam laughed. 'What were you going to do? Rose or skull?'

'Neither,' she replied, meeting his smile and feeling suddenly warmed by it.

He was even more handsome when he smiled. In fact, it completely transformed him. She felt a tug of something in her core. Something inviting. Something she couldn't quite place. She glanced away quickly, feeling flustered suddenly.

'I'd rather not ruin the surprise in case we go back to all that and it *does* escalate to that level,' she said, getting her thoughts back on track. 'But it was rude, and it was going to go here.' She pointed to her forehead with a grin.

Sam shook his head with a groan. 'You're *dangerous*. If I'd realised this when we first met, I'd never have got on the wrong side of you.'

Kate looked down at her mug. As kind as he'd been to her tonight, and as much as she appreciated that, Sam was still the same guy he'd been an hour ago. One heroic act didn't change a whole person, and she needed to remember that. There was a short silence, and then he spoke quietly, his words taking her by surprise.

'I'm sorry for the way I've treated you since you arrived here, Kate. The person you've seen really isn't who I am. I don't know what came over me these last couple of weeks.' He shook his head and turned to look out of the window. 'I know it probably doesn't look like it to you, but I loved my aunt very much.'

Kate waited for him to continue, listening with interest.

'They took me in when I was twelve, after my parents died. It was a rough time. They had to fight to get me outta the system after the state threw me in there.' Sam stared into the distance for a moment. 'But they did. And they gave me a home and a family and treated me like I was their own. They were just like that. If they had something to give, they'd give it, without question. Especially kindness. *Always* kindness.' He smiled, looking down at his mug. 'The day my aunt died, I was with her. I held her hand.' He swallowed hard. 'It was the hardest goodbye I've had to say, and I've had to say a lot. I needed to get away from everyone after; couldn't stand the sympathy and the attempts to help. I just needed some time to process things on my own. So I took off to one of my empty projects and camped out for a few days.'

'Projects?' Kate asked.

'I build affordable, sustainable eco houses and solutions,' he explained. He looked up at her with a half smile. 'I know you had me pegged as a careless bum, being around here so much lately, but not the case, I'm afraid. Sorry to disappoint you.'

Kate stared at him, surprised. That *was* a turn-up for the books. Or was it? She hadn't actually asked him, after all. In fact, if she was being brutally honest with herself, she'd really just assumed that because it fitted best with the picture she'd wanted to create of him.

'I spent a week up there, trying to come to terms with it all,'

Sam continued. 'Then I drove back to get cleaned up the day before her funeral.'

'Oh my God,' Kate groaned as the penny dropped. 'And before you could get home, you ended up crashing into that tree and meeting me.' She covered her eyes with her hand, his reactions suddenly making a lot more sense.

'Yeah,' Sam confirmed. 'Which doesn't excuse my behaviour at all. I just wasn't dealing very well, and then *there you were.*' He grimaced.

'*There I was,*' she repeated quietly. 'Wait, did you say the funeral was the next day?' She frowned.

'Yeah.' He scratched the back of his neck. 'Jenna organised it all. She just wanted it to be a good day, and after the day before, I just...' He struggled to finish his sentence and made a sound of reluctance.

'You thought I'd be better locked up in *jail* than roaming the house where you were holding the wake,' she finished. She pursed her lips. 'I can't pretend I agree with that, but at least it was for a better cause than a *date*. Why did you tell me it was a *date*?'

Sam laughed. 'I didn't – you just assumed. You asked me if I'd left you in there so I could drink wine with a woman, and technically I had. So I said *yes*. You were a crazy stranger. I didn't feel like sharing something that personal with you.'

Kate shook her head. 'Well, your methods of dealing with things are terrible, but I guess you aren't as awful as I thought you were,' she admitted. 'Which means I'm going to have to rethink *all* my evil plans.' She exaggeratedly rolled her eyes. He laughed again, and she smiled, thinking back over all their interactions. 'OK, I have more questions.'

'Go on,' he said warily.

'That police officer who arrested you – what did you do to him to make him hate you so much?' she asked.

'I was born,' he answered with an awkward laugh. 'When I

moved here, he gave me a hard time. Found out the last home I'd been in had been in a trailer park and told everyone I was trash. Which wasn't fun. Not least because the people in that trailer had been really kind to me. They were good people. So I stood up to him, and the more I did, the worse it got. That's when I met Mike and Jerry. They had my back, and things started to change.'

Kate frowned in disgust. 'What a douchebag! That must have been so hard, with everything else you were dealing with.'

'Ah, life's full of people like him,' Sam said, brushing it off. 'I got my own back, anyway. Couple years later I became popular with the girls and dated the head cheerleader for a while. I was her first love, as she still tells everyone when she's had a few margaritas.'

Kate grinned. '*Please* tell me she's Healy's wife.'

'She's Healy's wife,' Sam confirmed.

'Ha!' Kate slapped her hand on the back of the couch and laughed. 'That's amazing! Oh, he must hate you *so much*.'

'He does.' Sam grinned. 'OK, *my* turn.' He eyed her for a few moments. 'I don't *get* you,' he said eventually.

'That's not a question,' she told him.

'OK. So you're clearly *very* smart, and you're passionate when you're fighting for something you care about. But then it's like you...' He put down his drink and tried to condense a ball of air between his hands. 'I don't know, like you try to *contain* it in a neat little box.'

Kate frowned, feeling defensive. 'I like to be *organised* and *prepared*. But there's nothing wrong with that.'

Sam nodded. 'OK. So what makes you tick? What makes you feel alive?'

Kate faltered, stumped, and realised no one had asked her that question in a really long time. She tried to pinpoint the last thing that had made her feel something genuinely positive, but neither *the snow* nor *jetting off the runway on a plane* actually answered Sam's questions.

The silence stretched on too long, and Sam cleared his throat.

'Sorry, that was a big one to throw outta the blue. It's not always easy to put that kind of thing into words, I know.' He offered her the out so politely that it only made her feel even more embarrassed that she couldn't answer.

She touched her ring, looking down at it with a touch of guilt. She should have said that Lance made her feel alive. Or that what made her tick right now was the wedding.

'When's the big day?' Sam asked, gesturing towards her hand.

'Oh, um, New Year's Eve,' she replied, forcing a smile.

'Oh, it's close!' Sam exclaimed. His gaze lingered on the ring. 'That's an impressive rock, by the way.'

'Yes, it's...' Kate bit the inside of her cheek. 'It's something.' She looked back up to see Sam staring back with a frown, and quickly smiled.

'You must be pretty desperate to finish up here and get back then, I imagine?' he asked.

Kate nodded with a sound of agreement, but Sam's curious frown remained. 'There's just still a lot to arrange,' she told him, by way of explanation for her lack of enthusiasm. 'It's all happened very fast, you see, and I just haven't, er, haven't really got my head around it all.'

*What are you doing?* she screamed at herself. *Why are you telling him this?*

'I mean, *no*, I-I don't mean my head, I mean more like, you know...' She started rambling, feeling flustered. 'I mean with things to organise still, it's stressful. That's all. I haven't even got a *dress* yet!'

'No?' Sam scratched his stubble. 'There's a dress place in town I know. Round the back of the old water mill. Jerry's wife works there. I could talk to her if you like, see if I can get you in to look around? Probably the least I could do, after the whole jail thing.'

'And the water,' she reminded him.

He nodded. '*Yup.*'

'And the noise torture,' she added.

'Mhm,' he agreed.

'*And*' – she narrowed her eyes – 'the *milk*. You do *not* get in between a Brit and her tea. *Not cool.*'

Sam threw his head back and laughed.

Kate took another sip of her drink, then looked down at her hands for a moment. 'I'm sorry, too, by the way. For your wallet and for driving you to break down a *wall*.' She glanced over at the jagged hole around the TV. 'I didn't realise you felt *quite* so strongly about watching the game.'

Sam let out a rueful sigh. 'I don't, actually. But one of the guys, Dave, his wife left him recently. Took the kids and the dog and moved downstate with some guy she'd been seeing behind his back.'

'Ouch.' Kate winced.

'Yeah.' Sam looked down at his cup. 'He's not coping well. We've been taking turns to keep an eye on him. Game night is the only thing he looks forward to, so...' He trailed off and looked at the hole.

Kate suddenly felt like the biggest jerk in the world. She closed her eyes.

'I'm so sorry, Sam,' she said quietly. 'I'm an idiot.'

'No, you weren't to know,' he said, brushing it off. 'You were just giving back what I deserved.'

Kate shook her head. 'Still, I should have handled that better. This isn't how I deal with things. It's not who I am at all.'

'Seems we've been bringing out the worst in each other, huh?' Sam said quietly.

Kate nodded, and they studied each other for a few moments.

'I'm glad you're not who I thought you were,' Kate said suddenly.

'Ditto,' Sam said. 'It'll be nice to sleep with *both* eyes closed again.'

Kate laughed and tucked her hair back behind her ear. 'Affordable sustainable eco houses, huh? That's amazing. Most people only care about how much profit they can make. It's refreshing to see there are still people out there trying to make a difference in the world. It must be very rewarding.' She smiled, feeling a pang of envy. She couldn't remember the last time she'd worked on something that felt rewarding.

Sam nodded. 'It is. I'm all for working hard for the things you want in life, but people shouldn't have to struggle for basic things like safe living conditions or have to choose between things like heating the house and feeding their kids.' He sighed. 'When people don't have money, they often end up in a more expensive rut than people who do.'

'What do you mean?' Kate asked, intrigued.

'I don't know what it's like in England, but here, if you're down on your luck, it's almost impossible to drag yourself back out, and the cycle goes way deeper than people realise. For example, if you're poor, you buy cheap foods, which are pumped full of stuff you wouldn't throw at a dog, but they're hidden in the mile-long list of ingredients, so you don't know, and that's what you eat. What your *kids* eat. The lack of nutrition slows them down, so they focus less and get worse grades, which has a knock-on effect on their future. It slows *you* down, too, but at the same time, you're picking up more hours at work to pay the bills. If you *have* a job.'

He sat forward, growing more impassioned. 'Imagine the only place you can afford is a run-down dump. There's mould on the walls, the washer's packed up, the landlord doesn't care and the bills just keep mounting. You work harder, eat worse, breathe in that toxic air, grow more stressed and run-down until you end up ill – and then you either don't have health insurance or it doesn't cover what you need. You're faced with the choice of crippling debt or leaving your health to deteriorate until you can't work or, as is often the case, just die.'

Kate blew out a long breath. 'That's a depressing picture.'

'That's the reality for a lot of people,' Sam replied. 'But if they have access to safe, sustainable, affordable dwellings, that changes things. Not everything, of course, but it's a start.' He shrugged.

Kate watched him for a moment, her grudging admiration for him growing. 'Well, you certainly sound like you've found your purpose in life.'

'Everyone needs one, right?' he asked, his piercing gaze meeting hers. 'My aunt used to say that so long as you have a purpose and something or someone in your life that makes you feel alive, that's all you need. I'm lucky that my work ticks both.'

Kate nodded. 'That makes sense.'

His gaze flickered to her ring, then back to her face, roaming around it like he was reading all its secrets. As though he could see right through her carefully perfected mask and knew she wasn't as together as she liked to make out. She looked away.

A few more seconds passed, and then Sam cleared his throat. 'Listen, let's wipe the slate clean. Put all the craziness behind us and start over,' he suggested, reaching out a hand. 'Hi. I'm Sam.'

Kate looked at his offered hand and then took it in hers with a smile. 'Kate.'

# TWENTY-SEVEN

'He's away at the moment, I'm afraid,' the reedy voice on the other end of the phone informed her. 'Won't be back now for a month.'

'A *month*?' Kate exclaimed, putting her free hand to her head in despair. 'Is he reachable at least? Is there a number I can try? It really is quite urgent.'

She'd been trying to get hold of Edward Moreaux all week, after the incident with Aubrey and Evelyn, but it was proving to be almost impossible.

'I'm afraid not – he's at a health retreat. No phones. Only emergency calls allowed to the main number. Is it an *emergency*?' the woman asked, the unsteady wobble in her voice betraying her more advanced years. 'Where did you say you were calling from again?'

'From Morris and Sch—' Kate clamped her mouth shut to contain her seething frustration. 'I'm his late brother's lawyer, Kate Hunter. I've called a few times. It's about his brother's estate.'

'*Whose* lawyer?' she asked, sounding even more confused.

Kate closed her eyes and counted to five. 'Edward's brother William.'

'Oh, *that* brother. He died years ago.' Her voice became suspicious. 'Who are you *really*?'

Kate pressed her fingers and thumb into her temples. 'When will Edward be back?'

'He's back sixteenth of December, so you'll have to call back then,' came the reply.

Kate closed her eyes and slumped forward over the kitchen island, pressing her face to the cold marble as she mentally watched all hope of tying this up before Christmas wave merrily goodbye and walk out the door.

'Hello? *Miss*? Are you there?'

'Yes, I'm still here,' Kate replied, her words mumbled from where her nose and mouth were still squashed against the countertop. 'Sixteenth, OK. I'll call back then, thank you.' She ended the call and groaned, not moving.

'It's fine,' she muttered with dramatic self-pity to the empty room. 'There probably won't be a wedding anyway once they all learn I'll *still* be tied up here. And even if there *is*...' She raised her hands and held them out helplessly, feeling too defeated to lift her head. 'Well, my mother will probably just put me in peach to show her passive-aggressive disapproval. Bell sleeves, giant flowers all around the neckline from Nanna's old curtains...' She could visualise it now. 'She'll invite everyone she's ever met and turn it into a circus, where *I'll* be the main attraction. As *penance*. And *then* she'll tell me I brought it on myself and to get out and perform. *Dance, monkey, dance!*' She waved her hands around above her head to mimic a pair of performing monkeys, then let them drop heavily back to the counter.

The crunching sound close by nearly made her jump out of her skin, and her head darted up. She froze, mortified, as she clocked Sam standing directly in front of her across the island with an apple in his hand. He stared back with a deeply concerned pucker between his dark brows as he slowly chewed. Holding her gaze, he walked back out with slow, deliberate steps, not saying a word.

She waited until she heard his door close before she shut her eyes and let the burning shame ride free. 'Of *course* he heard that,' she muttered under her breath before glancing up to the heavens. 'Can a girl not catch a *break* down here?'

Her phone pinged, and she looked down expectantly. It was a voice note from her mother. 'I guess not,' she muttered wryly. She opened it up and pressed play.

'Kate? It's your *mother*, *Eleanor*,' came the voice, each syllable accentuated as though she were talking to someone almost completely deaf.

Kate shook her head. She'd explained voice notes to her mother a thousand times, but it just never seemed to take.

'When you're not working, you need to call me. On the *telephone*, not on the What'sUp app, OK, darling? *Call* me. On the *telephone*.'

'Eleanor, she can hear you perfectly clearly. You don't need to repeat everything like she's a small child,' her father said in the background.

'Henry, be *quiet*, I am *trying* to send a recorded message!' Eleanor sighed irritably, and Kate grinned, amused. 'So, as I said, darling, do *call me* when you can. On the *telephone*. We need to talk about *the flowers*. Amy's had some rather strange ideas that I don't like the sound of, at *all*. And *call Lance*, if you haven't yet today, Kate, won't you? Don't forget. *Call Lance*. Oh! And Harriet Parsons – you know the one: *Harriet*, from the big *bluebell fiasco* last year – she's been asking around for my secret Christmas cake recipe. Absolutely shameless. I'm just telling you, darling, so that you know. So if she tries to contact you and asks, I have *not* sanctioned this. I repeat, *do not give up any information.*'

'Oh, for crying out loud, Eleanor,' Henry exclaimed. 'No one is going to contact Kate to try and steal your recipe. And even if they did, Kate knows the score, OK? You trained her well. She's ready to withstand any and all torture tactics before handing over your state secrets.'

Eleanor tutted, and Kate let out a short laugh at her father's mock serious tone.

'You're not taking this *seriously*, Henry. Harriet could easily *lie* to get what she wants, which is why I'm telling Kate now. So she's prepared. And we don't have *state* secrets; we're *British*. Our secrets are *national*. Just because Kate's over there, it doesn't mean *you* can start acting American.' She sighed. 'Kate, I have to go. Your father's trying to be *funny* again. Call me later.'

Kate chuckled and held down the record icon.

'Hi, Mum. I did actually know it was you, as your name came up with the message. And, of course, I'm rather familiar with your voice. But thank you, anyway, for the in-depth clarification.' She grinned. 'And don't you worry, your delicious Christmas cake secret is safe with me. I mean, as *if* I would give that up to *Harriet Parsons!*' *Whoever she is*, Kate added silently. 'I'm tied up at the moment but I'll call you tomorrow to talk flowers.' Her smile turned to a grimace at the thought of that conversation. She couldn't face it today. Not after the one she'd just had with Edward Moreaux's secretary. 'Love to you both. Catch you soon.'

She ended the call and stared out of the kitchen window, feeling deflated. She usually loved this time of year. Usually, she'd be fully into the Christmas spirit by now, planning parties and presents and everything in between. But then again, usually she'd be in England, around family and friends. She wouldn't be living in a stranger's home in a town where she knew no one, planning a wedding she hadn't expected nor wanted from halfway around the world.

Running a hand back through her long dark hair, Kate bit her lip and stared at the phone screen, feeling a twang of guilt in her chest. She'd been putting off calling Lance, more and more often. But that really wasn't fair on him. Plus, she'd promised herself she was going to move forward with a better mindset towards things.

She unlocked the screen, scrolled to his number and pressed the video call sign.

Lance's face lit up her screen, and she straightened up, giving him a broad smile. 'Hi, how's things?'

'They're good. Great, actually,' he replied.

A loud, obnoxious laugh she recognised all too well sounded from behind him. It was his boss, Nigel. A man she absolutely abhorred. Someone she privately called *the megalodon*, as although Nigel was one of the largest sharks in London's legal waters, he was also a dinosaur, in all the worst ways. A man who grieved *the good old days* when there were fewer rules, and who kept himself just a careful hair's breadth away from a sexual harassment case at all times.

'Sorry, I didn't realise you were out,' Kate said with a tight grin. 'I'll call you later.'

'No, stay,' Lance insisted. 'Tell me all about your day.'

'*Yes*, Kate Hunter, tell us about your day!' parroted Nigel as Lance was suddenly demoted to half the screen. 'How's life over there in the backwaters of America?' He guffawed at himself.

'Nigel,' she said tightly. 'How are you? And how's your lovely wife? Is she there, too?'

'*Christ, no!*' Nigel looked horrified, then laughed again. 'We're out at the estate. Boys' hunting weekend. Managed to rope in this old boy as you're out of town. Couldn't leave him moping around London getting lonely.'

'How thoughtful of you,' Kate replied. 'I'm sure you'll have a lovely time.'

'We will indeed. And you should *know*, Kate, you're very privileged to be speaking to him right now.' He pointed a thick sausage-like finger at the screen. 'There are no wives allowed on boys' weekends, not even on the phone. It's a contractual clause of the verbal invite acceptance, you see. Now, I'll make an exception for you, as you're technically still unmarried, but make the most of it, because come the first of January...' He trailed off with a waggle of his eyebrows and then chuckled loudly at himself again.

Kate nodded along, gritting her teeth as Lance joined in. '*Got it*. Though if I manage to grow a *penis* after that point, where do we stand? Does that constitute as a clausal loophole?' She smiled politely.

Lance froze. Nigel abruptly stopped laughing and frowned with a look of distaste.

'Kate, you're far too pretty to be that vulgar, and I'm certain Lance could do without that image in his head. Leave the jokes to your husband, will you?' he said with a low chortle. 'There's a good girl.'

The angel on her shoulder Hollywood dived over to the other side and grabbed the little devil round the waist just as she lunged towards the phone with both fists at the ready. She dragged the other furious imaginary entity, still kicking and punching the air, around the back of Kate's neck, giving her an encouraging thumbs-up before disappearing.

Kate took a deep breath and exhaled slowly, reminding herself that Nigel held Lance's career in the palm of his pudgy hand. 'Yes, you're right, of course,' she said smoothly. 'That wasn't very ladylike at all, was it. Anyway, I'd best go. You guys have a great weekend. Lance, we can talk Monday. It's really nothing urgent.'

'OK, if you're sure, sweetheart,' Lance said warmly, pushing his glasses up his nose as he came back into full view. He walked away from Nigel and his smile turned to an accusing frown. 'Kate, what *are* you playing at?'

'I'm sorry, but the guy is just so damn *obnoxious*,' she replied.

'*Yes*, he *is*,' Lance said, stressed. 'But he's earned the *right* to be!'

'*Excuse* me?' Kate exclaimed. 'You think obnoxious is something you *earn the right* to be? Like it's some sort of *goal*?'

Lance tutted. 'That's not what I meant, Kate, and you know it. I just mean when you've earned a professional track record as impressive as his, you expect to be allowed a little leeway on the odd thoughtless comment.'

Kate stared at his face on the screen, feeling bitterly disappointed by his response. 'To be honest, I'm really failing to see the difference,' she said flatly.

Lance let out a deep sigh. 'Kate, I don't want to fight with you, OK? All I'm asking is that you don't offend my boss, the man who could make or break my career at will. Is that really too much to ask?'

'No,' she replied quietly.

'*Thank you*,' Lance said with emphasis. He turned his head away for a moment at the sound of someone calling his name. 'Look, I've got to go. I'll catch you later.'

'Sure. Catch you later,' Kate echoed.

The screen went black, and she stared at it for a few more moments. In his haste to jump to Nigel's defence over her apparent offensiveness, it hadn't seemed to have even crossed Lance's mind to jump to hers. Not that she *needed* defending. But the fact he'd been more bothered by Kate ruffling Nigel's feathers than by the rude behaviour that had prompted her to do so didn't sit well with her.

Pursing her lips, Kate put the phone away and tried to push it out of her mind. There was no point dwelling on it. She had enough on her plate already without adding anything more.

She pulled a deep breath in, exhaled loudly and pushed her hand back through her hair.

There was a creak as Sam's door reopened above, and a few moments later, he reappeared in the kitchen wearing a smart dark-green shirt. He buttoned the sleeves and tilted his head upwards. 'Hey, what are you doing tonight?'

Kate shrugged. 'Working, I guess. Might walk to Main Street later. Why?'

'Well, there's a party at Jack's, the bar on Main. Jenna hired it out to celebrate Matthew reaching fifty years at the company. Everyone from Coreaux Roots is going. There's a good band, open bar. Wanna go?' He waited expectantly.

'Are you sure they'd be OK with me coming?' she asked.

'Yeah, I mean...' He paused and frowned. 'You're *not* one of the *wives*, and they're the only people we ban from these things, so...' A slow smile crept up his face.

'Oh, very *funny*,' she said wryly, rolling her eyes. 'You heard that then?'

'I wasn't trying to, but these walls are pretty thin,' he replied. 'So, you wanna come?'

Kate hesitated. 'Will Aubrey be there?'

Sam shook his head. 'She hates them as much as they hate her.'

'OK then.' Kate smiled. 'Give me a minute to pack up here and I'll go change.'

'Great.' Sam walked back out into the hallway. 'By the way, if you manage to grow that penis earlier than planned, let me know, will ya? I'll switch back to leaving the seat *up*.' He glanced back with a mischievous grin, and Kate closed her eyes.

As he disappeared around the foot of the stairs, she turned to a small picture of Cora on the windowsill and shook her head with a sigh. 'You know, Cora, I'm not sure this fresh start is actually doing me any favours. Sam's keeping his slate pretty clean, but I've racked up two crazy points today already.'

'Walls are still thin, Kate,' Sam called out.

Kate's eyes widened. *Three*, she mouthed at the picture as she pulled her things together.


Kate watched Jenna swing her two children around on the dance floor with a smile. Like everyone else, they were having a whale of a time at the party.

Matthew's speech about his time at the company, and his friendship with William and Cora, had been emotional, but soon after the band had started to play and the atmosphere had livened. Now the party was in full swing.

As Kate stood watching from the sidelines, Matthew walked over to stand beside her with a lopsided smile. 'Glad you could make it,' he said.

'Thanks for having me,' she replied.

''Course. Can't have you home alone on a Friday night when there's a perfectly good party going on.' Matthew took a sip of his beer and leaned sideways against the wall. 'Coreaux Roots is a family. We're one whole, don't leave no one out. You might not work onsite, but you're still our lawyer, which means you're *part* of this family.'

Kate felt touched by the sentiment and gave him a warm smile. 'Thanks, Matthew. I'm honoured to be considered that way.'

He nodded and took another sip of his beer. 'How's it going, anyway?'

Kate sighed. 'Not as smoothly as I'd hoped,' she admitted. 'I met Aubrey last weekend.'

'I heard,' he said.

'It wasn't very pleasant,' she added.

'I heard,' Matthew said grimly.

Across the room, Sam put down his beer and allowed Jenna's daughter to pull him onto the dance floor. He swung to the music and twirled her round and round, making her laugh. Kate smiled as she watched him, then Jenna danced over with her son, and as she turned, Sam gripped her hand and twirled her around, too.

A strange pang of wistfulness yanked at Kate's core as she saw the way they looked at each other, and she blinked, surprised by how it had made her feel. It wasn't jealousy though. Of course it wasn't. Sam didn't mean anything to her in that sense. He was just a friend, at best, and Kate was engaged. She looked over at Matthew and saw him watching her.

'Sam's good with Jenna's kids,' she remarked. 'They seem to think a lot of him.'

'Yep,' Matthew commented. 'They're like brother and sister. Cora pretty much raised 'em both.' He pushed off the wall and straightened up. 'Sam looked after Jenna a lot when they were kids, being that bit older. I think he always felt that it was his job to get her through, both of them being without a mom.'

Kate smiled. 'He's like Cora then?'

Matthew's smile widened fondly. 'He is a lot like her, yeah. He cares about people. But he's more like Will. Has the same big ideas about changing the world and the same stubbornness to make 'em happen, too.'

The softness of his smile at the mention of Cora's name suddenly prompted Kate to wonder exactly how deeply his love for Cora had run. *Was* it just with the fondness of a close friend, or could it be something more than that? M was still very much the focus of Cora's diary, from what she'd read so far. *Matthew* started with an *M*, and he'd told her himself that he'd been around from the beginning. What if Cora had never given up this secret love of hers? *What if…* She studied the side of his face for a moment, then dismissed the idea. It was ridiculous. Of course Matthew wasn't M. She needed to stop letting her imagination run riot.

Kate turned back to the dance floor, her gaze resting on Sam curiously. 'Whose side of the family did Sam come from?' she asked Matthew. 'I wasn't sure, with his name being Langston.'

Matthew exhaled slowly. 'Well, I guess it's no secret. Sam came from Will's side. His father was the youngest of the three brothers. Jimmy.' He shook his head with a grim expression. 'As bad an egg as I ever did see, I'm sad to say.'

Kate frowned. She'd assumed Sam was William and Cora's great nephew. That he was the same generation as Aubrey. As if he'd read her mind, Matthew's next words answered her unspoken wonderings.

'Jimmy was a lot younger than Will; a good decade or so. And then he was nearing forty when Sam came along,' he told her. 'Don't think he'd ever planned to have kids, so Sam was a surprise for all of us.'

'I see.' That explained the wide age gap between Sam and his uncle and aunt. 'So was Langston his mother's name?' Kate asked.

'Yep,' Matthew confirmed. 'Jimmy was, er...' He made a small sound of discomfort. 'Well he put Sam and his mother through a lot, from what I understand. He was a bully with a gambling problem. I remember him from the early days, before Sam came along.' He shifted his weight from one foot to the other. 'I guess Sam wanted to honour his mother, rather than him. He was very close to his mother before she died. And he's done a *lot* in her honour. Always trying to make things better for folks. Those houses of his, the cellulose film...'

'That was *Sam's* idea?' Kate asked, turning to him with a frown.

'More than just the *idea*,' Matthew told her. 'Sam set the whole operation up, from start to finish.'

Kate frowned. 'But I thought he didn't want anything to do with the business?'

'Hey, Matthew! Look who made it!' someone called over, and he turned.

'I'd best go say hi,' he said, smiling and raising a hand to the woman who'd just walked in. 'You alright here?'

'Of *course*! You go – I'm fine,' Kate replied with a smile.

He tipped his head and walked away, and Kate turned her attention back to Sam with a sad frown. He'd been through more trauma and heartbreak in his tender youth than any child should have to suffer. Her heart went out to the little boy he'd once been, but as she looked now at the man he'd become, she realised that the more she learned about him, the less she understood. He'd loved his aunt and uncle and clearly cared deeply about people. He wanted to help people. He'd set up an incredible and cutting-edge new venture within the company. He was the ideal person to take over Cora and William's legacy on all fronts. So why was he so dead set against it?

# TWENTY-EIGHT

Hours later, Kate and Sam said goodbye and set off back to the house. The sky was crystal clear, so although the moon was barely a sliver, the stars shone brightly enough to light their way. The snow glistened, reflecting the starlight with an ethereal silvery dance as they walked down Main Street, and their breaths frosted the air, drifting off in small white clouds.

Kate rubbed her gloved hands together and glanced up at the streetlamps. 'How come they're not on?' she asked.

'It's past midnight.' Sam checked his watch. 'Yeah, ten minutes ago. That's when they switch them off.'

'Midnight? That's early for a weekend. They don't have very rock 'n' roll expectations of the people in this town,' she commented, instantly yawning.

Sam glanced at her wryly. 'Can't imagine why.'

'Hey, it's five a.m. as far as my British body clock's concerned. It doesn't get much more rock 'n' roll than that,' she told him.

'Mhm.' Sam shot her an unconvinced look.

They walked on for a few moments in silence, then Kate glanced sideways at Sam. 'Hey, can I ask you something?'

'Sure,' he replied.

'Why don't you want Coreaux Roots?'

Sam shrugged. 'I just don't. It's a wonderful place and I love it, but it was my uncle's dream, not mine.'

'But don't you want to look after it for *them*?' she asked. 'After everything they've built, everything *you* invested? Matthew told me the wood fibre plastic stuff was all you – don't you want to keep it going?'

Sam frowned. 'No. I don't.'

Kate frowned, too, confused. She cast her gaze forward, trying to understand him and failing. It was such a gift to have been left. And one he'd clearly been heavily involved in.

'The Coreaux Roots family means a lot to me,' Sam told her. 'But the idea of going in there every day, sitting in an office to continue someone else's dream kills me on the inside. It makes me feel *trapped*. Like I'd be stuck in a cage while the life I really want is still out there, you know?'

Kate looked away into the darkness. 'Yeah, I do,' she said quietly. It was something she understood all too well, in fact.

They passed the bandstand, and Kate nodded at a half-built stage beside it. 'What's that for?'

Sam glanced over. 'That's where the nativity scene goes each year. Santa's grotto usually sits behind it. Mike's Santa this year.' He grinned.

'Oh *wow*,' Kate replied with a laugh and a look of joking concern.

'Actually, he's surprisingly good at it,' Sam told her. 'Calls it his missed calling in life. Likes to tell people that if the police gig doesn't work out, that he'll—'

'What?' Kate cut in with a grin. 'Become a year-round Santa?'

'I think more just a general actor,' Sam answered, his expression matching hers. 'Like, a really good local Z-lister. I mean, there's always a call for *some* sort of seasonal character. You've got the Easter bunny...'

Kate nodded. 'True.'

'*Cupid.*' He raised an eyebrow as if to jokingly suggest this as a perfect fit. 'I can see Mike as a cupid, spreading the love in a toga and wings.'

'It's the baldness that makes it work,' Kate agreed with mock seriousness. 'That and his height.'

'It helped Danny DeVito's career,' Sam added.

Kate laughed, reaching up to tuck her hair back behind her ear, then lowered her hand to see Sam staring at her with a small smile. 'What?' she asked, giving him an odd look.

'Nothing, you just look really nice when you're happy,' he replied, his tone warm. 'When you smile – your *real* smile, I mean, not that other one you do – you look, well, beautiful.' He held her gaze, and for a moment something changed, and she felt a strange skitter run through her core. Then suddenly he turned to look forward again with a shrug. '*Almost* human.'

Kate forced a laugh. '*Almost,*' she agreed.

They carried on down the road to the corner.

'You know, Mike could always hire himself out for parties between seasons, too,' she said.

Sam nodded, glancing sideways at her with an unreadable expression. 'True. Plus, there's bar mitzvahs and funerals.'

'I really don't know why he's still wasting his time on the force,' Kate replied with a grin. 'Oh, look at that.' She stopped. 'They must have decorated this while we were out tonight.'

She stared up at the large freshly decorated fir tree in the front garden of the house next to them. The twinkling lights reflected off the bright shining baubles and a golden-haloed angel looked down from the top. The quiet tones of 'Silent Night' drifted across the night sky from somewhere nearby, and as it filled the air, Kate smiled, feeling like she'd stepped right off the path and into Christmas Day itself for a moment.

'I love Christmas,' she breathed. 'It's so full of magic.'

Kate closed her mouth suddenly, realising she'd let her guard down. She didn't usually share such fanciful thoughts with people. She'd clearly had more to drink than she'd realised. But Sam didn't laugh at her words, the way she'd expected him to. The way most people would have hearing those words coming from the mouth of a thirty-five-year-old woman. Instead, he just stared up at the tree with her.

'My aunt and uncle always saw the magic in everything,' he replied. 'And they taught me how to see it, too. Something I'm eternally grateful for, having spent my earlier years thinking all there was in this world was cold, hard reality. Life's pretty grey for those who can't find the magic.'

'I always thought that, too,' Kate said, turning to look at him.

Sam stared up at the tree, the lights reflecting brightly in his blue eyes and a ghost of a smile lifting the corners of his mouth. A dimple creased into the dark stubble between his strong jaw and cheekbones, and for a moment, Kate caught a glimpse of the boy inside the man. The boy filled with the same wonder and joy she still felt for Christmas, too. She smiled softly, feeling a sudden warmth towards him she hadn't before.

He turned to face her, surprise lifting his brows as he briefly glanced upwards. Kate's gaze followed his, and she realised a sprig of mistletoe now hung from the branch of a large tree, just above. As she moved her gaze back to his, a few snowflakes fell from the branch above and danced around them in the breeze, and Kate felt something shift. Their gazes locked, and she stared at him, frozen, momentarily suspended, unable to move either forward or back. They stood there together under the stars in their shared bubble of Christmas magic. But it was more than that, she realised somewhere in the back of her mind. She didn't let the thought go further. Because it felt good, being in this strange bubble. The air around her seemed to almost tingle with electricity, and yet at the same time, she felt so relaxed she could barely think.

They lingered there in the silence, Sam's azure-blue eyes pulling Kate in as though they were a gravitational force. And in that moment, as the gentle music, soft lights and the heady mix of his aftershave and the beautifully decorated pine filled her senses, she wondered, just for an instant, what it would be like to throw caution to the wind and lean in.

As the thought registered, Kate jumped with a small start and pulled in a sharp breath, looking away to the tree. The bubble was shattered, and the feeling of joy and contentment she'd felt just moments before gave way to hot shame and anger. What on earth was she doing?

She put a hand to her head, vaguely aware of Sam turning back towards the tree, too. 'I, er...' She wetted her lips, moving her hand to her burning cheek. 'I think that rum punch hit me harder than I realised. I'm really feeling it suddenly. Feeling really, um, really spaced out.' It was a thin cover at best, but if Sam saw through it, he didn't let on.

'Yeah, Jenna packs that punch a lot stronger than it tastes. The fresh air always brings it home.' He gestured vaguely around and then pushed his hands down into his pockets, still staring at the tree. 'We should get out of the cold. That punch don't just lie about its strength; we're not as warm as we think we are.'

'*Yes!*' Kate jumped on board the life raft with both feet. 'You're right. I actually read about that recently. The added risks of hypothermia when drinking alcohol in cold temperatures because it only gives the illusion of warmth.'

Sam started walking towards the house, and she fell into step beside him.

He glanced at her, looking amused. 'You read that recently?' he clarified.

'Yes,' Kate answered. Sam chuckled and shook his head, and she frowned. 'What? What's funny?'

'Nothing. You British really don't get much snow over there, do you?'

Kate narrowed her eyes. 'Why do you say that?'

'Because over here we learn basic survival tips like that in kindergarten,' he replied.

'Oh, I see. Well, we don't have the need to learn things like that, no. But if you ever need an expert on how to keep calm and carry on in constant rain, you won't find *anyone* more prepared than a Brit, I can assure you.'

She nodded sagely, and he laughed, the sound much more relaxed now, as they walked away from the mistletoe and the perfectly decorated tree.

'I'll be sure to remember that, lawyer girl,' Sam said seriously. 'I'm just glad I met you when I did. Who knows *what* I'd have done next time it rained.'

'Not kept calm and carried on, that's for sure. At least not well,' Kate replied. 'You really are very lucky.'

They exchanged a grin and continued in companionable silence. But although she'd regained her outward composure and had hidden herself well behind the witty banter, inside, Kate was still a confused, mortified mess.

What had just happened? she lamented. She was weeks away from her wedding. And she was a grown woman – an *intelligent* woman – one who was in full control of her thoughts and emotions. This wasn't her. This wasn't who she was at all. It had to be this place, she decided. With its charm and romantic Christmas displays that people seemed to go all out on popping up everywhere, it was getting to her, that was all. She was off centre, being so far away from home and from everyone. And she'd drunk more than she'd meant to tonight, as well. All of that together was just messing with her head.

Though even if all that hadn't been true – which it *was* –

there was one factor to consider that overrode anything. She would *never* cheat. Not in a million years. *That* she knew right in her very core. There were certain things Kate had never and would never compromise on, and being able to look herself in the mirror without shame was one of them. She had morals, and she would stick to them no matter what.

But although she knew this, as she slid her gaze towards Sam, she still had to wonder what she'd find in her reflection after tonight. Because whether she'd acted on it or not, and whether she liked it or not, for one brief moment there had been a part of her that had very nearly made a very big mistake.

# TWENTY-NINE

The weeks following Matthew's party passed in a blur, which for the most part Kate filled with paperwork and legalities, trying to keep herself busy and her ever more frantic mother at bay. A lot of the time she was alone, as Sam disappeared sporadically for days at a time to one or another of his projects.

She'd spent time with Jenna in Sam's absence, too, and had learned a lot from her about the way the business worked and how close different people had been to Cora and William. Each day she'd made a little more progress with Cora's estate, and each night after speaking to Lance, she'd delved deeper and deeper into Cora's old diary.

As the year of 1955 had progressed, so had Cora's predicament. M, the sweet-talking mailman, was no longer working that particular job by the summer and would disappear for weeks at a time. Cora's entries would become wistful and sad, despite poor William doing his best to cheer her up with treats and trips. But despite Kate's hopes, M would always end up returning and pull her back in with whispered promises before William had a chance to win her heart over fully. Kate knew it was only a matter of time before he got there though. History didn't lie.

Eventually Kate couldn't put off a visit home any longer, her excuses having run too thin to remain believable, and as December arrived, so did her scheduled flight back to London. Her feelings had been mixed as the date had loomed. On the one hand, she was looking forward to going back. It was her home, after all, and she missed her loved ones greatly. But the thought of having to face the reality of the wedding – and get through all the plans they'd made for her to attend with a smile – left her already jagged nerves hanging by a thread.

She flew back on a Friday. Lance met her at the airport and they went for a late dinner, taking some time to catch up properly, then Amy arrived first thing the next morning with a big hug, a detailed itinerary and a tray of double-shot coffees. Though nervous at the sight of the itinerary, Kate knocked her coffee back and pushed forward, determined to make the most of every second with her best friend. She'd missed her hugely.

Frogmarching Kate out of the building, Amy took her to meet Eleanor and Beth, who were waiting with a thick file and a tray of tea in a nice hotel nearby. Kate had barely sat down before Eleanor jumped straight into it.

'OK, now, *Katherine*...' She leaned forward over the table between them with a serious expression. 'First things first, have you put on any *weight* since you've been living in Boston?'

Kate raised her eyebrows incredulously.

'*What?*' Eleanor asked. 'It's a valid question! We need to track any changes since you left so we can predict how much it's likely to change between now and the *wedding*.'

'Let's get the girl a cuppa first though at least, hey, Eleanor?' Amy said jovially.

'*Thank you, Amy*,' Kate replied pointedly.

'Though...' Amy winced and tipped her head sideways. 'We *do* kind of need to know.'

Eleanor held her hands outwards with a roll of her eyes, as if to say, *Exactly*, and Amy gave Kate an apologetic grimace. Beth shook her head at the both of them, shooting Kate a look of solidarity.

Kate pointedly took off her coat and poured herself a cup of tea from the tray before answering.

'*No*, Mother.' She picked up her teacup and saucer and sat back against the overstuffed sage-green sofa. 'I haven't put on any weight. And I've been in *Vermont*, not Boston. As you well know.'

'Whatever, darling. It's all the same continent, no need to get technical. So, what *do* you weigh?' Eleanor asked, clicking the top of her pen and picking up a notepad.

'I don't know,' Kate replied.

'*OK*.' Eleanor sighed loudly. 'How much did you weigh before you left?'

'No idea,' Kate responded.

'But you *must* have weighed yourself at *some* point?' Eleanor asked, getting visibly perplexed.

'No. Not recently.' Kate shrugged and took a sip from her cup.

Eleanor dropped her pen with a loud tut. 'I really don't know why you're being so *difficult*, Katherine, I'm only trying to *help you*. How can you know if you've put on weight or not when you haven't *weighed* yourself?'

'*Because*, Mother, my *jeans still fit*,' Kate replied with a childishly defiant look at Eleanor that silently added, *So there*.

Eleanor's brows knotted together. 'But Katherine, what *kind* of jeans?'

Kate glanced up to the heavens. 'Really?' she muttered.

'Well, *darling*, jeans can have a lot of stretch these days,' Eleanor exclaimed. 'Pamela from my community watch club – you know the one: Pamela, from the Bundt cake debacle – she absolutely *brags* about a pair of hers that she bought when she was a size ten and can still get into now, and she's at least an eighteen. We're seventeen members strong now, Katherine. Did your father tell you? Anyway, I just don't think jeans are a very trustworthy measure.'

'Well, these are non-stretch, so you needn't worry,' Kate replied.

'Are you sure?' Eleanor raised a doubtful eyebrow. 'I've seen your jeans – none of them look particularly sturdy.'

Kate bit her lips together and stared back at her mother as her little devil poofed up on her shoulder.

Amy hastily jumped in. 'You know what, Eleanor? I think we'll be fine. The stretch is all in the legs really, anyway. The waistbands don't move.'

'Oh, OK, that's fine then,' Eleanor replied, her frown disappearing. 'Katherine puts on around the middle first – always has done. OK, next on the agenda...'

Kate pulled an expression of wry defeat.

'Actually...' Beth checked her watch. 'What time did you say the fitting was, Amy?'

Amy looked at her watch. 'Ooh, yes! Let's go!'

Eleanor's face lit up, and she quickly gathered everything together. 'How exciting. OK, let's go, girls. Drink up, Katherine, chop-chop!' She stood up and practically danced towards the exit, dragging Amy along with her.

Kate quickly drained her teacup, pulling on the coat she'd only just taken off.

Beth waited to walk with her. 'What's the community watch club?' she asked as they followed Eleanor and Amy down the road.

'It's a bit like the neighbourhood watch, in that it's a group of women who spy on everyone, then share everything they've seen, only it's completely made up and run by my mother because she felt the neighbourhood watch rules were too restrictive,' Kate told her. Beth shot her an incredulous frown and she laughed. 'Yep.' She shook her head. 'Hurricane Eleanor will be stopped by no one.'

'I'm sorry... *What?*' Her expression shocked, Amy leaned in towards the woman at the front counter of the bridal boutique.

The woman shrugged. 'There's no booking on the system.'

'But I *did* book it,' Amy insisted. 'I booked it *weeks* ago. I have a confirmation email, look.' She pulled out her phone and scrolled to find it, then brandished it triumphantly in the woman's face. '*Here!* See, I *told* you.'

The woman took it with a polite smile and peered at the screen with a frown. Her lips then thinned, and Kate realised what was about to happen with an internal groan.

'Er, *miss*?' The woman waited for Amy's attention with a cool fixed smile.

'Yes?' Amy asked.

'You *did* book an appointment with us...'

'Yes, *as I said*,' Amy replied, a touch sharply.

'For the seventh of *January*,' the woman finished.

'*What?*' Amy exclaimed. 'Let me see that.' She grabbed the phone back and frowned at the screen. 'Oh *shit!*'

'Amy! *Language*,' Eleanor scolded.

'Oh, Kate, I'm so sorry,' Amy said, horrified, ignoring her.

Kate brushed it off with a shake of the head and squeezed Amy's arm. 'Don't worry – mistakes happen. It's no big deal, honestly.'

'*No big deal?*' Eleanor exclaimed. 'It certainly *is* a big deal. You're only three— *Ugh...*' She bit her lips together, catching herself on the edge of freefall into total panic, then turned to the desk with a pleasant smile. 'I'm so sorry about all this, er, *Mandy*,' she said, glancing at the woman's name badge. 'Gosh, look at us all standing here feeling foolish. This really is *quite* a to-do!' She let out an awkward laugh, but the woman didn't warm to her the way she'd clearly hoped. She cleared her throat. 'Listen, my daughter has flown all the way over from America for this weekend. It took her *eighteen hours,* poor thing. Is there anything you could do to squeeze us in?'

'I'm sorry, madam,' Mandy replied, clearly not sorry at all. 'We're fully booked weeks in advance.'

'What if someone's late?' Eleanor pushed. 'I noticed you checked your little screen there with a frown when we came in, which means the person due in now isn't here yet.' She glanced up at the clock. 'Which means, if the appointment is for eleven, they're five minutes late. How late would they need to be to count as a no-show?'

'I'm sorry, madam, but the slot is *taken,* even if they arrive late,' Mandy replied firmly.

Eleanor's face tightened. 'What if they get *run over* crossing the road outside? What about then?'

'OK, we're done,' Kate said, not doubting for a second that her mother really would consider running over a group of strangers to get the spot. 'Let's go.'

Amy nodded and pulled Eleanor towards the exit by the arm. 'Right, well, thanks for nothing, Megan,' she called back.

'It's Mandy,' the woman replied.

'Whatever, Michelle,' Amy shot before the door slammed closed behind them.

The four women stood in a silent line outside on the pavement for a moment.

The door to the building across the street opened, letting out a waft of laughter and background music.

'Pub?' Amy suggested, staring at it.

'*Pub,*' Kate confirmed.

They crossed the road, and Kate held the door to The Coach and Horses open for the others. As they disappeared inside, she glanced across the road at the bridal boutique with a troubled frown. She'd never really believed in signs, but suddenly she found herself wondering.

'Hey.' Kate turned to see Amy looking back at her. 'You OK?'

Kate bit the inside of her cheek, searching Amy's face. 'I'm fine,' she lied, letting the door close behind her. 'Absolutely fine.'

# THIRTY

'And *this* one, Lance, look at *this* one,' Eleanor said excitedly, turning the screen of her laptop towards him.

'Oh, yes,' he replied. 'That one *is* lovely.'

He caught Kate's eye over the coffee table while Eleanor wasn't looking, and Kate hid a grin. She had no idea what her mother was showing Lance, but whatever it was, it definitely wasn't hitting the mark. They were at her parents' for Sunday lunch before she had to jet back off to Pineview Falls the next morning, and so long as she tuned out her mother's constant talk of the wedding, it was a day she was truly enjoying.

'Have I shown you my new amaryllis, Kate?' her father asked.

'*Katherine*,' Eleanor corrected him, barely breaking away from the stream of ideas she was sharing with Lance to do so.

Henry ignored her and simply stared at Kate expectantly.

'I don't know, Dad. Which ones are they again?'

Henry rolled his eyes with a pained sigh. 'Honestly, I don't know *how*, after all those years of my attempts to brainwash you into being a gardener, you *still* don't know one end of a flowerbed from the other.' Kate laughed, and he grinned back.

'Come on.' He stood up. 'I'm going to give it one more shot, and if it doesn't work, I'll have to try some Chinese water torture on you.'

Kate laughed again and dutifully followed him out. They wandered in companionable silence down to her cherry trees and sat together on the bench. Kate pushed her hands down into the pockets of her long red coat and looked out at the view.

'Where's this armadillo then?' Kate asked.

'*Ha ha*, very funny,' he replied, nudging her with his shoulder. 'You won't be laughing when you've been kidnapped by a spy from one of the competing villages and they're torturing you, screaming, *Just tell us where the amaryllis is and we'll let you live* though, will you?' He raised his eyebrows in mock seriousness.

'I do worry about that *exact scenario*, actually,' she agreed. 'I hear it's really common.'

Henry nodded. 'Very serious business here in the Cotswolds. The war of the rosebushes has been going on years,' he said sagely. Kate glanced at him, and they both grinned. 'There is no amaryllis,' he admitted. 'I made it up to escape. I've had to listen to that same wedding list of your mother's about eight times. She just *restarts* whenever someone new walks through the door. I don't think I can take another round without losing my sanity. Now *there's* a good torture tactic. Your mother would be a fabulous asset for the government if we ever end up at war again.'

Kate nodded her agreement.

'*You* looked like you were going to fall asleep, too, so I thought I'd drag you out for some fresh air. You alright, love?'

He sounded concerned, and she rushed to reassure him. 'I'm fine, Dad, honestly. It's just been a busy weekend.'

'Hmm. OK.' Henry didn't look convinced, but he didn't push her, either. He looked up at her cherry trees for a few moments. 'Do you remember when you planted these?'

'Of course I do,' Kate replied with a grin. 'Mum went *mad!*'

Henry nodded with a wry smile. 'She was absolutely *hopping.*'

Kate shrugged. 'I didn't know she had plans for this area.'

'Oh, *you knew,*' Henry said to her surprise. He chuckled.

Kate frowned. '*Did* I?' She tried to think back, but the memory was in snippets now, too old to recount clearly. 'That doesn't sound like me.'

'It was *exactly* like you. Back then, anyway,' he told her. 'You were always a good kid, but you had this rebellious streak that would flash up now and then. I used to love watching you in action. It drove your mother insane.' He smiled at the memories.

'Did it not drive *you* mad, too?' Kate asked, intrigued.

Henry shook his head. 'No. Like I said, you were a good kid. You had your moments, but you knew right from wrong. You never rebelled just for the sake of it; you'd only get fired up over something that really meant something to you.'

Kate thought back, his words stirring memories she hadn't recalled in years. 'I guess,' she mused. 'Gosh, that was a long time ago now.'

'Seems like only yesterday to me,' Henry replied. 'But I suppose it was. Back before you grew up. Before you were taught to prioritise fitting into society, like all kids are eventually.' He eyed her for a few moments, then looked back to the trees. 'I watched you plant these, you know. From the house.'

Kate let out a surprised laugh. 'Did you *really*?'

'Yes. I came across you cultivating them in your room and mumbling to yourself that it was *your* garden, too, and that no one ever asks *you* what you'd like in it. And I thought to myself, *Yes. She's right.*' He shrugged. 'So I just kept watching you, quietly egging you on. I even strategically placed what you'd need to plant them in your path.' Kate gasped, and his eyes danced with a mischievous twinkle. 'Then, the day you decided to do it, I even hid your *mother's* garden tools so she couldn't do anything before I had a chance to intervene.'

'You are *such* a *plotter!*' Kate exclaimed. 'Forget *Mum, you're* the one who'd make a good spy.'

Henry shrugged. 'Who says I'm *not?*'

'What else don't I know that you helped me with?' Kate asked suspiciously.

'Quite a lot, actually,' he replied. 'But you know, I felt truly *sad* when that rebellious streak of yours got buried. I'd always felt it was what kept you true to yourself, to what made you happy.' He gestured to the trees. '*That's* why I helped you with these. No, they didn't fit in with your mother's idea of a perfect garden. Or mine, actually. But it was *your* idea of perfect. It was the garden that *you* wanted. And *that's* what I wanted to fight for.'

Kate didn't reply, suddenly suspicious that they were no longer talking about trees or gardening at all.

Henry met her gaze. 'You know, I go along with your mother most of the time because it's *easier*, and because most of the time, I really couldn't care less about the things that mean a lot to her. So the way we work *works*. For both of us.' He moved his gaze over to the rockery between the trees. 'But I want you to know that I will *always* fight for the girl who planted these trees. You're my daughter. I will always support you in *any* decision you make for your own happiness. No matter what that is or what your mother, or anyone *else*, thinks of it.'

Kate felt a lump of emotion rise to her throat. 'Thanks, Dad,' she said softly. 'That means a lot.' She reached out and squeezed his hand, wanting to reassure him. 'You know I'm OK though, don't you? Because I am.'

Henry patted her hand with a smile. 'You'll always be OK, Kate. You're too clever not to be.'

She smiled and gave him a sideways nudge. 'Careful – all these compliments are going to start going to my head.'

'That's OK,' Henry replied. 'If you get *too* big for your boots, I'll just bring you back down a peg by telling you you're starting to sound like your mother.'

Kate gasped and recoiled.

'You're not really,' he told her, standing up. 'Come on. She should be wrapping up about now, and we should probably save Lance.'

'True.' Kate followed him up the garden, tucking her arm into his as they walked. 'You do *like* Lance, don't you, Dad?'

'Of course,' he replied, sounding surprised. 'Why do you ask?'

Kate glanced at him. 'Just checking.'

'He's a nice guy.'

'He is,' Kate agreed.

'Successful, too,' Henry added.

'Yep.' Kate nodded.

'Your mother tells me he's handsome, but I couldn't comment personally. Never been much into blondes myself,' he joked.

Kate grinned. 'Well, yes, he is,' she confirmed. 'Nice, successful, tall, blonde and handsome, and good at handling Mum. Looking at the big picture, he ticks every box,' she joked back.

But this time Henry frowned.

'And what *is* that, to you?' he asked her.

'What's what?' Kate asked, confused.

'The big picture,' he replied.

Kate gave him an odd look. 'You know. The picture of the future, of *life*, I guess.'

'Hmm.' Henry frowned. 'I've always hated that phrase. *The big picture*. It doesn't actually exist, you know. That a single snapshot could somehow encompass all the layers and nuances of a life in one single frame – it's a ridiculous concept. A life that hasn't even been lived yet.' He shook his head. 'Life is too unpredictable. It very rarely goes to plan, so how could anyone paint a reliable picture ahead of time?'

They reached the house, and Henry stamped the leaves and mud off his shoes on the outside mat. 'Someone once told me, many years ago, that – studies and career paths aside, which do need an element of planning – the best thing you can do is live in the moment. Pick a direction and make sure the little things along the way make you happy. Because one day, you'll realise *the big picture* was never a goal.' He studied her face with a warm smile. 'It's something that you look back on, made up of all the little moments in life strung together. And if you're *lucky*, like I am, you look back and realise you made one hell of a masterpiece along the way. One you're incredibly proud of every day.'

Realising he meant her, Kate felt her eyes mist over, and she leaned her head sideways onto him as he wrapped his arm around her shoulders. Henry squeezed her warmly, then gently released her.

'Thanks, Dad,' she said quietly.

He nodded.

The door in front of them suddenly flew open, and Eleanor stared at them expectantly. '*Well?*' she demanded. 'Are you coming in, or are you going to just stand out there on the doorstep all day? I didn't cook this chicken for *fun*, you know.'

'Coming, dear,' Henry said placatingly.

He walked inside, and Kate looked back at her cherry trees for a moment before following her father inside and slowly closing the door.

# THIRTY-ONE

Kate walked out to Lance's car, feeling a wistfulness for her parents and childhood home almost instantly. Usually she'd be looking forward to returning to London, but this time she knew she wouldn't see them again until she came home for Christmas, and after seeing all the decorations up in the house and breathing in the familiar scent of cinnamon and nutmeg around the house from her mother's baking, she felt her absence more keenly than ever.

Henry hugged her extra tight as they said their goodbyes. She'd already had her goodbyes with her mother, and Eleanor was now fussing over Lance as he tried to politely get away and into the car.

'Did you notice the plastic tree in the living room this year?' Henry asked her.

'Yes. I always thought Mum hated the idea of a fake tree,' Kate replied.

'She does, but I just couldn't pick a tree without you. It didn't feel right,' he replied. 'We argued, of course. Your mother suggested I take Lance to pick it instead.' Kate's eyebrows shot up in outrage, and Henry nodded his agreement. '*Exactly*. So I gave her a choice. Either we got a plastic tree or she had to release you from one of the wedding trips this weekend and take Lance to *that* so you and I could pick the tree together, as always. Obviously, she wasn't going to agree to such a lopsided prisoner swap, so plastic tree it was.' He shrugged.

'Well, I appreciate you sticking to our guns, Dad,' Kate replied, walking a couple of steps away before looking back with a suspicious squint. 'You know, that comment I made earlier about you making a good spy…'

'Yes?' Henry asked.

'You said, *Who says I'm not,*' Kate recalled.

Henry arched an eyebrow. 'I'm not hearing an actual question.'

'You really do use a *lot* of military analogies for someone who works for a bank,' she replied.

'That's still not a question,' he told her.

Kate squeezed her gaze further. '*No*, it's *not*,' she said in a suspicious voice. She pointed her index and middle finger towards her eyes and then his. 'I'm watching you, Hunter.'

Henry laughed. 'Ahh, if only I *was* a spy, Kate. What fun that would be. Banker and flower enthusiast by day, double-O by night.' He put on his best Sean Connery voice. 'One bottle of Miracle-Gro, please, Miss Moneypenny. Shaken, not stirred.'

Kate laughed. It *was* ridiculous, now he said it out loud. 'No amaryllis thief would get away with their antics in *these* parts again,' she joked.

'Nope,' Henry agreed. 'Of course, you'd never know if I really *was* a spy. The families never do.' He winked as Kate's gaze resharpened. 'Safe flight back, love. Touch base when you can.' He smiled and then turned back to the house as Lance called out from the driver's seat.

'Are you ready? Kate?' He paused as Kate stared at her father's retreating back. '*Kate?*'

'Coming,' she said, finally registering. 'Sorry.'

She walked to the car and turned to give her parents one last wave, just as Henry reached Eleanor on the front step and rested his arm across her shoulders. Kate frowned slightly through her smile, then got in the car and closed the door. As they drove off, she watched them through the wing mirror.

'Everything OK?' Lance asked, reaching across to hold her hand.

'Mm,' she murmured. She turned to him as they rounded the corner. 'Hey, if my dad was secretly a spy, what *tells* do you think there would be?'

'*Henry*? A *spy*?' Lance let out a loud, sharp burst of laughter. 'For who exactly? The horticultural society?'

Despite the fact she'd made a similar joke just minutes before, Kate felt herself bristle at Lance's words. When *she* said it, it was with love. From Lance, especially in the mocking tone he'd used, it just sounded disrespectful.

Henry was far from perfect, but it didn't matter how long a stretch of time or space it had been, what she was going through or what her mother was doing, he was her reliable constant. An anchor through the storms and crazy winds of life, always calm, understanding and supportive when she most needed it. So he was someone Kate felt particularly protective over.

'Never mind,' she said, turning to look out of her window.

'I'm only joking,' Lance said, sensing her disapproval. 'Come on – where's your sense of humour?' He sighed.

Kate twisted her mouth to the side. Perhaps she *was* being a touch oversensitive. Coming back this weekend had been harder than she'd thought it would be, and the fully packed schedule had exhausted her. She turned to look at him with a reconciliatory smile and squeezed his hand.

'Sorry, I'm just really tired.' As if her body was listening, she instantly let out a huge yawn.

She frowned as Lance turned off the road.

'This isn't the way out. This is a dead end.'

'Is it?' he asked in a strange voice.

He smiled broadly, a twinkle in his eye, and it immediately left her feeling uneasy.

'What's going on?' she asked.

He pulled up on the side of the road and cut the engine. 'I want to show you something.'

'What?' Kate's concern increased further.

'Come on.' Lance got out of the car and walked around to open her door.

He took her hand and led her over to a large house, and Kate's stomach flipped horribly. She shook her head in horror as he pulled out a key, and as he opened the front door, her hands flew to her face.

Lance took her reaction as amazement, and his smile widened. 'Isn't it something? You're speechless, I know. But you haven't even seen inside yet. Come on.' He guided her forward into the house, and she let him, lost for words.

The hallway alone was almost the size of her little London flat. A curved oak staircase stood at the centre of the house, and the state-of-the-art kitchen and the manicured garden that she could see beyond were both huge.

'It's the *dream*, Kate,' Lance said excitedly. 'The absolute *dream*. Five double bedrooms, three with en suites, and a walk-in wardrobe off the master that you'll *love*. There's a games room, built-in cinema and another room down here I thought we could turn into an office.' He opened a set of double doors. 'Look at this. Look at that view, Kate. I think this one even rivals your *parents'*.'

'Whose dream?' she muttered, feeling sick.

'What was that?' Lance asked.

Kate looked at him, her shocked expression finally darkening into a deep frown. 'I said, *Whose dream*? *Whose dream* is this, Lance? Because it is *definitely* not mine.' She put her hands up onto her head as she looked around, then dropped them, turning to face him in anger. 'Tell me you haven't *bought* this? *Please*. Tell me you haven't.'

Lance recoiled as if stung. 'What is the *matter* with you?' he asked. 'Why on *earth* are you yelling at me?'

Kate just shook her head and leaned over, trying to pull in a deep breath, which suddenly didn't feel possible. She hadn't realised she was shouting. She recognised this feeling though. She was having a panic attack. 'Lance, I need to get out of this house. *Did you buy it?*' she asked, trying to keep her voice calm.

'No,' he answered coldly. 'I didn't. I just arranged to have the key to show you around. I wanted to see what you thought of it. Well.' He turned away, placing his hands on his hips. '*Now I know.*'

'Yes, now you do,' Kate responded, closing her eyes. 'Can we please go now?'

'Yes,' he replied curtly, marching away to the door without bothering to look back at her.

They drove out of the village in silence, and Kate stared across the fields with her arms crossed over her middle, feeling thoroughly miserable.

Lance eventually looked over, still furious. 'Are you going to tell me what that was all about?' he demanded. 'Because right now, I'm completely in the dark.'

Kate's frown deepened. 'Why did you do that? Why didn't you talk to me about it?'

'Because I was trying to do something *nice*!' he exclaimed. 'I was trying to make it *fun* and *exciting*. I thought you'd be happy.'

'But *why*?' she asked. 'What about that did you think would make me happy?'

Lance's face twisted into an incredulous frown. 'Are you serious?'

'Very,' she responded. 'I *hate* surprises, which you know. And if you'd ever actually *asked*, you'd know that the idea of moving back to the tiny village where I grew up fills me with dread.'

'*What?*' Lance asked. 'That's *insane*. It's one of the most sought-after places to live in the *country*. What's got *into* you?'

Kate stared at him, wondering how they could be on two such completely different wavelengths. '*Nothing's* got into me. That's just how I *feel.*'

Lance lifted a hand off the wheel and let out a sound of hopelessness, then dropped it again with a shake of his head. '*Right*. OK. I can't pretend to understand that in the slightest, but if that's how you feel, *that's how you feel*. We'll look elsewhere. I just thought you'd want to be close to your parents when we had kids, that's all.'

Kate rubbed her forehead, her nerves still scattered and skittish from the panic attack she was still only just holding at bay. She was exhausted, physically *and* mentally, and she knew that probably had a lot to do with her particularly emotional reaction, but knowing that didn't make her feel any better. She felt Lance's hand move across her back.

'I'm sorry,' he said in a gentler tone. 'I should have spoken to you about it – you're right. I was just missing you, and I guess I just got carried away with the idea.'

Kate leaned into his arm, burying her head in his shirt. 'It's OK,' she said. 'I'm sorry I flipped out on you like that. Admittedly, that wasn't the best reaction. I'm just tired and stressed right now.'

Lance kissed the top of her head. 'I know. Not long now though, right? You'll be done soon, and you can settle back properly. Maybe take some time off, if you can. I think you need it.' There was a short silence. 'Kate?'

'Yeah, maybe,' she managed to reply.

But as the panic reared up again, like a wild horse fighting against the reins she gripped in her blistered mental hands, Kate knew it wasn't just the house. This panic attack wasn't going to calmly melt away because it was about *all* of it. The wedding, the future, the responsibility she had to everyone around her, the loss of control over her life, *everything*. It was all suddenly far too real, and she had no idea what to do about it. What *could* she do about it? It was too late. There was no way out of this whirlwind she'd slipped into. Not without blowing up her entire life and everyone in it. Not without destroying Lance and her mother and even Amy, with all that the four of them did together.

A tear escaped her eye, and Kate quickly rubbed it away before it rolled onto Lance's pristine white shirt. The wedding was booked – it was *paid* for. Everyone had been invited; everybody they knew was watching them and counting down the days. This was it, she realised. She had no choice but to keep calm and carry on, like the good old British war slogan. And there had to be something in that, she reasoned hopefully. If it had pulled a whole country through a war, surely it could see her through this. It *had* to.

Because in three weeks she was getting married, and after that they would buy a family home and work out a timescale for children. That was the plan, it seemed. The wheels were fully in motion and the train was now steaming towards the platform.

Kate's mind reeled as she just about held on to the reins. In just over three weeks, she would walk down the aisle. And there was no way out.

# THIRTY-TWO

*4 August 1955*

*It finally happened. W asked me to marry him. The sad part is that the proposal was the sweetest proposal there could ever have been. He took me out on a boat to the little island in the middle of the lake for the afternoon. We took sandwiches and lemonade, and the weather was truly beautiful. We'd had a lovely time, talking and laughing together, but then he got down on one knee and everything changed. He talked of my beauty and grace, and about how my smile lights up his day. He declared that he wants to take care of me, make me happy every day for the rest of my days. Then he told me, in that quiet way of his, that he knows I don't love him the way he loves me, but that he's OK with that. Because he knows I love him enough, and that I will grow to love him more once we are married and he has earned it.*

*That broke my heart, because that man is one of the kindest souls I know, and he shouldn't have to earn anybody's love. He already deserves it. And for one fleeting moment, those words made me feel a flutter of something more. They truly did. But that fleeting moment passed, a mere drop in the wide ocean of tides that wash over my heart every day for M. If I'd never met M, I imagine I'd be happy with W. But I did, and I can't change that any more than I can stop the sun rising in the sky.*

*Mother spoke with me long into the night, begging me to make the right choice. She has never admitted it out loud, but I know that she knows about M. I suspected a while back, but now I am sure. She told me stories of hardship she endured when she first married my father. She told me how they stripped the shine off of their love for one another. And whilst I can't imagine anything so unimportant as hardships ruining what M and I share, I must imagine that she also didn't believe that at the time. Which does give me some cause for hesitation. The rest of my life is a very long time. And as all mothers like to say, those married in haste repent at leisure.*

*I stand at this momentous fork in the road not knowing what I should do. Do I trust my wild heart, or is it the fickle creature of so many women's tales, which will turn like the tide at the first storm? Or if I trust sense and logic, is it sure to bring me contentment down the line, or will I feel unfulfilled with a husband who'll grow to resent me when he realises he will never be enough?*

*How, in the name of all that is holy, am I supposed to choose?*

# THIRTY-THREE

A few days later, after settling back into life at Pineview Falls, Kate ventured out to the Christmas market for some fresh air and a distraction from her spiralling thoughts. Having been suitably distracted from the moment she arrived, and unable to resist all the mouth-watering smells filling the air, she trudged back up the snowy hill a couple of hours later laden with paper bags fit to burst with delicious seasonal treats.

It wasn't just the market that had brought back her smile though. It was also eager anticipation for the trip she was taking to one of Sam's housing projects that afternoon. Since learning what he did for a living, she'd been more and more intrigued, and eventually she'd worked up the courage to ask him if she could go along and see it in person. Sam had been surprised but more than happy to let her come along. Kate could hardly wait. Hearing about all the inspiring things that Sam was doing here interested and excited her in a way nothing else had for a long time. The creative things he'd developed fascinated her, but the more she thought about it, the more she realised her excitement lay in what these things meant for the people they helped. She admired what Sam was doing and realised she envied him, too.

She envied him the gift of waking up every day knowing he was going to make a difference to someone. Someone who needed it, rather than some penny-pinching CEO trying to hide failing parts of their business in the paperwork of a complicated deal.

Lost in thought and humming the tune to 'Deck the Halls', Kate didn't initially notice the car slow to a crawl behind her. She heard the window wind down though and glanced back. For a moment, she assumed it was someone looking for directions, so she stopped and turned properly. But then she saw who it was and froze.

'What do *you* want?' she asked coldly.

Aubrey moved alongside her and leaned out the window with an angelic expression of sorrow. 'I want to apologise,' she said humbly. 'I really don't know what came over me that day – I swear to God, it was like something just *took over* my body. I wasn't seeing sense. I wasn't seeing anything at *all*. All I can remember is that we were having a nice talk over a cup of your *lovely* tea, and then my grams arrived, and – and then suddenly Sam was there and there was water all over the floor, and when I learned what I'd nearly *done*. Oh my *gosh...*' She put her hands to her cheeks and shook her head, looking stricken. 'Kate, I just *cannot* bear it. Can you find it in your heart to ever forgive me? I *can't* forgive myself, but if I know I have your forgiveness along with the good Lord Jesus on my side, then I may just get there someday.'

Kate made a sound of derision. '*Ugh...* Don't use *Jesus* as part of your scam this close to his birthday, Aubrey. It's really *not* good form.'

She turned and carried on up the hill, glad that it was still daylight and that other cars were regularly driving past. The luck on her side was that with the snow, Aubrey probably couldn't mount the pavement with her car, so Kate was at least safe from being run over. But she still felt tense with the woman so close behind her.

The car moved to keep pace alongside Kate.

'Kate, it's the truth,' Aubrey insisted. 'I'm really not a bad person. I feel horrible. Honestly, I think it was seeing my grams. There's all sorts of bad childhood trauma there, you see.'

'Mhm,' Kate murmured. 'With a *grams* like yours, you'd think your acting skills would be a little better.' She turned to face her. 'But even if they were, that excuse isn't even *close* to believable. Childhood granny issues don't cause someone to *accidentally* try to blackmail a lawyer with violence and permanent scarring. What *you* did was... *ugh...*' Kate recalled the dark, vindictive look on the woman's face as she'd gone for her that day. 'That was something else entirely.'

A glint of annoyance flashed across Aubrey's face, even as she tried to keep up the act, and Kate shook her head, a fierce feeling of protectiveness for Coreaux Roots sweeping through her like a hot tidal wave.

'Look, you're not getting any part of Coreaux Roots, Aubrey,' she said suddenly. 'Not you *or* your grandmother. That's what you've come sniffing around for, so you might as well know that now. *Neither* of you understands what that company really is or cares about it at *all*! Which means neither of you are worthy of it.' Kate watched as the mask dropped and Aubrey's face contorted with bitter sparks of hot rage. She reined her emotions back in and suppressed a shiver. 'You need to leave now.'

'You self-important, *stupid* little *bitch*,' Aubrey hissed.

Kate kept her expression carefully neutral, pointedly aware of how unpredictable and dangerous Aubrey could be. They were almost at the house now, and Sam suddenly walked out and down the drive towards them with a frown.

'Think what you like of me, Aubrey,' she said calmly. 'It makes no difference. To me *or* the outcome of this case.'

She heard Sam's boots crunch in the snow as he strode the last few feet behind her.

'I thought I told you to stay the hell away?' He glared at Aubrey darkly.

Aubrey moved her hateful gaze between the two of them, eventually resting it on Kate. Her mouth widened into a cold, sly smile.

'Thanks for showing your cards. We've already gone through our options with our *own* lawyers and will now act accordingly.'

'Good luck with that,' Kate responded, unfazed. It had been inevitable.

'I mean it, Aubrey – *get out of here*,' Sam ordered.

She ignored him, her gaze still burning a hole into Kate. 'Expect to be served before Christmas. Time is money, after all. And it is *my* money we're talking about.'

Spinning her wheels on the snow, Aubrey drove away.

Sam watched her leave with a dark look, then took the bags from Kate's arms and turned back towards the house.

Kate fell into step beside him. 'Thanks.' She glanced back over her shoulder. 'I'm glad you happened to see us. That woman really puts me on edge.'

'Well, someone prepared to burn your face off will do that to you,' he replied. 'But, actually, I was waiting for you.'

'Oh? How come?' she asked.

'You left your phone,' he replied.

Kate's hands flew to her pockets, finding them empty. 'Oh! I didn't even notice.'

'It rang a couple of times. First one was your mom, so I left it,' he told her.

'*Wise*,' Kate muttered.

'Second one was a local number, so I picked up in case it was urgent. It was odd.' He frowned. 'Some old lady who told me I sounded suspicious and said she'd only give me the message in code.'

Kate laughed, realising it was Edward's secretary. 'What did she say?'

They walked into the house. 'I wrote it down on the pad in the kitchen.'

Kate walked through, taking off her gloves and other layers as she read the note.

*E.M. 26<sup>th</sup> 14:00*

She frowned. That couldn't be right. *Boxing Day?* She picked up her phone and dialled the last incoming number, waiting for the old lady to pick up.

'Hi, it's Kate Hunter,' she said. 'I just...'

'*Who?*' the woman asked.

Kate closed her eyes. 'Kate Hunter. The lawyer who—'

'Yes, *yes*, I know who you are. What do you want?' she asked, cutting Kate off irritably.

Kate looked up to the heavens. 'I just got your message. Am I reading it correctly – is it the *twenty-sixth* of December?'

'Yes, that's right.'

'OK.' Kate frowned. 'Is there any *other* day he can do? Only with it being Christmas, I'm not going to be here, so—'

'I thought you said this was urgent?' came the impatient reply.

'Yes, it is, but—'

'Well then, that's all he can do. He's extending his stay at the retreat until Christmas, he'll be around that day and then he leaves for New Zealand to visit his son. It's either then or not at all,' she told her.

Kate sat down on one of the bar stools, aghast. How could she tell Lance and her mother that she wouldn't be home for *Christmas*? How could she even get her *own* head around that?

'Well? What'll it be?' the woman prompted.

'I...' Kate raised a hand and then dropped it defeatedly. 'OK. I'll have to take it.'

'Very well. Now please don't call *again*.'

The line went dead, and Kate put her phone on the side, then dropped her head into her hands, feeling thoroughly deflated. How was she going to explain it to Lance? And, even worse, to her mother.

# THIRTY-FOUR

'Hey, thanks again for arranging this,' Kate said as she and Sam arrived at the door of the bridal boutique. 'I really appreciate it.'

The trip to the housing project had been postponed after Sam had received a call from Jerry's wife. He'd spoken to her, as promised, and she'd finally had a last-minute cancellation. In truth, Kate would have preferred to decline and carry on to the project, as planned, but with no time left, she knew she had to find a dress.

'It's fine,' Sam said with a shrug, pressing the buzzer on the door. 'Jerry owed me a favour.' he studied her thoughtfully as they waited. 'So, I thought the dress was one of those things you girls liked to have sorted in advance? You seem to be cutting it kinda close.'

'Most girls, I guess,' Kate answered reluctantly. 'And yes. The dress appointment back home fell through, so...' She trailed off and shrugged.

Sam nodded, looking at her with a slight frown she couldn't quite read. He opened his mouth to say something, but then the door swung open and a tall blonde woman with a warm smile and twinkly blue eyes looked out at them expectantly.

'You coming in or what?' she asked.

'Well, it ain't *what*,' Sam replied cheerfully. He walked inside, and Kate followed.

Sam and Sarah exchanged pleasantries and a little banter, and Kate liked her almost instantly. She had a friendly warmth about her and possessed the great mixture of a gentle voice with a big laugh and a ready smile that naturally put people at ease.

'So, can I get you guys something to drink?' Sarah asked.

'I'm good, thanks,' Sam replied. 'Kate?'

'I'm OK, too. Thank you though.'

'Well, let's get you started. Now let me just get a quick look at you.' Sarah held Kate back at arm's length and ran an experienced eye over her. 'OK, so you're what, about a six?'

'Er...' Kate winced, trying to remember the conversion.

'What are you back home?' Sarah asked.

'A ten.'

'OK, then yeah, you're a six. Come with me – I'll show you what we've got. Sam, you stay right there.' Sarah ushered her further inside with an excited twinkle in her eye. 'We have some *really* nice ones in right now.'

'Sounds great,' Kate replied, forcing a smile.

She looked at the rows of dresses. There were so many of them! More than there had been in the shop in London.

'Here we are.' Sarah waved her hands over several of the racks. 'All of these are your size. What styles do you like?'

'Er, I guess something simple and classic. Nothing frilly or lacy,' Kate said.

Sarah nodded and gave her another quick once-over. 'OK, what about one of these...'

She picked out three dresses and hung them on the wall. Kate smiled appreciatively. They were stunning designs. All quite different, but all fitted the bill.

'See anything you like?' Sarah asked.

Kate nodded, her gaze resting on the middle one. It was an

off-the-shoulder creamy satin gown with a plain fitted bodice, a sweetheart neckline and a sweeping A-line skirt.

'*That* one,' she said.

'That was my favourite for you, too,' Sarah told her. 'It'll sit really nice on the neck. You've got the perfect shape for it.'

'That's encouraging,' Kate replied.

'Are you comfortable with me helping you?' Sarah asked, moving her into a changing room.

'Sure.'

'Great, OK.' She closed the curtain. 'Turn away from the mirror while we fit you up, so you don't ruin the full effect when you see it on.'

'OK.' Kate turned away.

She lifted her arms and moved as instructed, waiting patiently while Sarah tugged and zipped and pulled it into place before finally standing back with a wide smile.

'I think we're all set. OK.' She met Kate's gaze, her blue eyes twinkling once more. 'Can you trust me on something?' Kate nodded. 'Don't look in this mirror. The one in the main room has three angles and *all* the light. Can I walk you through to do your first look there?'

'Sure. You're the expert,' Kate replied.

She caught the swiftly veiled puzzlement in the other woman's face and looked away. She really liked the dress and *was* glad to be here, but she just couldn't force herself to be excited by all of this. She really had tried, but it just wasn't happening.

'Perfect. Let's go.' Sarah led her out, avoiding the mirrors, and pulled the curtain aside to let Kate through.

As Kate walked into the main room, the first thing she saw was Sam's reaction. He did a swift double-take and quickly sat upright, his eyes and mouth widening as he was rendered speechless. His eyes moved slowly over her in open awe and then back up to meet her gaze. As their eyes connected, Kate felt something stir inside her. The same thing she'd felt the night of Matthew's party under the mistletoe. She stopped walking and just stood there in front of him, not wanting to move. Not wanting to break the strange connection until she could at least understand it.

But a bright flash suddenly crossed her vision, and they both turned, startled. Sarah pulled the instant photo out of the retro Kodak camera and waggled it around in the air.

'Oh, don't mind me. I'm just cashing in on a bet,' she told them, her eyes moving from one to the other with a knowing smile.

Sam cleared his throat and looked back at Kate, his bright blue eyes serious now and guarded with a sad tightness. He smiled encouragingly, but it didn't seem to reach his eyes.

'Now that's a *dress*,' he said quietly.

'Yes?' Kate asked nervously. Nervous for reasons she couldn't even name, rather than because of the actual dress.

Sam nodded. 'Yeah,' he confirmed. He smiled again. 'Turn around. See for yourself.'

Kate nodded, wishing she didn't have to turn away from him but reluctantly doing so anyway, as she knew was expected.

'Oh.' Her eyebrows rose in surprise. The dress fitted like it had been made just for her, and she smiled, feeling, for the first time since the whole wedding nightmare had started, like a princess. Her eyes flicked across to meet Sam's through the glass.

The flash went off again, and she twisted towards Sarah, who was wiggling a second photo in the air.

'Alright,' Sam said. 'What *is* this bet?'

'Jerry bet me five hundred dollars that you'd never set foot in here. So I took it.' She grinned.

Sam shook his head with a short chuckle. 'Why on earth did he bet you that?'

Sarah waved it off with a grin. 'Long story, but he lost. Here, honey...' She walked over to Kate and handed her the picture. 'You can keep this one.'

She held Kate's gaze for a long, loaded moment, then moved away. Kate frowned and looked down at the photo in her hand. It was of her in this beautiful wedding dress looking softly into the mirror. But as she followed her eyes, her heart jumped. Because it wasn't herself she was staring at with such a mesmerised look.

It was Sam.

# THIRTY-FIVE

By the twenty-third of December, Kate had successfully organised, listed and legally bound all parts of Cora's estate. The only thing left to do was officially note who it would be going to, but Kate wasn't able to do that until at least *after* she'd met with Edward Moreaux. Frustratingly, Kate knew as little about him now as when she'd arrived. She'd found it odd that no one ever seemed to mention him in the small town that was so greatly centred around his brother's life's work, but she'd not been able to bring him up.

Everyone knew who Kate was and why she was here, and they all also knew the details of the contract, thanks to Aubrey. Legally she had to be very careful. She wasn't allowed to share any details yet and had to be *especially* careful that she didn't accidentally share something about one interested party with another. Aubrey had made her interest public and linked herself to Kate before she'd even arrived, so there'd been no harm in asking questions about her. But Edward was another story.

Having done all the work she could for now, Kate had taken the day off and was now laid back under a blanket in the lounge armchair thinking about life. There was a lot to be said about just lying there. She'd always felt guilty taking time to do this back home, like she should be doing something else. Something worthwhile. Lance detested the act of lying about. He said it was lazy. But she didn't agree, and she'd now decided to let herself rest like this a whole lot more, going forward.

The front door opened in the hall behind her, then closed again. She heard Sam stamp his boots, then he paused by the door. Kate craned her neck to look backwards over the arm of the chair.

'Hey, how's things?' she asked.

'Good. And you?' Sam came in and sat in one of the other chairs.

'Fine. I was just contemplating life,' she said simply.

'That bad, huh?' he joked. 'What particular part of life are you contemplating?'

'All of it,' Kate answered with a shrug.

'That's a lot to process in one go – no wonder you needed to lie down.' Sam laughed and ran his hand back through his dark salt-streaked hair, releasing a long breath. 'Actually, it's not a bad idea. I'll join you.'

Kate watched him close his eyes for a moment, wondering how often he just sat and did nothing.

'Did you know they call stress the silent killer?' she asked him, recalling a warning her father had given her years before.

Sam opened his eyes and looked at her with a tired flicker of amusement. 'I did. My uncle drummed it into me when I was younger. Made me promise to take time to rest and for myself in life. Not take it too seriously.'

Kate smiled broadly. 'My dad did, too!'

'Yeah?' Sam grinned. 'Well, they can't *both* be wrong.'

'No.' Kate's smile lingered as she looked up at the ceiling.

Her phone rang, and she glanced at the screen. It was Lance. Her heart dropped, and the little buzz of worry he incited in her these days awoke in the pit of her stomach. It continued ringing, and she bit her top lip anxiously. She *should* answer. But she didn't. It rang off, and she relaxed again, looking back up to the ceiling.

She could see Sam watching her from the corner of her eye and was aware he'd have seen the screen.

'Everything alright?' he asked carefully.

Kate nodded. 'I'm just busy right now. Relaxing is important.'

'It is,' he agreed. 'It's good to have time to do that with no distractions. Very healthy.'

'Yep,' she replied simply. She tapped her fingers together with a slight frown, and there was a short silence.

'*Still...*' Sam murmured.

'Yes?' Kate prompted eagerly.

Sam looked sideways at her, a slow grin creeping over his face and deepening his chiselled dimples. 'I do have *one* other idea...'

Two hours later, Kate threw her head back, laughing maniacally, her hair whipping back and forth across her face as she spun in circles and hurtled down the steep hill in a slick circular sledge.

'*Woo-hoo!*' she yelled, raising her arms up high and laughing as the echo bounced back at her.

She slid to a slow stop at the bottom and was tossed out at the last moment by a stubborn snowdrift. Standing back up, she grabbed the sledge and began to jog back up the hill, panting slightly from the exertion.

'What's the matter?' Sam asked, overtaking her on the way up with a challenging grin. 'Have I worn you out already?' He wiggled his eyebrows and sped up.

Kate laughed again, feeling wonderfully carefree as they

played away the afternoon. The slope Sam had taken her to was deserted but for the two of them. A remote hidden gem that none of the local kids knew about.

'Not a chance. It takes more than a few sprints up a hill to wear *me* out,' she told him, catching him up at the top.

'Yeah?' He looked down at her, his breath freezing in the air between them. 'That sounds like a challenge.' He cocked an eyebrow.

Kate pulled her long dark hair back from her face and looked up, her frozen breath mingling with his. She felt the magnetic pull of him that she'd stopped trying to pretend didn't exist and bit her lip, stepping away from him with a grin of her own.

'No, *this* is a challenge,' she said, stepping up to the steepest part and getting ready to dive down on her sledge. 'Bet you can't beat me to the bottom.'

Sam's grin widened, and he let out a low chuckle as he followed her with a determined glint in his eye. 'Oh, you're *on*, lawyer girl.'

Kate shrieked as he sped up. 'Winner gets to cook the turkey!' She dived off the edge just as he reached her.

'Whoa, the stakes have been *raised*!' Sam dived after her.

Kate cackled with glee as she looked back. A moment later though, she realised he was catching up with her. '*No!*' she wailed. 'I take it back! The turkey's off the table!'

'No way – too late,' Sam shouted as he slipped past. 'Weight *always* wins at sledding, rookie!' He turned onto his back for the last part of the slope and laced his hands behind his head, shooting her a grin.

She let out a sound that was half laugh, half frustration as Sam became the clear winner, but then her attention sharpened as she realised they were running too close together. 'Hey, watch *out!*' she called.

Sam looked back just in time to see the upcoming collision,

and he pushed off his board, grabbing hers and instinctively shielding her in a bearlike grip just before impact. Kate turned into him, letting her board fall away, and they rolled over and over for what seemed like an age, until they finally came to a stop in a mound of deep fluffy snow.

Unsure which way was up after their dizzying fall, Kate blinked and tried to blow the crazy mess of hair off her face, scraping it back with her hands when that didn't work, and as her line of sight cleared, she met Sam's stunned gaze above her. They stared at each other for a moment and then burst out laughing.

'Oh my God, that was crazy!' Kate exclaimed.

'That was *reckless*,' Sam added with another shocked laugh. 'We really should have thought about that before we jumped.'

'Well, we're alive, so...' Kate trailed off, suddenly incredibly aware of the weight and heat of Sam's body on hers.

He was still holding her close to him in his tight, protective grip. She looked up at his handsome, chiselled face as their cold, white breaths mingled in the air and saw his expression change as he registered it, too. The air suddenly seemed heavier, this thing between them that kept rearing its head whenever she let her guard down filling every pore of her body and every inch of space around them like it was liquid. A warm and dangerously addictive liquid. Kate pulled in a deep breath, but that movement didn't break the bubble this time. This time, the invisible pull just seemed to grow more intense than ever.

'Yeah,' Sam murmured, his voice low. 'We are.'

It was different this time. Harder to pull away, with the heat of him pressed against her and her own traitorous body begging not to be peeled away. But although it took every ounce of energy she had, Kate ripped her gaze from his and slowly pulled back. She might not be able to control her feelings, but she could still control her actions. Even if doing so felt physically painful.

Feeling her move spurred Sam into action, and he instantly released her, pushing back to give her space. He looked away, quickly shielding his expression, but not before she caught the brief troubled frown.

'Sorry, I must be crushing you,' he said, standing up and shaking himself off.

'No, not at all,' she replied. There was no evidence of how shaky she really felt in her voice, she realised thankfully.

Shaking the snow out of her hair, she turned away for a second to get a more solid grip on her composure. Taking a deep breath in, she turned back around with a bright smile.

'Well, I think I've had my fill of near-death experiences for today! Shall we head back?' She waited, praying he didn't try to convince her to stay. She needed to get away from him for a while and clear her head.

'Sure,' he replied. 'I'll grab the boards. You head on back to the truck.' He pulled the keys out and threw them to her.

'Thanks,' she said, catching them.

Kate watched him walk away, her smile dropping to a worried frown. This was becoming a problem. A very real one. She'd tried reasoning these feelings away and shutting them off, but neither was working. She needed to get away, get him out of her head completely. She needed that headspace to focus on her other worries. On her *real* life. And hopefully, in a few more days, she'd be able to do that. She just had to get through Christmas. Because Christmas was now one *more* thing they were going to share.

When he'd learned she was staying in Vermont, Sam had officially invited her to spend the day with him. Kate had been surprised, assuming he'd have plans with friends or family. Jenna, at least. But Sam admitted that he'd turned down all the invites that had come, wanting to just be at home one last time, surrounded by his memories of his aunt. Kate's guilt had hit an all-time high, and she'd instantly tried to book a hotel, apologising for encroaching, but Sam had stopped her, insisting she stay. He hadn't actually wanted to be alone, he'd told her. He just hadn't wanted to be anywhere else. And so Kate had accepted, quietly resolving to try to make this first Christmas without Cora easier for him any way she could.

But as she watched him now, yet another problem on top of all the others she was already juggling, she wondered how on earth she was going to get through Christmas without totally cracking under the pressure of it all herself.


As Sam pulled onto the drive and switched off the engine an hour later, Kate was so lost in her tangled thoughts that for a moment she didn't move.

'Kate?' Sam prompted gently.

'Hmm?' She looked around. 'Oh. Right. Sorry, miles away.'

They got out of the truck, and Kate turned back to gather her things.

'Excuse me, ma'am?'

She looked around and saw a young man walking up the drive towards her. Sam had taken the boards to the door, but he returned now with a frown.

'Can I help you?' he asked.

The man ignored him, his beady gaze still on Kate. 'Are you Ms Kate Hunter?'

'*Wait...*' Sam put his hand out in warning, but it was too late, as Kate spoke at the same time.

'That's me. Can I help you?'

She realised what was happening just a second too late. The envelope was thrust into her hand, and a flash went off as the guy took a picture. 'Consider yourself served,' he said, walking off quickly now that his job was done.

Kate groaned, annoyed at her own stupidity.

Moving to stand beside her, Sam watched the man leave with a grim expression. 'Aubrey wasn't bluffing then.'

'I never thought she was,' Kate replied with a sigh.

'Well, that's that then,' he said, turning back to the house. 'I guess you're taking this battle to court.'

'Yeah,' Kate replied heavily. 'I guess I am.'

# THIRTY-SIX

Christmas Eve arrived, and Kate kept busy for most of the day, managing for the most part to avoid Sam and keep to herself. She had to work hard at keeping her spirits up, with the court summons niggling irritably at the corners of her mind and the homesickness coming in unhappy waves. She couldn't even *think* about the wedding. It was now just a week away. *One week.* And now, being that close, the whole thing felt oddly unreal, like it was happening in a film or to someone else and she was merely a spectator. Because the whole idea that her *actual wedding*, a legal ceremony binding her to someone else for life, was happening in a few *days* was just insane.

Kate had spoken to everyone back home on video calls earlier in the day, one after the other, and with the rest of the items on her to-do list already ticked, she stuck on Michael Bublé's Christmas album, poured herself a hot mulled wine and set about wrapping her gifts.

Sam arrived home just as she finished and headed straight down to the basement. She briefly wondered what he was up to, then stood up to stretch and cleared away her mess.

Carrying the freshly wrapped gifts up to her room, Kate put

them aside and then ran herself a bath with a generous dollop of the luxury bubbles she'd treated herself to the day before. She tied up her hair, lit a candle and slipped into the velvety embrace of the deep hot bath. As she closed her eyes and relaxed back with a contented sigh, there was a loud thud from somewhere downstairs. A staccato series of similar thuds shortly followed it, and she opened her eyes with a frown.

'What on earth is he doing?' she muttered curiously.

After half an hour of trying to work it out, Kate finally gave up on her relaxing bath and ventured down to find out. She smiled as she realised that Sam had put up the big tree she'd seen in the basement, and that he'd dragged up several boxes of ornaments. He'd set the tree by what she'd thought, up until now, was a purely ornamental fireplace. The roaring fire now burning merrily away, however, proved that theory well and truly wrong.

Sam walked into the room from behind her, carrying one more box. He smiled as he saw her. 'Hey. Wanna help me decorate the tree?'

'I absolutely *do*, *yes*,' Kate replied with feeling. She kneeled down beside Sam eagerly as he opened the first box. *Now* it felt like Christmas.

They spent the next hour decorating the tree and the house and sharing Christmas stories. Kate put some festive music on, and they had a heated debate over whether or not the Pogues had written the best Christmas song of all time. (They had, of course.) Then once the boxes were all empty and they'd packed the fire with some more logs, they collapsed on the sofa with some mulled wine and carried on talking, their conversation eventually coming back around to the upcoming court date.

'So explain it to me,' Sam asked. 'Because I don't fully understand what it is that she's doing.'

'OK, so Aubrey and Evelyn have made it clear they're a team now. They've obviously realised they have a stronger claim together than apart,' Kate started, putting her wine down on the side table. 'They're going to drag me through court to try and show I've not done what I'm supposed to in the contract, and that I've not acted in the company's best interest. The court date is the fifth of January.' He nodded, and she could see further questions brewing in his eyes. 'There *is* more to it than that,' she explained. 'But I can't share details with you just yet. I'm sorry. The one thing I *will* tell you is that I think I'm close to making a decision and that it's in the best interests of everyone. Touch wood.' She touched the top of her head.

Sam nodded again. 'OK.' He looked over to the tree and at the gifts they'd each stashed underneath. 'I don't know what your tradition is, but we used to give our gifts to each other on Christmas Eve. You up for it?' he asked, changing the subject.

Kate smiled. 'Definitely! We always have to wait for Christmas morning in my house. It's *torture.*'

Sam laughed, and they both jumped up then kneeled beside the tree.

'Mine first,' Kate insisted before he could get in before her.

Sam closed his mouth and accepted her win with grace. 'Thank you.'

He took the package and pulled the green ribbon and gold paper away. Kate felt a swell of excitement and nerves. She really hoped he liked it.

Sam ran his finger down the wooden carving with a smile. It was of a man holding an umbrella over a smaller woman or girl, his free arm resting protectively on her shoulder.

Kate bit her lip. 'It made me think of you and Jenna,' she told him.

'This is a truly lovely gift,' he said, sounding touched. 'Thank you, Kate. I love it.' He looked up at her, his words heartfelt, and Kate felt her cheeks grow warm under his intense, unreadable gaze.

She nodded and looked away, her emotions beginning to churn a little too deeply for comfort.

'OK, my turn,' Sam said, reaching under the tree.

Kate took the gift he held out with a smile. 'Thank you,' she said, pulling the twine and unwrapping the blue tissue paper. Inside was a small box, and as she opened it, her expression widened in surprise. 'Oh, Sam, *thank you*. It's *beautiful*.'

She touched the necklace, a delicate gold chain with an intricately woven key pendant hanging down, covered with a pattern of tiny vines.

'I thought of you when I saw it.' He looked down at it. 'I thought maybe when you look at it, it might remind you that sometimes you have to let yourself out of that cage you lock yourself in. Because when you do, that's when you bloom, Kate Hunter. When you let yourself go and you say and do what you want.' He looked up at her again, holding her gaze. 'That's when you're *magnificent*.'

Kate stared back at him for a long moment, feeling the intensity behind his words deep down in her core. How did he do that? she wondered. How did he get under her skin and bury in so deeply? But then just like that, as though someone had flicked on a light, she saw it. The realness between them. The truth. The deep connection that had somehow bonded them these last two months, without her even realising. And she wanted to give in to it suddenly so badly. So *desperately*. But though every atom in her body buzzed towards him with fierce intensity, she forced herself to remain still. She couldn't do it to Lance. She *wouldn't*.

With the same difficulty of pulling one industrial-strength magnet away from another, Kate pushed backwards away from him. She swallowed hard and closed the lid of the necklace box.

'Thank you,' she managed. She cleared her throat and stood up, looking back down at the box. 'This really is beautiful.'

Sam nodded, rubbing the back of his neck as he cast his gaze to the wooden carving. 'Thank you, too,' he said quietly. He looked back up suddenly, his eyes seeking hers. 'You know it's *you* I see under that umbrella, Kate. Whenever I look at this, it will *always* be you that I see.'

Something hard pushed painfully up through Kate's chest and lodged in her throat, and she had to work to pull in her next breath. She didn't trust herself to reply. She could feel herself shaking. Or perhaps it was the vibration from the rush of energy now racing through her veins. She wasn't sure – she couldn't think straight. All she knew was that she needed to get out of this room before she did something she'd regret. She swallowed hard.

'I, um, I need to go to bed.' She edged around him towards the hallway as though he were some dangerous animal she was scared to get too close to. And she *was* scared, she realised. But not of him. She was scared of *herself*. 'Big day tomorrow,' she muttered. 'Goodnight, Sam.'

And without waiting to hear his response, she turned and fled up the stairs.

## THIRTY-SEVEN

After an hour of pacing her room and sitting at the window looking out at the gently falling snow, trying to snap herself out of this emotional mess she'd let herself get into, Kate stared at the bed debating whether or not to try to sleep. It was late and she was tired, but her mind and her heart were still racing. Her gaze drifted to Cora's diary, and she stared at it for a few moments, unsure whether she was in the right frame of mind. Then, deciding to try it anyway, she walked over to pick it up. She propped herself up on the bed and thumbed through to the last page she'd read.

The tides had finally begun to turn for William in Cora's young mind, and Kate had found this change of heart a great comfort to read, a balm for her nerves whenever she worried about her own upcoming marriage. If Cora had finally come around, there was no reason to think that she wouldn't soon, too. Time was clearly the key. Her and Cora's tales may have been seventy years apart, but seeing Cora and William's wonderful, happy life together and knowing it had been born from a marriage based on friendship, sense and logic reassured her. Because she and Lance had so much more than just friendship. They'd chosen to be together. They loved each other.

Perhaps that had been the real reason she'd ended up out here. The universe had *clearly* chosen to test her at this junction in her life, but perhaps it had also placed this story in her path to bolster her faith in her future with Lance. Maybe Kate had just needed this reminder that sense and logic really were the best ingredients for a happy life.

In an entry Kate had read the week before, Cora had finally accepted William's proposal. The mystery M had fought, asking her to wait for him while he made something of himself, then asking her to run away with him, as Cora was forced to make a decision. He'd told her his love for her ran so deep, there was nowhere on earth he wouldn't go for her, and once more Matthew's face had flickered through her mind. It was Cora's mother who'd finally managed to make her see sense and marry William. And as her wedding day had approached, Cora had thrown herself into it with all her energy. Kate had stopped reading just before the big day, saving that entry to read on Christmas Day as a little gift to herself. But she needed it *now*. She needed to soothe herself with Cora and William's happy ending. Or rather, their happy beginning.

Settling back against the pillows, Kate started reading it eagerly, already feeling her jagged nerves begin to calm as she delved back into their story.

*5 October 1955*

*Today is the day I chose to get married. For weeks now I have lovingly prepared every single last note of the song that is today. My beautiful dress was made and the shoes to match. I woke up with the shakiest nerves I have ever felt in my body. For my nerves knew, it seems, more than I just how momentous a day this would turn out to be.*

*I knew from the moment I picked it that today would be the day my life changed forever. The day I forged a new path. I packed up my bags last night, ready to take to the home of my new husband, to spend my first night there as man and wife. And I'm so glad I brought my diary. I so very nearly didn't, for memories can be troublesome things sometimes. But the past and the future are all linked by the present. It is all one big journey, rather than what was and what will be.*

*It was late last night, as I tossed and turned in my bed, that I felt so restless I could barely think. So I put on my coat and I went for a walk. I just needed some air. I needed to breathe. It felt so stifling in that room, under the shadow of my wedding dress. And my feet carried me without asking where I wanted them to go. I was not thinking of minor things like geography just then. I was thinking about life and death and love and the universe. And then suddenly, there I was, by our old tree. Mine and M's. And what was more, I was not there alone. For there on the branch was a man. A broken man, his head hung low. And that's when I knew so much more had aligned for us both to be there that night than just my restless feet. It was something that ran much deeper. Much wilder and more alive in my veins than anything else could ever be in this world.*

*I got so close I could touch him before he realised he wasn't alone. And when he turned, the relief in his eyes met with mine and we knew we could not be apart again. Not for another day. Not another hour.*

'Er, *what*?' Kate exclaimed out loud. She turned a wary frown towards Cora's picture before sitting up straight to read on.

*I agreed there and then to go with him wherever he wanted to go. I no longer cared about anything else. I no longer had the strength to hide my unhappiness and be the woman my mother wants me so desperately to be. I know she means well, and her lessons come from a place of love, but my body is not worth preserving if the heart inside it has died. And so we walked back to the house and I picked up my bag. I picked up my wedding dress and my shoes and I left.*

*I left her a letter to explain and to tell her I love her. M urged me to wait and tell her in person, but he doesn't know my mother like I. She won't understand. She'll need some time before she can accept or forgive this.*

*I sent just one more letter. An apology to W along with my heartfelt wish that he find a girl much more deserving of him than me. And he will do, I'm sure of it.*

*M and I walked and talked all night, our need for each other's company stronger than any need for sleep. We made our plans and our promises. And then first thing this morning we found a little church, far away, where the vicar was happy to marry us. And we stood in front of God and those stones and we said our forever vows. To have and to hold each other, for our whole lives through. For better or worse, now and always.*

*Now, I belong to M, and he to me. But of course, I no longer have reason to fear writing his name. For today I became Mrs M. Today I so proudly and ecstatically became Mrs William Moreaux.*

Kate's mouth gaped, her eyes as wide as saucers and the diary dropped to her lap. It was *him*. It had always been *him*. M had been William all along. She'd been wrong about *everything*. This incredible life Cora and William had built, the deep, inspiring love they'd shared, wasn't built on sensibilities and logical choices; it was built on passion and chance and the bravery to take a leap out of the normal lanes and into the unknown, for what made them feel alive!

Kate's heart thumped hard in her chest, and she stood up, feeling as though the rug had just been pulled from right underneath her. She began to pace tensely from one side of the room to the other, one hand on her hip, the other rubbing the back of her neck. This was a disaster. She couldn't get her head around it. Her mind began to whirl. What did this mean for *her*? Cora and William's story had been the proof she'd been clinging to that she was doing the right thing marrying Lance. That tick boxes and practical compatibilities were the right tools to measure the best future. It had made *sense,* proof of an already logical argument. But now that proof was gone. It had never even existed. And more than that, what she knew *now* seemed to stack proof of the exact *opposite. Now* it seemed that Cora and William's incredible life was built on blind faith and by ignoring all sensibilities entirely.

The enormity of the situation, of everything becoming the polar opposite of what she'd previously trusted in, suddenly overwhelmed her. She sat down feeling lightheaded and tried to calm her reeling thoughts, tried to think straight for just a moment. But then a sound in the hallway made her freeze and look up. It was Sam. He'd paused outside in the hallway. She held her breath and stared at the door, then his steps continued, and she heard the squeak of his door opening and shutting as he retired for the night.

She continued staring at the door for a few moments, her mind whirling in a chaotic tangled mess of contradictions. All the many waves of panic she'd felt about Lance and the wedding that she'd pushed down since he proposed now reared back up, all at once, no longer prepared to be ignored now that the logic she'd used to subdue them was gone. Every decision she'd made for the greater logical good, every internal scream she'd subdued with her silence, every doubt she thought she'd defeated with reason, all came flying back, hitting her in the gut with so much force she had to physically catch her breath.

They flew around and around in her core and her mind, growing faster and louder until they were one big roar of confusion, and suddenly something in Kate snapped. She mentally grabbed hold of the tornado of thoughts and threw them out of her mind with force, leaving just one lone whisper behind. The *truth*. The raw, unspoken truth that she'd never allowed herself to hear. The whispered truth that what she really wanted, what she *needed*, was to do something that was just for herself. Something that wasn't designed around other people's expectations or desires. Something she didn't adapt to fit someone else's happiness over her own. And as she finally set that desire free, Kate suddenly saw, with stark clarity, that she hadn't made a choice in her life that was actually for herself in years. The realisation was simple but devastating, and she felt something inside her shift. She felt something awaken.

Slowly, and not entirely sure that she knew what she was doing, Kate walked across the room and opened the door, stepping out into the dark hallway. Light spilled out of her room, throwing just enough glow on Sam's door for her to make out the grain of the wood. She touched her fingertips to it and felt her pulse quicken in both fear and excitement combined.

*What am I doing?* she asked herself in despair.

The angel on her shoulder beseeched her to turn back, but the devil rested a hand on the angel's arm and shook her head.

*Something for me*, Kate told them calmly. *Something entirely for me.*

## THIRTY-EIGHT

Kate stared thoughtfully across the kitchen at Sam the next morning as she finished up the icing on the chocolate log. She put the spoon in her mouth and savoured the leftover chocolate, trying not to laugh when Sam caught her and his face opened up into incredulous accusation.

'That's full-on *gross*, Miss Hunter,' he admonished.

'Why? I'm done – I'm not putting the spoon back on the log,' she replied in defence.

He grinned and shook his head. 'Cora would have you shot on the spot. She was always very particular when it came to kitchen hygiene.'

'Oh yeah?' Kate kinked an eyebrow and dipped her finger into the spare chocolate icing. 'And what would she think of this?'

She shot him a mischievous look and then flicked the chocolate over the counter at him. It hit him square on the nose, and she burst out laughing at the shock on his face.

'Alright,' he said, nodding with a grim smile. 'You asked for it.' He leaped around the counter, diving for the icing, and Kate shrieked, grabbing the bowl and darting out of the way.

Despite the fact she'd not had much sleep, Kate felt a lot better this morning than she had in a while. She hadn't walked into Sam's room the night before, realising as she'd stood there in the dark hallway that the thing she needed to do for herself was not *him*. Not right then, at least. It had been hard to turn back round, having got so close to giving in. But hard and frustrating as it was, she'd realised she wasn't prepared to lose her self-respect. Especially not for such a fleeting pleasure as a one-night affair.

No. She knew she needed to do something for herself that would last. Something great. Something worthy. So she'd stayed up long into the night working out exactly what that was and exactly how she was going to get it. And as Christmas morning finally dawned, Kate had the outlines of a plan. A plan of something she could be proud of and that truly excited her.

'OK, OK, I surrender!' Sam called, lifting his arms in the air as Kate pelted him mercilessly with leftover sultanas.

'Really?' she asked, pausing with a look of suspicion.

Sam thought it over with a tilt of the head and then nodded. 'Yeah. I could take you, but I'm honestly too tired. Truce?'

'Absolutely not,' Kate retorted indignantly. 'I won fair and square.'

Sam laughed. 'Fine. Take it. You win.' He shook his head, and the pair of them set about collecting all the rogue food bullets now scattered around the room.

Kate watched him as they worked in natural sync, a small smile playing across her lips. She'd thought a lot about Sam, too, overnight. About the way he made her feel. Then she'd thought back to her father's words about the bigger picture, about the fact there was really no such thing. That life's *big picture* was really just a collection of moments all strung together. When she looked back over all her memories with Lance across the last few months, she'd been surprised to realise all she could see was stress and unhappiness and restraint. And this was a pattern that went back much further than his surprise proposal. They'd had their good times, but they'd come at a cost Kate hadn't realised she'd been paying.

She'd realised, as she analysed it all now from this distance, that over time she'd become less and less herself in a bid to become what he wanted her to be. It had been even more sobering to realise that she'd been doing this to herself for much longer than Lance had been around. She'd been trying to live up to everyone else's expectations of her for far too long. And she had no idea when she'd started sacrificing parts of herself that way, but she knew it was time for her to stop. No matter *how* terrifying that prospect was.

When her thoughts had then wandered back over her time with Sam – their initial mutual hatred aside – she realised she'd felt happier and more inspired in this time than she had in as long as she could remember. And while she knew it was easy to feel positively about someone new, she also knew that this was different. They hadn't started off in the rose-tinted phase of most new relationships. They hadn't even started off on the right foot. They'd suffered the worst of each other's ugliest side and had been through more together than some people go through in a decade. And yet despite all odds, and their best efforts not to, they'd grown closer and had become a genuine source of happiness in each other's lives. But this wasn't something she could allow herself to think about just yet. She had a few more pressing things to deal with right now.

Sam looked sideways at her, and she caught his gaze with a look of question. 'What's up?'

'Listen, about last night,' he said, his tone a trifle awkward. 'I don't want to overstep the mark and ruin anything today, but I just want you to know that whatever I – that – *ah*...' He turned to face her but looked away, struggling to find the right words.

Kate's stomach did a small flip, and she carefully neutralised her expression as she waited, not quite sure if the feelings his words had stirred up inside her were of hope or panic. She couldn't have this conversation with him, not yet. No matter how much part of her wanted to.

'I think, er, I think it's pretty clear that I think a lot of you, Kate,' Sam continued. 'I just want you to know that I wouldn't ever – I wouldn't – I just – *look*... I know you're getting married in just a few days, and I want you to know that—'

'Sam.' Kate couldn't stop herself reaching out, and they both stared at her hand on his for a moment. 'Listen.' She bit her lip, torn as his eyes moved up to meet hers. 'Things aren't exactly the way they seem. Or the way they *were*, perhaps. I don't know. I, um...' Kate shook her head. 'Look, when I get back to London—' she started carefully, but the rest of her sentence was cut short as a loud knock sounded at the door.

They shared a confused glance, and then Sam stepped back.

'Are you expecting anyone?' Kate asked, relieved at the interruption.

Sam shook his head. 'No.' He moved away from her reluctantly. 'I'll see who it is.'

'OK.' Kate turned back to the counter with a deep, calming breath.

Whoever it was, they couldn't have come at a better time.

She walked to the fridge and pulled out the custard she'd made earlier and took it back to the island with a determinedly bright grin. It was Christmas Day, and *that* was what she would focus on. Hopefully their guest would stay a while and be the distraction she needed from the words that remained – just about – unspoken between her and Sam.

'We have enough food for a small army, by the way,' she called out as she heard Sam open the door. 'So if whoever it is wants to stay for food, they're more than welcome, though I'd possibly avoid the custard.' She grimaced at it.

'Well, that's certainly good to hear,' came a familiar voice. 'Because after *that* journey, I'm absolutely starving.'

Kate twirled around with a gasp and dropped the spoon to the floor with a clatter. The lumpy custard splattered up her favourite oversized beige jumper and onto her cheek. But she didn't notice any of that, because Lance was standing in the doorway, all dressed up in his Armani suit. He smiled at her, and Kate's heart plummeted. She glanced past him to Sam, trying to gauge his reaction, but it was unreadable. Then Lance walked forward, blocking him from view entirely. He held out a bottle of champagne with a big blue Tiffany's box.

'Merry Christmas, darling.'

# THIRTY-NINE

'Here you go,' Kate said, handing Lance a glass of wine across the table. 'Sorry for the wait. I just had to sort out some last-minute bits.'

She'd also run upstairs and silently cursed behind her closed door before walking back down with a serene smile. She felt awful for Sam. Aside from their near moment being totally quashed by Lance's arrival, he was just trying to enjoy his last Christmas in his home while Cora's memory was still fresh and around him. The man was grieving and trying to understand their earlier half-managed conversation, and then, of all people, *Lance* shows up. Possibly the last person in the world Sam wanted to be forced to entertain right now.

Lance, she knew from the set of his cool smile and the way he'd been studying the other man with his courtroom tactics, had already taken against Sam. And it was natural, she supposed, to some degree. His future wife had been living here for months with this other man he didn't know anything about. Of course he'd feel guarded.

'So, Sam,' Lance said, with a cool, lofty smile, 'tell me, what

is it you do?' He helped himself to some potatoes, then exaggeratedly stared at Sam's checked flannel shirt. 'Are you in *trade*?'

Sam held his gaze levelly for a moment, but Kate saw him
tense at Lance's subtle condescending tone. 'Yes,' he answered.
'I am.' He reached for the parsnips.

'Oh, fantastic,' Lance replied with a slight laugh. 'That's
great. Katherine, could you pass the salt?'

Kate hid a frown at the use of her full name. Why was he
being so weirdly formal? He didn't even call her Katherine in
front of her mother. She passed him the salt with a tight smile.

'Thank you. Is there a lot of work for you around here,
Sam?' Lance continued with exaggerated politeness. 'Is it
domestic work you do or commercial? Skilled or...?' He let the
question hang.

Sam's face twitched as he forced a smile back, and Kate
frowned, annoyed at them both. Lance was acting like a face-
tious snob, and Sam was playing the game he'd played when
*she'd* first arrived, giving nothing away and letting Lance
mislead himself. Well, it might be a game *he* enjoyed, but *she*
certainly didn't. She butted in ahead of him before he could
answer, taking on Lance's challenge herself as she served them
both slices of turkey.

'Actually, Sam's selling himself short,' she told him. 'He has
a successful business specialising in the design and build of
affordable, sustainable eco houses and eco solutions.' She smiled
and turned Lance's attention back towards Sam with a flourish
before walking back out to the kitchen for the gravy. She took a
moment around the corner to roll her eyes. This was the worst
Christmas dinner *ever*.

'Oh, how interesting.' She heard the wind leave Lance's
sails as he discovered there was nothing about Sam's business he
could look down on without sounding like a complete idiot and
cheered up slightly. 'One-off sort of stuff or bigger sites?'

'Yeah,' Sam said, sounding resentful that he'd been outed

for exactly who he was. 'Both, but mainly bigger sites. I've got a couple going at the moment, so...' He trailed off.

'Great, great,' Lance said glumly. 'So when you say *solutions*, what do you mean exactly?'

'You know, like energy sources and facilities, a few of the appliances. I use solar panels, ground-source heat pumps, things like that. Put in filtered wells. Dishwashers here and there.'

'You can make sustainable *dishwashers*?' Lance asked, devastatingly impressed. 'Did you design them yourself?'

'After a fashion,' Sam admitted reluctantly. 'And yeah, I designed them.'

Kate grinned at how disappointed they both sounded, now she'd scuppered their passive-aggressive attempts to rub each other up the wrong way. Picking up the jug, she walked back into the room and sat down with a bright smile.

'Gravy anyone?'

Over the course of the meal, Kate continued to direct the awkward conversation as best she could, but things became increasingly strained.

'So you're a lawyer, too, Lance?' Sam asked, eventually slipping out from under Kate's constant prompts towards his line of work. He wiped his mouth with a napkin and put it down on his empty plate.

'I am, Sam, yes,' Lance replied, leaning back and twisting the stem of his wine glass.

Sam nodded, obviously trying to be polite for Kate's sake. 'And do you do the same sort of thing as Kate? Is that how you two met?'

The arrogant smile returned to Lance's face. 'Er, *no* actually. *Katherine* works in corporate law; I work in criminal defence. The *fun* side of lawyering,' he joked. 'A lot more court, a lot less desk.' He raised his eyebrows and lifted the glass of wine. 'Darling, have you got anything a bit stronger? I must admit, this isn't really cutting it today.'

'No,' she said, feeling annoyed. 'And for the record, *Sam*, *my* side of lawyering is quite fun, *too*.' She pursed her lips.

'Oh, you know I'm only messing around,' he said jovially. 'But you must admit, it's definitely sexier solving high-drama murders in court than it is checking off clauses in a contract.'

She raised her eyebrows, feeling needled at the way he was putting her career down, even if it was just *messing around*. She felt tempted to bite back for once, rather than ignore it the way she'd grown used to doing, but for Sam's sake, she didn't. This was his home, his first Christmas without Cora. Lance's presence was already unfair on him, all things considered – he didn't need her making it worse by starting an argument.

Seeing her annoyance at Lance's putdown, Sam cleared his throat and spoke up. 'You get some court action, too, though, don't you, Kate?' Lance laughed, and Sam frowned at his rudeness. 'Well, you've got that one in January coming up, at least.'

Sam was just trying to stick up for her, she knew, but Kate closed her eyes as Lance turned to her with a flash of dark annoyance.

'Where?' he asked. '*Here?*' He waited, his frown deepening by the second.

She sighed. 'I was only served papers the night before last and I didn't want to ruin your Christmas, so I was going to wait and tell you tomorrow.'

'You have *got* to be kidding me!' He sighed loudly.

'Oh, I'm sorry,' Sam said awkwardly. 'I didn't realise. I apologise.'

'Of course you didn't.' Lance stared coldly at him before he broke out a tight smile and let out a little laugh. 'It's fine,' he said, looking back to Kate. 'It's fine. Whatever it is, we'll deal with it. We'd better just hope we're not on our *honeymoon*.'

Kate saw him watch for Sam's reaction to his words, the slight squeeze of his eyes the tell-tale sign, and she saw Sam show his hand, looking down and away at Lance's talk of the wedding. Lance noted this with interest and moved smoothly on, and Kate sighed internally.

'Where do you want to go, anyway, Katherine?' he pressed. 'Your choice, darling, anywhere you want.'

'I can't think about that right now,' she answered shortly. 'We'll talk later.'

There was an awkward silence, then Sam stood up, slapping his hands on his thighs.

'*Alright*. We've sat here long enough, I think. Lance, are you a whisky man? I think I have some in the back of the cupboard.'

'*Now* you're talking,' he replied.

'Great.' Sam walked out of the dining room and through to the kitchen, Lance following shortly after.

Finally alone, Kate looked around sadly at what remained of their Christmas dinner and took a deep sip of her wine. She looked over to one of the pictures of Cora and William, the guilt weighing heavily on her chest. 'I'm so sorry,' she said quietly. 'This is *not* the Christmas Sam should be having this year.'

She stood up and walked to the kitchen, realising she shouldn't leave them alone for too long.

'*Smugglers' Notch*,' Lance read. 'Local, you say?' He put the bottle down and smelled the amber liquid he was swirling around in the glass before sipping it.

'Yeah, not too far south of here, actually,' Sam confirmed. 'This is one of their special reserves.'

'It's *good*,' Lance said with grudging approval. 'Katherine, come try it. I think you'll like this one.'

'Oh, you like whisky, Kate?' Sam asked, looking surprised.

Lance smiled. 'She *loves* whisky.'

'Nice,' Sam commented, shooting her a smile. 'I didn't know that about you.'

'Well, why *would* you, old boy?' Lance said with a cruel laugh. 'You don't actually *know* her at all.'

So *that* was why he was calling her Katherine. It suddenly

clicked. Lance was trying to create some sort of distance between the Kate Sam thought he knew and his Katherine from London. Except *that* version of her wasn't real. It was just another one of Lance's courtroom manipulation tactics to make people see things from a heavily altered alternate perspective.

Kate had reached for his glass, but she paused at his scathing words and this realisation, and Lance took the opportunity to wrap his arm around her. He pulled her to his side, leaning over to kiss her deeply on the lips. Kate tensed, not in a position to pull away as Lance had her in a tight grip, but not happy at being used to prove a point like this at all. When Lance finally let go, she shot him a sharp frown, but he simply turned back to Sam with a smile.

'Can you believe in just one week I'll be marrying this incredible woman, Sam?' he asked in a bright tone. 'She'll be Mrs Kate Cheyney by the first of January. Then comes the rest of the fun. Starting our home, our *family*.' He raised and dropped his eyebrows suggestively. 'What a *great* adventure we're on the cusp of, eh, Katherine?'

She stared at him with a cold expression, too furious with his games to answer. If she hadn't been desperately clinging on to the attempt to keep this Christmas Day a civilised affair out of respect for Sam and his home, she'd have let rip with what she really thought. Her cheeks burned with anger, and as she looked over to Sam, she tried to convey a silent apology, but he looked away with a nod and a forced smile.

He lifted his whisky glass in a toast. 'Well, here's to *you*, Kate.' He looked back at her for a moment, his expression disappointed. 'One week from now you'll be going from *Hunter* to *Chains. Congratulations.*'

'It's *Cheyney*,' Lance said, the double meaning behind the change totally lost on him.

'Cheyney, *so* sorry,' Sam said. He downed the rest of the liquid in the glass and put it down on the counter beside his wooden carving. 'I gotta head off. Got some things to sort out, so I'll just grab a couple of bits and leave you guys to it.'

'*What?*' Kate stepped away from Lance, removing his hand with hers firmly. 'Sam, *no*. It's Christmas *Day*. You need to be *here*.' She frowned and started after him as he jogged up the stairs, but Lance grabbed her arm and pulled her back.

'Leave the man to do his *thing*,' he insisted with a painfully forced laugh, trying to secure her again under his arm. 'I'm sure he has people to see in his *own* life. His *own* friends and family.'

Kate rounded on him with a glare. 'Just *stop it*,' she demanded. 'What's got *into* you?' She twisted round as Sam jogged back down, the backpack he usually took to work slung over his shoulder. 'Sam, *wait...*'

'Can't, sorry. I'll catch you later, Kate,' he called as he walked out the front door.

It closed behind him as she tried to pull herself out of Lance's grasp, but he didn't immediately let go. 'Kate, *stop*. Come *on* – turn around,' he said.

'Lance, *seriously*,' she said, raising her voice now as her temper began to turn molten. 'Get *off of me!*'

She yanked her arm out of his hand and ran through the hall to the front door, but by the time she got it open, Sam's truck was already off the drive and setting off down the road. She looked around for her boots, then made a sound of frustration as she realised they were upstairs. She put her closed fist to her head and the other hand on her hip as she watched him drive away, knowing she had no chance of catching him now. She could have run for her boots, but her car was still halfway down the hill, as she'd never bothered to buy chains.

She shut the front door, leaned her forehead against it and closed her eyes. 'I should have bought those bloody chains,' she muttered.

Lance walked through and stood behind her. 'Kate, I think we need to have a talk.'

Kate ignored him as guilt flooded through her. It had been her job to make sure Sam was OK today. To make sure he got through without feeling alone or getting bogged down in the darker circles of grief. But she'd *failed*. More than that, she'd ended up making his day *worse*.

'If I'd just *got* the stupid chains, I'd have *caught* him. *Ugh*, I'm such an *idiot*,' she muttered, banging her forehead against the door a few times in quiet frustration.

'What on earth are you talking about *now*?' Lance asked, tutting impatiently. 'Can you turn around, please? I'm serious – we need to have a discussion.'

Kate opened her eyes and narrowed them with a look of disbelief before turning round to shoot that look towards him. '*No*, I'm *not* an idiot,' she said, striding towards him with a pointed finger. '*You* are.'

'Excuse me?' Lance asked, annoyance flashing across his face. 'What a thing to say to me!'

Kate shook her head. '*No*. This is where I'd usually just *take it*. The chains were under *my* control so therefore the fault must be that, not *you*, right? That's what I usually do. But it *was* you.'

'Kate, *nothing* you're saying is making any sense to me right now,' Lance told her.

He was suddenly calling her Kate again, now that Sam was gone, she noted. She shook her head. 'What are you even doing here?' she asked. 'Why aren't you at home with your mum? It's Christmas *Day*.'

'Because I was *trying* to spend it with *you*. My future wife.' Lance held her gaze accusingly, and she shook her head.

'No, that's not it. I was set to fly home the day after tomorrow. You wanted to come out here and stamp your territory,' she accused.

Lance exhaled and pushed up his glasses. 'Well, what if I *did*?' he asked. 'Is that really so awful? You've been gone nearly two *months*, shacked up with some guy I don't know – who's apparently the Hulk's younger cousin. Can you really *blame me* for wanting to check up on you and puff my chest out a little? Especially as it seems maybe I *did* have something to worry about. Because instead of focusing on *me*, the fiancé who just travelled for eighteen hours to surprise you on Christmas Day, there you are running off to chase the latest *Magic Mike* recruit. I mean, seriously, Kate, the *sheer size* of the guy!' Lance blew air out through his cheeks and shook his head. 'Tell me *you'd* feel happy about me all cosied up with the *female* version of that.'

Kate exhaled and sighed unhappily. 'Lance, if you were stuck on a job living with the all-time hottest *Page Three girl* for two months, I would still trust you without doubt,' she told him sadly.

She walked past him to the lounge and sat down in one of the armchairs, rubbing one cold hand over the other slowly and looking down at her engagement ring as a heaviness settled over her like a blanket. Lance took the seat opposite her. He opened his mouth to speak, but she stopped him.

'No, I'm going to talk. Lance, you came here because you didn't trust me. And I've had chances to cheat on you, you know, if I wanted to,' she said truthfully. 'But I never have and never would, because I'm not that kind of person, and *that's* something I thought you knew.'

Lance had the grace to look ashamed, and he nodded. 'I do,' he said, his voice heavy. 'I do know that. And I do trust you.'

Kate shook her head. 'What was worse though was the way you came in here and treated *Sam*. This is his *home*. And he lost his aunt, the woman who raised him as her own son, just a few weeks ago,' she told him. 'She was the only family he had, so today was his first Christmas *alone*. His first Christmas without a *family*.' She shook her head. 'You were callous and rude and unkind, and it's just not OK. I get that me being here hasn't been easy for you, but Sam's been through a lot worse, and I honestly can't believe how badly you just treated him.'

Lance shrugged. 'OK, fine. I'm *sorry*. You're right, it was rude, but I saw how the guy was looking at you, and it got my back up.'

'Yes, well, it really doesn't matter now.' She sighed tiredly.

'What's *that* supposed to mean?' Lance asked with a frown.

Kate studied him for a moment. 'Lance, why did you ask me to marry you?' she asked.

He frowned. 'What sort of question is that?'

'A simple one,' she replied. 'We don't even live together – what prompted the sudden proposal?'

Lance sighed, looking stressed. 'Alright. It was at Rick and Amy's wedding, when your mother started making all those comments. Thing is, Kate' – he spread his hands outwards – 'she made *sense*. I want a family. I want the nice house and the children. And you're *thirty-five*. You know, you act all startled about these things, but you're a *woman*. You have a time limit. I'm sorry, but it's *true*. So I thought about it and, yes, it needs to be *now*. And we'll look back and thank ourselves, down the line, that we did.'

'I have a time limit?' Kate let out an incredulous laugh. 'Lance, do you realise you've not once actually asked me what *I* want?'

'Of *course* I have,' he said dismissively.

'When?' Kate waited as the cogs behind Lance's eyes began to whirr.

After a while his eyebrows flicked up in brief surprise. 'I guess I didn't, did I?' Kate shook her head. 'Well, what *do* you want?' he asked. 'We can make a plan to make it work for both of us. I *love you*, Kate. Obviously, I want to make you happy.'

Kate sighed, and she looked away sadly. 'You *have* made me happy,' she told him. 'For a while I think we made each other happy. And I don't doubt that you do love me, Lance, but we need to start being honest with ourselves. We aren't right for each other. Not really. You and I want completely different things.'

'No.' Lance shook his head. His eyes darted around her face, and fear coloured his frown as he saw what was there. 'Come on, Kate – don't do this to me. To us.'

'Lance, to make a marriage work, you both have to *want* it, but I *don't*.' She winced. 'I *don't* want to marry you, and I'm sorry that hurts you, but I can't change how I feel. Believe me, I've tried. The thought of a big family home and kids *terrifies* me.' She shrugged. 'And maybe some therapist will figure out why one day,' she said with a weak grimace. 'But either way, that's just not what I want.'

'You'll look back on this with regret, Kate. Throwing away what we have,' he argued. 'Come on – this isn't you. This is just cold feet, a blip, but we can work through it. I *know* you can see how foolish it would be to walk away from what we have here. Just take a second and look at this practically. We *get* each other. We're on the same path, the same level and we get on wonderfully when we're actually on the same continent. We are the *perfect match. Come on – snap out of this.*'

When she didn't answer, he moved off the chair onto his knees and grasped one of her hands between both of his in her lap. 'Kate, these last couple of months have been hard, I know. It's all moved fast, and you've been out here, away from me, away from your home and family and friends. And that must have been so hard for you. It's certainly been hard on *us*. But just think back to how you felt when we first got engaged. Remember the *real* us, before this distance and the stress muddled things up. That's *all this is*. Just come home and marry me. I promise you, in a couple of months, you'll look back on this and be glad that sense took over.'

Kate looked down into his bright hazel eyes with a sad smile. For a moment, she wondered if she really was being a fool. But then the words from Cora's diary stirred in her memory, and her resolve strengthened.

She squeezed his hand. 'Lance, if we settle for each other now, we'll both miss out on finding the greatest adventure of our lives.'

This was the end now. She knew it with the strangest certainty, and she knew that Lance knew it, too. She gently pulled her hand away and took off her ring, placing it on the coffee table.

'Kate, *don't*,' he begged, his low voice breaking pitifully. 'We can work through this. I'll – I'll...' He trailed off and hung his head with a defeated sob.

Kate felt her own eyes well up, and a tear fell down her cheek. She'd never wanted to hurt Lance. She'd never wanted to hurt anyone. But she couldn't keep holding them all up at the expense of herself.

'You're going to find someone amazing, Lance,' she told him gently, meaning every word. 'And while I'm sorry it couldn't be me, when you do, I'll be happier for you than you'll *ever* know. Because I want you to find that happiness.'

Lance looked up at her, tears still running down his face and his heart breaking in front of her eyes.

'*Christ*, Kate. I can't believe this is happening,' he said shakily.

Kate nodded sadly, but she didn't reply. Because she already knew and had come to terms with the sad knowledge that this was the right decision for them both.

# FORTY

Kate woke up feeling groggy and bleary-eyed, forgetting for a moment why. Forgetting, too, why the room around her didn't look quite right. Then suddenly it all came flooding back. She lifted her head, looking around the room for Lance. He'd been next to her when she'd fallen asleep. But she quickly realised that she was alone on the deep sofa she'd spent the night on. She lay back with a deflated sigh and rubbed the sleep from her eyes before staring up at the ceiling.

She felt a strange hollowness inside, like the space Lance had filled in her life still held his shape out of habit. But the feeling wasn't a bad one. It felt more like a weight had been lifted. Like in his place was an empty canvas, just waiting for whatever she chose to create in her life next. She still couldn't quite believe she'd done it. That she'd taken that huge leap for herself, despite the fallout that would inevitably follow. That wasn't going to be fun. But she'd realised, through Cora, that life was both too long and too short to spend without something or someone in it that set your soul on fire. And she wanted that. She wanted it desperately.

Kate sat up, and her gaze fell to the note on the coffee table. She reached over and picked it up.

*Kate,*

*I'm not good at goodbyes, especially ones I never wanted to say.*

*I love you. And I'm not sure how I'll ever get over coming so close to making you my wife, only to lose you at this eleventh hour. But it seems I shall have to try. If I'm to have any chance of succeeding though, I must beg one simple kindness. Don't call me or ask us to be friends. I could never be friends with you. You mean far too much. If you ever find yourself in need of me, I'll be there. Always. But otherwise, from here I shall say goodbye.*

*Good luck with your court case. Not that you'll need it. You're an incredible lawyer, Kate. And an even more incredible woman. And much as it will kill me when you do, I hope you find whatever it is you're looking for.*

*Yours always.*

*Lance*

A stray tear escaped and ran down her cheek as she read his heartbroken words, then she carefully folded the letter in half and put it away. She looked up to a picture of Cora on the wall. Cora stared back with her solid, knowing smile, and Kate took a deep breath in. This wasn't going to be smooth sailing once the news hit back home. There were storms ahead, and Kate hated that her decisions were going to hurt people she loved. But it was done and done for good reason. For better or worse, she'd chosen her path. Now she needed to embrace it and take the leap, with her head and her hopes held high, into the great unknown.

. . .

A few hours and several coffees later, Kate walked into the coffee shop on Main and looked around at the people seated. It didn't take more than one sweep to spot him. Even if he hadn't raised his hand to catch her attention, he looked so similar to William that he would have been hard to miss.

She walked over and held out her hand with a smile. 'Hi, Edward? I'm Kate.'

Edward nodded, shaking her hand briefly before withdrawing it. 'I know who you are,' he said. 'Please, sit.' He gestured to the chair opposite.

Kate looked over to the counter. 'Can I get you a drink or anything first?' she asked.

'No, I'm fine, thanks,' he said, pointing to his bottle of water.

Kate nodded and ordered herself a tea before taking the seat opposite him. She assessed him subtly. He was a little over average height, slightly stooped with the standard old-man half ring of fluffy white hair on the sides and back, with a handful of whiskers still clinging to the top. His eyelids were very drooped, but his eyes were still beady and alert. He wore a smart suit and tie that he seemed at ease in, and he held good eye contact. Erica had worked out that he had to be eighty-four. Which wasn't an *ideal* age to be taking over a lively company such as Coreaux Roots, that was for sure. But what other choices did she have? She took a deep breath in and gave him her brightest smile.

'Thanks for meeting with me,' she said politely. 'So, you obviously know why I'm here in general. And firstly, really, I'm just trying to get a feel for you as a person, talk to you about your interest in the company and whether you were close with your brother, that sort of thing. So tell me everything you need me to know.' She pulled a pen and notepad from her bag and gave him an encouraging nod.

Edward scratched his cheek. 'There's not a lot that's important that you shouldn't already know, but alright,' he said. 'I'm Will's younger brother. I run a printing press over in Hillier Valley. We're just a local paper but a good one. I have a team of thirty-eight people working for me now. And I know that ain't the hundreds Will had,' he said with a chuckle. 'But those thirty-eight have been with me *years*. I know how to manage people, how to look after them and how to keep the company running strong to keep them earning money,' he told her firmly. 'And at the end of the day, that's what it's all about. Your community. Your family.' He held his hands out in a small shrug. 'Will and I were very similar in our approaches. And that's *why* I asked for the company to be given to me.'

He paused to take a sip of water. 'I'm eighty-four, Kate. I'm not looking to take companies over for the money or the power. I've not got long left here. But I *know* what's been going on.' He eyed her hard. 'Those two on Cora's side. Nasty bits of work, the both of 'em. If they get hold of the company, or any part of it, they'll destroy it. And it will be the workers who suffer. *That's* what I don't want. That's what Will never wanted.' He stared out through the window for a second.

'It definitely sounds like your visions were aligned,' she agreed. She clicked the pen on and off under the table a few times. 'What would you do with it later on?'

He chuckled, a wide grin spreading across his face. 'You mean when I've *had it*,' he translated. 'I have a son in New Zealand. We've talked, and he's agreed to move over to learn the ropes, if I'm awarded the company. I'll train him up to take over. That's my plan, anyway.'

Kate nodded. It was certainly the best plan she'd heard so far.

She looked down at her notes, pondering what she should do next. It seemed pretty cut and dry at this point. Though really, she wanted to run it past Sam, now she'd made a potential decision.

'I leave on the thirtieth, by the way,' Edward said to her. 'For New Zealand. If I'm going to get things in motion with him, I'll need to know by then.'

Kate nodded. 'I'll keep that in mind. Do you have a personal mobile or direct line I can take?' she asked suddenly, remembering his doddery gatekeeper.

'Yes, here, take one of these,' he said, reaching into his inside pocket. He handed her a business card, and she slipped it into her bag.

'Thank you. I'll be in touch,' she said.

'OK then,' he said, abruptly standing up. 'Goodbye.'

Kate blinked as he turned and left without another word. 'Right,' she said to herself as no one else was there to say it to. She picked up her bag. '*OK. That's it then. Time to make a decision.*'

# FORTY-ONE

Kate walked outside, zipped up her coat and walked down Main Street in the opposite direction for a change. Pulling out her phone, she wandered down a bit further, then leaned against a wall at the end of a row of industrial buildings that ran the length of a small side road as she scrolled through her contacts to Sam's number. She pressed dial and waited.

At the same time her call connected, she heard the shrill ring of Sam's ringtone resound through the air. She frowned and pulled her phone down to look at the screen, confused. She put it back to her ear, but the shrill ring continued. She looked around, wondering who it was. It would be just one of those random coincidences, of course. Two phones connecting at the same time. It was a fairly common ringtone. Still, it was annoying her not knowing where it was coming from. She frowned, stepping forward and circling back for a better look around as she waited for Sam to pick up. As she leaned to the side and glanced down the industrial side road, she almost missed it, but then suddenly he moved his arm.

Kate darted her head back across, her eyes widening under her frown. Just a few metres down there was an opening into the building she was leaning on. And *someone* was leaning against the inside frame of that opening, facing away from her. *Someone* with a thick khaki coat and a mass of dark hair. *Someone* with his hand coming out of his pocket holding a phone. And as *someone* checked the phone and rejected the call, simultaneously ending *her* call, Kate's mouth opened in a wide O of indignant shock.

She almost marched down there to confront him, to tell him she was only calling out of concern, to make sure he was OK after he'd not returned the night before. But then the swish of blonde that flicked out made her pause. She frowned and leaned around a little more. Was that Aubrey? They were talking, she realised in shock, their voices low. What the hell was going on? This made no sense. Sam hated Aubrey. And why would they meet somewhere like this? Somewhere so secretive?

Aubrey's arm suddenly came into view, too, and Kate instinctively ducked. But neither of them looked her way.

'*Listen* to me...' Aubrey's voice grew louder momentarily, and Kate leaned further, her eyebrows shooting up as she heard her own name. '... just checking Kate doesn't *know*.'

'No,' Sam replied firmly. 'She doesn't. Not *yet* anyway.'

'Good,' Aubrey purred, wrapping her arm around his neck and, from what little Kate could see, pressing her body to Sam's. 'Keep it that way, you absolute *animal. God,* you're hot.'

Kate recoiled like she'd been stung. What was *happening? This can't be what it looks like*, she told herself. *It just can't.* But as Aubrey's words and the image of her arm around his neck looped on replay through her mind, she knew she was just trying to fool herself. Feeling sick to her stomach, Kate rolled back around the end of the building, unable to look anymore.

'*Listen*...'

As she heard Sam's voice again, she glanced down the road, debating whether she should leave or stay. She didn't want to hear any more of this. The thought of him being with *her* of all people felt like a punch to the stomach. The shock alone had knocked her for six. She needed to leave, she decided. She couldn't hear any more. But she wasn't quick enough to evade Sam's next few words, and as he spoke, it felt like he'd stabbed a knife right into her chest.

'Once Kate's done what I need her to, I don't care what she knows. It'll be done. Legally sealed.'

Kate gasped and then clapped a hand over her mouth, realising too late that she'd been too loud. They stopped talking.

'What *was* that?' Aubrey snapped. '*Go*,' she ordered. 'Check it out.'

Kate panicked and looked around desperately for somewhere to hide. She heard Sam turning around and, realising she had maybe three seconds at best, threw herself under the branches of a large overhanging wall plant. It didn't cover her fully, long thin vertical gaps between every branch, but her long weather-friendly coat was bright white, and they were surrounded by snow. She squatted down and pulled her hood up, quickly tucking her hair in and huddling down.

She froze, the sound of her breath suddenly horribly loud in the silence. She pressed her mouth under the zipped part of her coat in the hope it hid both sound and clouded breath as she heard Sam walk out onto the road. She moved a fraction of an inch, just enough to see Sam's brown boots. He stood just feet away, turning in a circle and pacing away as he looked around. Then suddenly the boots turned in her direction. Her eyes widened, and she froze as he stopped just a step away. He was so close she could have reached out and touched him, and if he thought to check inside this bush, the game would be up. Her heart thumped, and her breathing hitched, and it was all so loud she was *sure* he had to have heard her. But then he turned and just walked away, back to Aubrey.

'Nothing there,' Kate heard him say.

With the danger over, she heaved in a deep breath and

released it heavily. Tears stung her eyes as she thought about what she'd just heard. They'd been working together all along, she realised. They'd set her up together. Aubrey had acted out the threat, and Sam had saved the day. It was so cleverly simple, when she looked back. Aubrey had never been the real enemy. She'd just been a distraction. The wall of smoke and mirrors. *Sam* was the enemy. He had always been the enemy. From the very first second until now.

She pressed her hands to her eyes as she thought about how hard they must have laughed at her. Kate had gone from hating Sam's guts to seeing him as a shining hero within the space of a minute. She was such a *fool*. Sam had never stopped playing the game at all. He'd just upped *his*. And Kate had played right into his hands.

# FORTY-TWO

Looking down at the delicate gold necklace Sam had given her just two days before, Kate felt a hot prickle at the back of her eyes. Sitting on the bed, she blinked it away angrily and snapped the box shut, turning it around in her hands. How had she been so stupid? She should have *known* it was just another elaborate prank. She should have been more suspicious of it all from the start. Sam had proven himself to be an awful person several times over before he'd swooped in and pretended to save her from Aubrey, so why had she believed him so easily?

*Because he's hot*, the devil on her shoulder whispered.

*No, because she's a nice person who looks for the good in people,* the angel countered.

'No,' Kate whispered furiously. 'I'm just a fool.'

Her phone vibrated in her pocket, and she pulled it out with trepidation. Seeing it was Amy, she felt a wave of relief and swiped to answer the video call.

'Hey! Merry Boxing Day, you gorgeous thing, you!' Amy cried with a cheerful smile.

Kate had thought she had her emotions under control, but suddenly seeing her best friend's face after the last two awful days seemed to break through the dam holding them in. A hard lump formed in her throat, and tears filled her eyes.

'Kate?' Amy's smile dropped, and she leaned in closer to the screen with a deep frown. 'Oh my God, *Kate*, what's happened?'

Kate shook her head as the tears began to fall. 'I, ugh... I don't know. *Everything.*'

'OK, lovely, I'm going to need a little more than that,' Amy said. 'Where's Lance? Is he with you? What's happened?'

Kate closed her eyes for a moment and wiped the tears off her cheeks, more replacing them a second later. 'Just *so much.*' She sighed, wondering where to start. 'I've called off the wedding.'

There was silence on the other end of the phone as Kate took a deep breath and waited for Amy to shout at her.

'Good,' Amy responded, nodding seriously through the phone.

Kate blinked, surprised. '*What?*' she asked slowly. 'That wasn't exactly what I was expecting. I thought you loved Lance? And why don't you sound surprised? Did he already tell you?'

'No, he hasn't told us,' Amy said, then stood up and crossed the room. 'And yes, I do love Lance, but *you* don't. Not enough to go through with this, anyway. And it's all going to be fine. I have a wedding escape plan ready to go. A built-in back door to most of the arrangements that I didn't tell anyone about. So don't worry, OK? I'll sort everything.'

'*What?*' Kate asked, unsure whether to feel amazed or horrified by this.

'Yeah.' Amy rifled through a drawer and pulled out a notebook. 'I had a go-bag ready for you, for the day, too.'

'That's...' Kate shook her head incredulously.

'Kate?' Amy sat back down and looked at her with a sad smile. 'I stayed quiet about the engagement because I thought you'd want to marry Lance. It was only at the party afterwards that I realised things weren't right. You looked so, I don't know... *trapped*.' She shook her head. 'You flew out the next day, and the only time I've seen you since, we've had other people around and we've been running around sorting this wedding...' She sighed. 'So I planned the wedding and just made some room for an exit in case you needed one.'

Kate nodded miserably. 'It's just been crazy, you know? And it all happened so fast, and everyone was really happy about it—'

'Just not you,' Amy said quietly. 'So what's the situation now? Have you postponed it or...?'

'No.' Kate shook her head with quiet resolution. 'We're over.'

'Oh!' Amy's eyebrows shot up, *this* part surprising her.

'Lance and I just want completely different things,' Kate explained, running a hand back through her long dark hair. 'He wants the perfect house, the two-point-four children, the stay-at-home wife...' She trailed off with a grimace. 'That just isn't what I want.'

'And what *do* you want?' Amy asked.

Snippets of the last two months flickered one after the other through her mind. The things she'd learned about Cora, and about life. The things she'd planned as she lay awake contemplating life on Christmas Eve. 'I want to make a difference. I want to wake up every day and feel like I'm helping other people. Like I'm making things better.'

Amy nodded. 'Yeah, that sounds like you.'

'Does it?' Kate asked.

'It does. You've always wanted to save the world, remember? That's why you got into law. Do you remember when we were kids, you'd agree to play weddings with me, but only if I played heroes with you after?'

Kate laughed at the memory. 'I do. I wanted to fly so badly.'

'You made me call you *Super Kate, the bad-guy hunter,*' Amy reminded her.

Kate tilted her head with a look of appreciation. 'Not a bad play on words.'

'Meh, it could use some work,' Amy countered. 'But the point is, you wanted to save people even then. And fly all round the world on adventures. But then life happened, and you got all caught up in contracts.'

'Thanks, Amy,' Kate said.

'What for?' she asked.

'Just being you,' Kate told her.

Amy shrugged with a nonchalant smile. 'Anytime, Supergirl. Being me is what I do best.' She winked. 'Anyway, what else is going on?'

Kate's expression darkened as she was reminded of Sam. She told Amy everything, leaving no detail out, and watched as her friend grew more and more angry with each word.

'That *pig!*' she seethed. 'I can't believe this! What do you think they're plotting? It's obviously to do with getting hold of the company, but I can't work out the angle. It doesn't make sense.'

'Yeah, I don't know, either...' Kate felt the pain gnaw at her insides again and bit her bottom lip to ward off the tears. She felt so betrayed. She'd truly *trusted* him. But she couldn't share that with Amy right now. Not over the phone. 'Look, I need to go. I'm packed up and booked into a local hotel. I want to get out before he gets back.'

'Alright, but call me later, OK?' Amy asked.

'Sure.' Kate looked away, knowing she wouldn't. It was too painful. 'See you soon.'

She ended the call and stood up, looking around the bedroom she'd lived in for the past two months one last time. She cast her eyes from the freshly made salmon-coloured bed to the diary neatly laid on the table beside it to the picture of Cora on the wall and finally to the scissors still next to the sewing machine on the desk. She smiled sadly, feeling a tug in her chest.

'Goodbye, Cora,' she whispered. 'It was really good getting to know you.'

She picked up her suitcase, pausing only to place the boxed necklace on the bed, then turned and left for the last time.

## FORTY-THREE

Two days later, Kate stepped out of the car and stared up at the Coreaux Roots building. Burying herself in work, the way she always had when she needed to distract herself from the harder parts of life, she'd written up all the paperwork and sealed off all loose ends. She'd set it all up to make Edward Moreaux the sole owner of the company and all its assets, other than the house, which she'd left to Sam. Whatever he'd done to her had nothing to do with this. Cora would have wanted him to have the house, and Cora was who she was here for.

Another car pulled up beside her, and Kate put on a professional smile as Edward got out and stretched his legs. She walked over to him and waited politely for him to gather his cane and turn towards her.

'Thanks for meeting me here,' she told him. 'I've got all the contracts with me; we just need to sit down and go over a few things in the office, get it signed and then we're done.'

'And then it's all legally mine?' he queried, glancing at the building critically.

'Yes,' she confirmed. 'Well, as soon as I've filed it, which I'll do this afternoon. Shall we?'

They walked into the building, and Kate led the way to Cora's old office. She had a key now, which had been sorted out after she'd made Jenna acting CEO.

'I'll run through some basics with you, but most of what you'll need to know you can find out through Jenna, the office manager. She's been acting CEO in this interim and knows how to run everything better than anyone here on the office side of things. And if I were you,' she added, 'I'd promote her with a pay rise as soon as you can. You can't afford to lose her, and she's more than earned it.'

Edward's gaze flickered sideways at her, and he gave a strange smile. 'We'll see,' he replied. 'I'll keep your personal feelings in mind, but I like to judge people's worth myself. I imagine this place comes with rather a lot of dead weight, too.'

Kate frowned but didn't reply. As the company lawyer, it wasn't her business to get involved past the point of signing things over correctly, but that comment didn't fill her with confidence.

'There are a handful of senior site managers on the operational side who, again, will be of great help. They've been running this place for years. One of them celebrated fifty years here last month.'

'*Did* he now?' Edward asked, lifting an eyebrow in interest. 'That is a long time indeed.'

'It is,' Kate agreed. 'And very impressive. Right, here we are.'

She opened the door and gestured for him to enter ahead of her. Cora's office was a big bright room with a wide desk and a cosier, less formal seating area to one side. Kate imagined this was where Cora used to look after Jenna as a baby, a thought that always made her smile. She moved towards it but then realised Edward had gone straight to the desk. He sat down behind it and ran his hands over the polished wood with a quiet chuckle.

Kate watched him for a moment, seeing the exultation in his smile and hating it. It was understandable, she supposed, to feel excited and happy at inheriting such a big and lucrative company. But some show of modesty wouldn't have gone amiss out of respect for Cora.

She walked over to the desk, pulled the first of the two contracts out of the envelope and handed them over.

'It's all there, and my signature is already at the back.' She flipped to the last page to show him. 'Feel free to take some time to read it over, then sign whenever you're ready.'

He nodded and pulled out a pair of glasses from his inside pocket.

Leaving him to it, Kate crossed her arms and wandered over to one of the windows to look out at the view. The office overlooked the front car park and part of the winding drive up from the main road before it disappeared behind trees. Everything was still covered in snow, which glistened like a million tiny diamonds under the bright midday sun. As she looked, a car appeared in the distance. Not really surprised, as there was still a skeleton staff in today to keep things ticking over, she watched it approach, but then her eyebrows rose as she realised whose car it was.

Jenna parked up and looked at her car and then Edward's with a small frown before heading in through the front door. Kate glanced back at Edward, who was still skimming the pages of the contract. She hadn't yet had the chance to tell Jenna what was happening, as she'd gone away for Christmas, so this was actually perfect timing.

'I'll be back in a moment,' she said, walking to the door.

He grunted and didn't bother looking up.

She made her way back through towards the front and met Jenna in the hallway behind the admin office. 'Hey!' She smiled. 'I thought you were off until tomorrow?'

'I was, but I wanted to get the new year shifts booked in,'

Jenna replied, for once not returning Kate's smile. Instead, her dark eyebrows were puckered in concern. 'Kate, whose car is that next to yours?'

'Well, that's what I need to talk to you about,' Kate replied. 'That belongs to the new owner of Coreaux Roots. Edward Moreaux.'

Jenna's eyebrows shot up, and her eyes widened as she visibly paled. 'Edward Moreaux, as in William's brother? As in the old man with the newspaper, Edward?'

'Yes, and I know what you're thinking,' Kate replied. 'He's eighty-four and that doesn't exactly shout company stability, but he's bringing his son over to—'

'Kate.' Jenna grabbed her forearms urgently, cutting her off. 'Where is he? Have you made it official?'

Kate blinked. 'He's in the office. He's signing the papers now.'

Jenna paled and let go, putting her hands to her mouth for a moment.

Kate felt a sense of panic as she saw the other woman's face. 'Jenna, what is it?'

'Kate, I don't know what he's told you, but the only reason he wants this company is to destroy it. He hated William. He was so jealous of William's success that it led to a big falling-out years ago. He threatened then to destroy all they'd built, one way or another. He's tried all sorts of things to sabotage this place, though luckily failed. But if he has control of it...'

'Oh my God, what have I done?' Kate breathed. She stepped backwards and turned, speeding up into a run. 'Quickly! There may be time!'

Jenna followed hot on her heels, and Kate felt her heart beat painfully fast against her chest as the implications of what she'd done began to hammer down on her like the weight of the world. This couldn't be happening. After everything that had happened here and the trust William and Cora had placed in her via their will, she couldn't be the cause of everything crumbling to the ground. She just *couldn't*. All the faces of the people who worked here, the townsfolk, the family the Moreauxs had created, flashed through her mind, and she pressed on faster, pushing through the door and into Cora's office.

She stopped, Jenna skidding in beside her, and her heart dropped as they watched Edward sign the last page and put the pen down with a smile.

# FORTY-FOUR

Edward's eyes flickered from Kate to Jenna and then back again with a little flash of something dark. Looking back to the freshly signed document, he then picked up his phone and stared at the screen for a moment before typing something out, ignoring the two women entirely.

Kate glanced at the document and edged towards him, trying not to seem as worried as she really was. All she needed to do was get it back and tear it up, then this was all just a horribly near miss that one day they could all look back on and joke about. Or at least talk about without permanent scarring, anyway. He glanced up as she neared and smiled, so she forced a smile back. Reaching the desk, she paused and half turned to look back at Jenna. Jenna stared back at her with a stricken expression, and Kate gave her a subtle nod to reassure her that she was dealing with it.

'All in order, Mr Moreaux?' Kate asked politely.

'Oh, yes, I'd say so,' he replied, slipping his phone into his inner jacket pocket and standing up.

'Here, let me take that.' Kate reached over for the contract, but as she gripped on to it, he quickly grabbed the other end.

'No, I think I'll have my *own* lawyer file this one,' he said, watching her with a crafty gaze.

Kate's heartbeat quickened, but she held on to her end of the document tightly. 'As the lawyer for Coreaux Roots and whose signature is on this contract, I actually need to be the one who files it, Mr Moreaux, sorry,' she lied.

'Unless you're a particularly *bad* lawyer, we both know that's not true, don't we?' he replied smoothly. 'It doesn't matter who files it once it's been signed and witnessed, which, thanks to you, it now *has*. So very helpful of you to sign your part *before* our meeting, Miss Hunter. Very helpful indeed.'

His dark gaze bored into hers and danced with amusement at the little game they were playing. He knew, she realised. He knew that his cover was blown.

'*Ugh*, sod this...' she muttered. Gripping the contract with her other hand, too, she swiftly yanked it away from him, no longer interested in keeping up the pretence. Jenna ran forward, and Kate handed it to her. 'This needs to be destroyed immediately.'

'*Gladly*,' Jenna replied with feeling.

Edward chuckled. 'I'm afraid you're too late for all that,' he told them. 'Oh, Miss Hunter, really... You have me down as that stupid? I took photos of every page, and the second I saw you blast back in here with Cora's favourite little minion and that look on your face, I sent them all over to myself on email. They're long gone, and there's nothing you can do about *those* now, is there? And with your signature all over it, what better evidence of my viability as CEO here could there possibly be?'

Kate closed her eyes and felt her heart sink to the bottom of her stomach.

'That doesn't mean anything without the original though, right?' Jenna asked urgently. 'Kate? It doesn't, does it? I mean, he can't file with a *picture*.'

Kate reopened her eyes and glared at the devious old man,

his smirk making her blood boil. 'No, he can't file. But that's not the only way he could use it.'

She placed her hands on her hips and turned away with a sound of frustration. How could she have done this? How could she have made such a colossal mistake? She should have asked them about him. Jenna at least. She'd been too cautious after the incident with Aubrey, too careful. So caught up on keeping herself clean so the woman had nothing on her when things got messy that she didn't dig deep enough for the case. And perhaps, she admitted to herself, she'd also let herself become too distracted by the situation with Sam to think it all through thoroughly enough before going ahead. Either way, this was all her fault. She had royally dropped the ball. She pinched the bridge of her nose, stressed.

'What do you mean?' Jenna asked. 'How can he use it?'

'What she means, *Gemma*,' Edward replied, pointedly using the wrong name, 'is that I can use it as evidence in court. And it just so happens that there is already a court case coming up about who should be given control here in just a few days, isn't there, Miss Hunter?' He grinned coldly at Kate. 'That crazy sister of hers and the airhead great niece. I think I'll fare pretty well in comparison now, wouldn't you agree?' He rounded the desk and walked towards the door, reaching up to mimic the action of tipping his hat to them as he passed.

'*No,*' Jenna said, her voice low with simmering anger. 'No. You're not getting your hands on this company. I've watched you try to destroy us for years. The people you sent to plant things in here that could have us shut down, the forest fires you started, the machines you messed with...'

'All hearsay,' Edward replied easily, not bothering to pause. 'Nothing ever proved, was there, child?'

'No, but only because your brother was better to you than you deserved,' Jenna shot back. 'William *had* proof that could have put you away more than once, and he chose to let you go.

Because he was a good man. He cared about people even when they didn't deserve it, and *that's* why he ended up being so much more successful than you – the thing you're so bitter about. Because he earned people's respect and their loyalty.'

'Huh!' Edward turned to face her and rested both hands on his cane. 'The only reason my brother did so well was because he got a good deal on land before people realised the worth of this place, and he convinced a few gullible locals that he was the second coming, getting them to do his dirty work. He never deserved *any of it*. And he should have put me away when he had the chance. Because when I get my hands on this place – and I most certainly *will* now that Miss Hunter here has been so helpful – your beloved little wood shop will be stripped down piece by piece until there's nothing left. And the *land*, all these miles and miles of forest surrounding that twee little toy town my brother built you all, will be sold off pocket by pocket to steel factories, mining companies and cheap motel chains. By the time I'm done with it all, you'll barely see sunlight for all the industrial smog, and the only reason anyone will mention my brother and his wife's name will be to curse them for coming here in the first place.'

Jenna's bottom lip wobbled and her cheeks turned scarlet as furious tears began to fall down them. She opened her mouth to reply but couldn't, and clapped a hand over it instead, turning her head away.

Edward continued walking away from them, and Kate cursed as he reached the door, furious with herself. 'You'll regret this, Edward, I assure you. And if you turn up to that courtroom, I will tear you to shreds in front of them all.'

Edward paused and looked back with a cold, hard glint in his eye. 'I look forward to watching you try.'

# FORTY-FIVE

Kate's phone rang, interrupting the deep spiral of despair she'd been circling after the catastrophic mess she'd made at Coreaux Roots. She looked down at the screen. It was her mother again. Closing her eyes, Kate rubbed them tiredly. The news had gone down about as well as she'd known it would when she'd rung to tell her parents she'd ended things with Lance the day before. Eleanor's hysterics had escalated to such a degree that, in the end, Kate hadn't been able to make out any words at all – but not before she'd told Kate what a colossally stupid mistake she'd made. Not before demanding she find Lance and apologise for how awfully she'd treated him , and that she beg him to take her back. Not before she made the depth of her disappointment in Kate crystal clear. Kate had taken her mother's heartbroken rant with quiet resignation, it being exactly as she'd expected.

Eventually her dad had wrestled the phone from his sobbing wife and had simply asked Kate if she was OK. That had been her undoing, and she'd promptly burst into tears. But she'd quickly got her emotions back under control and assured him she was fine, and after she'd fielded a few more questions of concern, he'd allowed her to retreat.

Eleanor had been calling her repeatedly to continue the conversation, but Kate hadn't picked up, unable to deal with any more guilt or shame or general argument over Lance right now. With everything she had going on, Kate felt thoroughly depleted. All her emotional reserves were spent. She was tired, she was anxious, and she felt horribly and deeply alone. And she knew this was just a rocky part of her journey. It would get easier in time. But right now, she was finding it hard to figure out a way forward.

The call rang off, and Kate let out a breath of relief. A second later, a message pinged through and she glanced down, expecting it to be from her mother. This one, however, was from her dad.

*Pick this next call up. Please. Trust me. Dad Xx*

A few seconds later, the phone started ringing again, and she grimaced. With a deep sigh, she braced herself for the onslaught and answered the call.

'Hi, Mum.' She put the call on speaker and placed it on the desk, then leaned back in her chair and waited.

'*Finally,*' Eleanor exclaimed. 'Katherine, I've been worried *sick*. You need to stop ignoring my calls. I'm your *mother*.'

'I know, Mum. I'm sorry – I didn't mean to worry you,' Kate said tiredly.

There was a short silence, and when Eleanor spoke again, her voice was unexpectedly gentle. 'You don't need to be sorry.' She sighed. '*I* do.'

Kate blinked, and she squinted at the phone, sure she must have misheard. Eleanor's apologies weren't *quite* a thing of myth, but being as confident as she was that she was always right about absolutely everything, they were certainly a thing of great rarity.

'You know how much I think of Lance,' Eleanor continued.

'He's a wonderful man and one I'd have loved to see you happily married to. But there is *no one* in this world I'd ever want to see you *unhappily* married to. So I'm sorry for how I reacted when you told us.' Eleanor's voice grew smaller somehow, and Kate realised she felt ashamed.

'It's OK, Mum,' she said.

'No, Katherine, it's not,' Eleanor replied firmly. 'All this time you've been with Lance, I've been so pleased you found someone who we liked so much that I stopped paying attention to how *you* felt about him. I didn't notice how unhappy you were.' She sounded so sad that Kate felt a lump begin to form in her throat. 'I thought it was just wedding jitters. You're truly *awful* with surprises, and that proposal was a huge one. I thought you were just feeling off centre and that deep down you'd *want* that future, once you'd got past that. *That's* why I've been trying to keep you on track and why I tried to get you to go back and fix it. Not because *I* wanted you to marry Lance. I know it probably looked like that, but I was just terrified you'd done it for the wrong reasons and would look back with regret. The last thing any mother wants is her child to live a life of regret.'

'I appreciate that, Mum. And I know you meant well,' Kate replied, blinking away the mist in her eyes.

Eleanor sighed. 'I realise I can be a bit vocal with my opinions and that there are some, *very rare*, occasions where I don't get things entirely right – not that you are *ever* to repeat that in hearing of *any* of the neighbours.' Kate shook her head with a fond smile. 'But even when it doesn't look like it, the most important thing in the world to me is you. It always has been and always will be, Katherine. Having you was the best thing I've ever done. I want you to remember that. Because I've realised, after a lengthy talk your father and I had today, that there are times I must have made you feel that you *weren't* the priority.'

There was a pause, and Kate heard her mother struggle to hold back her tears. One fell down her own cheek at this, and she wiped it away.

'So if you ever feel like that again, I want you to tell me. OK? Because I never want that. I want you to know you can talk to me and that I'm here for you. Like I am now. If Lance wasn't the one, he wasn't the one,' Eleanor said.

Kate smiled, touched by this unusual display of openness and solidarity from her mother. 'Thanks, Mum. That means a lot to me.'

'And you can just ignore all those things I said about being single at forty, by the way,' Eleanor added. 'Not that you're anywhere near it yet, but even if you *are* still single at forty, you *won't* look tired around the edges. But if you do look a *little* bit tired, there are all sorts of wonders available to change that now. So we'll just look into your options.'

Kate had to throw herself face down onto the bed to muffle the laugh that rose up and exploded at her mother's words. Only Eleanor could come out with something like that with wholehearted, loving sincerity.

'Katherine? Are you still there?'

Kate lifted her face from the pillow. 'Yep! I'm here,' she confirmed, looking at the phone with a fond smile. 'I love you, Mum. And I'm really glad we had this chat.'

'I am, too,' Eleanor agreed. 'We don't properly sit down and talk to each other enough.'

Kate thought about it and realised she was right. There was always something else going on, keeping them busy while they exchanged brief snippets of information, or they were with other people and got carried along with the conversational flow of the group. They rarely spent time just the two of them. In fact, now she thought about it, Kate realised that the run-up to Christmas was probably the only time of year they ever truly made time for that. They talked on long walks and over games of cards by the fire. Over lazy breakfasts and late-night eggnogs. She realised suddenly that this was what she'd *really* been missing every time she felt a pang of nostalgia for their traditions of Christmas. It wasn't the lingering smell of nutmeg or the taste of her mother's famous Christmas cake. It was what came with those things. That proper uninterrupted time with the people she loved the most.

'Well, maybe we should do that more,' she suggested. 'Meet up more regularly, just us, to catch up.'

'I'd love that,' Eleanor replied.

'OK then.' Kate bit the inside of her cheek. 'I should have told you how I felt about Lance the day he proposed. I just panicked, and then it all spiralled out of control. The truth is, Lance and I want and value very different things. He's a great guy, but we're not right together. And I know you really want to see me find the right man to settle down with so I can give you grandchildren, but I need to be honest: that's just not something I'm even thinking about. There are some other things I want to focus on right now.'

'Oh, that's OK,' Eleanor said, surprisingly chirpily. 'I don't need grandchildren yet.'

Kate frowned. 'You *don't?*' she queried. Eleanor had been openly lamenting her lack of grandchildren for quite some time, so this was a surprising response.

'No. In fact, I don't think I could have one in the house anyway, darling, for quite some time, so you hold on to those eggs,' Eleanor told her.

Kate blinked. 'Right. I'll, er, I'll do that. *Have to ask*' – she squeezed her gaze – 'why couldn't you have one in the house?'

'*Because*' – Eleanor drew the word out excitedly – 'your father has bought me a *puppy!*' Her voice rose on each syllable until it reached an excitable squeak. 'He's a King Charles spaniel and he's absolutely *gorgeous*, Katherine. You're going to *love* him. I'm calling him Mortimer. Morti for short. We're off this afternoon to get all the things he needs, then we pick him up tomorrow morning!'

Kate's jaw dropped in stunned amazement. 'You...' She put a hand over her mouth as she pieced together what her father had done for her. 'A *puppy*? As in a real baby dog?'

'Well, I'm hardly talking about a seal pup, Katherine, am I?' Eleanor replied.

'Well, that's *great!*' Kate exclaimed. 'I can't wait to meet him.'

'Right, I have to get off, darling, or Morti won't have a bed to sleep in,' Eleanor told her. 'I'm here if you need me, OK?'

'Thanks, Mum. Happy shopping!'

'Thanks, darling. Ciao for now!'

The line went dead, and Kate quickly opened her messages.

*You bought her a \*puppy\*??!*

She pressed send and thought back to the last time they had a dog. Her dad *hated* dogs. He'd grudgingly agreed to the one dog they'd had when she was little because Eleanor had assured him he wouldn't have to do a thing. He'd ended up doing nearly all the daily walks and scooping all the poo from the garden as Eleanor complained it wasn't very ladylike for her to do it. He'd made it very clear that he would never, *ever* have another dog in the house again, after Pippi died. But now here he was, making the ultimate sacrifice to save Kate's metaphorical bacon with her mother.

*Yes. A puppy. A small, yappy, untrained one. You owe me. Big time.*

Kate bit her lip and stifled a grin as the second message followed shortly behind.

*BIG Xx*

She smiled and started typing.

*I love you, Dad. I know how much that must have hurt. Thank you. Xx*

The response came straight back.

*I love you, too. Now go and make sure my pain and suffering is worth it. Get all the adventures your mother will disapprove of in that you can while she's distracted. Because once it's not a puppy anymore, she'll be right back on you – and I am NOT giving in to her request for us to start salsa lessons. Xx*

Sending back a heart, Kate smiled and looked out the window, feeling uplifted and more energised than she had in days. Feeling, finally, like she wasn't so alone with her troubles, after all.

# FORTY-SIX

The next few days passed in a blur as Kate threw all her energy into making things right at Coreaux Roots. As it was all her fault, she'd made the decision to do something she'd once vowed she'd never do, and that was to outright lie on the stand. It went against the oath she'd sworn upon becoming a lawyer. It went against everything she stood for, but she knew that if it offered a chance of putting things right, of saving this incredible place and the livelihoods of all the people within it, then she had to try. So, with Jenna's help, she'd fabricated a story as to why and how Edward had forged her signature, and would just have to pray that it didn't come back on her in court.

The problem was, this court would have no choice but to make a decision of some sort on who should take over, as she hadn't been able to fulfil the requests within the will. Kate had ideas of her own as to who should be awarded the company, and she'd put together a strong argument for why. But they were not blood relatives, and she'd be hard pushed to get that accepted in the face of three contenders who were.

As New Year's Eve came round, Kate had done almost as much as she could to prepare for court, but there was one place she still hadn't yet looked for evidence against the people now trying to destroy or run the business into the ground. Cora's diaries.

She'd put off going back to the house so far, not wanting to run the risk of bumping into Sam. They still hadn't spoken since he'd walked out on Christmas Day, and she didn't feel up to breaking that streak now. But she'd taken a couple of detours around that way over the last couple of days and was pretty certain that he hadn't been home. The snow was piled high on the drive, no track marks to indicate he'd parked there recently. So after psyching herself up, she'd decided that today was the day she'd risk it. Better sooner rather than later.

An email from Bob popped up at the corner of the screen. Kate clicked on it and skimmed the contents until she reached the part she'd been waiting for right at the bottom.

And as for your request, I'm happy to report that it was granted by the board, and by unanimous vote, too. This is certainly going to be interesting, and I, for one, look forward to seeing what the future holds.

Best regards,

Bob

She smiled, the words lighting her up on the inside for a moment, allowing her temporary relief from all the stress and worry. It was something good in a sea of bad, but it was also something that would have to wait. Because she knew if she didn't go to the house to read through Cora's diaries now, she never would.

After closing her laptop on her small hotel-room desk, Kate stood up and shrugged on her coat with a sigh. She reached into her pocket and checked she had the right keys, then opened the door to leave. But as she moved forward to step out, she almost instantly jerked back with a small yelp, because right there in the hallway, facing her with one hand raised as if about to knock, stood Amy.

'Oh my *God*! What are you *doing* here?' Kate cried.

Amy threw both woolly mittened hands up in the air and made jazz hands with a wide, dazzling grin. '*Surprise*! We didn't get a chance to exchange Christmas gifts this year, what with you not coming home, so I thought I'd bring yours to you.' She grabbed the handle of her suitcase and rolled it inside before pulling Kate into a one-armed hug. 'It's me,' she added as she squeezed. 'I'm the gift.'

Kate laughed with joy as Amy let her go and carried on into the room. This was one surprise she could actually get on board with. 'Well, that's the best gift you could have ever got me.'

'I know, right?' Amy joked, looking around. 'Nice digs.' She took off the pale pink mittens and matching earmuffs. 'I still need to book myself a room, but I just had to come up and see you first. It's been such a long crazy journey.'

'Yes, I know. You must be exhausted,' Kate replied. 'But don't bother booking a room – just bunk in with me, like we used to.'

'Yeah?' Amy smiled and ran her fingers through her blonde wavy hair. 'I was rather hoping you'd say that. So much more fun that way.' Her smile softened a little. 'Plus, I didn't want to leave you alone, tonight of all nights.'

Kate smiled back sadly. Today was supposed to have been her wedding day. 'How's he holding up – do you know?'

'He's coping,' Amy replied. 'Rick's with him. They went up to Scotland. They're doing something tonight with big burning torch things. I don't know.' She shrugged. '*Man make fire*.'

Kate smiled. 'That sounds fun. And good, as long as he's OK.'

Amy nodded. 'He will be. You both will.'

Kate nodded. 'I know.'

But while she knew she'd made the right decision for them both, she still worried about him and felt guilty for the pain she knew she'd caused.

She glanced at the door and back to Amy. 'Listen, um, I hate to do this when you've just arrived, but I was about to pop out for a bit. I just need to shoot to Cora's house to check some things out, and I don't want to leave it too long in case Sam comes back. Why don't you grab some rest now for a bit and then we'll go out somewhere for dinner when I get back?' she suggested.

'No chance!' Amy exclaimed, immediately pulling the mittens back on. 'I'm coming with you!'


An hour later, Kate sat back on the floor of her old bedroom, poring over the box of diaries Cora kept, searching for any useful snippets of information about Aubrey, Evelyn and Edward. She'd found a couple about Aubrey and one on Edward, but nothing too damning so far.

'Is this the bat you terrified Sam with that first night?' Amy asked, sticking her head back around the doorway and brandishing it.

'That's the one,' Kate replied, amused. Amy had been roaming the house, shamelessly poking around, since they'd got here.

'Ooh, I wish I could give him a whack or two with it. I bet it really hurts,' she said, eying it up.

'Yeah.'

Kate's eyes flickered up to the spot on the bed where she'd laid the box with the necklace inside. It had disappeared, so Sam must have been back and taken it at some point. It made her feel strangely empty that it was now gone. Even though it had clearly never meant anything to begin with, just a meaningless prop in his and Aubrey's big plan, whatever that plan was. The thought of them together and how much they must have laughed at her turned her stomach, and she looked back to the diary in her hand.

'You find anything useful yet?' Amy asked, walking into the room and wandering over to look at the photo of Cora.

'Yes, a few things. Nothing massive though.' She kept reading, her eyes skimming the pages swiftly for any sign of their names. Turning the page, she carried on, almost flicking to the next when something interesting suddenly caught her eye. She went back and read it slowly, excitement dawning in her eyes. 'Hang on...'

'Hmm?' Amy turned to her. 'What is it?'

'It's...'

Kate trailed off, and they both froze as they heard the front door open and then close below. Footsteps trudged through to the kitchen, and Kate and Amy locked eyes. Amy's gaze slipped down to the bat in her hands, and with a fierce glint in her eye, she retightened her grip and set off out of the room.

'*Amy!*' Kate hissed, quickly standing up. 'Amy, where are you going?'

She went out to the hallway just in time to see Amy rounding the bottom of the stairs, then with a deep, screeching warrior cry, Amy ran towards the kitchen with the bat held high.

'Oh *shit...*' Kate ran down the stairs after her, alarmed, turning the corner just in time to catch the shock and fear on Sam's face as he registered the second, crazy, British, bat-wielding banshee coming to attack him unexpectedly in his home this winter.

'*What the hell!*' he yelled, jumping out of the way of the swooping bat as Amy attacked. She raised the bat again, and he hastily set off at a run around the kitchen island. '*Jesus Christ, what is going on? And who the hell are you?* Ow! *Ouch!* Ow!'

'Take *that*, and *that*, and *that*!' Amy roared, hitting him whenever she caught up with him.

'*How did you even get in*? Oh. Thank God. Kate, can you *help me a little here, please?*' Sam begged, spotting her.

Watching him get a little taste of his comeuppance though, Kate wasn't sure she wanted to help him, after all. 'Mm.' Kate rocked her head from side to side, pretending to consider it. '*Nope.*'

'Kate? *Kate!*'

Amy managed to corner him and began jabbing away with the end of the bat. 'How do you like *that* then, tough guy, huh? And *this!*'

'I don't!' he yelled between ouches.

After a few more decent hits, Kate pulled Amy gently back. 'OK, I think that's enough.'

'Yeah?' Amy checked, breathing heavily from the exertion. 'You sure? I can do more.'

'I think we're good. Thank you though,' Kate smiled at Amy, and Amy smiled back.

'No problem.' As Amy's gaze turned back to Sam, her smile dropped to an evil glare, and she pointed two fingers towards her own eyes and then his as she walked away.

Sam watched her with a deep wariness as he straightened up. 'What the *hell* is going on, Kate? What *is* this? And why are you *here*? Why aren't you getting *married?*'

Kate ignored the last part and lifted her icy gaze to his. 'What's *going on* is I know exactly what you've been up to, Sam. About your partnership with Aubrey to manipulate me into doing what you want with the paperwork for the company.'

'*What?*' Sam frowned.

'Don't play dumb, please,' Kate snapped. 'I saw you. I heard you talking. The game is up.'

'What *game?* There is no ga— *Oh...*' Something occurred to him, and he froze for a moment as it finally clicked.

Kate looked at him coldly. 'We're all on the same page now, yes? Good.'

'It's not what it looks like,' he said, following her as she walked through to the kitchen.

'No?' Kate asked, not bothering to turn round. 'It wasn't that you're working together to manipulate me into doing what you want with the business.'

'*No*, it's *really* not,' he replied, standing at the kitchen island.

'Oh, OK. Great. So it wasn't you absolutely playing me into having feelings for you, while you and Aubrey laughed behind my back, either, right?'

'*No*, of *course* not!' Sam exclaimed, his face crestfallen.

'Oh, please,' she scoffed. 'Save me the dramatics. I *know* you played me, and you might not be able to tell me why, but I'm *certainly* not going to fall for it again.'

'Kate, I'm serious.' He moved towards her but swiftly moved back again with his arms in the air as Amy shot a warning swing. 'Please, just hear me out.'

'*Why*, Sam?' Kate demanded. 'You lied to me and treated me like a fool.' Tears prickled at her eyes. 'You made me believe there was something between us, and all along it was just cruel lies. I really should have known better the first time, but I sure as hell won't be making the same mistake twice.'

'That's what you *think*?' Sam demanded, anger clouding his handsome face as he took a step towards her. 'That all of it was just a lie?'

Kate held his gaze, ignoring the hurt she could see there. He was good at faking it. 'Yes,' she said strongly. 'That's exactly what I think.'

Sam took another step forward, growing closer to her now, frowning down at her with a look of betrayal. 'You think *all of that* was nothing? All our talks and the things we shared. That moment on the slope when we crashed, Christmas Eve – that was all *fake* to you?'

Kate's lip wobbled as he brought the pain all flooding back to the surface, and she turned away to the hallway. 'I can't do this.'

'Well, you're going to have to,' Sam thundered, following her out and grasping her arm. He tugged her back round and glared down at her. 'Because if you want to walk away now, that's fine. I'll respect your choice. But I sure as *hell* won't have you deciding it was because of me. That it was because I wasn't genuine.' His bright blue eyes held hers with a deep fire burning within. 'I don't feel things for other people easily, Kate. Not romantically, at least. It's a hard thing to let someone in, after the childhood I had. And I didn't want to let *you* in, but you bulldozed in there anyway, with all the ease of a damn hurricane, messing up my life and tossing my world around so I don't even know which way is up anymore. And then you *left*. To marry some guy who doesn't deserve or understand you one bit. And I *still* held my tongue because that was your choice.' He pulled a deep breath in and pointed a finger at her. 'But don't you dare try to tell me those moments between us weren't real. Because they were. Or at least they were for *me*.'

Tears streamed unbidden down Kate's face now. 'Then explain what that was with Aubrey.'

Sam pulled back, instantly closing up. 'I *can't*.'

'*Tell me*!' Kate screeched, losing control of her patience with all this entirely.

'*Fine*!' Sam yelled back. 'You really want to know what I was hiding? I was hiding the will, Kate.' His voice deflated as she gasped and stepped backwards. 'I was hiding the damn will. The one you were looking for. I've known where it was all along.'

# FORTY-SEVEN

The town hall slowly began to fill up with people as the clock struck twelve. All of the Coreaux Roots employees had been asked to attend the emergency meeting, along with Aubrey, Evelyn and Edward. As Edward arrived, he spotted Kate and walked over with a small, nasty smile.

'I'm guessing this is all to rally the troops against me – turn their collective hatred my way in the hope it has enough power. Well, it won't,' he told her confidently. 'You can rile them up all you want, but it won't make a difference in court.'

Kate looked back at him levelly, choosing not to answer. 'Please take a seat, if you're staying. Otherwise, the door is behind you.'

Edward smirked and turned round, taking a seat at the very back.

Feeling nervous as she looked out at the room full of people, she straightened her suit jacket and smoothed her hair.

Jenna came over and gave her an encouraging smile. 'You've got this, OK? Whatever this *is*,' she added with a small laugh.

She hadn't told anyone what was happening here today, only that they all needed to come. Not one person in this room had a clue what was about to happen. Her eyes flickered back to the door for a minute as Aubrey and Evelyn walked in and took seats not far from Edward.

'Thanks, Jenna,' she said with a tight smile. 'How are we doing? Do you think we've got most people here?' She looked around.

'I'd say that's pretty much everyone,' Jenna confirmed. 'Go for it.'

Kate nodded and walked up onstage to the microphone. As she reached for it, the crowd fell silent, all eyes on her. She cleared her throat, casting her eyes slowly over the people of this small, incredible town. The town Cora and William had built from nothing with their bare hands. With sheer grit, love and determination. The sea of faces fuelled her fire, and she felt the fierce pull of responsibility she'd come to inherit from Cora. Cora couldn't protect them anymore. But Kate could. And she sure as hell *would*, too.

'As many of you know, I'm Kate Hunter, the lawyer for Coreaux Roots,' she began. There was a light round of applause, and she smiled. 'When I first came here to sort out Cora Moreaux's will, I thought this was going to be a pretty straightforward job. A paperwork exercise. Tick some boxes, draw up a couple of contracts then move right on. *But...*' She turned and paced to the side, tilting her head towards the listening crowd with a wry smile. 'It certainly turned out to be anything *but* that.'

There was a light laugh from those who knew some of the battles she'd fought. She met Jenna's eye, and her smile warmed.

'You see, the Moreauxs added a clause in the contract when they placed that will with my firm that stated I had to stay here for a minimum of six weeks and get to know the place and the people here. Which was unusual and sounded a little over the top, to be honest. But then I started getting to know who Cora and William were and what they'd created in this beautiful town. I discovered the incredible community they'd cultivated and how their goodness lives on in the heart of this community, even now they're gone. I got to know some of *you,* the people they cared about most.' She shook her head. 'You know, I didn't realise places like this existed. Places where you could genuinely see the incredible difference someone has made all around. In fact, I don't think there's anywhere else in the world quite like it.'

There were some rumbles of agreement and nods from the audience.

'But the reason I'm up here sharing all of this like some teenage girl verbalising her diary isn't just to flatter you all. Though do feel free to take that, anyway.' She smiled as a few more people laughed, then wandered back to the central stand. Turning to face them, her expression grew more serious.

'You all already know that Coreaux Roots isn't just a company. You all know it's so much more than that. It wasn't built and expanded out of corporate greed. It was developed to sustain and serve this town. To help everyone in it rise and grow. It's given so much to so many, and it's a place people are proud to be a part of. It became the glue of a true family. It became a living breathing thing.' Her gaze moved to meet Jenna's as she recalled their very first conversation. 'The business and all of you who run it are the body and soul combined. You're one whole. And that's what makes it so special. *That's* what Cora and William wanted me to learn when they put that clause in the contract.' Kate turned and paced to the other side. 'Once I understood all that, I knew Coreaux Roots had to be protected at all costs. Which meant I had to be sure whoever I signed it over to was going to do just that.'

She took in a deep breath and let it out slowly. 'As you all know, Aubrey Rowlings was hoping to be awarded full owner-ship.' There was a low ripple of unease throughout the crowd, and Kate kept her voice carefully neutral. 'Aubrey feels she is

best placed to take on the mantle of leader and that she's ready
to step into Cora's shoes. She is, I must admit, the only one of
the three who put in a claim who's worked there and has at least
a basic understanding of how the company operates.'

The volume of the disgruntled murmur in the room
increased, and Kate waited, noting the smug lift of Aubrey's
chin as she watched from the back.

After a few moments, despite looking as worried as the rest,
Matthew stood up from his seat in the front row next to Jenna
and turned with a stern bellow. 'Pipe *down*, everyone. We're all
here to find out what's happening, so y'all just let Kate say what
she has to say.'

The room fell silent, and he turned back to Kate with a
sharp nod before sitting back down.

Kate let the tense peace stretch for a few moments before
continuing. 'As the Coreaux Roots lawyer, I'm forced to follow
a legally defined path, no matter what my personal views. As a
family member and one with a connection to the company,
Aubrey has a decent claim should she take it to court, which she
now *has*.'

'*What*?' several voices cried out.

'What does that *mean*?'

'She won't *win*, will she?'

Kate held up her hand to call for silence. 'Aubrey is taking me
to court in three days' time, where she will ask to have the legal
responsibility for Coreaux Roots taken from me and awarded to
her, under a specific clause in the legal contract between the
Moreauxs and my law firm, which allows her to do that if she
believes I'm not working in the best interest of the company.'

'That's *hogwash*.' The angered cry came from Matthew
himself this time as he stood up and dashed his hat through the
air as though wanting to throw it. 'Not *nobody* can say that
about *you*. Judge'll see that straight away. Right?' He turned to

gather support from the crowd. 'Won't they?' Some joined in his assurances, but most fell silent, looking scared.

Kate shrugged, looking grim. 'If it comes to that, it could go either way. A judge won't understand or take into account all the things we know. They have to judge on cold, hard facts. And some of those cold, hard facts will be that I've been here for two months with three viable options and haven't acted on any of them.'

Aubrey's smile broadly widened, and she stared at Kate, not bothering to hide her smugness as Kate voiced what she knew Aubrey's lawyer would have already told her.

'Well, who're the other two?' Matthew asked.

Jenna leaned forward in her seat and put her head in her hands. 'I feel sick.'

Matthew sat back in his seat and patted her gently on the back.

'We'll get to that,' Kate replied, ready to start turning the tables. 'But first, did I ever tell you about the first time I met Aubrey?' She lifted her eyebrow in question and scanned the room. 'She turned up at the house one day and tried to burn me with a hot kettle, threatening to scar me for life unless I drew up paperwork to legally hand her everything.' There was a wave of shocked gasps, and she paused, enjoying the satisfying look of discomfort on Aubrey's face. 'Her grandmother, Evelyn, one of the other two who put in a claim for the Moreaux estate, just stood by and watched her do it. She even backed up Aubrey's threats at one point.'

Aubrey suddenly stood up as people began to vocalise their shock. 'This is an absolute lie!' she cried. 'This woman is out for her own gain. Don't listen to her.'

'Unfortunately, Aubrey, there was a witness there that day, and I took photos of the wounds you left on my arm. I put my statement into the police today, and Jerry here is now going to escort you – and you, Evelyn – to the station to answer a few questions.'

'*What*?' Aubrey screeched, turning pale. 'You can't do this!'

But Jerry and another officer pulled the two women away, ignoring their complaints. Kate watched them go with a smile and the deepest feeling of satisfaction she'd felt in a long time. The atmosphere in the room lifted, and hope began to shine through people's expressions again.

'So what does this mean?' Jenna asked, hope and fear warring with each other in her eyes as she looked up at Kate. 'The court case can't go ahead without her, right?'

Kate's gaze flicked up to the back of the room at the cold pair of eyes staring back at her above a cold smile. 'Actually, it could, if someone else took Aubrey's place for the same reason.'

Jenna looked back over her shoulder, following Kate's gaze, and her expression darkened.

'But while we're on the subject of criminal activity, there's one more person here today who was planning on taking the company by any means necessary. Edward Moreaux.' There was another murmur of general discontent. 'It sounds like some of you know him already. For those who don't, Edward is William's brother. The one who hated him. Edward *also* plans to fight me in that courtroom. He told Jenna and me that once he gets hold of Coreaux Roots, he plans to strip it down until nothing's left, and then he'll sell the land to industrial developers, until the entire local area is destroyed.'

Everyone started talking at once, some cursing, some panicking, some of them asking questions. She raised both hands this time, urging them to let her continue. 'Now, it's no crime to threaten something like that. But *arson* certainly is.'

Edward had been watching the room warily as she'd riled them all up, but now he narrowed his eyes, and his gaze swept back over to meet hers. He lifted his chin, and she could almost see the cogs turning in his head as he assessed her.

'Once I learned all the ways Edward had tried to sabotage the place over the years, and that William had let him go more than once, despite having the evidence, I figured that evidence had to be somewhere. So I went looking for it. I found an entry in one of Cora's old diaries that led me straight to the CCTV footage William hid of Edward setting fire to outbuildings and stock.'

Edward let out a low chuckle and gave her a look that said he knew she was bluffing.

Kate smiled and turned her attention back to the rest of the room. 'But I've run off track. I wanted you all to know what I've been fighting against because this is what *you're* all going to be fighting against soon, too. It's been my responsibility to protect Coreaux Roots through this transition, but when I'm gone, that responsibility is going to fall to all of you.' She looked around, feeling her emotions swell up. '*Protect* it. *Fiercely.*' She hit her fist against her chest. 'With everything you've got. Because this is *your* legacy now.'

Edward let out a derisive snort, then stood up and leaned on his cane. 'Did you really drag them all here for these useless empty words? To raise their hopes for no reason? This *legacy* belongs to no one right now,' he said coldly. 'But it will, once I've dealt with you in court.'

'No,' Kate replied, a buzz of excitement zooming around her body as she neared the moment this had all been building towards. 'I don't believe in doing *anything* without a reason. Which is why I have an announcement to make.' She moved her gaze across the crowd. 'The will I was working from was a very old one, entrusted to my firm before the Moreauxs knew what their family would look like. But Cora and William made another will, much more recently.'

There were a few gasps of surprise, and people looked around at each other, intrigued and confused. Edward frowned, and his eyes darted around as he processed her words.

'In this will they were much more specific,' Kate confirmed with a warm smile. 'It took a long time to find it.' She turned to look back into the corner behind where Sam stood silently watching and smiled. 'But we got there in the end.'

'You're lying,' Edward spat, though she could hear the uncertainty in his voice.

'No,' she replied, looking over at him with open contempt. 'It's real. And very well tied up, too, from a legal standpoint. They took no chances with this one. And you probably have yourself to thank for that. You were probably exactly who they were protecting themselves from when they wrote it.' She lifted her chin a little higher. 'So you won't be getting your hands on this company – or anything of theirs. Not today, not in court. Not *ever*.'

'Really?' Jenna breathed as excitement began to buzz around the room. 'We're safe?'

'I think so,' Matthew replied.

Edward glared back at her, his cheeks turning red and then a deep shade of purple as his chest heaved up and down with rage. 'I don't believe it. It's a fake. I'll take it to court. I'll rip it to shreds. I'll—'

'Be my guest,' Kate told him, cutting him off. 'It's iron clad, so waste all the time and money you want. But that will all have to wait because you have a prior engagement to attend first.' She raised two fingers to signal the man waiting patiently in the corner nearest the door.

'What are you talking about?' Edward shot back crossly.

'I was serious about that CCTV footage. And after all you've done and all you planned to do to the people he loved, I figured William wouldn't be averse to me using it. This is Mike.' She nodded to the officer just as he reached Edward's side and slapped a cuff over one of his wrists.

'Get your hands *off* me,' Edward shouted angrily.

'Mike will be escorting you to the station to discuss that video further,' Kate continued.

'I will not be manhandled. I said get *off* me!' Edward tried to struggle, but he was no match against Mike, who twisted him around and started frogmarching him out of the building.

'Alright, buddy. Let's go.'

His complaints continued in a stream until the door finally closed behind them.

Kate glanced back at Sam. This was it now, the final surprise. The last piece of the puzzle about to be slotted into place before she signed and sealed it all off for good. And that knowledge both thrilled and crushed her, all at the same time. She took a deep breath and then, looking out at the crowd, she stepped back.

'My job here is almost done,' she said, forcing a smile. 'But I'm going to hand you over to Sam to tell you this last part.'

There was a round of applause as she moved aside and Sam took the floor. He looked around at everyone, taking his time to find the right words.

'My aunt and uncle cared about the people of this town more than anything else. All they ever wanted was for the company to be carried on by people who cared as much as they did. Who knew, as Kate said earlier, exactly what it means.' He looked down with a small smile. 'They actually left the company to me.' He held his hand up to still the cheers that began to erupt, shaking his head. 'No, no, let me finish. They left it to me but with their blessing, if I don't want it, to decide who it *should* go to and to award it accordingly. And *this*, with Kate's legal help, is exactly what I now plan to do here today. I never shared in their dream. At least, not in this way. But I *care* about their dream deeply. And I see their dream in so many of you every day. I see their leadership qualities, their heart, their sense of family. So to make sure that lives on for many, *many* more years, I will be handing equal percentage of the company over to the following people.' There was a short pause and a collective holding of breath as everyone waited to hear what Sam was going to say. 'Matthew Springer, Andy James, Joe Barnes and Jenna Napoli.'

Kate watched as Jenna's jaw dropped and her face paled in shock. Matthew shook his head and then looked down as his bottom lip wobbled slightly. Then all of a sudden, a loud, heart-felt, resounding cheer filled the room and grew into a huge crescendo. Jenna's shock turned to joy and Matthew's wobble turned into a watery smile as everyone around them began to celebrate.

Sam jumped down, and Jenna turned to him, her face alight with emotion.

'You have no idea what this means to me,' she said, her tear-filled words barely audible over the excited hubbub throughout the room.

'Oh, I do,' he shouted back. 'You four will lead Coreaux Roots forward into the future. Honestly, there is no one who could do it better, Jenna. You deserve this. You all do. It's what Aunt Cora would have wanted.'

Jenna's lip wobbled, and he pulled her into a one-armed hug before turning to let the celebrating crowd offer up their elated best wishes.

Kate watched from the stage and wiped away a happy tear of her own. She'd *done it*. It hadn't been easy, and her life had been turned upside down along the way, but she'd carried out Cora's last wishes in a way she knew the woman would rest easy looking down on. She'd left this town safe and protected. This small corner of the planet where good things happened and good people lived. Where two people who'd dared to dream and take a leap of faith, so many years before, had created something magical. A place that changed everyone within it for the better. A place where hope could be found. A place truly worth fighting for.

Amy sidled up from where she'd been quietly sitting to one side and squeezed her in a quick sideways hug. 'You are amazing, do you know that? Honestly, Judge Judy eat your heart out. *That* was riveting!'

Kate laughed, and Amy followed her gaze towards Sam. 'Have you told him yet?'

'Not yet,' Kate replied. 'But I will.'

She watched Sam and felt the familiar pull in her chest, and as he looked up at her, she smiled back with every open inch of her soul.

# FORTY-EIGHT

Hours later, after signing and sealing all the paperwork with each new owner to make it official, Kate made her way over to Cora's house. Or rather *Sam's*, as it was now. She paused on the porch and knocked, no longer being a resident with the right to use a key. He opened it almost instantly and led the way inside to the lounge.

'Drink?' he asked.

'Er, no. Thanks,' she replied, trying to decide how to start what she wanted to say.

When Sam had revealed the will, he'd explained that the reason he hadn't shared it was because Cora had told him about the old contract. She'd told him the newer will left it all to him and suggested that if he didn't want it, to let the original fall into play. He'd assumed Kate would figure out who to give it to herself but hadn't realised exactly how much she would be up against in her attempts to do so.

Aubrey knew about the more recent will after eavesdropping on a conversation years before, and she'd worked out it would be in her favour for Sam to keep it to herself. She'd simply been checking in to see if he was still staying quiet.

What Kate had missed was Sam telling her very plainly never to corner him into meeting like that again.

Kate had been annoyed with him over the will at first but had grudgingly understood his actions after she'd calmed down. And she'd felt a deep relief when she learned the truth about Aubrey. Relief that her instinct to trust Sam hadn't been off. That she hadn't been played so easily, after all. She'd felt a little guilty about jumping to conclusions, too. But there had been no time to deal with that. She'd been against a ticking time bomb and had needed to get all her ducks lined up before the date of the court case. Now though, it was all finally over. Which meant now she had time to talk to him for her own reasons. She fiddled with her bracelet, suddenly feeling nervous. All the fires around them had been put out and the obstacles removed, meaning there were no distractions to escape to or walls to hide behind. All that was left were the two of them.

The fire behind Sam crackled as the silence stretched on, and she glanced at the flames, finding them easier to hold than his eye as she began to speak.

'You, er, you asked me the other night why I wasn't back home getting married.' She swallowed. 'I called it off. The whole thing.'

'I'm sorry,' he replied levelly.

'Don't be,' Kate told him. 'You were right. He wasn't the right person for me. And I wasn't the right person for him, either.'

She fiddled with the bracelet and walked over to the window, looking out at the falling snow. 'I realised a while ago that I wasn't happy with my life, but it took me a long time to figure out the reasons why. And it wasn't just Lance.' She turned back to face him now. 'The main reason is that I haven't been living for myself. Somewhere along the way, I started living for everyone else, fitting into their idea of who I should be, putting their needs of me before my own.'

She shook her head with a small shrug. 'I've always wanted to use my skills to help people. I want to make a difference, and I want to travel the world. But so far I haven't really done either. I got stuck in that rut of pleasing people rather than helping them and forgot what *I* wanted from life. But I've remembered now. I woke up. And that's mostly down to you and your aunt, actually. And after I realised what I wanted...' She blew out a long breath through her cheeks with a small smile. 'Well, I just went and turned my entire life upside down and changed absolutely everything to make sure I started living my life for *me*.'

'Oh?' Sam asked, his eyes sparking with interest.

Kate nodded, taking a few hesitant steps towards him. 'I asked my boss in Boston to let me set up a non-profit sector of the business. It's a decent tax break for them, and it gives me the backing I need to do some real good in the world. They agreed.'

Sam's eyebrows shot up, and he gave her a slow nod of approval. 'That's amazing. Where you setting up – in London?'

'Somewhere over here, actually, in Vermont,' she told him, walking towards him until she was just one step away. 'I've grown kind of fond of this part of the world. It's beautiful. And it's a good base to jet out on adventures from.' She looked up into his eyes as he leaned a little closer. 'I don't know exactly where this idea of mine will lead yet, but I'm really excited about it. And it's the first time I've been able to say that about something in far too long.'

His gaze locked with hers, warmed by his smile, and Kate smiled right back, feeling their connection ignite. It was still there. That pull. That feeling of live energy between them like a pulse that couldn't be stilled.

'Yeah,' he said huskily. 'I know what you mean.'

Biting his lip, Sam drew back and reached into his pocket. He pulled out the box she'd left on her bed. 'I found this, after you'd left. I thought you might like it back.' He held it out.

Kate nodded. 'I would,' she replied. 'But only if you come

with it.' She reached out and touched the front of his shirt, hooking her fingers in between two buttons. 'Adventures are always better with the right person beside you. And I think my right person is you, Sam Langston.'

Sam's mouth curled up in a slow grin, and he wrapped his hands around her waist, pulling her close. 'And what else do you want, Kate Hunter? I want to know. Tell me.' He leaned closer, his breath warm on her face, and it took all her self-discipline not to melt right into him there and then.

'I want you to take me as I am,' she answered, her voice barely more than a whisper as their lips hovered achingly close to each other's. 'I want you to live in the moment with me and make every one of them count. And I want you to keep being you, exactly as you are. Because you're incredible and inspiring, and you make every day a little brighter just by being in it.' Kate's heart sang like a bird as she finally declared her feelings out loud. 'All in all, I guess what I'm saying is that I'm pretty mad about you. Utterly crazy for you, in fact, despite all my best attempts not to be.'

Sam smiled, his face lighting up as his eyes roamed her face and drank her in. 'Well then, yes, I do come with the necklace,' he confirmed, reaching one hand up to stroke her face. 'And I'm crazy about you, too. But you're the inspiring one, Kate. From the moment you arrived here, you tore up this town in all the right ways, and your passion lit up the dark in this house like a blazing inferno.' He looked down at her hand on his shirt and took it in his. 'You lit up the dark in *me*, too.' He fell silent for a moment, a mixture of emotions playing out on his face. 'I'm yours, Kate,' he told her simply. 'Completely, fully yours. I think I have been since the moment you flashed me those murder eyes of yours the day I drank your milk.'

'*What?*' Kate laughed, and he joined her before pulling her in towards him.

'Not really,' he admitted, his easy smile still warming his face. 'I just really like to see you laugh.'

And it was in that exact moment that Kate felt her heart surrender to him completely. She smiled, looking back to those early days of furious pranks with a quiet sound of amusement. 'They really *were* murder eyes, you know,' she told him. 'I genuinely considered murdering you that day. Just for a millisecond, but it was definitely there.'

Sam threw back his head and laughed as she shrugged, then he looked back down at her with a bright twinkle in his eye. 'Well, life with you is *always* an adventure, Kate Hunter. And I wouldn't want it any other way.'

Unable to resist him a moment longer, Kate pushed up on her tiptoes and pressed her lips to his. Sparks flew as they connected, and as Sam took her in his arms and kissed her even deeper, pure, unharnessed bliss flowed through her veins like it was a fluid mix of magic and silk and the joy of every Christmas she'd ever known combined. The world around them slipped away. The fire, the tree, the falling snow outside, all of it. And there in that perfect moment, as her heart soared and her soul sang, Kate knew that whatever happened now, whatever life may throw at her, spectacular things were ahead.

Because she'd done it. She'd let her heart lead her forward in all parts of her life, with nothing but hope and blind faith to guide her. And taking those leaps, those paths not yet tried and tested, was what made life an adventure. That was how all those tiny fragments of her big picture would be coloured with joy and fulfilment. It was what would make Kate feel truly free and alive.

And *that,* at the end of the day, was what made a life truly worth living.

# A LETTER FROM EMMA TALLON

Dear reader,

Firstly, thank you so much for reading my book. I really hope you enjoyed it! I've been writing for nearly a decade now, but after fourteen dark, gritty crime novels, this is actually my first venture into the brighter, more cheerful side of fiction. I'd really love to hear what you think of it – what you loved, what made you laugh, what you may have taken away from it – so please, if you can spare a moment, leave a review and let me know!

*www.bookouture.com/emma-tallon*

I always read and greatly value every review, page comment and message that comes through.

When this story first started floating around my mind, it was Kate who really stuck out to me. I couldn't get her out of my head. And although her story naturally morphed and evolved as it went from idea through to final draft, the most important part of it (for me) never changed. Kate's journey from keeping everyone else happy (as we too often find ourselves doing) to creating a life that made *her* happy.

I love her relationship with Sam (*Of course you do*, I hear you say, *you wrote the book*!), but he was always going to be the added bonus, rather than the point. Because in reality, whilst love will always be what we humans live for, in one way or another, there's really only one person responsible for creating true happiness in our lives. Ourselves.

The curtain doesn't fall when the girl gets the guy. Life continues, things change, sometimes things work out, sometimes they don't.

Romantic love isn't the fairy tale. *Life* is. And the moment we realise that *we* hold the reins and *we* control our stories, *that's* the moment it really begins.

Hopefully, we meet again soon, reader. But for now, stay safe, stay happy and make every moment of *your* story count.

With love,

Emma X

 facebook.com/emmatallonofficial
x.com/EmmaEsj
 instagram.com/my.author.life

# ACKNOWLEDGEMENTS

I'd firstly, and most importantly, on this one in particular, like to acknowledge and thank my amazing editor, Helen Jenner. This book wasn't just a new journey for our heroine, Kate; it was also a bit of a new journey for Helen and me, too. It was a first book in this genre for us both.

So, Helen, thank you for being my partner in non-crime this time. Thanks for your endless patience (even when I know you must be pulling your hair out behind the scenes at the chaos I throw into your order). And thanks for another great adventure. Our fifteenth book together – how crazy is that! I look forward to the next one.

Thank you to my two incredible best friends, partners in crime fiction and all-round epic women, Casey Kelleher and Victoria Jenkins. For keeping me sane when I'm losing the plot, for always knowing exactly what to say in every ridiculously frequent crisis, and for your endlessly supportive and inspiring friendship. I don't know how I'd get through the craziness of life – professionally *or* personally – without you!

I have to put in a special mention here for the amazing crew at the Moxy, too. I spend so much time typing away there, that you guys see me more than my own family do, some weeks. There've been so many times that I've been utterly defeated or overwhelmed with this book, only to have you spur me on with your kind, upbeat and unwavering support. I can't tell you how much I value that. You guys are honestly awesome and I love that I've got to know so many genuinely cool people through simply rocking up with my laptop. (Side note for head office – they all deserve pay rises.)

Lastly, I'd like to thank my dad – yes, *you*, Dad, if you've actually read this one and have got this far without complaining that it's *no Jack Reacher* and switching me out for Lee Child instead.

Thanks for passing on the half-decent side of your sense of humour and for always being up for a round of banter, even in the most serious of situations. The lifelong entertainment and character building has been priceless. And, of course, it's given me plenty of material to use in the relationship between Kate and Henry throughout this book. You'll hopefully have noticed those snippets of us in there. (Lee Child hasn't put you in any of *his* books, by the way. Just saying.)

All humour aside, though... thank you for seeing and understanding me better than anyone else ever has and probably ever will. Thank you for always being there when I need you and for always having my back. When the skies of life are sunny, you're the best kind of storm. But when dark clouds roll in, you're always my shelter, steadfast and calm. I'm more grateful to you for that than you know. Thanks just for being you, Dad. I love and appreciate you so much.

... even if you *are* a cantankerous old boomer who's always wrong about everything. *Especially* UK politics.

—Tallon version 2.0 *out!* \*mic drop\*

## PUBLISHING TEAM

**Turning a manuscript into a book requires the efforts of many people. The publishing team at Bookouture would like to acknowledge everyone who contributed to this publication.**

### Commercial
Lauren Morrissette
Hannah Richmond
Imogen Allport

### Cover design
Head Design Ltd

### Data and analysis
Mark Alder
Mohamed Bussuri

### Editorial
Helen Jenner
Ria Clare

### Copyeditor
Ian Hodder

### Proofreader
Laura Kincaid